THE FORSAKEN CIRCLE

PARANORMAL ARCHAEOLOGY BOOK 3

ERNEST DEMPSEY

138 PUBLISHING

PROLOGUE

PROLOGUE, AD 100, BRITAIN

Conall didn't enjoy being on the night patrol.

Except in the brief months of summer, it was always cold. The strength of the chilly weather depended on the season. In fall, it was annoying, like a bad itch. But in the depths of winter, it gripped him with an icy fist, offering no relief no matter how many layers he donned.

This was one such night.

He pulled the cloak around his shoulders tighter to seal off the chill, though the act changed little.

Beyond the discomfort of the weather, the darkness offered even greater threats, unseen while protecting the village at night.

Dangerous creatures lurked in the shadows of the forest's skeletal trees. Most were the usual predators, but Conall knew some of the threats skulking through the darkness weren't of a natural kind.

He'd heard stories of monsters that roamed this land, tales of beasts that could tear even the strongest men apart. And there were others—stories of dark magic, of supernatural beings that crossed over from the Otherworld, beyond the borders that protected the earth.

He said a silent prayer of thanks to Cernunnos, his favorite deity, protector of the forests and wildlife, the Lord of Wild Things.

During his short time on the night patrol, Conall had never seen any such dark beings; he'd never laid eyes on any monsters. But he believed the stories. They'd been passed down by those who had witnessed terrible things during the hard times, when the portals between this realm and the Otherworld had been breached and the evil beyond spilled across the border.

He thought he detected movement in the forest to the west, about one hundred paces from where he stood.

The full moon hung in the sky, casting its eerie glow across the hills, meadows, and woods, but refused to illuminate whatever he'd seen.

Conall turned in that direction and pulled his bow from his shoulder. Within two seconds, he'd notched an arrow and raised it toward the area he'd seen the anomaly.

"Who's there?" he asked, caught between the uncertainty of whether he should stay silent to maintain some element of surprise and the fear that by saying something whatever was out there might run away.

He stalked in that direction, glancing back over his shoulder toward the village at the top of the hill. He knew there were men atop the wall standing watch, all young like him. It was a rite of passage. The youngest over the age of fifteen guarded the village at night, while the older men protected it during the day.

Conall couldn't wait until he was eligible for the day guard. The only time he felt the warmth of the sun on his face was when he was helping in the fields or preparing meat the hunters had brought in during the morning hours.

A branch snapped in the direction his bow was aimed, and he nearly loosed the arrow out of instinct. But his fingers maintained their grip, and he tightened the string, pulling back to its fully cocked position near his ear.

He still didn't see what caused the sound.

His feet moved, as if on their own, toward the woods. He left the path he'd trodden hundreds of times that encircled the village and wandered into the tall, thick grass of the meadow. The blades grazed against his trousers and plucked at his tunic.

The grass proved useful for stalking. It cushioned every step, producing little to no sound to alert an enemy of his approach.

He kept his eyes on a thicket between the trees. The movement had come from there, or at least he thought it had.

Stories began to creep into Conall's mind—tales of monsters, creatures of unimaginable size and strength that lurked in the shadows of these forests. They were only stories. That's what he told himself. The elders told them to children around bonfires in the evening. Conall had heard them when he was younger, and even into his teenage years. As far as he could guess, the older members of the clan used the tales to keep young ones from venturing too far away from the village. There were, after all, very real threats out there beyond the boundaries of their land.

But during his time on the night watch, he'd never seen anything such as had been described in the scary stories around the fire.

He crept forward, keeping his pace steady and deliberate. The edge of the forest was so close now he could hear the rustling of the few leaves that remained stubbornly clinging to scraggly branches.

A limb cracked from somewhere deep in the woods. Conall adjusted his aim and loosed the arrow. He hadn't seen anything, and he quickly realized he'd fired the arrow out of panic. Cursing himself for his carelessness, he drew another from his quiver and notched it on the bow.

"Steady, Conall," he said to himself barely above a whisper. "Probably just a rabbit or something."

He knew a rabbit couldn't have caused a branch to crack that loudly. Only two things would have caused that. Either a limb had fallen from a tree, or something heavy stepped on one that was already on the ground.

Nothing had broken off a tree. Had that been the case, there would have been other noises that followed, including the sound of the object hitting the ground.

That meant this could only be one thing.

"Perhaps a deer," he whispered hopefully.

But that didn't make much sense either. Deer weren't clumsy animals and weren't typically prone to making much noise. Stealth was a big part of how they survived.

So the question lingered in Conall's mind: *What made the noise?*

He froze when he reached the edge of the woods, where the tall grass ended and the undergrowth began. Dried leaves covered the ground. A few weeks ago, snow had blanketed the world around his village. But the weather had warmed to an unusual level leading up to the solstice, which just so happened to be today.

That was another reason for Conall's restlessness.

Strange things were always rumored to happen on this day, though in his short time on the night watch, he had yet to witness anything beyond explanation.

He took a breath to steady his nerves and stepped across the boundary into the forest.

The moment his boot touched the ground, a frigid breeze swept into the woods. It cut through him like the tip of a sword, piercing his layers of warm clothing he'd donned to protect himself from the winter's icy grip.

He hesitated to take another step. The cold wind seemed a warning to go no farther. But his curiosity held him firmly in place, unwilling to let him retreat back to the safety of the meadow.

Maybe I should go get help, he thought.

He turned to look back at the earthen wall surrounding his village. The pyres still burned brightly against the darkness of the sky beyond.

He couldn't go back. If there was a threat here, it was his job to take care of it. He'd been trained for this, and despite his young age, Conall could handle himself with a bow, and with a sword.

His right foot extended out, and he took another step. Then another. Soon, the trees behind him blocked out the view of the fires in his village. The moon shone brightly in the sky, piercing through the branches overhead. He kept his eyes forward, bow lowered around his waist but ready to snap into position at any moment.

Conall swept his gaze from left to right, fully aware that whatever was out here might ambush him from behind a tree trunk, attacking from his flank.

His feet continued forward.

He glanced back over his shoulder and found the meadow completely blocked off by the dense growth of trees. More thoughts of turning back pummeled his mind. It was the safe thing to do. He could return to the village, recruit a few of his fellow guards, and return with torches and weapons to investigate.

Yet for some reason, he pushed ahead.

After a few minutes of slow movement, he froze at the sound of something.

Leaves crunched. And he wasn't sure, but he thought he heard footsteps. Not the light gallop of a deer. This was something heavier, much larger than one of those animals, or any animal he knew to be native to this area.

He raised his bow again, drawing the arrow back.

The footfalls were more pronounced now. And he couldn't tell if whatever was in the woods was running from him or toward him. As they grew more distant, he knew it was the former and immediately pushed forward at pace.

Whatever was out here, he had to handle it. If he didn't, the threat could escape and return to cause problems later on—perhaps even kill one of his friends on the night watch when it was their turn to patrol the perimeter.

The noise ahead continued, yet Conall could still not see what was causing it.

He picked up his speed to a near-run. Low-hanging branches snapped against his shoulders and arms. One twig striped across his face, scratching his skin—an irritation that was exacerbated by the frigid temperatures.

Conall suddenly stopped between a pair of oak trees and listened.

The movement had ceased, and up ahead, probably fifty paces

away, he saw a light radiating from beyond the dense forest, the trees silhouetted against the blue glow.

What is that? He wondered, unconsciously taking another step forward.

The sapphire light pulsed in a rhythm like a slow heartbeat, its cadence steady.

Conall pushed ahead, carefully navigating fallen branches and leaves littering the forest floor.

He stopped next to an ancient oak tree and leaned his left shoulder against it, keeping the bow raised. Whatever had been moving around in the woods before had abruptly stopped, leaving him wondering what it was and where it went. If the creature knew he was following it, it may have run off, or perhaps it was standing still somewhere in the darkness, hoping Conall wouldn't find it.

After a few seconds of waiting and gazing toward the light, Conall refocused and checked his surroundings. There was no sign of his quarry. He kept wanting to believe it was nothing more than a rabbit that had disappeared underground. But he knew no rabbit would make that much noise. He'd already been through that discussion in his mind a few minutes before.

He craned his neck out around the thick tree trunk and looked to the left. Then he froze. What he saw both terrified and mesmerized him.

In the shadows, a mere thirty paces from where he stood, a creature unlike anything he'd ever seen before stood on the edge of the forest, peeking around a tree.

Conall had heard stories about monsters since he was a child. The tales came from all over the world, from places he'd never heard of and would probably never see with his own eyes. Legends of creatures with serpents for hair, or the head of a lion and the tail of a scorpion, or of the banshees that wailed before the death of a loved one, and dozens more.

This one, though, was a monster from Celtic traditions that he'd learned about since he could speak.

"A Fomorian," he mouthed, not daring to make a sound.

Conall knew too well the threat that stood before him.

Fomorians were some of the earliest inhabitants of Celtic lands, embodying chaos, darkness, and wild, untamed nature. They were said to be in constant conflict with other races of Celtic myth, such as the Tuatha Dé Danann, representing the clash between order and anarchy, as well as the struggle for control of the land.

Their origin was shrouded in myth, with various accounts suggesting they were born from the depths of the sea or came from distant, shadowy lands. Often described as deformed or grotesque, the Fomorians could have animal-like features. They were a symbol of the unpredictable and destructive aspects of nature, with their appearance representing the imbalance between man and the unknown.

The Fomorians were led by powerful and terrifying kings, such as Balor of the Evil Eye, a giant whose gaze could kill or destroy entire armies. Balor's presence was especially fearsome, as it was said that only through a special intervention could his deadly eye be opened, causing untold devastation.

Balor's grandson, Lugh, would eventually rise as a hero of the Tuatha Dé Danann and fulfill a prophecy by killing Balor during the Second Battle of Mag Tuired, a significant confrontation between the Fomorians and the Tuatha Dé Danann.

This battle, also known as Cath Maige Tuired, was a pivotal event in Celtic mythology. It represented the victory of light and order (embodied by the Tuatha Dé Danann) over the dark, chaotic power of the Fomorians. Despite their defeat, the Fomorians were not entirely eradicated but were instead driven back to the margins of the world, where they continued to haunt the edges of human consciousness—a reminder of the ever-present threat of chaos.

The Fomorians were not merely monstrous enemies; they also had complex relationships with other races. Some Fomorians inter-married with the Tuatha Dé Danann, blurring the lines between friend and foe. These unions produced offspring who often inherited great power, such as Bres, who became a king of the Tuatha Dé Danann. Bres was known for his beauty but also his unjust and oppressive rule, a reflection of his mixed heritage and the tension between the two races.

All of these details raced through Conall's mind. He'd never believed he would actually see one. And now, he wished he never had.

From a distance, the Fomorian loomed like a twisted remnant of an ancient nightmare, half-shrouded in the forest's shadows. Its goat head, crowned with curving, gnarled horns, was the most striking feature—a grotesque blend of beast and malice. It turned around, and for a moment, Conall feared the thing had seen him. The creature's eyes were narrow and glowing, flickering with a cruel intelligence that seemed to pierce through the haze. Its snout was long and scarred, lips pulled back to reveal jagged yellow teeth, each breath escaping in visible puffs that smelled of damp decay.

Just as quickly as it had looked back Conall's way, it turned around and stared toward the light.

The Fomorian's body was unmistakably human yet grotesquely disproportionate. Its sinewy muscles bulged beneath the darkened steel plates of its armor; each piece forged with wicked intent. Spiked pauldrons jutted from its broad shoulders; their serrated edges stained with the remnants of past conquests. The chest plate, hammered roughly into shape, bore the runes of ancient power—symbols that glowed faintly, pulsating as if alive. Beneath the armored segments, blackened chain mail draped its form, rattling with every step as it trudged across the ground.

The Fomorian's massive arms held a weapon that matched its sinister presence—a brutal war hammer, the head of which was jagged and pockmarked, forged from obsidian-dark iron. It wielded the weapon with terrifying ease, the haft wrapped in strips of cured leather, worn smooth by years of battle. Around its waist, a belt of bones hung loosely, each vertebra carved and adorned; trophies of fallen enemies that rattled like macabre wind chimes with its every movement.

The goat-headed beast's stance was as if it were prepared to attack, its hooved feet rooted firmly on the leaf-covered ground. It swept its gaze from left to right, as if searching for its next victim, its nostrils flaring to catch the scent of fear. Its armor clanked and creaked, each movement deliberate, filled with an ancient, remorseless purpose—an echo of a dark age when chaos reigned, and monsters like it were feared above all else.

I really should have gone back for help, Conall thought. *What is it looking at?*

The beast appeared to be staring at something beyond the forest, perhaps the source of the light.

Conall wanted to get a closer look, but to move would risk catching the monster's attention.

As if on cue, the Fomorian stepped forward and away from the cover of the tree, and moved closer to the forest's edge.

Conall didn't wait. He quickly picked his way through the trees, closing the distance between himself and the creature, while also bending around to the Fomorian's right flank. Only when Conall neared the edge of the forest did he see what had drawn the monster to this place.

The trees gave way to a circular glen. He crouched low at the edge of the woods, his heart pounding in his chest as he peered through the shadows of the underbrush into the meadow beyond. The stone circle loomed in the moonlight, the colossal standing stones towering over the robed figures. The stones' surfaces were rough and weathered, etched with symbols that seemed to shift in the dim light, the air around them almost humming with an energy as old as time itself.

Within the circle, twelve Druids stood, their forms cloaked in dark gray robes that billowed gently in the wind. They were arranged in a perfect circle, each one an equidistant part of a larger whole, their faces obscured by deep hoods. They raised their arms in unison, palms open to the sky, as if drawing down the power of the heavens. Their chanting was low and rhythmic, a murmuring that seemed to blend with the rustling leaves and the distant call of a night bird. The words they spoke were lost to him, but he could feel their weight, an incantation that thrummed in the marrow of his bones.

At the center of the circle stood a stone plinth, no wider than four inches on each side, and rising four feet from the earth. It seemed almost delicate compared to the massive standing stones that surrounded it. Atop the plinth, something glowed—a strange, pulsing blue light that bathed the Druids in an ethereal glow.

Conall squinted, trying to make out the source of the light, but it shifted and twisted, as if it were not entirely of this world. The object looked mostly like a cube, but it shifted, making its form impossible to fully grasp, edges folding inward and outward, a geometric impossibility that hurt his eyes if he stared too long.

The blue light pulsed in time with the chanting, each beat sending a ripple of energy through the meadow. He could feel it, even from where he hid—a vibration that resonated in the earth beneath him, making the hairs on his arms stand on end. The Druids moved slowly, their hands lowering as they turned toward the plinth, their voices rising in intensity. The light atop the plinth flared brighter, casting their hooded faces in sharp relief, the glow revealing glimpses of features that seemed almost otherworldly—eyes that glimmered, mouths moving with an unnatural precision.

He swallowed hard, his breath catching in his throat. There was a power here, something ancient and raw, something that felt beyond the understanding of mere mortals. The meadow seemed to hold its breath, the air thick with anticipation, as if the earth itself waited for what would come next. He dared not move, dared not make a sound as he watched the Druids, the blue light, and the strange ritual unfolding before him.

Conall sensed movement to his left. He cursed himself for being so drawn in by the vision before him. He'd nearly forgotten about the monster lurking nearby.

He turned and peered at the creature, keeping his bow and arrow ready.

What are you doing?

The Fomorian stood there, the blue light only grazing over it, not fully illuminating its hideous form.

The beast watched the Druids, staring at the scene. Conall wasn't sure if the monster looked hungry, or curious. It seemed to be a strange blend of both.

The light pulsed quicker now, and the Fomorian inched its way out of the shadows and into the glen. Now he could fully see the creature. It held a battle ax in each hand, its huge muscles easily bearing the weight. Conall knew he would have trouble wielding one of the heavy weapons in both hands.

The Fomorian stood taller than any man Conall had ever seen, easily over seven feet. The thing dwarfed him and all the Druids in the meadow. It stalked toward the circle, carefully moving toward its victims without making a sound. The Druids were so focused on their chants, and ceremony, they didn't notice the monster approaching.

Conall had to do something. If he just stood there, the Fomorian would tear through the ranks of the unarmed Druids within seconds.

The creature drew closer to its targets. The drumbeat grew louder.

"Turn around," Conall breathed. "How are they not seeing this thing?"

He watched in horror as the beast neared the circle, holding its axes out, ready to strike.

Conall couldn't sit idly by any longer. He pushed aside his fears, raised the bow, and aimed at the creature. He pulled the string to his right cheek and let go.

The arrow zipped through the crisp air with blinding speed, striking the Fomorian in the right hamstring, where no armor protected its leg.

The monster howled. It was a terrible, ghastly sound like the howls of a hundred banshees.

The Fomorian dropped to one knee, twisting its head around to see who dared to attack it.

Conall stared into the monster's glowing red eyes, another arrow already notched. The beast started to stand, but Conall loosed another arrow, this one striking the creature in the left hand.

The Fomorian roared again, dropping the ax at its feet. It looked down at the arrow sticking through its hand and tried to stand using its one good leg.

For a terrifying second, Conall thought the monster was going to charge him—or at least limp toward him. But behind the Fomorian, the Druid circle opened. The drum had never stopped beating, the chants never ceasing.

The light brightened to near blinding, and Conall had to shield his vision with the bridge of his hand to withstand it.

The creature howled into the sky as the light changed to a pinkish purple color. Conall watched as the light wrapped around the monster like a giant ethereal hand. The Fomorian struggled, trying to free itself, but the light dragged it away from Conall toward the center of the circle.

The creature dropped its other ax, kicking and squirming to free itself. But the light continued to pull it toward the plinth.

Suddenly, the light formed a circle in the middle of the air. Conall peered into the swirling lights. It was as if a door to the beyond had been conjured right before his eyes. He stared at the Fomorian as the light drew it closer to the portal.

With one last screaming protest, the monster stretched out its left arm toward one of the Druids as it passed.

Conall reacted instantly, raising his bow once more and firing an arrow.

The missile struck the Fomorian's wrist and caused the creature to snap the arm back just before the light sucked it through the portal.

Then, as quickly as it had appeared, the hovering vertical circle disappeared. The light went out, and Conall found himself standing alone in the darkness.

He looked around, still uncertain the threat was gone.

It took a minute for his vision to adjust to the dark, but when it did, he saw the Druids still standing amid the giant stones. Only now, they were looking directly at him. Fear crawled across Conall's skin.

Have I done something wrong?

He was only trying to help, and had he not taken those shots, some if not all of the Druids would be dead right now.

One of the hooded figures stepped away from the others and extended their right hand. "Come," the woman said.

Conall guessed she was the head priestess, and wondered if he would be punished for interfering.

He reluctantly stepped out from his position among the trees and walked forward. The woman pulled back her hood, revealing a pale, beautiful face. Her lips were full and dark red, contrasting the face around them. Her hair was blonde like thick strands of gold, tied up in two braids that hung down past her shoulders. She was younger than he expected, possibly only five or six years his elder. Her expression seemed welcoming, even appreciative, which eased his anxiety a little.

The other Druids lowered their hoods too, some men, some women, all of them staring straight at him as he approached.

When he was a full stride from the priestess, he stopped, and looked around at the others.

"Who are you?" the young woman asked, a muted smile creasing her lips.

He bowed his head low. "My name is Conall, son of Diomosagh. I am with the night watch."

She inclined her head. "That was brave of you."

"I didn't want that thing to hurt anyone."

"Noble," she mused. He got the feeling she didn't need his help, but she didn't say that. "Do you know what that was?" She motioned absently to the stone plinth.

"It was... a Fomorian, wasn't it? I thought those were only legends, stories the elders told the young."

She shook her head. "No. They are real."

"Where did it go?"

Conall noticed several of the other Druids holding what looked like stone heads in their hands. He hadn't seen them before. Had he? They couldn't have just appeared.

"It was sent back to its realm," the priestess answered.

Concern overwhelmed Conall. "Will it ever come back?"

She shrugged. It was a slight, almost unnoticeable gesture. "Only if someone brings it here."

"Someone brought that thing here from another realm?"

"There are those who would see the world burn if they could. Such is the evil that dwells in the hearts of men. They would sell their souls to these abominations in hopes of gleaning the scraps from their table. There will come a day when someone will seek to open portals to the Otherworld to bring the armies of darkness into this world."

"How do we stop that?" Conall asked.

"We have done all we can for now." The Druids behind her dispersed, each walking away in a different direction. "Go, return to your village. Live a good life, Conall of Diomosagh. You've nothing to fear now."

"Nothing to—"

She turned, raised her hood over her head, and walked away into the darkness of the forest.

"When will they come back? How will we fight them?"

He started to follow after her, but she disappeared into the shadows, untouched by the pale glow of the moon.

He took a step forward, but his boot kicked something hard on the ground. He looked down and saw one of the stone heads similar to the ones some of the Druids held.

He picked up the heavy object and stared into its hollow, lifeless eyes. It was a bust of sorts, but he didn't recognize the person.

"You forgot your..." His words faded, and he realized he was completely alone.

As he trudged back into the woods, heading toward the village, he carried the stone head under his right arm, wondering about the meaning of the priestess' cryptic prophecy.

1

PRESENT DAY | SOUTHERN GOBI DESERT, MONGOLIA

D r. Felicia Lowe knew she was on the verge of the discovery of a lifetime. Now, all her research and toiling in the unforgiving heat of the dig site had finally yielded fruitful results.

Dr. Lowe stood atop the dusty plateau overlooking the Flaming Cliffs, her gaze fixed on the horizon where the desert met the sky. For years, she had scoured this remote region of the Gobi Desert, drawn by whispers of unexplainable phenomena and ancient mysteries buried beneath the sands. The setting sun hung low over the rock formations, casting the cliffs in hues of fiery reds and oranges that had given the landscape its name.

Just a few weeks ago she'd been on the verge of giving up. After countless hours of searching, digging, sifting, and analysis, she'd found almost nothing of note here in this mysterious place. At the precipice of throwing in the towel on her life's work, fate intervened.

A rare thunderstorm swept through the area. The hard downpour driven by gusty winds peeled back layers of hardened dirt and sand along the cliffs, revealing a section of rock face that had been concealed for centuries, and exposing a series of glyphs that hadn't been seen by human eyes in perhaps thousands of years.

Intrigued by the unusual markings, Felicia directed her team to focus their excavation efforts there. Days of careful digging beneath the glyphs unveiled a large stone slab intricately carved with patterns that bore an uncanny resemblance to Celtic knots—an astounding anomaly in this part of the world.

Now, as the last rays of sunlight bathed the cliffs, Felicia carefully brushed away the remaining dust from the slab's surface. Her fingers traced the grooves of the carvings, feeling the subtle shifts and indentations that hinted at movable sections. She pressed gently on one of the larger symbols, and to her astonishment, it depressed slightly under her touch. A series of faint clicks echoed from within the stone.

Her heart pounding, she called over her assistant, Chen. "I think there's a mechanism hidden inside this," she said, her voice barely above a whisper.

"What do you mean?" the young man asked, his eyes poring over the stone surface.

"I pushed on this. It's like a button."

The assistant's confused expression deepened, but he could offer nothing except a blank stare.

Dr. Lowe ran her fingers over the surface and in the grooves carved into the ancient rock.

"What does it mean?" Chen asked.

"I don't know," she said, puzzling over the find. She was tempted to press on another section of the stone but hesitated. "These are Celtic symbols, just like the ones on the wall there." She indicated the nearby rock. "Neither of these things should be here."

Upon discovering the markings on the wall, Dr. Lowe had immediately suspected the glyphs to be fraudulent—some kind of sick prank. But it would have been an elaborate hoax, performed thousands of years ago. She couldn't come to accept that hypothesis. Why would anyone go to so much trouble way out here in the middle of nowhere just to play such a trick? The odds of anyone finding it were exceedingly low, which meant, at least in her mind, these engravings and markings were legitimate.

But that conclusion flooded a series of new questions into her mind. She was far from an expert on Celtic culture and history. At the University of California, Berkeley, she'd studied both anthropology and archaeology, earning degrees in both. There had never been any discussions or studies regarding the Celts exploring beyond the bounds of Europe, though her coursework had barely touched on that civilization.

Dr. Lowe probably had several people in her network who were experts in the field, but she couldn't think of anyone off the top of her head.

The notion that the Celts had somehow made their way into Mongolia seemed ludicrous on the surface, but perhaps the history books had missed this piece of the human story, as they so often did. Vikings were explorers, nomadic in nature, and had traveled farther than initially believed. She'd seen much evidence supporting the idea that they had even reached the Americas. But this? This was different.

Had there been an ancient Celtic settlement here thousands of years ago? Did that mean this area was their true place of origin? Or was it merely a tribe that happened to pass through? So far, she and her team had uncovered little evidence of a village in this area. She knew, based on research and her gut instincts, that this place had once served as a home for people who lived long ago. But Lowe had figured—rationally—that they were Mongolian, or the predecessors of those people.

This, however, had shaken everything she thought to be true to its core.

Dr. Lowe continued analyzing what she guessed were more of the slab's interactive components. After several minutes of quietly pressing and turning various symbols, something clicked within the slab. She leaned back for a second, fearing she may have just done something horribly wrong. Instead, a rectangular section of the stone popped open.

She glanced over at Chen, who stared at her with widened eyes. "It looks like a lid," he said.

Lowe agreed with a nod. "I guess we should open it."

She wedged her fingertips underneath the lid. For two seconds, she considered that maybe this thing wasn't supposed to be opened, that it had been sealed long ago, perhaps to keep something terrible locked away from the prying eyes of humanity. Then again, why would those ancient people put something dangerous in a place where it could be found, and with a way to open it?

Lowe cast aside her paranoia and lifted the lid. Ten seconds passed as she and Chen stared into the open container. Inside lay a compact device made of an unfamiliar metal, its surface adorned with rotating rings and dials, all etched with similar enigmatic symbols. From its appearance, the object appeared to be untouched by time and weather, as if it had been created the day before.

Felicia reached in with both hands, then paused when Chen touched her on the shoulder.

"Are you sure about this?" he asked.

"No," she shook her head. "But I don't think we were meant to just leave it here."

She tried to lift the device carefully, its weight solid and heavy in her hands. Veins rippled across her forearms as she set the contraption down on the slab's surface. But the object wouldn't move.

The device was a curious amalgamation of ancient craftsmanship and inexplicable engineering. It was roughly the size of a large grapefruit, spherical but flattened at the poles, giving it an oblate shape. The outer surface was composed of interlocking metal plates, each adorned with intricate Celtic knots and spirals etched with remarkable precision. The metal itself was unlike any she had seen—its hue shifted subtly between burnished bronze and deep iron, depending on how the light struck it.

Encircling the device were three concentric rings, each capable of independent rotation. These rings were embedded flush with the surface, their edges marked with a series of Ogham inscriptions and cryptic symbols representing elements and celestial bodies—that much she could decipher. Tiny gears and mechanisms were visible within narrow gaps between the rings, hinting at the complexity hidden beneath the surface.

At the very center lay a recessed dial set with a single gemstone that glowed faintly—a light neither reflected nor refracted but emanating from within. The gemstone changed color as she manipulated the rings, cycling through shades of sapphire blue, emerald green, and fiery red.

What fascinated Felicia most were the subtle vibrations she felt when the device was in motion—a gentle hum that resonated through her fingertips, as if the artifact were alive with latent energy. Despite its apparent antiquity, the device showed no signs of corrosion or wear; the metal was smooth, almost warm to the touch.

Intricate patterns on the rings aligned to form larger symbols when rotated correctly, suggesting that the device was a kind of combination lock or astrolabe. Yet it seemed to interact with forces beyond mere mechanics, bridging the gap between the physical and the mystical. It was a masterpiece of ancient ingenuity—a puzzle waiting to be solved.

As she began to manipulate the outer ring, aligning it with one of the symbols on the inner dial, a low hum resonated through the air. Suddenly, the sky above the Flaming Cliffs ignited with ethereal lights—brilliant streams of color weaving and dancing against the twilight.

"Chen?" she said, staring up at the lights.

He didn't answer at first. Instead, his gaze remained fixed on the bizarre, inexplicable display.

Members of their team began gathering around the two, all eyes transfixed on the lights over the cliffs. Muted murmurs trickled through their ranks. Some were asking what it was, what caused it, and what it meant.

Others remained stoically silent, taking in the spectacular, otherworldly vision.

Felicia stared in awe for nearly a minute before she snapped out of the trance. The mysterious lights, previously a rare and unpredictable spectacle, were now intensifying and shifting in direct response to the adjustments she made on the device. Swirling patterns formed overhead, mirroring the symbols on the mechanism —spirals, knots, and serpentine shapes glowing in vibrant hues.

Her fingers worked faster now, moving the pieces around to see what would change in the lights' patterns.

"Unbelievable," Chen whispered, his eyes reflecting the celestial display.

Felicia's mind raced. This was more than a remarkable archaeological find; it was a gateway to understanding forces long thought to be mere legend. She continued to experiment, noting how each movement of the device altered the lights' configuration. Aligning two specific symbols caused the lights to converge into a radiant beam pointing westward, as if indicating a direction.

She wondered what else this thing could do, but she realized there could be numerous combinations with this device, and she had no clue what each could mean, or do.

Felicia knew she had reached the limits of conventional archaeology. This phenomenon intersected with the realms of the unexplained—a specialty of the Paranormal Archaeology Division working under the umbrella of the International Archaeology Agency.

She needed to call her colleague Tommy Schultz, the founder and director of the agency. She wondered if he would come here in person to investigate this wild anomaly.

Part of her hated asking for help. She almost never did that unless she was in a jam with no clear answers to a problem. In this instance, it wasn't a problem so much as the end of her expertise. At the very least, maybe the PAD agents could help decipher the Celtic glyphs and symbols.

"We need to document this and reach out to specialists," she decided. "There's a team that might be able to help us decipher this."

Chen looked over at her with concern dripping from his eyes. "Are you sure? Shouldn't we get this area secured? I imagine there are many people out there who would like to get their hands on this."

"We don't know what this is," she countered. "And almost no one knows we're out here. If I know Tommy, I'm sure he can have his people out here within the next forty-eight hours."

"That's a long time to keep this under wraps," Chen cautioned.

"Well then, you and the others don't go on social media and post pictures and videos of this. Call everyone together. We'll have a little meeting about all this, and what our next steps are."

Chen acknowledged her orders with a nod, stood, and started making the rounds with the onlookers from their team, explaining that this needed to be kept secret.

As night fully enveloped the desert, Felicia and her team set up recording equipment to capture the ongoing celestial display. The device remained cool to the touch, its mechanisms humming softly as if alive. It was strange. She felt a sort of distant connection to the makers of the device, even though she had no idea who had actually crafted it.

Once everything was set up, she dispatched the team to their tents and stood there alone for a few more minutes, soaking in the unusual sight. She didn't know how to turn the lights out, or if that were even possible. In a way, she didn't want to. Felicia was afraid if she did that, she might not be able to get them to come back on.

They'd erected a barrier around the device and the slab to keep any curious members of her team from getting too close in the middle of the night. Not that they couldn't get around it, but some deterrent was better than none.

A few minutes later, back in her tent, she took out her phone and typed a quick message to Tommy Schultz. The Starlink connection worked flawlessly, allowing the email to go through in seconds.

Satisfied for now, she started making preparations for bed despite knowing that there was no way in the world she'd be able to sleep tonight. She was too excited, too full of wonder to ever calm down enough to surrender to slumber.

Felicia would continue her investigations in the morning. Maybe she could figure it out on her own.

Deep in the recesses of her mind, though, worry trickled through her thoughts, wondering if she should have opened the slab to begin with, and what the repercussions could be.

2

CHICKAMAUGA, GEORGIA

Tara and Alex both silently wondered what they were doing here. They'd been wondering that since the second their boss, Tommy Schultz, asked them to make the ninety-minute drive from Atlanta to Chickamauga.

As the two head field agents for the Paranormal Archaeology Division of the IAA, they were accustomed to the bizarre and unusual. Over the years, their division had received thousands of calls regarding what people called paranormal events. From alien encounters to seeing unusual lights in the sky to even reports of ghosts, Tara and Alex were inundated with them all.

It had, initially, hurt their research, taking them away from the lab more than they would have preferred. But after bringing in two new agents to help shoulder the burden, they'd been able to pass off some of the more suspect reports, which allowed them more time to stay in the laboratory conducting analysis or running support for Sean, Tommy, and the other IAA field agents.

This one, however, Tommy had requested they handle personally, in part because the other two agents were already out on assignment in different parts of the world.

At least the drive wasn't too bad, and both of them enjoyed getting out into the country and away from the city traffic—and all the people.

Tara flicked her gaze toward Alex as she drove, the last rays of dusk streaming through the windshield, catching in her green eyes, sharp and analytical, the same way she examined every detail of an artifact. Her auburn hair, pulled back in a loose ponytail, gleamed like polished copper in the daylight. Even now, with one hand on the wheel and her thoughts likely running three steps ahead, there was a measured precision to her movements, the same focus she applied to deciphering centuries-old mysteries.

Alex sat across from her with one elbow resting against the door, his thick, dark brown hair slightly tousled from the warm breeze rolling through the open window. His beard, neatly trimmed, framed a face that was always on the edge of either amusement or deep thought—depending on whether he was solving a problem or enjoying someone else's attempts to do so. His dark brown eyes, nearly black in the midday sun, missed nothing, trained to pick up shifts in body language, inconsistencies in stories, the smallest cracks in a well-constructed lie.

The car rumbled down a narrow two-lane road, flanked by rolling green fields and dense patches of oak and pine, the occasional fence line cutting through the countryside. A white farmhouse sat far back from the road, half-hidden by the tree line, a reminder that this land had seen centuries of history long before roads cut through it.

Tara adjusted her grip on the wheel, her jaw tightening the way it always did when something wasn't sitting right.

The last stretch of the drive into Chickamauga was quiet, the kind of silence that grew with the deepening dusk. Tara watched the trees blur past her window as the SUV left the main road, the comforting hum of the tires changing pitch as they turned onto a narrower, two-lane route. The asphalt bore the wear of years, its edges crumbling slightly where grass and weeds reached inward, reclaiming territory.

The sun had nearly dipped below the horizon, casting a dusky orange light that spilled across the landscape in long, fading streaks. Shadows deepened between the trees, and the temperature seemed to drop with the light. Tara flipped on the headlights, the beams casting sharp silver cones ahead of them, cutting through the creeping dark.

The road wound through town slowly, almost as if time moved differently here. They passed modest homes, some clearly dating back to the late 1800s, their wooden porches slouched and railings chipped with age. Others were mid-century, post-war builds with concrete steps and peeling shutters. A few newer houses stood among them, out of place but not unwelcome—like guests who'd arrived decades late to a quiet reunion.

There weren't many shops. The occasional antique store sat tucked between old brick buildings and corner lots with faded signage. A barber pole spun in front of one squat structure, though the windows were dark, the business closed for the day. They passed a small church with stained glass windows that glowed faintly from interior light, a modest diner with a flickering open sign, and then back to stretches of quiet homes with dark yards and tall trees.

The pace of life here was clearly slower. There were no sidewalks in many places, just gravel shoulders and weathered mailboxes. In one yard, a cast iron bench sat beneath a pecan tree, empty. In another, the rusted frame of a bicycle leaned against a chain-link fence. Dogs barked distantly, the sound carrying on the breeze.

As the last of the sun disappeared beyond the treetops, they came to a turn marked only by a small, worn wooden sign that read: Gordon Lee Mansion. Tara eased the SUV onto the gravel lane, tires crunching softly as they followed the curve of the drive.

The woods grew thicker here, the trees older and taller, their branches arching overhead like a cathedral canopy. The headlights illuminated thick trunks and low-hanging limbs, and every now and then the reflective eyes of a raccoon or fox flashed from the under-brush before disappearing into the shadows.

Then, the trees opened. Gordon Lee Mansion stood at the center of a wide clearing, its white-columned facade bathed in the remaining light of dusk. The manor was grand but aged, its Greek Revival architecture unmistakable: tall, fluted columns supported a wide portico that led up to the main door. The paint was slightly weathered, and ivy crept along parts of the foundation, but it held a kind of solemn dignity that made it appear untouched by time.

The grounds around the mansion were quiet. A circular driveway looped in front of the house, flanked by boxwoods and old stone markers half-sunk into the soil. A detached carriage house stood nearby, its shape dark against the trees. Beyond that, the woods resumed, dense and dark.

Tara pulled the SUV to a stop, the engine ticking quietly in the hush that followed. The mansion loomed above them, silent, the kind of silence that hinted at memory. Alex stared out through the windshield, then turned to her slowly.

"This place feels... older than it is," he said.

Tara nodded, her hand still resting on the key. "Yeah. Like the ground remembers more than it lets on."

She stepped out of the vehicle, her boots crunching softly against the gravel. The air smelled of damp leaves, woodsmoke, and something older still—like stone and dust and time. Lights glowed from the windows, warm and inviting. But around the edges of the property, the darkness gathered, patient and still.

A figure stepped out from the shadow of the porch as they approached. He stood beneath one of the columns, hands in his coat pockets, watching them with a stillness that suggested he'd been waiting for a while. The porch light cast a soft glow over his weathered face and gray beard.

Tara gave him a polite nod as she stepped out of the SUV. "You must be Martin Hensley."

The caretaker gave a small smile and dipped his head. "Evenin'. You must be the ones from the IAA. People said I was crazy. But I knew there had to be something to this. Y'all are a little younger than I expected."

"Not as young as we used to be," Tara said with a smile.

"Ain't that the thruth for us all."

Alex joined her, extending a hand. "Alex, and this is Tara. We appreciate you meeting us."

Hensley shook his hand with a firm grip. "Glad to do it. Not many come out this way after dark."

Alex glanced toward the tree line and then back at the old man. "We'd like to see the spot, if that's okay with you."

Hensley gave a slow nod and gestured toward the side of the house. "Follow me. It's just through there. Won't take long. But watch your step. The ground's uneven, and the trees don't always like visitors."

"So you said it happens around this time every night?" Alex asked the caretaker.

The burly man in a black polo and tan khakis standing next to him nodded. "Well, not every night. But when it happens, it's around this time."

He slowed to a stop, and peered straight ahead, his wide eyes glowing in the pale moonlight. His thick, almost fluffy beard bounced slightly when he spoke.

"Are there any other things that happen that coincide with these appearances?" Tara asked.

"Not that I know of," the man said.

"I do have to ask why we're hiding in the forest," Alex said.

The caretaker looked over at him as if the answer should have been plain. "I don't want it to see us."

"The ghost. You don't want the ghost to see us?"

"Yeah, man."

Alex blinked slowly, peering into the man's eyes for a few seconds before the guy turned away to continue searching for the apparition.

The caretaker of the Gordon Lee Mansion had called the IAA to report unusual paranormal activity occurring at this time of night just on the other side of the historical home. He'd claimed that a shimmering, translucent woman appeared there, roaming around the edge of the lawn as if searching for something, or someone.

He described the woman as appearing sad, and wearing a dress that would have been popular fashion in the 1860s.

The Gordon Lee Mansion and the property around it had played a significant role in American history, particularly during the Civil

War. It had served as a military headquarters, and later on as a hospital. One of the more macabre facts regarding the mansion's role as a hospital was the overwhelming number of limbs buried around the property. Some estimates suggested as many as nine wagon loads full of amputated body parts.

It was an unsettling thing to consider, especially while standing on the edge of the forest in the dark of night. But the fact also highlighted how deeply gruesome that war had been, both on and off the field of battle.

Tara and Alex had been skeptical of the ghost sightings. Not only of the claims but also about being sent here to begin with. They weren't the Ghostbusters, or those ghost hunters from some of the popular reality television shows, even if they did investigate those kinds of things now and then.

They had both witnessed supernatural things that 99.9 percent of the public hadn't, never would, and would never want to. But as far as ghosts were concerned, neither of them had ever seen anything to prove ghosts were real, at least not in the sense people claimed them to be.

They'd heard a hypothesis once that apparitions were actually imprints of residual energy on the fabric of space-time that appeared around the same time of day or night when something significant happened in that person's life.

Others suggested that these ghosts were around because time is vertical and not linear.

They were interesting concepts, both insinuating that there wasn't necessarily a consciousness attached to the apparitions. Tara and Alex could get more on board with that than most of the traditional thoughts on the subject, but even still, they remained highly cynical. Which only made their being here that much more tedious.

But it was part of the job. A big part, actually. More often than not, leads turned out to be cold, with no evidence of the claimed paranormal activity.

Alex and Tara had already discussed their protocol before getting out of the car. They'd give it ninety minutes before leaving to head back to their home in Atlanta.

Alex casually checked his watch, trying to stay discreet. He didn't want to insult the caretaker, or make him feel like they thought they were wasting their time, but the two agents weren't going to stick around all night in hopes of seeing something spooky.

Martin, the caretaker who'd made the call, continued to watch the darkness beyond the mansion as if his intense gaze would summon the otherworldly figure.

"What is your theory about this ghost?" Tara asked, trying to both pass the time and glean more information.

Martin glanced over at her. "Folks around here have several ideas about that. Some say she's the mother of one of the men killed in battle during the war. Others say she was a wife of one of them."

"Does this ghost resemble anyone from the family that owned this residence?" Alex wondered.

"Not that I can tell. And I have seen all the pictures of the family through the generations. She doesn't look like any of them."

"So, who do you think it is?"

Martin shrugged his bulky shoulders. "I've thought about this a lot, ever since I first saw it. I never really believed in that kind of stuff. Always thought it was nonsense or people lying about seeing things to get attention. You know, like the people who claim to have been abducted by aliens."

The two listened quietly without interjecting.

"Best I can figure," he went on, "if it really is a ghost, it must be one of those two things I mentioned—either a wife or a mother of one of the soldiers who died here."

"Hard to imagine a more harrowing, life-altering experience than to lose your son in battle," Tara whispered.

"Yeah, and it's possible there was more than one. There could have been brothers. That was pretty common. Entire family lines were wiped out in that bloody war. Some of the stories I've read and heard are just awful. Horribly sad stuff."

"Something so profound could apply to that idea about energy being imprinted on space-time," Alex said.

Martin glanced over at him; his expression vague. "I don't know much about those sorts of things, so I'll have to take your word for it."

"The greater the energy of emotions, the more powerful the effect on the fabric around us that holds everything together."

The explanation didn't seem to make a dent on Martin's face.

"Think of it this way," Tara jumped in. "If you press an ink stamp gently against a piece of paper, you'll get a light impression. Or none at all. But if you press really hard on it, you'll get an easily visible, dark imprint. The same with human energy and emotions. The fabric of space-time is the paper, except it's all around us in 3-D. This woman you described, if she experienced such a traumatic event, it's possible that event was recorded residually on that paper, or three-dimensional fabric."

Martin blinked a couple of times before looking back toward the mansion. "Yeah, I suppose that's possible. To be honest, I've never heard anyone say anything like that. Are you two some kind of physicists or something? I thought y'all worked for an archaeology agency."

Tara and Alex smiled.

"No," Alex said. "We're not physicists. But we do study the fringes of that subject both out of curiosity and necessity."

"What archaeology would cause you to dive into that topic? Most of what I see from your line of work is people digging in holes and scraping away layers of dirt, and using those sifting boxes to find little fragments of artifacts."

"That's true," Tara confirmed. "For most archaeologists in the field. We're more the back-end type, the ones who analyze artifacts in the lab, and try to piece together answers."

"Well, you ain't finding any artifacts on this trip. I can tell you that much. Everything around here has already been pulled up a long time ago. And there won't be any permits to allow more digging."

Suddenly, a blue light radiated from the woods beyond the mansion. It was dim at first, a sphere hovering amid the trees. The glowing ball began moving toward the mansion, drifting between the tree trunks in a straight line.

For several seconds, neither Tara nor Alex could find a word. Martin remained silent too, simply watching the sphere as it continued through the woods.

"Uh... Martin?" Tara said. "Do you always see that before you see the ghost?"

He shook his head. "No, ma'am. I've never seen that before."

Alex leaned forward, trying to get a closer look. "It looks similar to some of the descriptions of Foo Fighters from the 1940s."

"What?" Martin asked. "The rock band?"

"No. Same name. They had to have gotten it from the references to glowing orbs following American and allied pilots over Germany."

"Wait. You're telling me American pilots saw this thing way up in the sky while they were flying?"

Alex took a breath to maintain his patience. "Yeah. And there's a lot more to the story than that, but I want to know what this thing is doing here."

"It could also be a wisp," Tara offered.

Alex arched an eyebrow and looked over at her. "As in the will-o'-the-wisps? From Celtic mythology?"

She rolled her shoulders. "Yeah. Sure. Why not? We've seen stranger."

Alex directed his attention back to the bloating sphere. "That's for sure."

"What's a wisp," Martin asked in a hushed tone as if speaking too loudly might frighten the orb away.

"In Celtic traditions, wisps are sometimes associated with spirits trapped between worlds or elemental beings connected to the earth. They might guard ancient sites or serve as omens."

"And you think that... thing might be one of those?" He pointed his finger in the general direction of the glowing orb.

"I wouldn't say that's my top guess, no. But with what we do, you have to have a pretty open mind about a lot of things."

The sphere emerged out into the open over the lawn and

continued another fifteen feet before it stopped in midair, hovering in place.

"What's it doing?" Martin wondered.

"Your guess is as good as ours," Alex hissed.

Then, four beams shot out of the glowing ball. They started out horizontal, one of them passing closely by the three onlookers. After a few seconds, the beams began to move toward each other until they nearly formed a single, powerful one.

Martin held his breath in an animated fashion. A quick look told the couple he was trying to hold back a sneeze.

They both shook their heads at him, silently pleading for him to hold it in.

He nodded then sneezed internally, barely making a sound.

Tara and Alex let out a collective sigh, but as they turned back to observe the sphere, Martin sneezed again, so loud it echoed through the forest and across the meadow.

Instantly, the sphere reacted. The beams disappeared, and the glowing ball raced back into the woods, then vanished.

Tara and Alex stared after it, hoping it would reappear. But after ten seconds of watching, they realized that wasn't going to happen. Both turned their gaze upon Martin, who looked back at them as innocently as he could.

"I'm sorry, guys. I couldn't help it."

They couldn't be angry with him. It wouldn't do any good. He couldn't help it. When you had to sneeze, there wasn't much that could stop that force of nature. Still, it had been exceedingly ill-timed.

"Don't worry about it, man," Alex said. "This gives us something to go on. We didn't see the ghost you talked about, but this is every bit as intriguing."

"The way it rushed away from us is definitely a wispy trait," Tara noted.

The two men looked at her with clear skepticism on their faces.

"What?" She held her arms out wide. "I'm just saying, based on the lore, that's what wisps do. And they have been associated with things that people might construe as ghosts or elemental beings."

"Anything is possible," Alex half agreed. He turned back to Martin. "We'll need some time to process this and come up with some theories as to what it is."

"Don't y'all have some kind of device that detects weird stuff like this?"

Tara's eyebrows sank. "You mean like in *Ghostbusters*?"

"Yeah."

"No. No we do not."

"Oh," Martin said, dejection drooping his facial muscles. "That would have been cool if you did."

Both Alex and Tara exchanged a look. It told the other that they could elaborate on the fictional aspects of those kinds of tools, but they decided to let the guy have his dream.

"We need to get going," Alex said. "It's a haul back to Atlanta, and I think we've seen enough here for one night."

"So, you're going to look into it?" Martin sounded almost desperate.

"Yeah, obviously. What we just saw definitely fits into our area of investigation. We'll let you know if we figure out anything, and we will be in contact again. I think we would both like to take another look at this, perhaps with some video equipment."

"Sounds good. I appreciate y'all coming up here."

"No problem," Tara said.

The caretaker walked them back to their vehicle, where they said their goodbyes one more time before Tara and Alex climbed into their SUV. Martin watched them back out of the spot and pull away, his face and body illuminated by the red taillights.

"Was there something off about him?" Alex asked once the man was out of view.

"Yeah, I got that too. I can't put my finger on what, exactly."

"Right. But hey, what we thought was going to be a pointless trip here turned out to be pretty awesome. I can't wait to dive deeper into this."

Tara nodded, looking out the window into the darkness.

"You okay?" Alex asked after a minute of silence.

"Yeah," she answered. "I'm good. Just thinking."

Alex looked over at her, silently pleading for her to tell him.

"It's just weird, right?" Tara said. "We're there to see whatever this guy claims to have witnessed, and instead we see this glowing blue orb."

"Yeah. It is weird. What's your point?"

"Of all the nights, why tonight? Why was tonight the anomaly?"

Alex turned left onto the next road, passing old family homes on large lots the way they were built decades before the more modern approach of packing as many cookie-cutter houses as possible onto overdeveloped lots.

"If you're thinking this has something to do with you, and your experiences, I wouldn't worry too much about that."

"Why wouldn't I worry about it? Ever since Bolivia, strange things continue to happen around me."

"I know. But nothing weird has happened lately, right? Unless you haven't told me about it."

"No. Nothing strange lately. Maybe you're right. Maybe I'm just a little paranoid about it."

"Hey, it's okay." Alex consoled her. "But I'm with you on the timing of it all. It's certainly curious. That guy said he'd never seen anything like that before."

Tara considered the problem for a moment. "Maybe there is a solar storm hitting right now. I seem to remember reading something about that recently."

"Could be. Those have weird effects on everything. Like the one that happened over the summer and turned the whole night sky pink."

"Yeah. Maybe that's it. Either way, we'll need to get Malcom to do some digging."

Tara pulled her phone out of her pocket, ready to open the app to their state-of-the-art AI known as Malcom. She noticed a new text message and decided the AI could wait for now.

She tapped on the messaging app and read the text from Tommy.

"Sounds like Tommy has another oddity for us to check out," she said after finishing the message.

"Oh yeah?"

"Yeah. Says it's in Mongolia, Gobi Desert."

"Mongolia? The desert? Seems like a long way to travel to go out to the middle of nowhere in the Gobi Desert."

"He wants us to call him."

Alex bobbed his head. "Sure. Call him up."

She hit the Call button and then switched the audio to speaker.

The phone rang three times before Tommy answered. "Hey, Tara. How's it going up in Chickamauga?"

"Hey, Tommy. You're on speaker with me and Alex. We're actually just leaving."

"Yeah? So, anything interesting?"

"Actually, there was. But not what we expected. No ghosts, but we did see a glowing blue sphere emerge from the woods."

"Really? Fascinating. Did the orb do anything?"

"It moved through the trees in a straight line then stopped over the lawn for a minute. Martin, the caretaker, sneezed, and it fled back into the woods before it disappeared."

"Unusual," Tommy said, his tone thoughtful.

"Yeah, it was. Was there anything strange going on in the atmosphere tonight?" she asked. "Solar storm? Something else?"

Tommy hummed for a few seconds. "No, I don't think so. I can check. But it seems like I would have heard about it."

"Okay. We just wanted to check the easy answers first. So, what's up with the Mongolia thing."

"That's an interesting one."

"Why's that?" Alex asked.

"An archaeologist messaged me earlier asking for help with something she found there at a place known as the Flaming Cliffs. Said they uncovered an ancient stone slab that contained some sort of device. She was pretty minimal on the details, but she claimed when she manipulated the device, strange lights appeared over the cliffs."

"What kind of lights?" Tara pressed.

"Again, she didn't give me a detailed rundown of all that happened. Apparently, part of her team's discovery entailed several Celtic markings and glyphs, both on the cliffside and on the stone slab."

"Celtic markings?" Alex clarified. "In Mongolia?"

"Yeah. It's weird. We have no records or even any theories from modern scholars about the Celts traveling to that area. Definitely worth checking out if you two are up for it."

Alex and Tara glanced at each other. They were tired, and could use a good night's sleep, but that didn't mean they weren't up for the challenge.

"When do we leave?" Tara asked.

"Tomorrow if you can do it."

"That'll work. We taking the plane?"

"Come on. Did you think I was going to make you fly commercial?"

3

MONGOLIA

D r. Lowe hadn't been able to sleep for the last forty-eight hours. Not much, anyway. The excitement of the find two days ago was too much to contain. Thoughts, ideas, and theories sprinted around her head like hot rods on a NASCAR track. She'd dozed off a few times, her imagination carrying her to a place beyond this realm, where wild dreams shone on the screen of her mind. But those sleepy moments were few, and she found herself roused again by that bitter temptress of anxiety.

Felicia had tried to tell herself to relax, that there wasn't a timeline for this. Maybe she didn't need the IAA's help. She was extremely intelligent. She could figure out the device on her own.

But they'd spent all day yesterday trying to figure out how the device worked, and what it meant. Most of her team had continued to work in other areas of the site—digging, sifting, cataloging—while she and Chen diligently toyed with the mechanism without results.

They were still able to see the mysterious lights in the daytime, but that hadn't helped matters. There was something she was missing, and Felicia couldn't figure out what.

It was a constant assault in her mind the last two nights until the sun's faint glow began to illuminate the tent walls. Now, even though she was wide awake, and knew the rest of the camp would be starting their day soon, Felicia wanted to stay in bed, wanted to finally fall asleep long enough to recharge her batteries.

She knew that wasn't going to happen, but it was nice to think about.

Rolling over onto her left side, she looked at her phone sitting on a camping stool. The wires ran down to a solar generator that fit neatly in the corner.

She let out an exasperated sigh, as if seeing the time on the screen added to her misery. *There aren't enough pots of coffee in the world to shake this fatigue*, she thought. But she would try anyway.

After using her jet stove to heat a pot of water, she poured the steaming liquid over the grinds at the bottom of a French press and placed the lid back on top. While the coffee brewed, she slipped into a clean pair of tan shorts and a white moisture-wicking T-shirt. Sounds from around the camp began to filter into her temporary dwelling.

She looked over into the back-left corner opposite her cot and frowned at the growing pile of laundry. Without access to machines out here, they had to do things the old-fashioned way—other than the eco-friendly detergent they'd brought along. Laundry was done in plastic barrels fed by the only source of water available in this remote location, a spring that flowed out of the base of the cliffs nearby.

The thought of cleaning her clothes today felt unbearable against the wall of fatigue in her mind and body. Felicia wasn't usually one to procrastinate, but today... she'd allow it.

After putting on her hiking boots, she returned to the French press and pushed the screen down until it reached the coffee grounds in the bottom. Then she reached for one of the two mugs she'd brought with her and filled it almost to the top.

With a deep breath, and her cup in hand, Dr. Lowe walked over to the entrance of her tent and stepped outside.

The sun was still low over the horizon, and the air was cool and dry—a pleasant way to start a day she knew would turn unbearably hot before noon.

Chen was already up, sitting at a table under a canopy, working on his laptop. A black mug of coffee sat next to his computer.

He'd been a great asset to the project, and to others they'd worked on together in the past. And since he'd originally come from this part of the world, having him here was invaluable in communicating with the locals, getting permits, and even securing supplies.

He looked up as she approached, his thick, black hair tousled from a night of slumber. He saw her drawing near and ran his fingers through his hair in a futile attempt to straighten it.

"Good morning," he said, putting on his best weary smile.

"Morning," she answered. "What are you working on?" She raised her mug to her lips and tested the coffee to make sure it wasn't so hot that it would burn.

"Just looking at the aerial maps of the site. I'm trying to see if there's anything we missed with the layout here."

"Like some kind of clue that could tell us how that device works?"

"Right," Chen confirmed. "Sort of like the Nazca lines. Except with this, hopefully it leads us to a solution."

Felicia took another drink. "Sounds like a good plan."

He zoomed out on the map to get a broader picture of the topography. "When will the agents from IAA arrive?"

"They should be here in the next hour or two. Their plane landed last night. I received a message that they left their hotel earlier."

"Sounds like they're eager to get here to be up that early."

"Can't say I blame them. How anxious have you been the last two days?"

"I haven't slept much," he confessed.

"Same. But if we can get a handle on how this thing works…"

"You still won't be able to sleep because we'll have just stumbled onto something else that requires more investigation." He looked up at her and smiled.

"You know me too well, Chen," Felicia said.

He grinned back at her then resumed analyzing the map.

She stepped away from the table and stared up at the cliffs. They'd discovered a narrow path that led up to the top, but no one in her group, including herself, had investigated it yet.

"I think I may go up to the top of the cliffs and check out what's there," she said, her eyes still fixed on the rock formation.

"You want me to go with you?" Chen asked.

"No, you keep doing what you're doing. I doubt I'll be up there for long. I just want to see if there's something up there that's interacting with that device."

"Like what?"

She shrugged. "I don't know, honestly. But it seems like those lights all focus around that area. Maybe they're drawn to something. It's worth a look."

"Yeah. Sounds like a good idea."

"Keep it up. I'll be back down later."

"You going to eat breakfast?"

"Nah," she shook her head. "I'll grab something when I get back."

"Good luck," he offered.

"Thanks. You too."

Felicia meandered back to her tent, sipping on her coffee as she passed other members of the team. Some were carrying wooden boxes with fragments of artifacts in them. Others were hovering around tables, cataloging the finds from the day before. Some toiled in a couple of pits they'd excavated since arriving here.

It was early, and already her team was working tirelessly.

They were good people, and excellent archaeologists. Felicia had handpicked all of them, though most had come as a result of recommendations from her network. Only Chen and a few others had worked with her before on various projects. But everyone had come together quickly, and seamlessly worked their way into their routines within a day of arriving.

Felicia returned to her tent and once inside set her coffee mug back on the little table. She collected a few things she thought she might need—an insulated metal water bottle, a protein bar in case she got hungry before she returned, and a pair of binoculars, along with a map of the area she'd procured prior to arriving at the site.

She packed the handful of supplies in her day pack, slung it over her shoulders, and stepped back out into the morning sunshine.

Felicia left the perimeter of the encampment and walked over to the base of the cliffs, where the unusual inscriptions glared back at her, taunting her with messages from long ago that she couldn't interpret. Fortunately, figuring out what the glyphs said hadn't been as troublesome as it might have been a decade or more before. It was the one bit of progress she and Chen had made in the last two days.

With the use of their satellite internet connection, they were able to look up the meanings of most of the inscriptions written in the ancient Celtic language. The symbols revealed what appeared to be some kind of riddle, but it also read like a warning.

"The darkness sealed must not be unbound. The great guardians may only unlock it to destroy," she mouthed, recalling the interpretation. The translation after that was a little murky.

"Destroy what?" she wondered.

The next bit was even more difficult, and she didn't understand how it correlated with the warning, or whatever this was.

"On the twentieth day, cross of the warrior's belt, when the light defeats the darkness. Align the... heads? To open the door to the final battle."

Looking over the script again after taking a break for a day didn't seem to help much. She was still just as confused as the first time she laid eyes on the wall, even with the interpretation.

Felicia stood there staring at the emblems for another minute. With a frustrated sigh, she turned away from it and started toward the narrow path fifty yards away to the right. She glanced over at the busy encampment, watching her team working on their assigned tasks. No one complained. Most of them didn't even look tired. She wished she had their energy, and she also wondered how they did it with such a perplexing mystery right under their noses.

Then again, it wasn't their job to figure this stuff out. She wasn't sure if it was even hers. Felicia had been in this line of work for more than a decade since finishing her graduate work.

When she was younger, movies about this kind of stuff had reeled her into the profession, which she quickly realized wasn't about finding an X that marked the spot, or dodging booby traps in ancient temples.

It was hard work—in the books and physical archives, in online searches, conducting interviews with experts, and in the field, where the only actual dangers she'd encountered were the occasional spider, venomous snake, or dehydration.

She shivered at the thought of snakes. Felicia hated those creatures. She'd always had the mindset of kill first and ask questions later when it came to serpents. The people who told her there were good snakes and bad snakes seemed like lunatics to her, even though she knew they were correct. And the people who kept them as pets... They were even nuttier, in her opinion.

She'd heard stories about pet snakes that escaped their terrariums and slithered away to hide in hard-to-reach places of their owner's homes.

One particular tale sent shivers down her spine.

In Florida, a woman had a pet python that managed to get out of its glass cage and disappear. She thought the animal had somehow found a way out of the house and was now on the loose in the city—perhaps in a park. Months later, she went up into her attic to look for something and discovered snake skins littering the floor. And in the back corner, her pet sat coiled, ready to strike.

The serpent had grown to an astounding length, and was easily ten times thicker than when she'd last seen it.

Apparently, the snake had been hiding up in the attic, feeding on mice that had sneaked into the house. And with the perpetual warmth in the attic, her former pet had been quite comfortable with remaining up there.

Another shiver rippled across Felicia's skin as she reached the head of the narrow goat path.

The woman had been forced to call animal control, who removed the python and supposedly took it to a zoo.

Felicia wondered if that woman ever got another pet snake after the harrowing event. The lady had been lucky the thing wasn't sitting close to the top of the ladder when she'd ascended to the attic. It might well have considered her to be the meal of the century, and wrapped its body around her for the kill.

Taking a deep breath to purge the memory from her mind, Felicia began up the trail.

The path was barely more than three feet wide and wound its way up to the top through a series of switchbacks.

She reached the first turn and carefully continued her hike, wary of the loose rocks and scree underfoot. At the next bend, she paused for a moment and looked out over the encampment. The view would be even better from the top, but here she could still see everything laid out before her.

After seventeen treacherous minutes of climbing, she finally reached the top, where she paused to catch her breath. Her legs burned, and sweat rolled down the sides of her face and beaded on her forehead.

She removed the canteen from her bag and took a long drink. Out here where the air was as dry as David Spade's comedy, it didn't take much to dehydrate. The atmosphere seemed to suck the moisture out of her skin.

Felicia had been on multiple excavation sites with similar climates, and she always had to remember to pack extra lip balm. It only took one experience with cracked, parched lips near the point of bleeding for her to buy the stuff in bulk whenever she was heading out to a place like this.

The thought reminded her to slather on an application as soon as she finished taking a long drink.

After placing her bottle back in the bag and coating her lips, she took a slow breath and looked out across the desert. To many, it would seem more like a wasteland than anything else. She couldn't disagree with that sentiment. There wasn't much out here except dirt and rocks, and the occasional scrub, a random scraggly tree here and there. And there were few, if any, signs of life other than that coming from the camp.

Even so, Felicia found the view of the desert beautiful in its own way. This land had been touched by few humans, save for the settlement she was here to investigate. Most had thought she was crazy to do it. They called it a wild goose chase. Several peers told her she was wasting her time, that no ancient people had been at this place other than a few nomadic tribes who may have camped here a short while before moving on.

But what they'd found down on the plains had disproved all of that. There had been a permanent settlement here, a place where people lived millennia ago.

The one person who believed in her had been her mother. Felicia's father had died fifteen years ago from a heart attack, leaving her mother to raise their teenage daughter on her own.

Felcia grieved over her father's death and knew how hard it was on her mom. But she also counted herself lucky to be old enough to get a job and help out with the bills. Sure, it had kept her from living a "normal" teenage life—going out to parties on the weekends, seeing movies with friends, traveling—but she tried not to think about that, always keeping her nose down. That perseverance and focus had resulted in excellent grades in college, and she'd eased the financial burden for her mother.

Now, though, her mother was sick, and the bills were piling up.

Felicia had been forced to make a decision. Go back home to Cincinnati, give up on the discovery of a lifetime to help her mom, or stay the course in hopes of uncovering a lost civilization that would shake up the history books.

In the back of her mind, she knew publishing deals would follow, podcast appearances, and a new stream of income that could help her mother more than she ever could by simply giving up.

It hadn't been an easy decision, but now she felt vindicated.

"I wish you could see this, Mom," she whispered.

A warm breeze tickled her skin, almost as if her mother had responded from afar. It comforted her, at least a little.

Tears dammed in her eyes, but she choked them back and wiped them away before they could spill over. There wasn't time for that right now. She had work to do. And Felicia had learned long ago not to give in to her emotions.

She turned and looked back at the rocky terrain on top of the hill. "Isn't much to see up here," she said. "Other than the view."

Felicia wandered toward the center of the rock mountain, stepping carefully as she looked for anything unusual. She didn't even know what that might be—a pile of rocks that didn't belong there, a vertical cave entrance, perhaps the remnants of an altar beaten down by the hammers of time.

She paused after a few minutes of walking and lowered the brim of her hat to shield her eyes from the sun. Out here, her aviator sunglasses didn't seem dark enough against the unimpeded glare of the sun.

"There's something here," she muttered. "I know it."

The statement was just as much to purge her doubts as it was real confidence. If there'd been any ruins on the top of this big rock, she would have seen them already.

The undulating, uneven surface beneath her feet reminded her of images she'd seen from Mars. The entire area was like a Martian landscape, devoid of life or the ability to sustain it—other than the few terrestrial reptiles she'd encountered, her only reminder she was still on terra firma.

After walking around for ten minutes, Felicia found an unusual spot on the plateau. The hard, rolling surface flattened as if it had been carved by human hands. The area was circular, and while she couldn't be sure without getting a view from above, it appeared to be nearly perfect in its shape.

She crouched down and ran her fingertips across the smooth stone. There were no signs that ancient tools had cut it or ground it down to this state. The scientist in her insisted that it was only a natural formation, carved out over tens of thousands of years by the elements.

But as she peered around at the unusual shape, Felicia couldn't convince herself that was true.

She stood and walked around the edge, inspecting every inch. The circle was raised slightly above the rest of the rock around it, perhaps two inches higher. If someone wasn't paying attention, it might have gone unnoticed, though she doubted it.

"What is this?" she wondered. "Why would someone go through all the trouble of cutting away the rock around it then smooth this surface until it was almost perfectly level?"

Felicia moved to the center of the circle and spun around slowly, as if doing so would somehow give her the answers.

But none came, and no amount of theorizing provided any either.

She walked back to where she'd discovered the anomaly and studied it again. *This has something to do with those lights. I know it. But what?*

Thinking there might be another, similar formation, she pressed ahead, investigating the top of the mountain until she nearly reached the opposite end of where she began. The search was fruitless, unveiling nothing else like what she found before.

She turned and looked back. The other side of the mountain looked far away, and she realized how much distance she'd covered almost without realizing it.

Felicia took her water bottle out of her pack again, drank nearly half of it, then stuffed it back in its place and began the trek back to the goat path.

She paused when she reached the circle again, hoping she'd find something she missed before, but it all looked the same.

She panned across the unusual surface. If it had been carved out by Mother Nature, it was unlike anything she'd come across before— either in the field or in her studies.

Just as Felicia was about to give up trying to find a clue, a distant, unfamiliar sound reached her ears. It sounded almost like popcorn popping in a microwave, but with more punch to the noises.

Leaving the flat circle behind, she picked her way back across the top of the rock, heading for the end of the trail. As she drew closer, the popping sounded more like firecrackers she'd heard so often during Fourth of July celebrations.

Before she had time to wonder why her team would be setting off fireworks out here in the middle of the Gobi Desert, she reached the edge of the cliffs and looked down on the camp.

In an instant, Felicia's world turned into a nightmare.

4

She watched in horror as the scene played out below.

Several members of her team were lined up in a row, kneeling before armed men in gray tactical gear. Felicia was too far away to get a good look at any of the gunmen, not that it would have mattered. Their faces were covered in scarves and sunglasses.

She crouched behind a rock, trying to decide what she could do to help, but paralysis gripped her.

Her eyes panned the rest of the camp, and her chest tightened at the sight of five other members of her team lying motionless on the desert floor. She covered her mouth to keep from gasping, as if the gunmen below could hear such a subtle sound.

One of the gunmen raised a pistol and pointed it at a member of her team kneeling on the ground. The firearm popped loudly. Pink mist ejected out of the back of the person's skull before the woman toppled over.

Bile churned in her gut, ushered on by a wave of nausea. She managed to control herself and keep from vomiting, but just barely.

The gunmen with the pistol moved down the line to the next person, a guy named Raul who'd joined the team from Spain. The gunman said something to Raul. The answer the captive gave didn't satisfy the shooter, and he fired a round through the victim's head, just as before.

A tsunami of nausea blasted into Felicia, and she didn't think she could hold it back any longer.

Who are these people? What do they want? What can I do to stop them?

None of the questions rattling through her head produced any answers. She wondered if the gunmen knew where she was, if they'd sent someone up the trail to find her.

Her eyes darted over to the top of the trail, half expecting to see a man with a rifle appear any second.

Another pop echoed from below, and a third victim fell prostrate on the ground. The temptation to yell "no" or "stop" squeezed her mind. But it would do no good, and she knew it. To do so would only give away her position. She was unarmed, and as guilty as she felt about doing nothing, getting herself killed wouldn't help the situation.

Suddenly, she saw movement from one of the tents on the outer edge of the encampment. Two of the other members of her team took off in a dead sprint, running away from the camp toward the endless desert plains.

Two gunmen who'd been nearing the tent as they scoured the site for more victims saw the man and woman trying to escape. They hurried after them then stopped, braced their rifles against their shoulders, and opened fire.

The rapid popping of the weapons' report unleashed a volley of rounds at their targets. Dust and debris exploded in bursts around their targets' feet at first, and for the briefest of moments Felicia had the crazy notion they might get away.

But the shooters adjusted their aim as they continued to fire. Bullets struck both targets in the back multiple times, cutting them down midstride. They tumbled to the ground, writhing in agony.

The two gunmen trotted after them and stopped when they were over their victims. Then fired a shot into each of their heads to finish the job.

Felicia shuddered, tears spilling from her eyes and falling to the dry rock beneath her. Mingling with the overwhelming sense of fear and sadness was the feeling of helplessness unlike anything she'd experienced before.

More gunshots rang out, and she turned back to the line of those kneeling on the ground. All but one of them were dead. The last was a young woman named Sarah from Mississippi. Even from this distance, Felicia could see she was sobbing uncontrollably. Witnessing that ripped her heart in two.

The gunmen aiming at her looked up toward the cliffs, almost directly at Felicia. She ducked down behind the rock, fearful they spotted her.

She waited ten seconds before risking a peek. Three of the men in the group were on the move, and they were heading toward the base of the cliffs and the narrow path leading up to where she hid.

"Oh, no," she muttered and immediately began looking for a place to hide. She knew it was futile. There was nowhere up here. The entire top of the rock mountain was exposed.

Felicia felt a wave of panic rush over her. She only had fifteen minutes at most to find a place to hide, and as far as she knew, there were no other paths that led up here. Otherwise, she could descend down and find a place around the base to lay low until the men gave up and left.

It was wishful thinking.

Unable to simply stand still and allow her hunters to find an easy quarry, she turned and started running back toward the flat circle. Her heart pounded in her chest. Every step seemed too slow, as if the gunmen were somehow able to ascend the mountain in seconds.

She passed the round area and stopped just on the other side, where she scanned the layout again. This time, though, instead of looking for clues, she sought refuge. An idea popped into her head. It was a long shot, but it was better than staying out here, completely vulnerable.

Knowing there wasn't any place to hide on the top, she decided to check the sides. Felicia took off to the right, running all the way over to a point she'd noticed before that jutted out from the main surface of the plateau. She slowed down as she neared the edge and peered over the precipice. Directly below here was nothing but a sharply sloping rock face. But fifty feet to the left, she spotted a narrow ledge just wide enough for her to stand on, along with several gouges in the rock where she could grip with her hands.

She'd been a decent rock climber in college, and went out many times on the weekends with friends to test her skills. But most of the time she'd only done bouldering, and when she had ascended higher climbs, she'd always been in a harness with a friend belaying her from below.

Felicia had never done a lead climb, and had never free climbed anything taller than twenty feet. On top of all that, this wasn't a climb. It was a descent. One mistake, and she would fall to the desert floor far below.

Her hesitation only lasted for a precious minute before she darted to her left toward the spot she'd discovered. When she reached it, she glanced back over at the place she'd been hiding before behind the rock. The gunmen would be up here soon. It was either stand there and let them kill her—or worse—or she could take her chances on the cliff. Even then, they might check around the edges to see if she'd done something like that, but it was her only play.

Felicia could only hope the men weren't that thorough.

Her mind made up, she lowered herself down, dangling her legs over the drop-off. She carefully twisted her body, bracing most of her weight with her palms pressed into the rock, then gradually let her feet down while she adjusted her grip. Her fingers clenched a narrow lip in the rock until her head could no longer be seen from above. The toes of her boots dug into a crack in the rock wall, relieving some of the tension on her fingers and in her forearms.

She knew one slip would be the end. No matter how much she tried to think of something else, that thought alone dominated her mind.

She lowered her right hand to a crag that jutted out from the rock, gripped it tightly, and lowered her left foot down to the ledge she'd spotted before, then shifted her left hand to another crack just below the first.

Once her foot found purchase on the ledge, the burden on her hands and arms lightened. She moved her right foot down to join the other then fit the fingers of her right hand into the lower crack. The gap was wide enough that fitting her digits into it proved easy, though she feared there might be a snake or some kind of insect dwelling within the shadows of the opening.

She didn't have a choice. It was this or die at the hands of the gunmen.

5

Rolf pressed the rifle's stock against his shoulder as he swept the surface of the mountaintop, searching for the woman who'd supposedly come here earlier. Right away, he determined there was nowhere she could hide, save for the far end of the plateau where a slight rise could provide the most minimal cover possible. She'd have to be lying on her belly to go unseen.

He took five more long steps to reach the top of the trail then stepped aside for his two men to join him and fan out.

"No sign of her," Rolf said in a quiet tone, just loud enough to be heard over the wind rustling through their ears.

"Maybe the girl was lying," a man named Yuri offered in a Ukrainian accent. He was younger, in his late twenties, with tattoos on his neck that were visible above his collar.

"Perhaps," Rolf half agreed. "But we need to check everywhere just in case."

The Ukrainian nodded. The other man, Javier, remained silent, as was typical for him. He was known among their group as having a violent, fiery temper, but that rage simmered deep within like a long-dormant volcano that could suddenly erupt to life when provoked.

Rolf had witnessed the devastating power of the man's temper many times, and the carnage that remained in his wake. It was useful to have someone like that on their team, as long as he could control his emotions and follow orders. So far, after two years of working operations together, Javier had managed to do just that.

Still, Rolf feared the man was a ticking time bomb and could at any point make a huge mistake.

"Spread out," Rolf ordered. "Search the entire area."

"There's nowhere to hide up here, commander," Yuri protested.

Rolf leveled his gaze at the man, staring at him through his darkly tinted sunglasses. The glare carried an unspoken warning for his subordinate not to challenge his authority again.

Yuri understood and nodded reluctantly. "Yes, sir." He marched away to the left, while Javier moved forward to cover the center of the plateau.

Rolf watched for a few seconds then strode to the right. If the woman was up here, he'd find her.

He reached the edge of the cliff and looked down, keeping himself a safe three feet away from the drop. He checked the rock wall to the left but saw no sign of her. The mountain's face ran in a gently undulating pattern until interrupted by a section that stuck out farther away from the top, like a stone wave permanently jutting from the side.

"If she thought she could hang off the side of this and hide, she'd have had a long drop with a sudden stop at the bottom."

He turned and began stalking toward the other end of the mountain, his eyes staring straight ahead.

Rolf looked over at Yuri on the opposite side. He too was checking the cliff's edge as he pressed forward, but apparently saw nothing suspicious.

Javier had the easiest task moving up the center. With nowhere to hide, his job was menial at best. But Rolf was thorough in everything he did. It was why he'd survived combat situations where most of the men around him hadn't, and it was why he'd been recruited by his employer to head up this team.

He'd leave no stone unturned, even if there were no stones.

Rolf continued up the line until he reached the place where the anomalous point stuck out from the top of the rock. He started to walk out to it, but Javier called to him.

"Sir," he shouted over the wind. "Take a look at this."

Rolf looked back at him then noticed what had caught Javier's attention. He stood just outside a huge flat circle that appeared to have been carved out of the rock—and not by nature.

Forgetting his search for the moment, Rolf walked over to the strange carving and stopped next to Javier.

"What is it, sir?" Javier wondered.

"I have no idea." Rolf wasn't an archaeologist. He knew almost nothing about the field of study, much less about identifying artifacts, or in this case this giant circle.

"You think it has something to do with why we came here?"

"Possibly," Rolf conceded. "Or it could just be nothing. We're not up here to figure out the meaning of ancient rock formations or strange carvings. We're here to find the person who can."

Yuri had noticed the other two standing by the unusual formation and trotted over to join them. "What is this?" he asked, oblivious to the short conversation the other two just finished.

"We don't know," Rolf answered. "Any sign of her over there?"

The Ukrainian shook his head. "No. If she tried to hide on the side of the mountain, she would have fallen. There's nothing to hold on to." He paused then asked, "You think the girl lied to us?"

"Perhaps." The thought, however, didn't add up unless their last hostage was trying to buy time for the director. The more Rolf thought about that, the more it made sense. He and the other two hurried up here thinking they would trap Dr. Lowe, but if she'd headed out—possibly even in a vehicle—across the desert, she'd be long gone by now, and without knowing the direction, tracking her would be next to impossible without air support.

He peered off toward the far end of the mountaintop and pointed. "Come on, let's check the far side and see if there's any sign of her."

The three men left the circle behind and moved as a unit across the top of the mountain. Before they reached the other end, Rolf already knew they'd been tricked. Still, they pushed all the way to the end until they arrived at the edge. There, he craned his neck and looked down over the precipice. The woman was nowhere to be found.

Irritation flashed through him, and he squinted against the bright sun, scanning the horizon in every direction for any sign of Dr. Lowe.

If she'd taken a vehicle to escape, there should have been dust rising from the tracks she left behind. But there was none. Maybe she'd left before they made it on site, possibly to go get supplies. As far as Rolf knew, though, there wasn't anything near here except the city where they'd staged earlier that morning.

"Let's get back down to the camp and see if any of the others found her. Perhaps she was hiding out in one of the tents and our men simply missed it on their first sweep."

The other two nodded.

As they marched back toward the trail, Rolf couldn't help but feel like he was missing something, as if Dr. Lowe was here, right under his nose. But they were operating on a tight schedule, and time wasn't on their side. He knew that the team from the IAA would be here soon, and that could complicate matters.

His men could handle the Americans, especially if they weren't armed. But if the IAA agents sensed something was amiss, perhaps saw the guns from afar, they could turn around, head back to civilization, and call in reinforcements.

If Felicia Lowe had run on foot into the desert, she wouldn't last long without water. Getting anywhere would take at least a day or two. By then, the elements would have ahold of her, and she would more than likely die from exposure.

It wasn't a chance Rolf wanted to take, but he had to play the odds. Either way, he doubted his employer would appreciate the report, but he'd have to get over it. They'd done their job.

ORNAMENTLAL BREAK

WHEN THEY ARRIVED BACK at the camp fifteen minutes later, Rolf went straight to the SUV, where their lone living hostage had been stowed for safekeeping.

Rolf knew the man's name and background based on the dossier he'd been given prior to the mission.

He threw open the back passenger door to the SUV and stared into the eyes of the man in the back.

"She wasn't there," Rolf said in an accusatory tone. "And there was nothing up on that mountain except a circle carved flat out of the rock."

Chen looked back at him through weary eyes. "Not there?"

"You seem genuinely surprised. For a moment, I thought you might have lied."

Chen shook his head. "She went up to see if there was anything there related to the device we found."

Rolf narrowed his cold, blue eyes. "Show me this device. And hurry. Your friends from the IAA will be here soon."

He noticed the surprise on Chen's face and said, "You think we weren't tracking them?"

Chen shrugged.

"Come. Quickly. Show me this supposed device."

Chen nodded and climbed out of the vehicle. He lumbered over to a crate they must have kept the device in for the last few days. Rolf's men had already opened it in their search but left it alone until they received further orders.

"This is it," Chen said, motioning absently to the bizarre contraption he'd spent so many hours working with since its discovery.

"What does it do?" Rolf demanded, glancing back over his shoulder. The hands of time were winding faster than he'd like.

Chen reached down and twisted one of the dials.

Immediately, a light flashed from above the flaming cliffs. Its pink hue was barely visible against the clear blue sky overhead, but it was nonetheless there for all to see. The single beam towered over the top of the mountain like a pillar of light shining into the heavens.

"What does it mean?" Rolf asked.

"We don't know. I worked with this for hours. There are different colors, and the beams' directions can be changed, but as of yet I have no idea what it does."

Chen stole a second to glance around the camp. All of his coworkers were dead, their bodies littering the desert ground between the tents. A few lay out in the open. Rolf noticed his gaze and sensed the gravity of the slaughter hanging around his neck like thick iron chains. The look on Chen's face betrayed his nausea.

"Keep it together," Rolf said, his words sharp. "You're telling me you spent two days investigating this mechanism, and you still don't know what it's for?"

Chen nodded. "Yes. I tried many combinations with the dials, but it's produced no other results than the position or color of the lights."

Rolf stared at him, assessing the man to see if he was lying. The fear in Chen's eyes betrayed no falsehood. He didn't know what it was for, which was unfortunate—both for Rolf and for Chen.

"It would seem you are of no use to us," Rolf said, raising his pistol, pointing it at the man's face.

"No. Please. I'm close. I can do it. I... just need more time." He raised his hands in protest, but the forlorn expression in his eyes told Rolf he knew he was doomed.

"We are out of time. Your friends from the IAA will be here soon. I would rather not tangle with them right now."

Chen's expression changed slightly. "You're... afraid of them?"

Rolf snorted in derision. "Please. I fear no one. But they are connected. Well connected. One wrong move, and we could have agents swarming us. I can't have that."

He saw the gears turning in Chen's mind through the rapid shifting of his eyes.

"What?" Rolf demanded. "What are you thinking?"

"It's... Well, it's just that... we could wait and see what they do when they get here."

"What do you mean?" Rolf kept the pistol trained on his hostage, but he relaxed his grip a little.

"The IAA agents, they'll come here and find all this. They'll see what you've done. Obviously, they'll call in support."

"I'm waiting for your point."

"I'm saying you were sloppy, and now all this senseless violence is going to come back on your head." Chen's aggressive statement surprised Rolf, and not in an entirely unpleasant way. He actually respected the man more considering up until that point he'd believed him to be a soft soy boy beta male.

Rolf lowered his pistol, which appeared to surprise Chen.

Then he turned to Yuri, who stood just behind him off his right shoulder. "Round up the men. We're leaving."

He watched Chen's reaction. A frown, eyebrows tightening over his nose, watching as Yuri carried out the order.

"You're just leaving?" Chen asked.

"Yes," Rolf said. "At least for a while. Let the IAA team get here and see what's happened. As you say, they will be compelled to call for help. Of course, out here, who has jurisdiction? Who would they even call?"

Chen lowered his head dejectedly. He didn't have an answer. He doubted the Mongolian government would respond quickly, not out here in such a remote area. People died all the time in the wastelands and deserts, though not like this. This was murder. On a big scale.

"I'm willing to wager this group from the IAA will have to call in international support, probably from their own country. The investigation won't happen for at least a day or more. In the meantime, we'll wait and see if they can figure out your device. Who knows, perhaps we'll get lucky."

6

The SUV roared through the vastness of the Gobi Desert, kicking up clouds of dust and grit that curled in the sunlight before disappearing behind them. The old dirt road was barely a suggestion, a faint scar cutting across an endless stretch of sand and rust-colored earth. Tara's knuckles were white as she gripped the steering wheel, her foot pressing the accelerator hard, forcing the vehicle to barrel forward over every bump and dip in the uneven terrain. The tires bounced, jostling the occupants, sending shocks up through the seats with each jagged edge of the road.

Alex gripped the handle over the passenger-side window so tight his knuckles were ashy white. His body lurched side to side with each turn, his eyes wide beneath his sunglasses. The speed made every feature of the landscape blur into one continuous golden smear. He swallowed hard, his other hand bracing himself against the dash.

"You really like driving out here, huh?" he said, his eyes firmly locked on what passed for a road ahead.

Tara only answered with a sly grin as the SUV hit a hump and lifted off the ground several inches before slamming back down onto the dirt.

"Jeez!" Alex exclaimed. "Okay, you did that one on purpose."

"Pretty much," she said.

"Would you mind slowing down?" Fear riddled his voice.

"Why?" she asked. "It's not like I'm going to get a speeding ticket out here."

"It's not the cops I'm worried about."

She stole a sidelong glance, flashing a sardonic smirk. "Oh, you got something against a woman driving an SUV in the desert?"

"What?" he protested. "No. Come on. But you're driving like a maniac."

"Aww, is this a preview of what you're going to be like in your sixties? It's cute. At least for now."

"I'd like to live to see sixty."

"Come on, Alex! Where's your sense of adventure?" she called over the roar of the engine. Her hair whipped around her face from the breeze pouring in through the cracked-open window, sunlight highlighting her determined expression. She could feel the adrenaline coursing through her veins, her pulse pounding with the rhythm of the SUV's tires bouncing over the dusty path.

The landscape stretched out endlessly in every direction, a raw wilderness of sand, rock, and sparse clumps of hardy vegetation. Patches of sunbaked shrubs appeared here and there, their skeletal branches twisting upward, as if trying to catch a glimpse of the sky. The desert's palette was a stunning spectrum of reds, golds, and browns, the colors blending in waves as the sun arced overhead. The shadows were sharp and long, drawn out across the ground like dark fingers, contrasting with the brightness of the early afternoon sun.

The Flaming Cliffs, their destination, towered over the plains ahead. At first, they'd been visible only as a faint line of shimmering orange against the sky. But as the couple sped down the road, the massive mountain grew more imposing by the second.

The cliffs seemed almost like a mirage, their fiery hue dancing in the heat waves that rolled across the desert surface. Alex squinted at the horizon, trying to gauge the distance, but the heat distorted everything. The Gobi seemed to play tricks on the eyes, making the world twist and shift, mirages forming and fading in the distance, adding to the surreal feeling of being lost in an ocean of sand.

He could feel the vibrations of the tires reverberating through his bones. The SUV's shocks groaned as the vehicle sped over a particularly uneven patch, and Alex winced, letting out a low groan of his own.

"I don't know if this road even counts as a road anymore," he muttered, gripping the handle tighter. He glanced at Tara, her gaze fixed dead ahead, her jaw set. She looked as if nothing could faze her, her eyes locked on to the horizon as if it held some kind of promise she was determined to keep.

Sunlight poured down like molten gold, heating the world to a simmering haze. The sky above was a flawless expanse of blue, not a cloud in sight, just an unbroken vault that made the desert below seem starker and more isolated. It felt as though they were the only two people in existence, surrounded by the immensity of the desert, with nothing but the hum of the engine and the rush of wind to keep them company. The vastness pressed in on them, reminding Alex of how small they were in the face of such an expansive, indifferent landscape.

The desert stretched out in waves, rolling dunes in the distance broken by rocky outcrops and jagged ridges that seemed to rise out of nowhere. Occasionally, the remnants of ancient riverbeds carved lines through the sand, dry and cracked, their once-fluid paths now lifeless. The wind swept across the dunes, shifting the sand in gentle, mesmerizing patterns, creating ripples that danced across the ground like the surface of a golden sea. The road, if it could be called that, twisted and turned, skirting these natural obstacles, guiding them deeper into the wilderness.

The dirt road twisted sharply, skirting the edge of a shallow ravine that ran dry and cracked, its edges eroded into sharp angles. Tara took the turn hard, and Alex felt his stomach drop as the SUV tilted precariously before finding its balance again. He shot her a look, but Tara seemed undeterred. There was a glint of excitement in her eyes, a wildness that matched the harsh beauty of the desert around them.

The vehicle hurtled onward, leaving a swirling trail of dust in its wake that lingered like a faint ghost, dissipating slowly in the bright air. The roar of the engine echoed in the emptiness; the sound swallowed up by the desert almost as soon as it was made. The Flaming Cliffs seemed a little closer now, their jagged profiles growing more distinct with every mile Tara pushed through. The sandstone formations glowed a deep orange, their edges gilded in sunlight, standing in stark contrast to the pale blues and browns of the desert floor.

To the left of the road, a herd of Bactrian camels appeared, their large, lumbering forms moving in lazy procession. They stood out against the monotony of the landscape, their double humps swaying as they plodded across the arid ground. Tara pointed them out with a quick nod of her head, her voice raised above the noise of the SUV. "Look, Alex! Camels!"

He followed her gesture, his fear momentarily forgotten as he watched the animals. They seemed unfazed by the vehicle speeding past, their gaze calm, even indifferent. It was as if they had seen it all before, the desert's timeless inhabitants, unaffected by human endeavors. Alex allowed himself a small smile, the sight of the camels somehow grounding him amid the terror of the drive.

In truth, he shouldn't have been so worried. With no other vehicles out here, there was zero chance of a collision. But that wasn't the only kind of accident that could happen. If she lost control and veered off into an embankment, or worse, flipped the truck, they'd be stranded out here for who knew how long. And if they were injured in the crash, things could get bad in a hurry.

The sun beat down mercilessly, and Alex could feel the sweat gathering at the nape of his neck, soaking into the collar of his shirt. The air inside the SUV was hot, even with the windows cracked open, the dry wind offering little relief. The smell of sunbaked earth and dust filled his nostrils, mixing with the faint tang of gasoline and the metallic scent of the SUV's engine working overtime. He adjusted his sunglasses, wiping his forehead with the back of his hand, his gaze drifting back to the horizon.

The road only grew rougher as they neared the cliffs, the ground littered with loose stones and the occasional boulder that had tumbled from somewhere above. Tara navigated around them with ease, her focus unwavering. The Flaming Cliffs loomed ahead, rising from the desert floor like the bones of some ancient creature, their layered strata telling a story of ages long past, of a land shaped by wind and time.

Tara's hands were steady on the wheel, her eyes alight with a determination that Alex had seen many times before. She lived for moments like this, the thrill of the chase, the promise of discovery just beyond the horizon. He envied her ability to embrace the chaos, to find joy in the uncertainty. For Alex, the journey was something to endure, a means to an end, but for Tara, it was the adventure itself that mattered most.

The SUV rattled over a series of ruts, the tires skimming over the uneven ground, and Alex's teeth clattered together with each jolt. He glanced at Tara, her expression one of fierce concentration, her lips curved into a slight smile. He couldn't help but shake his head, a mixture of exasperation and admiration washing over him. "You really are something else, you know that?"

Tara shot him a quick look, her smile widening. "You say that like it's a bad thing," she replied, her voice filled with amusement.

Alex let out a breath, leaning back in his seat, his grip on the handle easing just a little. The Flaming Cliffs were closer now, their vivid orange and red hues standing out against the pale sky, the sun casting deep shadows that accentuated their rugged beauty. He could see the layers of sediment, the evidence of countless years etched into the rock, each stratum a record of the passage of time.

The desert seemed to hold its breath as they approached, the vastness of it all settling around them like a shroud. There was a sense of stillness, a quiet that contrasted with the roar of the engine, as if the world itself was waiting for something to happen. Alex felt a thrill of anticipation, a sense that they were on the cusp of something extraordinary, the kind of moment that defined everything that came after.

The Flaming Cliffs soared higher with every passing second, their jagged edges sharp against the sky.

From about a mile away, the encampment near the Flaming Cliffs came into view, a cluster of colorful tents and scattered vehicles against the otherwise barren landscape. But something about it seemed wrong. The first thing Tara and Alex noticed was the stillness. There was no movement—no bustling workers, no signs of life. The tents shimmered in the distance, tiny dots of orange, blue, and green appearing almost like an oasis in the vast, empty desert. Yet the camp looked strangely lifeless, devoid of the usual activity one would expect from an archaeological dig.

Tara squinted; her gaze locked on the camp as the SUV bounced along the uneven dirt road. The silence was unsettling. Normally, by now they should have seen people moving about, the flash of a reflective vest, or even the distant noise of machinery. But instead, there was nothing. It was as if the entire place had been frozen in time. The bright colors of the tents seemed surreal against the harsh backdrop of the desert, and the quiet was thick enough to feel tangible.

"Where is everyone?" Alex asked, his voice tense, his eyes narrowing as he scanned the horizon. Tara shook her head, her lips pressed into a thin line. Her excitement, which had fueled their drive across the desert, faded quickly, replaced by a creeping sense of dread. Her knuckles were even whiter against the steering wheel, her fingers gripping it tighter as they neared the camp.

The encampment looked small and vulnerable from this distance, dwarfed by the imposing cliffs that rose behind it, their fiery orange hue blazing in the bright afternoon sun.

As the couple drew closer, more details began to emerge—the angular shapes of scaffolding set against the rugged rock face, the vehicles parked at the edges of the camp, but still no movement, no people. The camp appeared deserted, its energy drained, an eerie quiet taking the place of what should have been a hive of human effort set against the indifferent backdrop of the desert.

"I have a bad feeling about this," Tara said.

Her stomach churned, and a chill settled into her bones despite the heat radiating off everything. Something was off. She exchanged a glance with Alex, and she could see the same unease reflected in his eyes. The closer they got, the more the eerie stillness seemed to press down on them, an invisible weight that grew heavier with each passing second.

The tents were positioned in a rough semicircle, forming a buffer around the excavation pits that lay at the heart of the encampment. The pits themselves became visible as the SUV approached, dark gashes in the golden earth marked by lines of rope strung between stakes. Tara could feel a knot forming in her stomach, her excitement quickly turning to concern. Where were the workers, the hum of activity? The entire place seemed unnaturally quiet, and a chill ran down her spine despite the heat of the afternoon sun.

As they neared the edge of the camp, Tara slowed the SUV, her eyes darting from one tent to another. The canvas flaps hung open, swaying slightly in the breeze, but there was no movement inside. A few of the vehicles were parked haphazardly, as if they'd been abandoned in a hurry. The generator, which should have been running to power the camp, was silent. The only sound was the faint rustle of the wind as it swept across the desert and through the open windows, carrying with it a sense of desolation.

Alex shifted uneasily in his seat, his hand resting on the door handle. "This doesn't feel right," he muttered, his gaze flicking to the excavation pits. There was something about the emptiness that felt deliberate, like a warning they were too late to heed.

The SUV rolled forward, the tires crunching over the gravel, and Tara's heart pounded in her chest. She could feel the tension building, a sense of urgency compelling her to turn around, to get out of there while they still could. But that wasn't an option. This was what they signed up for, coming to places like this, situations that could be dangerous. They'd trained for years with Sean Wyatt, learning how a former government agent handled nearly every scenario imaginable in the field. Even so, it seemed there were always surprises, things that they couldn't prepare for.

As the SUV rolled to a stop near the base of the Flaming Cliffs, Tara and Alex were greeted by a sight that made their blood run cold, and sent a blast of nausea through them.

Bodies lay on the ground, some dusted by the shifting sand, others out in the open, arranged in a grim, deliberate row. Their lifeless forms were dressed in their work clothes, as if they'd started the day as they would any other. Now, those clothes were their deaths shrouds.

There were no signs of a struggle, just a brutal efficiency that spoke of an execution.

"What in the world happened here?" Alex breathed, unable to take his eyes off the grisly sight.

Tara's breath caught in her throat, her fingers trembling as she turned off the engine. The sudden silence was deafening, and the world seemed to narrow to the scene before them. She could hear her own heartbeat, loud and frantic in her ears, and she forced herself to swallow, her mouth dry. Alex stared, his face pale, his eyes wide with shock.

"Who did this?" she whispered, her voice barely audible. The reality of what they were seeing settled in, and another wave of nausea rolled through her.

Whatever happened here was cold-blooded, calculated, and brutal. She glanced at Alex, his jaw clenched, his eyes darting around the camp as if searching for any sign of movement, any hint that someone might still be alive.

"Dr. Lowe," Alex said, his voice tight, his hand now gripping the door handle so hard his knuckles were white. "Her team." He couldn't form full sentences. He turned to Tara, his eyes filled with fear and urgency.

The two of them knew how to deal with fear, and for them to be afraid of anything anymore took something titanic. But they also knew when their surroundings could be dangerous. And at that moment, their danger meters were off the charts.

Tara met him with a determined gaze. "We need to call Tommy."

He nodded. "Yeah."

Alex took out his phone and found the last call with Tommy, then tapped the number. It rang three times before their boss answered on the other end.

"Hey, Alex. You make it out there okay?"

"Tommy, you're on speaker with me and Tara. Something happened here."

"What do you mean something happened?"

"There are bodies here, chief. Lots of them. No signs of life."

"The entire team is dead? Is that what you're telling me? What happened?"

"Not sure, but it wasn't natural," Tara said. "They were shot, from the looks of it. We haven't even gotten out of the car yet."

"Any sign of the killers?" Tommy asked.

"No. There aren't any other vehicles, and no signs of life."

Tommy sighed. They knew his brain had to be running wild back in the States.

"Okay. Okay," he repeated. "Are you comfortable securing the area?"

"Yeah," they both said at the same time.

"Good. Sweep the camp and check for survivors. Watch your backs, though. I don't want anything happening to you too."

"We'll be fine," Alex answered.

"All right. I'll get on the horn with my contacts in Mongolia and let them know what happened. It could take a while to get any teams out there to investigate, and to..." He didn't finish the thought, but both Tara and Alex knew what he was going to say. It referred to gathering the bodies—a macabre task that neither of them envied.

"Be careful," Tommy continued. "If you feel exposed, get back to the truck and leave until the cavalry arrives."

"Understood, chief."

"Okay. Check back in with me when you know more."

"You got it," Tara said. "Talk soon." -

Alex ended the call and looked over at her. Walking into a mass murder scene wasn't on the menu for a typical day in their lives. But they were equipped mentally and physically to handle it.

What had originally been an archaeological expedition had just morphed into a murder investigation

.

7

Tara killed the engine and sat perfectly still, her eyes scanning the desert around them. Alex did the same, sensing her concern that the killers might return, or were simply waiting just on the other side of the mountain to pounce on their next victims.

He opened the door and stepped out, pulling a scarf up over his mouth and nose to keep out the dust and sand blowing in the wind.

"Come on," he urged. "We better take a look around."

Tara nodded, her stomach churning as she scanned the encampment. The bright colors of the tents and tarps fluttered in the desert breeze, a jarring contrast to the lifeless bodies that lay beneath them. The dig site, which had once seemed like a place of promise and discovery, now felt sinister and dangerous.

They walked around to the back of the truck, opened the rear door, and flipped up a lid to a black gun case. Two Springfield XD 9mm pistols and two Springfield Saint AR15s rested in the foam within.

The couple removed the weapons from their cradle, holstered the sidearms, and slung the rifle straps around their shoulders. It paid to have connections all over the world. While most archaeologists and anthropologists were usually unarmed, Tara and Alex came from a faction that didn't fit inside the Bell Curve. Then again, most archaeologists never encountered the kinds of things they'd experienced.

"I don't know if we should be here," Tara said, her voice shaky but resolute. She quickly surveyed the camp for the umpteenth time, searching for any signs of life. The Flaming Cliffs loomed above them, their fiery colors now seeming to mock the horror that lay at their base. The once awe-inspiring landscape had taken on a malevolent quality, as if the very cliffs themselves were complicit in the violence that had taken place.

Alex nodded, his gaze fixed on the row of bodies, a chill running through him that had nothing to do with the desert air.

"Come on," he said. "We need to at least check for survivors."

Alex didn't have any misgivings. Whoever had committed this crime was thorough to a brutal level. He stopped a few yards from the row of victims lying on the ground, each with gunshot wounds to the head.

His instincts were to turn away, but he forced himself to scour the ground nearby. He immediately found what he was looking for.

"Shell casings," he said, pointing at the shiny, hollow brass cylinders.

"Nine mills," Tara confirmed. "They just lined them up and shot them in cold blood." Her voice trembled. "For what?"

Alex didn't answer immediately. He was preoccupied with looking around the camp, making sure they hadn't just walked into an ambush. The feeling that they were being watched pressed down on him like a barbell across his shoulders.

"I can only think of a few reasons," he said finally. "Could be a local warlord or guerrilla group, though I haven't heard about that sort of thing out here. Maybe they're a nomadic tribe."

"Or someone found out about what Dr. Lowe was working on out here," she countered.

Alex sighed. "Yeah. That's the other possibility I was considering. Let's keep moving. Dr. Lowe said she found a device that she wanted us to take a look at. Maybe it's still here."

Tara saw in his face that he didn't believe that would be the case. If whoever did this was after Dr. Lowe's discovery, surely they would have collected everything she had, and not just artifacts.

The couple moved toward the largest tent, figuring that was the center of activity. They paused outside the entrance, each taking up a position on either side. The flaps rippled in the warm breeze.

Alex and Tara shared a glance, then Alex nodded, raised his weapon, and waited while Tara raised the flap on the right. The instant it was open, he stepped into the tent, clearing the room left to right.

If there'd been anyone in there, he would have seen them immediately no matter where they were hiding. But the tent was vacant.

"Clear," Alex said, lowering his weapon.

Tara followed him inside and looked around. The tent's interior had been ransacked. Papers littered the ground around a table where they assumed Dr. Lowe conducted her research. A laptop bag and cord were next to the table, but there was no sign of the computer.

The cot in the corner had been flipped over and the pillow cut open. The blankets lay next to the mess in a pile.

Tara moved over to the table and picked up one of the sheets of paper. Dr. Lowe's notes were scribbled on it. It was mostly documentation of the things they'd found so far. Another sheet described her plans for the upcoming weeks and additional places she believed they should dig.

Tara set the page down on the table and looked back to her husband. "Looks like they were searching for something."

"And probably found it," he added, his eyes playing across the room. "Come on, we need to keep looking."

She nodded her agreement, and the two stepped back out into the sun. The camp's emptiness weighed heavily on them, and a thick, unsettling silence hung over everything. Tara took a deep breath, her heart pounding in her chest, and motioned for Alex to follow her as they began moving cautiously toward the other tents. They couldn't afford to ignore the possibility that someone might still be alive. But with every step, a gnawing dread settled deeper into Tara's gut. It was hard to imagine anyone could have survived what had happened here.

They approached the first of the smaller tents, the canvas flapping slightly in the breeze, moving shadows across the ground. Tara paused at the entrance, her hand hovering for a moment before she pulled the flap back, peering inside. The tent was empty—just a few scattered belongings, some tools, and a cot, the blankets half pulled off as if someone had left in a hurry. Alex came up behind her, glancing over her shoulder. The air inside the tent was stale, and there was no sign of life.

The two kept moving, their footsteps muffled by the sand beneath them. Tara led the way, her eyes scanning the ground, the vehicles, the surrounding excavation pits. The sense of unease wrenched at her abdomen, every gust of wind making her flinch. The camp, which had once held the promise of discovery, felt more like a graveyard.

She exchanged a look with Alex—his expression was grim, his mouth set in a tight line. Neither of them spoke at first, as if words would somehow make the horror more real.

At the next tent, Alex took the lead, pushing aside the entrance flap. He hesitated, his breath catching as his eyes fell on another body, this one slumped in the corner of the tent, a dark stain spreading beneath them. He swallowed hard, his stomach churning at the sight. The person—a man in his thirties—had been shot multiple times in the torso. His eyes stared vacantly at the ceiling. Alex took a step back, his head spinning, and turned to Tara, shaking his head. She didn't need to look to understand; she could see it in his eyes.

No matter how many times they'd seen the horrors of combat, or in this case—murder—in the field, it never got easier to handle. This man lying dead on the floor of his tent had a life, a family, friends, hopes, dreams, goals. His entire past, and his potential future, were entirely gone—snuffed out before his time, just like the others.

The couple left the scene and kept moving, checking tent after tent. Most were empty, abandoned in haste, with belongings scattered across the ground—half-packed bags, overturned chairs, notebooks lying open. Tara guessed the killers had searched every tent once they'd eliminated all the inhabitants.

The chaos on display in each dwelling spoke of fear, of people trying to escape whatever had come for them. But some tents held grim reminders of those who hadn't been fast enough. Tara found another body in one of the tents, a woman, her arm outstretched as if she had been reaching for something. Tara's heart sank further, the scope of the massacre hitting her with full force.

The sun beat down on them mercilessly as they made their way through the camp. Each new discovery only deepened the chill in the air, a sense of dread that refused to loosen its grip. There was something haunting about the stillness, the complete absence of any sound other than the wind and their own breathing. They found no survivors, just more signs of violence, more evidence of the brutality that had taken place there.

Tara paused for a moment, her eyes scanning the area. She noticed something off in the distance, beyond the edge of the camp, where the sand gave way to a rocky slope leading up to the base of the cliffs. Two shapes lay there, barely visible against the uneven terrain. Her breath caught in her throat, and she motioned for Alex to follow her. They moved cautiously, their steps slow, each one feeling heavier than the last.

As they approached, the shapes resolved into two bodies. They lay sprawled in the sand, facedown, their limbs twisted at unnatural angles. It was clear they had been trying to run, to get away from whatever horror had descended on the camp. Tara knelt beside one of the bodies, her eyes narrowing as she took in the scene. The man had been shot in the back, the blood dark against the bright fabric of his vest. She looked up at Alex, her eyes wide with fear.

"They tried to run," she whispered, her voice barely audible over the wind. The sight of the bodies, so far from the camp, made it all too real. Whoever had done this had hunted them down, had made sure there were no survivors. Alex knelt beside the other body, his eyes scanning the rocky terrain around them. He felt exposed, vulnerable—as if at any moment, the same fate could befall them.

"We shouldn't be here in the open," Alex said, his voice tight, almost a growl. He stood up, his eyes darting across the horizon, searching for any sign of movement, any indication that they were not alone. The Flaming Cliffs loomed above them, their fiery colors casting long shadows over the camp. The entire landscape seemed hostile now, as if the desert itself was a witness to the violence, holding its breath, waiting for the next act to unfold.

Tara nodded, pushing herself to her feet. Her heart was racing, the weight of the situation pressing down on her chest like a vise. She turned back toward the camp, her eyes darting from one tent to the next, her mind racing.

"We need to figure out what Dr. Lowe discovered," Tara said, her voice trembling but resolute. The sense of urgency was growing stronger, an instinctual need to flee, to put as much distance between themselves and this place as possible.

But Tara and Alex also felt the need to continue searching, like a duty. They moved past the rows of tents, retracing their steps, their eyes sharper now, searching for anything that might explain the horror. As they reached the far side of the camp, Tara spotted something odd near one of the excavation pits—a metal case, half-buried in sand, its lid slightly ajar. She exchanged a look with Alex, who nodded, and they approached it.

The case looked heavy. Tara knelt beside it, brushing away the sand that dusted its surface. The markings on the metal were faint, but she could make out some kind of logo—a symbol that looked familiar, though she couldn't immediately place it. With a deep breath, she opened the lid wider, revealing what lay inside.

It was a compact, stone-crafted device with movable parts—gears, dials, and rings intricately carved with Celtic symbols and patterns, an oddity in this Mongolian landscape. The carvings were detailed, and despite the device's age, it seemed surprisingly well preserved. The combination of stone and intricate mechanics made it look ancient yet advanced, as if it was meant to be both functional and ceremonial. Tara felt her pulse quicken.

"This is the thing she messaged us about," Tara realized, her voice a mix of awe and fear. "This is what Dr. Lowe found."

Alex crouched beside her, his eyes widening as he took in the sight of the device. "What is it?" he asked, his voice hushed.

"I don't know," Tara admitted. "But it's important. Important enough that someone was willing to kill for it."

"And for Dr. Lowe to send for us from all the way across the world," Alex added.

Tara reached out, her fingers grazing the edge of the crystal. A shiver ran through her at the touch, a feeling like static electricity that made her pull her hand back.

Tara examined the intricate carvings on the device, her fingers brushing over the gears and dials. "We need to figure out how this thing works," she said, her voice filled with a mix of awe and determination. The idea of leaving without answers wasn't an option, no matter how dire the situation. They needed to understand what Dr. Lowe had been so focused on.

Something else teased her mind as she considered the problem.

"Where is she?" Tara blurted.

"Where is who?" Alex asked.

"Dr. Lowe. I don't think any of the... any of the victims were her."

"I've never met her. But based on the picture in her dossier, I don't think we saw her either. Which means—"

"She either escaped, or was taken."

Neither one believed it was the former. The ruthless killers who'd come through here put on a chilling display of how efficiently they could operate. It was highly unlikely there were any survivors, and if there were, they'd be out in the desert, and with 360 degrees to search, finding them would be nearly impossible without search teams.

Both of them shared a grim glance.

"What?" he asked.

"I just feel like—"

"Don't move!" a new female voice shouted. "Both of you!"

The voice trembled and cracked, as if the interloper were the prey, and they were the hunters.

"Drop your guns," the woman barked. The voice came from just around a nearby tent behind where Tara and Alex knelt.

They did as they were told and raised their hands so the woman could see them.

"Who are you?" she demanded.

"I'm Alex Simms. This is Tara Watson. We're from the IAA. And whatever you're planning, you should know that we have already contacted our team, and support is on the way." He hoped the bluff would work, but he gave it less than a 10 percent chance.

"The team from the IAA?" The woman's voice didn't sound concerned. Instead, it rippled with relief.

"That's right," Tara confirmed, daring to twist her head around slightly.

She watched as Dr. Lowe emerged from her hiding place and stepped out into the clear. She held a rifle in both hands, lowering it as she moved toward the two. Her face looked drawn by exhaustion, fear, and grief, as if she'd aged five years in a day.

Tears began spilling from the corners of her eyes. Her toes dragged in the scree as she approached the two.

Tara and Alex moved toward her in time to catch the woman as she collapsed. They held her up while she sobbed. The emotions of what happened here erupted like a long-dormant volcano.

"It's okay, Dr. Lowe." Tara consoled her. "Everything is going to be okay."

8

For over a minute, the woman could do nothing more than weep, moan, and cough. Finally, she collected herself to regain the strength in her legs and stand on her own. She wiped her face, smearing the glistening tears across her cheeks and jaw. Her espresso hair hung in a ponytail with multiple strands dangling loosely to the sides. She looked as if she'd just run a marathon.

"They... they killed everyone," she managed.

"Who did?" Alex asked, trying not to pressure the woman.

She shook her head. Her glazed eyes stared forward between the two at nothing in particular beyond them. "I don't know. I... I've never seen them before."

Alex and Tara shared a concerned, sidelong glance.

"They arrived shortly after I went to the top of the cliffs," Lowe went on. She pointed absently up to the top of the rock mountain. "I'd gone up there to see if I could find anything relating to this device." She sniffled then acknowledged the bizarre contraption at their feet. "By the time I made it back to the trail, I heard the... the..."

Lowe couldn't continue. The tears returned, and she broke down again.

Tara took a water bottle out of her pack and offered it to the sobbing woman. Dr. Lowe accepted it and tried to drink. She managed to swallow a few swigs then sighed.

"Thank you. I never expected anything like this could ever happen. We're just archaeologists. Who would... do something so horrific to innocent people? Why?"

Her eyes pleaded with Tara and Alex for answers—answers they had no way of giving yet. But each knew they shared the other's commitment to find them.

"Come over here and sit down," Alex suggested, motioning to a set of four chairs, shaded under a tarp held up by strings and poles.

Lowe nodded, and the two helped her over to a seat where she let herself down slowly. The burden, both physical and emotional, eased visibly on her face. She took another drink from the metal bottle, and shook her head. "They were methodical," she began. "Killing was nothing to them. They may as well have been pulling weeds from a garden. They were cold, merciless." Lowe exhaled deeply. "My people never had a chance."

"How did you survive?" Tara asked, trying her best not to sound suspicious.

It seemed Dr. Lowe didn't take it that way. "I stayed up on the mountain like a coward. But there was nothing I could have done. I wasn't armed. I picked up that rifle from the tent of one of my locals. He kept it on hand in case we encountered any wild animals out here."

"Did they take anything?" Alex asked. He hoped sticking to more of an investigative line of questions would help keep Dr. Lowe's mind off the immense tragedy around them.

"I don't know. Some of my papers, I guess. And they took my assistant, Chen." Her red eyes welled, but no tears broke through. She'd cried them all. "I watched as they loaded him into one of their trucks. I have no idea what they want with him. We didn't find a treasure. Just artifacts. And they didn't take any of those."

"We'll figure this out," Tara said. "I promise."

She had no way of backing that up. All she had was the resolve to make sure she and her husband did all they could to make it happen.

"You're lucky to be alive," Alex said. "Really lucky."

Lowe nodded. "They sent three men up to find me on the mountaintop. I hid on the cliffs around that bend." She pointed at the right side of the mountain. "One of them was standing over me, but before he had a chance to look closer at where I was hidden, something drew him away. I remained there as long as I could until my forearms and toes couldn't anymore. Then I climbed back up. I expected them to still be there, and to kill me. But they were gone. They drove off that direction, away from the city."

"Yeah, we didn't pass a convoy on the way in," Alex confirmed.

"Do you have any idea why they would do this?" Tara asked.

Lowe shrugged absently. Her mind distant, somewhere mingling with the memories of those she'd lost in the brutal mass murder. "I don't know. Maybe they thought we had something they believed they could sell. They looked professional, like they were part of some kind of military group or maybe private security."

Alex and Tara shared a knowing look at each other.

"So, these weren't regional bandits or terrorists," Alex clarified.

"No. Their vehicles were all late models. And they wore matching clothes for the most part. Stuff like you would see military people wear, but not camouflaged."

"Sounds like either a government or a private group is interested in your work, Professor," Alex said.

"And my entire team died because of it," she answered, choking in the process.

Tara looped her arm around Dr. Lowe's shoulders and pulled her tight.

"We're going to find who did this," Tara said.

"Even if you can, what good will that do? These men were heavily armed. There are only two of you."

"There are never only two of us," Alex corrected. "You can be sure of that."

Lowe seemed confused by the statement but was too weary to ask.

Deciding to shift the subject, Tara indicated the device. "You sent for us because of that thing, yeah?"

Dr. Lowe nodded. "Yes. We uncovered it a couple of days ago. Chen and I fiddled with it for hours. The light show is pretty amazing, honestly. But we couldn't get any more than that out of it."

"Light show?" Alex asked.

Lowe nodded then shuffled closer to the mechanism.

"Why would they leave that here?"

"It's stuck."

"Stuck?" Tara wondered.

"Yes. It's rooted in the ground somehow, as if part of the earth itself. We didn't dig down around the sides to figure out how. It could be anchored to bedrock or something underneath. But we were more interested in what it could do rather than moving it."

She knelt down beside the device and twisted one of the dials.

Twin beams of light emanated from above the cliffs, pointing up into the clear sky.

"Whoa," Alex breathed.

"It's much more spectacular at night when the sun isn't diffusing the beams." She turned another dial, and the broad lasers turned in toward each other until they joined over the mountaintop.

"You can manipulate them?"

"Yes, but to what purpose?" Lowe answered. "If this is supposed to lead us to something, we weren't able to unlock it. Hence why we brought you in, along with needing to make sure this was kept safe. As I'm sure you're aware, the IAA has a good reputation for providing security for various kinds of artifacts."

"Tommy and Sean run a good outfit, for sure," Tara confirmed.

Tommy Schultz and his best friend, Sean Wyatt, had helped recover, secure, and transport artifacts from all over the world. Now and then, their work led them into trouble, usually the high-stakes kind that few others could handle. Sean had spent a great deal of time training Alex and Tara for just such events, and the skills they'd acquired had kept them alive more times than they wanted to count.

Sean and Tommy also had a knack for puzzles and riddles left long ago by those wishing to conceal their secrets.

When Tara and Alex first started working for Tommy in the IAA lab, they'd been surprised at how many clues to ancient mysteries were scattered all over the world. Now they almost expected to find such things—sometimes lying in plain sight.

Alex crouched beside her, his eyes fixed on the device. "So, you manipulate it with these?" He reached out to one of the carved rings, carefully twisting it. The gears clicked faintly, and both of them held their breath, watching for any reaction.

The lights over the mountain changed directions, splitting out to point opposite of one another.

"These Celtic symbols sure are a long way from home," Tara noted, observing the panel. "I wonder what this thing is doing way out here in the middle of nowhere Mongolia."

"That's what we were trying to understand," Lowe said.

It was a compact, stone-crafted device with movable parts—gears, dials, and rings intricately carved with Celtic symbols and patterns, an oddity in this Mongolian landscape. The carvings were detailed, and despite the device's age, it seemed surprisingly well-preserved. In the center, a large crystal pulsed with a dim, almost hypnotic light. The combination of stone and intricate mechanics made it look ancient, yet advanced, as if it was meant to be both functional and ceremonial.

Alex took out his phone and opened an app marked with a black M against a white background. He tapped on a camera icon at the bottom and took a picture of the device. Then he tapped on a microphone icon.

"Malcom, can you analyze this and interpret the meaning? It's some kind of ancient device, but we aren't sure how to use it."

"Certainly, Alex," a smooth, English male voice replied.

"Malcom?" Dr. Lowe asked, her curiosity overwhelming the grief that had gripped her since the two arrived.

"He's an AI assistant," Tara explained. "He's based in our lab back in Atlanta, but we created this app so we can connect with him from anywhere as long as we have an internet connection. And with the Starlink unit in the truck, we always have that."

"Fascinating."

"It can be helpful when we're in a jam, like right now," Alex commented.

"I have analyzed the image," Malcom said.

"Go ahead."

"This is quite the intricate puzzle. It appears to be based on the movement of constellations and planets. It also seems the lunar cycle plays a role in its solution. Unfortunately, I am only able to interpret some of the ancient scripts, and give you the meanings of the symbols. As far as a solution to the problem, I cannot offer any assistance."

"That's okay. Can you give me a list of the translations you were able to obtain?"

"Certainly. Sending to your phone now."

Alex's phone vibrated, and he opened the messaging app then tapped on the picture Malcom sent.

It looked almost exactly like the device, only reconstructed by the computer to display the rings and dials in new positions.

"How..." Dr. Lowe started to ask but couldn't finish.

"Okay, got it," Alex said.

He tapped on the message then opened the file attached to it. The screen filled with a row of symbols and the script from the device, and each one's meaning just to the right of it.

Tara knelt by the device while Alex lowered his phone screen so she could see it. Her eyes went back and forth between the phone and the ancient device.

"I see," she said. "Notice how these are just slightly off?" Tara pointed at the mechanism. "The constellations are out of alignment."

"You think it's that simple?" Alex questioned.

"You and I both know that sometimes the simplest solutions are the correct ones."

"It's worth a try," Alex said, rolling his shoulders.

Tara began manipulating the pieces on the board.

"Whoa," Lowe muttered, looking up at the lights above the cliffs. "I think it's working. It would be so much easier to see at night, though. Those beams are much clearer after dark."

"Yeah, well, I don't think any of us want to be hanging around here after the sun goes down," Alex said.

"No." The single syllable was drowned in sadness.

Tara may have been tempted to console her. She was a caring person in that way, but she remained focused and continued shifting the dials and rings until all of them were aligned.

"Malcom?" she said. "Can you show me those constellations as they appear in the night sky?"

"Certainly," the voice said from Alex's phone. A few seconds later, another message alerted the phone. Alex tapped on it and opened the next image—a map of the night sky. As she turned the last dial into place, something clicked inside the box. Over the mountain, the four beams of light joined as one.

"That's it," Tara said. "It looks exactly like the image Malcom sent. But it doesn't seem to have done anything except align the—"

Before she could finish her thought, a heavy thud followed by a deep rumble shook the earth beneath them. The three stood up and looked around as if concerned the earth might open up and swallow them.

The vibrations and the sound only lasted a few seconds, and then the stillness of the desert returned.

"What was that?" Dr. Lowe asked, her eyes wide with a mixture of fear and wonder.

"That didn't happen before when you were messing with this thing?" Alex asked, his gaze still shifting around to make sure the ground was stable.

"No. Nothing like that."

"Interesting."

Tara stared up at the top of the mountain, focusing on the lights above it. "When you were up there, did you happen to notice where those lights come from?"

Lowe thought for a moment then shook her head. "No. I didn't.

Strange, right? You would think there would be some kind of device or machine that shoots out the beams."

"Did you go up there when the lights were on?"

"Actually, no. Maybe I should have done that."

"Well," Alex said. "We can do it now."

9

Rolf sensed the unease of his two lieutenants before either of the men said anything. They'd been sitting here for hours, waiting, watching.

Rolf crouched in the shadow of a crumbling mudbrick wall; his back pressed against its rough surface. The coarse texture scratched through the thin fabric of his jacket, but he barely noticed. His attention was fixed on the endless expanse of the Gobi Desert that stretched out before him, a desolate ocean of sand and stone under the bright light of the afternoon sun.

The village, little more than a cluster of humble dwellings huddled together as if for protection against the vast emptiness, seemed suspended between worlds. Behind him, the faint murmurs of life carried through the still air; the muted clatter of a pot being set down, the occasional bark of a dog, and the singsong cadence of a woman's voice calling her children inside for a late lunch. The scents of cooking fires wafted through the air, mingling with the dry, earthy aroma of the desert. A faint trace of smoke stung his nostrils, layered with the pungent tang of fermented milk from a nearby yurt.

Before him, the desert was quiet but not silent. The wind swept across the barren landscape in restless sighs, lifting small eddies of sand that danced like specters in the fading light. The horizon was a jagged line where the rolling dunes met the distant hills, their edges blurred by the shimmering haze of the day's heat still clinging to the ground. Here and there, tufts of hardy grass and thorny shrubs clung stubbornly to life, their silhouettes sharp and black against the blazing hues of the sun.

The heat of the day would soon dissipate and be replaced by a creeping chill that bit at his exposed skin. From what Rolf knew, nights in the Gobi were merciless, the warmth stolen away by the same winds that now whistled softly through the cracks and crevices of the village. Rolf shifted his weight, pulling his scarf tighter around his neck to keep the dust out of his nostrils, and glanced over his shoulder at his men.

They were scattered in pairs among the shadows of the village, hidden behind walls, under the eaves of low roofs, and in the long shadows cast by the taller buildings. Rolf knew they stood out here in the quiet town, but for their part the villagers had left them alone. He assumed the locals understood not to disturb them when they'd first laid eyes on their firearms. Rolf and his team had made no effort to conceal their weapons. Fear was a powerful silencer, and out here in the wastelands, there would be no one they could call for help. No one close, anyway.

Rolf had briefed his men thoroughly, their orders clear: wait, watch, follow. And only move on his command. When the Americans arrived, they would be ready.

From what he understood, there were only two of them—a young married couple sent to investigate Dr. Lowe's discovery—an unusual device with bizarre symbols, dials, and rings on the panel.

He'd taken a look at the mechanism, even toyed with a few of the dials. But Rolf knew he wouldn't be able to solve whatever puzzle the thing presented. If Lowe hadn't figured it out by then, his chances were almost nil. And Lowe's assistant, Chen, had been adamant that he couldn't solve it, even with a gun to his head.

Rolf wasn't going to kill the archaeologist. Not yet. The man was worth more to them alive than dead, though Rolf felt certain that fact was tied to a ticking clock.

He'd considered digging up the box and bringing it with them, but Chen had warned them they'd have to dig deep down, and even then may not be able to uproot the ancient device. The archaeologist claimed he and his team had attempted to move it, but the thing wouldn't budge a millimeter, and so they'd resigned to experimenting with it on site until they could either figure out how it worked, or until the IAA team arrived to assist.

The village itself was a picture of rugged resilience. Low, squat buildings made of sun-dried bricks huddled together, their walls weathered and cracked from years of exposure to the desert's unforgiving elements. A few yurts or *gers*, the traditional round felt tents, dotted the outskirts, their smoke holes releasing thin tendrils into the sky. The people here lived simply, surviving on what little the desert provided. Camels and goats wandered in small enclosures, their bleats and grunts blending with the occasional distant howl of the wind.

From his vantage point, Rolf could see a narrow dirt track winding its way into the desert, barely discernible under the encroaching darkness. This was the road the IAA team had taken earlier. It lay quiet and empty, waiting for their return. The thought of it made Rolf's jaw tighten. They would be carrying either something, or someone, he wanted. And he wasn't going to leave without one or both.

He knew the waiting game could be a long one. In fact, he'd assumed it would be. If night fell and the team still hadn't returned, they'd switch to taking shifts throughout the dark hours and continue that pattern until the two agents came back.

Rolf doubted that would be the case. The couple wouldn't remain in the desert with all those bodies out there. They'd call for help from the nearest city or return in person to seek assistance.

But Rolf's employer had the utmost confidence in the IAA agents. Rolf had wondered if the man's belief in the two was misplaced. How could a couple of Americans simply show up and figure out the ancient device in a few hours that two expert archaeologists couldn't in two days?

A faint metallic clinking drew his attention. He turned his head sharply, his eyes narrowing as he located the source of the sound. One of his men was shifting his rifle, the sling's buckle tapping softly against the weapon's stock. Rolf raised a hand, his fingers forming a silent command. The man froze, understanding the warning.

Their task demanded silence, especially now. Rolf returned his focus to the horizon.

He drew a deep breath, letting the hot, dry air fill his lungs. It tasted of dust and smoke, the flavors of this barren land. There was a clarity to the desert air, a starkness that stripped away pretense and left only the essentials.

The plan was simple enough. When the IAA agents returned, Rolf and his men would acquire whatever they discovered—probably through the use of force. Unless he was directed otherwise. Before carrying out an ambush, his orders were to stay hidden, observe, and assess the situation. If he thought an attack necessary, he had been authorized to do so. But Rolf wasn't going to rush into anything. A firefight would mean witnesses from the town, which could cause problems.

They couldn't eliminate everyone in the area. Not without a great deal of effort. And there would always be someone who escaped.

As he peered out across the plains, he felt his men's patience wearing thin. Rolf wasn't like them in that regard. He could wait indefinitely for just about anything. He didn't possess the urge to take reckless action, which he knew was the reason several of his men had been booted out of their respective militaries.

He'd managed to harness those qualities to maximize the men's talents, but now and then the negative sides showed themselves, and it made things tenuous.

Rolf let his gaze linger on them for a moment. They were competent and disciplined, mercenaries he trusted—as much as a man like him could trust anyone. But he knew they were growing restless. The desert's oppressive vastness seemed to seep into their bones, its unending monotony fraying the edges of their patience. He would have to remind them soon why they were here, why the stakes were worth the wait.

Right on cue, Yuri was the first to speak up. "How much longer are we going to wait? And don't say as long as it takes."

"One can never know exactly when a fish will take the bait, Yuri. So, the fisherman sits for hours, waiting for his prey to bite."

"How philosophical. But that doesn't answer my question."

"You know the plan. We wait here."

"Yes. I know the plan. But what if they don't show up? Or what if they aren't able to decode the device?"

Rolf detected a hint of impatience from Javier as well, though he didn't vocalize it. The glint in his eyes told Rolf all he needed to know. He didn't fear a mutiny by his men. They would do as they were told, but not for the sake of loyalty. They were pure mercenaries, brought into the organization as employees. Their allegiance went only as far as their paychecks. Fortunately, their employer had plenty of money.

"Then we have a plan for that too," Rolf answered, meeting the gaze of both men for a moment. It was a look that commanded respect.

None of his men knew anything about Rolf's past, nor would they. While most of them bragged about their exploits from their previous lives or even the current one, Rolf kept his secrets locked away in a vault.

One of the reasons for his secrecy was that he didn't possess an innate need to brag. That kind of quality didn't do anything but stoke one's ego. The other reason for keeping his past hidden was more subtle. People had a tendency to fear what they didn't know or didn't understand. Men in his line of work had an especially strong fear of a lack of intel. Rolf knew how much leverage that gave him. After all, one of the most powerful motivators was fear.

Thankfully, Rolf's phone buzzed in his pocket, dragging him out of what would only be a pointless conversation, and thrusting him into a more important one.

He took the phone from his pocket and without excusing himself raised it to his ear. "Yes, sir."

"What is your status?"

Rolf stepped away from the other men and moved over to an abandoned alcove where he could have a little more privacy.

"We have the hostage. Still waiting for the IAA team to return."

"Good. I assume you eliminated the entire archaeology team?"

"Affirmative. Except the hostage."

"Then the IAA agents will arrive and find the carnage. You made sure to leave the device for them, yes?"

"Yes, sir. We didn't take anything. Just trashed the tents. Made it look like we were looking for something."

The man on the other end of the line hummed his approval. "Did you inspect the device?"

It was an unexpected change of topic, but Rolf didn't feel threatened. "Yes, sir. I... wasn't able to get anything useful out of it. I don't understand how it works." He shifted gears. "I did lead a team up to the top of the mountain to see if Dr. Lowe had maybe found something there, but there was only rock."

"Yes, well, based on the images of that device, it would take me considerable time to decipher the riddle. And I don't have that kind of time. We need those two to figure out where that device leads next."

"That's the plan, sir." He paused, then said, "And then we eliminate them?" Rolf asked.

"They will be taken care of when the time is right. Patience. As much as it would overjoy me to wipe those two off the planet, we must wait for the opportune moment."

10

lex noticed Dr. Lowe glancing back over her shoulders every ten to twenty seconds as the three ascended the narrow trail to the top of the mountain. The sun was halfway across the sky, and everyone knew they would need to head back to the nearest town for the night.

They could have done fine in the tents throughout the dark hours, but there was no way any of them were going to stay here with all those bodies.

Tara reached the top first, sweeping her weapon around to make sure no one from the attack party had hung around to lay an ambush. But there was no threat, and she lowered her pistol while the other two joined her.

"Well, that was quite the—" Alex couldn't finish his sentence. His gaze followed the two women toward the middle of the mountaintop. The four beams collided above a circle in the rock and shone a single ray down into a round opening.

"What in the world?" Dr. Lowe mouthed. "That wasn't here before."

"The opening in the rock?" Tara clarified.

"Yes. There was the circle, but it was solid stone. There were no seams or cracks."

Alex stepped forward, leading the way across the rocky surface to the strange opening. He stopped a foot from the edge and peered down, letting the sights on his pistol lead his search.

He found the shaft empty save for a stone box in the center surrounded by curved walls covered in strange emblems and symbols.

"I... don't understand," Lowe confessed. "This wasn't here earlier. It was just a big, flat circle." Her head turned back and forth. Bewilderment filled her eyes. "It didn't look natural. I thought it had to be man-made. Even so, I didn't expect this."

Tara looked up at the lights where they came together then followed the lone beam that shone on the stone box within the pit. "I guess whatever we're looking for here is in that box," she said.

"Yeah, but should we open it?" Alex questioned.

"What?" Dr. Lowe asked. "You came all this way, and my team...." She faltered for a moment. "My team and I spent too much time and effort to get to the finish line and not cross it. I want to know what is in that box."

Alex appreciated her sentiment. But he'd also seen too many dangerous incidents to be so reckless. "I'm just saying we should be careful. We don't know what's inside it."

Dr. Lowe wasn't about to slow down. She lowered herself down to the edge of the pit, sitting on the lip for a moment before dropping down the last few feet. The distance from the ground to the top was only about seven feet but would still require climbing out.

Neither Tara nor Alex was sure Lowe had considered that when she jumped in.

Upon closer inspection, Tara noted the tiny gaps around the pit's rim. The flat circle Lowe had seen before had pulled back into the curved walls. She wondered how long it would stay there.

"Looks like we can climb out pretty easily," Alex said. "What do you think?

Tara glanced around the rocky surface. It was littered with pocked holes and random shapes sticking up. "More than enough to grip climbing out, if we even need that. This lip isn't smooth at all, so getting back up should be easy."

Alex nodded. "Okay." From the sound of his voice, she could tell he didn't sound so sure.

So Tara crouched down then lowered herself into the pit as Dr. Lowe approached the stone box.

"You know what, just in case, I should stay up here. You know, if you two need any help climbing out."

"Good idea," Tara answered over her shoulder.

Alex watched nervously as the two women stood over the box. The ancient container was around two feet tall, two feet wide, and three feet long.

Tara knelt down on one side of it while Dr. Lowe crouched opposite of her.

"How should we do this?" Tara asked, letting the archaeologist take the lead. She'd been in a number of these scenarios, and on dig sites, to know that it was usually best to let the pros handle things when it was their field of expertise.

"Honestly, I was just thinking we slide the lid off," Lowe said. The obviousness to the answer caused Tara to chuckle.

"Yeah, that could work," she joked.

"Okay. Here goes." Lowe leaned closer and positioned her hands on the edge of the lid to her right. Tara copied her from the other side. "Okay, pull."

The two grunted as they tugged on the lid, but it didn't budge.

"Maybe you have to lift it," Tara suggested.

Alex might have been tempted to laugh were they not in such a potentially dangerous situation. They had no idea where the killers were, or if they might return. The more Alex thought about it, the more it would drive him crazy.

"I wonder if we have to press those stones on either end," Lowe suggested.

On either end of the container, a black stone was fixed near the seam between the lid and the main part of the box.

"Like buttons?"

Lowe shrugged. "Seems a little unnecessary if we managed to figure out how to find this thing."

"I was thinking the same," Tara agreed. "It's worth a try, I guess. That or we go back for a crowbar."

"I would rather not make that hike again." Dr. Lowe indicated the button on Tara's side. "Press that in and hold it. I'll do the same."

Tara did as instructed and reached down to the black gem. It was cold and smooth against her skin. She pushed against it and found the ancient button moved easily, sinking a centimeter into the side of the box.

Alex watched Lowe do the same. A click escaped the box, as if a lock inside it had been undone.

The two women looked at each other, then nodded and began to push on the lid again. This time, the slab moved easily. They scooted it over until it tipped off the container. The lid made a loud clinking sound as the edge hit the stone floor.

"What in the world are those?" Alex asked from above.

The two women stared into the open box, unsure how to answer.

"It's a couple of stone heads," Tara said after ten seconds.

"That's what I thought they looked like."

Lowe leaned in closer, wrapping her hand around the nearest bust. It, like the other, had been carved from sandstone, though her instincts suggested it was from far away. The detail was immaculate, though the heads didn't feature any distinguishing characteristics that would allow Lowe to place their origin. They were small, roughly the size of a couple of tennis balls. The eyes appeared to be equally apart from one another, and completely level. The nose was carved with utmost precision, as were the lips, chin, and jawline.

"Incredible craftsmanship," Tara said, as she started to pick up the second head. "Any idea who might have made it, or left it here?"

Lowe turned her head back and forth, never breaking her stare at the bust. She set the head back down. Tara was surprised she'd been able to hold it up for that long. The stone busts looked like they must have weight at least ten to fifteen pounds.

"What do these mean, though?" Lowe wondered. "Why would someone put a couple of stone heads here, in this place?"

Neither of the IAA agents had an answer for that. Not yet.

Tara lifted the other head and immediately found it to be lighter than she'd suspected. The bust still had some heft to it, but probably half the weight she'd expected. Her fingertips ran across the smooth head and left cheek. Then she turned it over and looked at the bottom.

"Hey, there's something written on here," she said, a trickle of excitement heightening her voice. "I can't tell what it says. But there's more Celtic symbology engraved into it as well."

Tara tipped it over so Dr. Lowe could see.

"Fascinating," Lowe said. She looked down at the head she'd been holding a moment before. "I wonder if this one has the same." She wrapped her hands around the bust and lifted again.

The ground beneath them suddenly started to shake, and the air filled with the deep rumble of stone grinding on stone.

The two women looked at each other then down into the box.

"What's going on?" Lowe asked.

"Hey, ladies?" Alex shouted. "The pit is closing!"

Tara looked up and to the right, and saw the lid that had receded into the rock now emerging again.

"Come on," Tara urged. "We need to get out of here."

Lowe didn't need to be told twice. But the massive pit's cover was moving quickly. Already, the ledge where Alex stood was inaccessible. He shifted sideways. "Hurry up!" he pleaded.

The two women rushed over to the side where Alex waited. Lowe held up the bust in her hands, and set it on the ledge. Alex dragged it out of the way then reached down his right arm.

"Grab ahold!" he barked.

"Get her first," Lowe said.

Tara set the second head up on the lip over the pit. The lid was closing, and was only a foot away when she reached up and took Alex's forearm. He wrapped his fingers around hers and pulled as she used the other hand to pull up on the ledge.

Within two seconds she was up and over.

But the closing cover forced Dr. Lowe to move to the last five feet of open space.

"Hurry, Dr. Lowe!" Alex shouted over the rumbling. "Take my hand."

Alex scurried over to where she stood and lowered his right hand down again. Lowe gripped hard with her fingers as she'd seen Tara do then grabbed the ledge and pulled.

Alex's left foot shifted slightly, and he lost his balance. He teetered over the edge, and fell down into the opening next to Dr. Lowe.

"Crap," he blurted then immediately moved to the wall. The cover was nearly over the entire hole.

"Quick," Alex snapped, holding his hands down at waist level. "I'll give you a boost."

"What about you?"

"Do it, or we both get trapped in here."

She didn't debate further and stepped up, planting her foot on his palms. Alex instantly lifted her as Tara grabbed her by the hand and pulled her up.

Alex had to react fast. He had mere seconds before he would be trapped, probably forever.

He turned and faced the wall with the only opening left, leaped toward it, then planted his left foot on the smooth surface. He only needed a split second, and used the wall to jump again, this time toward the lid sliding over the pit. Alex had never been into parkour, but in this case, it saved his life. He cleared the edge of the lid and rolled over into the center as the massive stone locked into place with a heavy thud.

He lay there for a few seconds, making sure he hadn't actually died or been trapped in the darkness. But the blazing sun and the two women rushing toward him reassured him that he was still very much alive.

"Alex?" Tara shouted, hurrying over to him. She crouched down when she reached him. "Are you okay?"

He coughed a little from a cloud of dust that had swept over him but nodded. "Yeah. I'm good. Piece of cake."

Dr. Lowe stood over the two of them, her head slowly turning back and forth in disapproval. "Is this the sort of thing you two get into on a routine basis?"

Alex arched his right eyebrow and smirked. "Yeah, pretty much."

"I wouldn't call it routine," Tara argued. "But we do encounter these kinds of things more than the average archaeologist."

"I'd say so."

Alex looked over at the two heads sitting on the outside of the circle. "I guess there was a counterweight in that box," he said.

Tara bobbed her head. "Yeah. Looks that way."

"That was dangerous," Lowe said. "We could have been trapped down there, or killed by that thing."

"Yeah," Tara half agreed, catching her breath. "But something tells me we needed both of those busts." She stared over at the two sandstone heads resting on the rock.

"Besides," Alex chimed in. "No harm, no foul. We all got out of there okay."

He stood up and headed for the two stones. Tara and Dr. Lowe followed him to where he stopped over the sculptures.

Alex bent down, picked up one of them, and tipped it over so he could see the bottom. "Could you show me the other one?" he said to Tara.

"Sure." She lifted the second bust and turned it over. The three scanned the engravings, and all came to the same conclusion.

"They're different," Lowe realized.

"Or," Tara offered, "two halves of one message."

"Can you get your AI to interpret that?"

Alex set his bust down and took out his phone. "No, the satellite Wi-Fi doesn't reach up here from the truck. We'll have to take a look when we get back down there." He peered out toward the horizon to the west, knowing they could quickly run out of time out here. They needed to get back to civilization, and figure out their next move, if there was one.

"There is more to this," he said. "I don't think this is all there is to find."

"Same," Tara agreed.

"Let's get a move on and get back to town. I think we'll all relax a little once we're away from this place."

Tara looked at the archaeologist as she stared toward the direction of the camp. "You going to be okay?"

"I don't know what I am right now," Lowe answered. "Kind of numb. I just... can't believe they're all gone, killed in cold blood. They were just here doing their job."

"I know the temptation is to blame yourself," Alex said. "But it isn't your fault. This shouldn't have been a risky gig."

"I've never heard of anything like this happening."

Tara and Alex nodded. They'd seen some terrible things in the field, and heard more from Sean and Tommy about their exploits. But their side of archaeology was different, and those kinds of things weren't all that common—especially a mass killing.

"We can't leave them all out here," Lowe said. "It's wrong. They deserve better than that. Their bodies will be..." She faltered, unable to finish the thought.

Tara reached out and touched her on the shoulder. "We can't bury them all, Dr. Lowe. That would take days. We have reinforcements coming. They'll take it from here."

Dr. Lowe nodded. "You're right. I know. I just hate it."

"I know," Tara echoed. "I don't like it either. But we don't have a choice."

"Okay. Let's do it. And please, call me Felicia. We're way beyond formalities."

11

lex's forearms and biceps burned. He set the stone head down behind their SUV and shook his arms to dispel the fire torching his muscles. He wiped the sweat from his brow with the bottom of his shirt and took a deep breath.

Tara set the other head down next to the one he'd carried and stretched her hands above her head.

"You know, those things aren't that heavy," he said, "but after a while, it gets to you."

"Yeah," Tara agreed.

Alex opened the cargo area, lifted the head up again, and placed it in the back. Tara did the same before securing the two busts behind a couple of rucksacks and the cargo net.

When she and Alex turned around, they saw Felicia staring toward where the row of bodies still lay just beyond one of the tents. The pain sagged her eyelids, and slackened her jaw.

She still couldn't believe what had happened. It was written on her face in deep lines—a frown that never seemed to flip—and dark circles under her eyes. The other two could physically feel the pain radiating from the woman.

Neither Tara nor Alex liked the idea of leaving all these people out here for wild animals or the elements to pick clean. But as they'd said before, there was no choice.

And they hadn't even mentioned the possibility that the killers could return after dark. Alex, in particular, couldn't shake the feeling that they were still standing in the middle of an elaborate trap.

He peered out across the plains, thinking that at any second he may see the killers' trucks on the horizon, roaring toward them with plumes of dust rolling into the sky.

Tara turned over the stones and took pictures of the script on the bottoms then repositioned the heads so they wouldn't roll around in the truck. Happy with her work, she closed the rear door and looked at the other two.

"It's time," she said, trying not to be indelicate in the situation.

Felicia looked back to the dig site. The pain of leaving her fallen friends behind, out in the open, drained the color from her face and reddened her eyes.

There was no need to reiterate the reasons for doing it. They'd rehashed that. Felicia knew there was no option. It was either return with the two IAA agents, find help, and hopefully figure out who did this . . . or stay here and possibly end up just like the rest.

The killers had come looking for her at the top of the mountain. Or perhaps they'd simply gone up there to see if there was anything of interest to find. Based on what Felicia heard, there was no way to be sure.

The two IAA agents let her have one more moment as she stared at the camp. Tara and Alex had no way to know exactly what or who she was looking at, or what she was thinking, but they knew it had to be a terribly emotional minute.

Felicia finally turned to face them, tears dripping from her eyes. "Let's go," she said, taking a big inhale. "Standing here and staring at them won't bring them back. The sooner we get to town, the sooner we can get them taken care of."

Alex and Tara nodded then moved toward the doors. Tara took the driver's seat, while Alex opened the back passenger door for Felicia and then the front door for himself.

"Would you prefer to ride up front with Tara?" he asked.

She shook her head. "No. I'll be fine in the back."

"Okay," he said with an understanding nod.

They climbed into the SUV, and Tara fired up the engine. "Here," she said to Alex, holding her phone in her hand. She sent the images she'd taken of the stone heads to him then set the phone down in a narrow groove in the door. "Those are the pics of the glyphs on the bottom of the heads. See what Malcom can make of them."

"On it. And I'll send them to Tommy too."

She shifted the truck into drive and stepped on the pedal. The rear tires spun for a second, kicking rocks and dust and sand out into the air before they found their grip and surged the vehicle forward.

Tara glanced back in the rearview mirror to check on Felicia. As she suspected, the archaeologist's head was turned so she could look back through the rear window.

The sight of her doing that at the back of the truck moments before, and now, tore at Tara's heart. She clenched her jaw and focused on the drive ahead.

Next to her, Alex took the images and sent them through Malcom's app.

"Message received," the AI's voice said. "Would you like me to analyze these?"

"Yes," Alex said into his phone. "We need to know what they say."

"Analyzing."

Tara cast another glance in the mirror. Felicia was facing forward now, wiping her eyes. Tara hoped this mystery would take the archaeologist's mind off things, at least for a little while. Then again, continuing to work on the project that had cost the lives of her team might only make the grief worse.

The SUV rocked in a steady rhythm along the bumpy path. Now and then, a particularly deep hole would jar the occupants. Alex held on to the handlebar over the window as he had before, still wary of the way his wife drove out here in the desert. He watched his phone in his other hand, waiting for Malcom to finish analyzing the messages on the busts. He needed something else to look at instead of the dusty road ahead. He'd rather watch his phone than that. At least the device didn't offer a new reason to be worried every five seconds.

"Analysis complete," Malcom announced.

"Can you put the translation on my screen?"

"Certainly, Alex."

The messaging app filled with the text from Malcom's work.

"Will you be needing anything else?" the AI asked.

"No, Malcom. Not at the moment. Thank you."

"You're welcome, as always, sir."

Felicia leaned forward, craning her neck to see the phone. "That AI is something else," she said. Curiosity had momentarily replaced the sadness in her eyes.

"Yeah. It's pretty amazing," Tara agreed.

"What did it say?"

Alex held it up so the archaeologist could see better.

"Looks like a riddle of some kind," he said.

Felicia read the message out loud. "Where the sands wail beneath the guardians of old." She frowned. "What does that mean?"

Tara and Alex both shook their heads. The truck hit a particularly large hump and nearly went airborne, causing Felicia to reach up and grab the handle over her window the same as Alex.

"Seriously," Alex said. "Do you have to do that?"

"Fine," she relented. "But only because we have a third party in the truck with us."

"Good enough for me."

"Where the sands wail," Felicia muttered, loud enough for the other two to hear over the steady moan of the engine and the ground rumbling under the tires.

"What was that?" Alex asked, looking back over his shoulder at her.

Felicia blinked rapidly. "I've heard of something like that before. Sands that wail. Sands that wail." She repeated the line as if that would somehow conjure the answer out of thin air.

"You know what it's talking about?"

She didn't respond. Instead, the archaeologist stared at the headrest in front of her, eyes darting back and forth, searching her mind for where she'd heard that phrase before.

"The Singing Sands," she exclaimed suddenly. "That's got to be it."

Tara flicked her a glance in the rearview mirror. "Singing Sands?"

"Yes." Felicia leaned forward. Excitement rippled through her voice. "The Singing Sands are in the Thar Desert. I've only heard about them. I never studied them."

"The Thar Desert?"

"It's also known as the Great Indian Desert. I had some friends who did some work there."

"India," Alex echoed. "First Mongolia, now India? What do those places have in common?"

"With the ancient Celts?" Felicia said. "I can't think of anything. This is an unexpected discovery. Then again, all of this was unexpected." Her voice turned somber again.

Alex opened a search app on his phone and typed in a question. The results populated with the AI answer at the top.

"The Thar Desert," he read, "spans approximately two hundred thousand square kilometers, primarily in the Indian state of Rajasthan, with smaller portions extending into Punjab, Haryana, Gujarat, and parts of southeastern Pakistan. It is one of the most densely populated deserts in the world." He looked up from his phone and out the windshield. "Still not sure why so many people would choose to live in a desert."

"Some folks like the lack of humidity," Tara answered.

"I guess." Alex looked down at the phone and kept reading. "The Thar Desert has been a cradle of civilizations, serving as a historical crossroads for trade and cultural exchange. The Indus Valley Civilization, one of the world's oldest urban cultures, thrived on the desert's periphery. The desert's ancient trade routes linked the Indian subcontinent to Central Asia and beyond, with caravans carrying spices, textiles, and other goods across the sands."

"Indus Valley Civilization," Tara repeated. She glanced over at

Alex then in the mirror at Felicia. "That's the group that mysteriously disappeared a long time ago, right?"

"Yeah," Felicia said. "No one ever really found evidence of what truly happened. Lots of theories. But nothing concrete."

"Sounds like something the IAA should be working on," Tara added.

"Indeed."

Alex continued reading. "The desert is dotted with historic landmarks, including the Jaisalmer Fort, a UNESCO World Heritage Site known as the Golden Fort for its distinctive yellow sandstone. Built in the twelfth century, the fort rises dramatically from the desert and houses palaces, temples, and bustling bazaars within its walls. Another notable site is the Sam Sand Dunes, famous for their ethereal beauty and the Singing Sands phenomenon, where the dunes emit a low-frequency hum when disturbed under specific conditions."

He looked back over his shoulder at Felicia. "Looks like you were right about the Singing Sands."

She nodded, but he could see she was hard at work thinking of something else.

"What's wrong?" Alex wondered.

"Just trying to figure this out," she answered.

"The Jaisalmer Fort," Tara said. "That may be a key point of interest."

"You think so?" Alex turned his attention to Tara.

"Unless there's something else near the Singing Sands. Sounds to me like if they put a fort there, it had to be an important place beyond being on an important trade route."

"Could be," Alex said with a touch of hesitation. He performed another search on his device and pored over the responses.

The Jaisalmer Fort, often called *Sonar Quila*, or the Golden Fort, one of the largest, and oldest fortresses in India.

"This could prove problematic," Alex grumbled.

"Why's that?" Felicia asked.

"Because it's a UNESCO site. Not exactly the best place to go snooping around. You can't even move a rock without getting a permit."

"Yes. That could prove problematic."

"Maybe not," Tara offered. "No sense in worrying about it before we get there. Maybe what we're looking for is out in the open." The other two could tell by the sound of her voice that she didn't believe that. It was beyond unlikely that some hidden piece to an ancient puzzle was sitting there for the world to see.

"Might as well be positive," Alex agreed.

"Either way, we know where we need to go next."

Tara peered through the windshield toward the horizon. It would be dark soon. But she was starting to rethink the notion of staying in the small town.

"If we know where we're going, maybe we should head there right away. It's not that much farther to drive to the city and the airport. We can rest on the plane."

"It'll take the pilot some time to get things in order," Alex said, "but it shouldn't be a problem. He can have it ready by the time we get there."

"I also prefer this plan," Felicia added. "With those men still out there on the loose, they could be waiting for us in that town, knowing we would return there. On top of that, there isn't much in the way of accommodations in that village. Honestly, our tents were better, other than having no running water or toilets."

"Sounds like it's unanimous. Guess we're heading back to Ulaanbaatar."

Alex smirked. "Say that five times fast."

The comment seemed to ease the tension inside the vehicle, even the dark emotions still resonating from Felicia.

"Do you think Tommy could help us get more access at the fort?" she asked. Her tone had turned to one of business.

Compartmentalizing stressful events, even tragic ones, was something Tara and Alex had learned through difficult experiences. Both of them had initially doubted Felicia would be able to use such a robotic talent. But maybe there was a dark past hidden somewhere deep inside her, something that had instilled that innate ability.

"It's possible," Alex answered her question. "He has contacts all over the planet. He may have someone in that part of India. And if not, maybe he can get someone there."

Alex and Tara were both aware of a previous mission in India that Sean and Tommy had taken on. Like so many of their field jobs, they'd ended up in a series of dangerous events that could have cost them their lives. But as always, they'd managed to survive.

Alex took out his phone and pulled up Tommy's number, then hit the call button.

He waited through three rings until Tommy answered on the other end. "Hey, Alex. You run into more trouble?"

"No. But we think there may be something to investigate in India —possibly near the Jaisalmer Fort. Do you know it?"

"I do. Interesting place. Kind of creepy, honestly. Lot of mystery around that place."

"That's what we're learning. We were hoping that you could help us out with access. It's a UNESCO site, so we figured someone like you calling ahead would be a good idea. Or if you have a friend or colleague in that region, maybe they could help us out. That way, we won't cause any problems while snooping around."

"Smart. Yeah, I know several people in India, including their national director of archaeology."

"Now you're just showing off," Tara said.

Tommy laughed. "I can put in a call to her and make sure you don't encounter any problems. It'll help to have a more local liaison too. I know a few folks who've worked that region before, so I'll reach out and see who I can get for you. I'll shoot you a text with the contact information as soon as I lock it down."

"Thanks so much," Felicia said, leaning forward so Tommy could hear her. "We really appreciate it."

"No problem. Just part of the job. You have transportation arranged yet with the pilot?"

"Not yet," Alex said. "We were about to call him and let him know where we're headed."

"I can handle that too if you like."

"That would be great if it isn't too much trouble."

"Not at all. I'll set it up." He stopped talking for a second, and the silence told the group in the SUV he was thinking about something. It was the kind of pause someone used when they were hesitant to say something for fear of upsetting anyone. "I made the other call. There should be a team of investigators heading toward the site. I'm sorry there isn't more I can do, Felicia."

"I'm... okay," she said, forcing back her emotions deep down. "Hopefully, the authorities will be able to track down who did this and make them pay." She thought for a moment and then added, "My assistant, Dr. Chen, was abducted by the men who did this. I saw them put him in the back of one of their trucks before they came looking for me. I don't know what they would want with him, or why they would kidnap him and kill the... the rest." Felicia faltered at the end of the sentence.

"That does add more questions," Tommy said. "Perhaps they wanted him for information."

Alex had different thoughts but kept them to himself: *If Chen had been abducted, and was still alive, that meant he was a hostage. But for what purpose? These people obviously wanted what Dr. Lowe was working on, or what she'd found.* He couldn't help thinking that he and the two women were doing exactly what they wanted, marching straight into a trap.

"Oh, by the way," Tommy said, "I got the image you sent of those two stone heads. Really unusual."

"You know anything about those?" Tara asked.

"I did a little searching, and they look exactly like the Hexham Heads."

"What are those?"

"The Hexham Heads were a couple of stone heads found near the town of Hexham in the United Kingdom. They were also made of sandstone like the two you found, and they look eerily similar in design."

"Great. Then we can compare the two sets. Maybe that will give us a clue as to what they're doing way out here in Mongolia, and why those guys were here."

"Unfortunately," Tommy countered, "they disappeared decades ago. No one has ever found them since. No leads. No clues. They just vanished. Whoever took them hasn't surfaced in all this time."

For a few seconds, no one in the SUV said a word, each contemplating the new layer to the mystery unfolding before them.

Alex spoke up first. "Do you think it's possible the men who attacked Dr. Lowe's site might be working for whoever took the original two? Maybe they're trying to collect the whole set."

"I would say it is entirely possible. And what's more, it seems whatever Dr. Lowe found there might be leading to another pair. I'll have to dig deeper into this, but I do know that the Hexham Heads unsettled a lot of people back in the seventies."

"Unsettled?" Felicia asked.

"Apparently, the people who first discovered them claimed strange things started happening, paranormal-type things. They were discovered by two young boys, Colin and Leslie Robson, who unearthed the heads while digging in their garden in Hexham, Northumberland. At first glance, these small, stone-carved objects seemed like ordinary artifacts—roughly the size of tennis balls and carved with rudimentary faces. One bore a frown, while the other appeared more neutral, even serene. Despite their humble appearance, the objects quickly became the center of a chilling mystery."

Tommy stopped for a second then went on. "Almost immediately after their discovery, strange events began to unfold in the Robson household. Objects reportedly moved without explanation. Doors slammed shut as if compelled by an unseen force. The family described an oppressive atmosphere, as though the heads carried a tangible, malevolent presence. The disturbances were not confined to the house, however. Neighbors claimed to witness a creature—described as a large, wolflike being with glowing eyes—prowling near the Robsons' home. This creature, said to straddle the line between animal and human in its appearance, left claw marks in the soil outside their property. Its eerie appearances coincided with the heads' presence and fueled speculation about a deeper, more sinister connection. The wife said she also saw a creature that was more like half-goat, half-man."

"Wild," Tara breathed.

"Indeed. As the Hexham Heads passed through different hands, the strange phenomena seemed to follow them. One notable account came from Dr. Anne Ross, a scholar of Celtic folklore and archaeology. She brought the heads into her home to study them more closely, and she too experienced unexplainable occurrences. Her daughter claimed to have seen a half-man, half-beast figure in their house, an entity that disappeared as suddenly as it appeared. Dr. Ross herself reported feelings of unease and dread whenever she was near the heads, and her family experienced frequent disturbances. The incidents grew so troubling that she eventually returned the objects, unwilling to risk further turmoil."

"That's saying something for a seasoned professional historian to get freaked out by something like that," Alex commented.

"I thought the same," Tommy agreed. "The growing legend of the Hexham Heads attracted paranormal researchers who sought to uncover the truth. Some theorized that the heads served as conduits for supernatural energy, possibly linked to ancient Druidic practices in the region. Others suggested they carried a curse, an idea often associated with ancient relics. Yet skeptics dismissed these claims, attributing the phenomena to psychological suggestion, mass hysteria, or even deliberate fabrication.

"Adding another layer to the enigma, a man named Des Craigie came forward in the late 1970s, claiming he had carved the heads himself during the 1950s for his children. This admission seemed to discredit the idea of the heads being ancient or mystical in origin. However, many refused to accept this explanation, pointing to the peculiar design of the heads and the inexplicable events surrounding them. To this day, no definitive answer has emerged, leaving the mystery unresolved."

Tommy sighed as he finished the mini lecture and allowed his audience to soak it in.

"And to this day," Tara said, "the whereabouts of the Hexham Heads remain unknown."

"Exactly. I would say it's a definite possibility that whoever attacked Dr. Lowe's camp might have been looking for those two heads. Why, I can only guess right now. All I can tell you is, be careful as you head to India. If those men were willing to go to such lengths searching for something, it's unlikely they've quit now. And if they have Chen, they're likely using him as a resource, or leverage."

"Okay, chief," Alex said. "Thanks for the information. We'll keep it in mind."

"And we'll be watching our backs," Tara added. "As always."

"I'm sorry I can't send you some help, but all of our field agents are, well, in the field. Including Sean."

"It's okay. We can handle it. We'll let you know the minute we learn anything new."

"Sounds good."

Alex ended the call and glanced back at Felicia.

"Looks like things are only going to get weirder. You sure you want to stick with us?"

She nodded. Her eyes held a piercing, determined stare. "Definitely."

12

Rolf's men had grown even more impatient. With every hour that passed, their fears that the Americans might not return to the village grew stronger.

Not all of them fell prey to the temptation of getting frustrated. More than half of them either accepted this was part of their job or looked at the time as a break from work where they simply got to do nothing for several hours.

But a significant portion of them were anxious.

Rolf likened a group such as this to the pirates of old. When things were running smoothly, the captain was loved by all. But the moment anything diverged from the norm, questions began to arise in the crew's minds, and thoughts of mutiny soon followed.

This was a different scenario in that the men were being paid no matter what they were doing minute by minute. So any impatience or questioning of leadership came purely from a source of childish impatience.

He likened it to kids in the back seat of a car asking if they were there yet a thousand times on a vacation.

He'd never ventured into that world, having kids. Rolf's life had been about nothing but survival since he left his family to join the military and then eventually to become a gun-for-hire.

After his parents passed, he had no other attachments in this world, which oddly enough was a good thing in his line of work. Attachments could lead to problems, and Rolf had more than his share of those—especially dealing with a group of guys who could, at any moment, turn on him and slit his throat.

He doubted any of these men would be so bold. They were well paid, and so far he hadn't failed them as a leader. Still, he could never let down his guard.

One of his men who'd been watching the desert from on top of a small shanty, slid down the tin roof and hurried over.

"Sir," the soldier said. "Headlights coming down the road from the mountain."

Some of the others heard the announcement and immediately perked up.

Rolf maintained his usual cool demeanor as he walked over to the edge of the building and peered out through the opening in the crumbling wall.

He raised a scope and peered through it, immediately locating the SUV as it charged toward the town, leaving a rising trail of dust billowing up into the night sky.

"Get ready," he ordered. "This is what we planned for. They'll probably stop here to refuel, and perhaps stay at the inn up the street."

The "inn" hardly qualified as that. It was nothing more than five derelict buildings with single, sloped roofs that looked like they could collapse at any moment. The exterior paint was a faded and cracked pale color that may have been white long ago.

Rolf had slept in places that most normal people couldn't. Such was the life of a merc. Even he cringed at the thought of staying in one of those buildings. They looked disgusting from the outside, and he loathed to think what they might look like inside.

The men scrambled into position. The ones in charge of driving hurried over to the trucks parked in the shadows of the building, hidden from the road that passed through the village just eighty meters away.

The engines revved to life, and the men loaded up their gear in the cargo areas before quietly shutting the rear doors.

"We wait until they go to bed for the night," Rolf barked. "Then we go in and find whatever it is they discovered back there."

He jerked his thumb in the general direction of the mountain where they'd murdered more than a dozen people.

Rolf looked back into the desert. The SUV was moving fast. Whoever was driving it definitely seemed to be in a hurry. That didn't surprise him. The agents from the IAA had come out to the desert to investigate an archaeological mystery, not a mass murder scene. He figured civilians such as they would freak out at such a macabre sight, turn tail, and hurry back.

But they hadn't hurried. They'd lingered out there in the desert for hours, only to return to the village now.

As the SUV neared the edge of town, it slowed down to a more reasonable speed before entering through the outskirts—a line of abandoned buildings that had once served as homes to some of the people from the area.

The Americans' truck rolled by, heading toward the inn at the middle of town. Rolf could see the place from where he stood and assumed that the SUV would stop there for the night.

Instead, the truck kept rolling, passing the lone gas pump and the inn.

He frowned. "Unexpected," he breathed.

"I thought you said they were going to stop there for the night," Yuri complained.

"I did."

"Looks like you were wrong, boss."

Rolf ignored him, moving toward the dusty street so he could keep an eye on the SUV. He watched for fifteen seconds as the taillights grew more distant, nearing the opposite end of town.

"Load up," he said. "They aren't stopping here."

"What do you man?" Yuri demanded. "Where are they going?"

"It would seem they have decided to go back to the city."

Javier picked up on what his leader was thinking. "Airport?"

Rolf nodded. "Follow them."

The men continued piling into the trucks, while Yuri and Javier remained close to the commander.

"You think they're going back to the States?" Yuri asked.

"Possibly. Or they may have found something with that device at the mountain." He turned to one of the other men who was walking by. "Mateo. It would seem our American friends are leaving Mongolia. I need you to find out where their flight is going."

The younger man with a mop of black hair on his head nodded and continued over to his assigned truck. Rolf knew the second he was inside, he'd flip open his laptop and begin hacking into the Chinggis Khaan International Airport's system.

Rolf stalked over to his truck and climbed into the passenger seat, while Javier and Yuri grabbed the prisoner, hauled him over to the truck, and stuffed him in the middle of the back seat, where they sat on either side.

Rolf turned around as the driver revved the engine. He peered into Chen's weary eyes. "It's time to see if you were right about those American agents you told us about."

13

INDIA

Alex and Tara kept their heads on swivels as they led the way out of Jaisalmer Airport and onto the sidewalk alongside the terminal. They hadn't noticed anything or anyone unusual inside, but it was the busy season, when tourists from all over the world came to see the incomparable fort and the Thar Desert beyond.

The Jaisalmer Airport was a small, regional operation, and from what Alex had learned, there weren't many flights in or out during the off-season. He half wondered if the place shut down for brief periods of time or if they had to lay off some of the employees, only to bring them back again when the next big season rolled around.

Tara stretched her arms and yawned before shrugging the backpack on her shoulders to make it more comfortable.

When they'd boarded the plane in Mongolia, none of the three expected they would get much sleep, despite the comforts the IAA private jet afforded. On top of that, the need to figure out who was behind the killings at the dig site still weighed heavy on their minds.

Felicia had seen the men from a distance but not clearly enough to give a remotely adequate description.

Eventually, the fatigue induced by both the emotional events in the desert and multiple days of travel bore down on the Americans, and within thirty minutes of taking off they'd all fallen into a deep sleep until the pilot announced they were beginning their descent into Jaisalmer.

Once they landed, the three collected their belongings and made their way into the terminal. The Jaisalmer Airport offered a blend of modern functionality and subtle nods to the region's rich cultural heritage. As travelers entered the terminal, they were greeted by a compact yet thoughtfully designed space. The walls, painted in warm, earthy tones reminiscent of the golden sandstone synonymous with Jaisalmer, lent the interior a welcoming and grounded feel. Soft lighting illuminated the space, creating a calm ambiance that contrasted with the lively bustle of arriving and departing passengers —and with the potential danger that still seemed to hang in the air around the Americans.

The floors were polished to a gleam, with clean lines and minimalistic patterns. Here and there, small seating areas dotted the space, their benches upholstered in earthy hues of brown and beige, reflecting the desert palette. Decorative touches included traditional Rajasthani artwork and murals, depicting scenes of the Thar Desert, camels, and the iconic Jaisalmer Fort. A few brass artifacts—perhaps miniature replicas of *havelis*, or mansions, and other intricately carved vases—were strategically placed on ledges and counters, providing travelers a glimpse into the region's artistic legacy.

Fortunately for the three, most of the people flying into Jaisalmer were coming from somewhere else in the country, such as New Delhi or Mumbai. Few if any major international airports offered direct flights to the small hub, and so their modest customs processing area was almost completely empty.

After going through the security gates and being processed for entry into the country, Alex led the way toward the exits, where signs directed travelers to cabs, rideshares, and pickup areas.

"We've never been here before," he stated, looking around to take in the scenery. "It's actually a pretty nice airport."

"Same," Felicia echoed. "I've been to India, but not to this area."

"Here for work?" Tara asked.

Felicia smiled and permitted a short laugh. "No. I was twenty-one years old, and trying to find my purpose. I came to India on a backpacking trip. We hit up some places in the Middle East, parts of Europe, deeper into Asia. It took two months. We called it a backpacking trip, but it was really more by train. The backpacks were just how we carried our things."

"You and some friends?" Alex guessed.

"Yes. Two of my girlfriends."

"And did you find your life's calling?"

"I did. I'd been studying history and archaeology in college, but getting out and seeing the real stuff, walking in the places where famous people from history walked... It made it all more tangible, more personal. So when the trip was over, I finished my degree, and here I am."

The last few words faded with a hint of sadness. Alex and Tara knew the pain of losing her entire team had returned to weigh on her heart.

Alex checked his phone. There was a message from their contact that said he would meet them in front of the terminal once they were through customs. Alex sent a quick reply to let the man know they were on their way and continued walking.

"Our ride is going to be out front in a few minutes," Alex announced.

Devong Anand was a historian from one of the nearby towns about thirty minutes away from Jaisalmer. True to his word, Tommy had reached out to Anand to request assistance for his team in navigating the red tape that wrapped around full access to the fort. It was still left to be seen how much the man could actually do for them in the way of examining all of the grounds, but it was certainly better than nothing.

Alex and Tara also knew that if figuring out this next piece to the puzzle did require such a thorough investigation, they would be here for more than a day. Fortunately, Tommy and his contact had made arrangements for the three visitors to stay at the esteemed Hotel Fifu.

Apparently, it was one of the nicer places in the area, and given the fact that it was a busy time of year, they felt fortunate to have been able to secure a reservation for two rooms.

Without the need to visit the baggage claim area, where mobs of travelers gathered, the three continued toward the exits.

The check-in counters and security areas were straightforward and efficiently organized, reflecting the airport's primary purpose of serving as a gateway for domestic travelers and seasonal tourists. A single snack bar offered a selection of beverages and light snacks, including packaged sweets like *ghewar* and *namkeen*, catering to both tourists and locals. The aroma of freshly brewed chai often lingered in the air, adding to the charm of the experience.

"Anyone want a snack before we go?" Tara asked.

Alex and Felicia shook their heads.

"I'll wait till we get to the hotel," Alex said.

"Fine by me," Felicia agreed.

They kept walking, looking around to both inspect the scenery and to make sure they weren't being watched.

Though modest in size compared to larger hubs, the Jaisalmer Airport's interior exuded a quiet charm that mirrored the city it served. It was not merely a transit point but a gentle introduction to the cultural warmth and unique character of the desert jewel of Rajasthan.

Alex reached the doors first and stepped outside into the bright morning sunlight. It had been decently warm in Mongolia, even in spite of the latitude. But down here, far to the south, the heat was on a different level.

He slipped on a pair of sunglasses and peered down the bustling street. Cabs and rideshare cars lined the curb, along with a smattering of ordinary drivers there to pick up new arrivals.

"Any idea what kind of car he drives?" Tara asked, stopping next to her husband.

"Red sedan. Honda Accord."

"Sensible."

A warm breeze blew from the southwest, carrying with it a forbidding sense of the heat to come later in the day.

The exterior design of Jaisalmer Airport reflected the city's timeless desert charm, blending modern practicality while still reflecting the heritage of the region. Situated amid the arid expanse of the Thar Desert, the airport's structure was crafted from sandstone-like materials, echoing the warm, golden hues of the iconic Jaisalmer Fort and the surrounding landscape. Its understated design complemented the natural environment rather than overwhelmed it, creating an inviting and harmonious first impression for visitors.

As travelers approached, the first thing they noticed was the simplicity of the airport's façade. Large rectangular windows punctuated the otherwise solid exterior, their frames casting sharp shadows on exterior walls baking in the desert sun. The entrance featured an intricately carved overhang, a subtle homage to the ornate craftsmanship seen in the city's havelis and temples. Above the main doors, a clean yet elegant sign in both Hindi and English announced the name of the airport, welcoming visitors with understated pride.

The locals neatly maintained the airport grounds too, with small patches of greenery adding a splash of life to the arid surroundings. Desert plants like bougainvillea and thorny acacia lined the drive leading up to the terminal, their hardy beauty symbolic of the region's resilience. The air was hot and dry, often carrying a faint scent of dust and sand, mingling with the occasional aroma of wild desert flora.

"I think that's him," Alex blurted, pointing to a red sedan approaching from the left.

The three shuffled closer to the curb, marking out their spot where a gap between a taxi and a gray compact Toyota were parked, waiting for their fares.

Alex waved at the driver, who immediately switched on his turn signal and deftly maneuvered behind a vehicle that was pulling out onto the main thoroughfare, and parked in its place.

The driver stopped and opened his door to greet the Americans.

Devong Anand carried an unassuming yet scholarly appearance, along with an understated confidence. His hair, mostly black but streaked with silver at the temples, was neatly combed back, lending him an air of dignified wisdom. His eyes, a deep, rich brown, held a warmth that contrasted with their sharp, perceptive glint—eyes that seemed to peer not only at the world but through it, uncovering layers of meaning others might overlook.

His skin bore the sun-kissed tone common to northern India, a warm tan that hinted at years spent in the field under the relentless sun. A neatly trimmed mustache, peppered with gray, framed his upper lip, further emphasizing his refined appearance. He wore a lightweight *kurta* in a muted cream color, the soft fabric adorned with subtle embroidery near the collar and cuffs. Over this, he had draped a dark brown waistcoat, its polished buttons and understated design lending him a professional yet approachable demeanor. Slim trousers completed the ensemble, paired with well-worn leather sandals that hinted at his practical nature.

"Greetings, my friends," he said, beaming at the newcomers.

He walked around the back of the car and flipped open the trunk.

As he spoke, his voice carried the melodic cadence. His accent was muted and contained a trace of educated British—a hint at India's colonial past.

The three Americans joined him behind the car and slumped off their backpacks.

He held out a hand and shook Tara's first, then Felicia's, and finally Alex's.

"I am Devong Anand. A pleasure to meet you, I'm sure," he said pleasantly. "May I take your things?"

"Sure," Tara said. "Thank you so much. I'm Tara, this is Alex, and Felicia."

"Of course. Tommy has told me so much about you and your husband." He proceeded to take Felicia's laptop bag she carried in her right hand, then continued packing the rest of the things as he spoke.

"Have you ever been to Rajasthan before?"

Alex and Tara shook their heads.

"No, first time," Alex answered.

"Same for me, I'm afraid," Felicia added.

"Oh, well then, welcome," he said with his seemingly perpetual smile. "Please, take a seat, and we will be on our way. This time of year, airport security doesn't like us to sit here for long by the curb."

"Felicia, you can have shotgun," Tara said. "I'll ride in the back with Alex."

The archaeologist obliged and walked around to the front of the car while Tara followed and climbed into the seat behind her.

Alex lingered a little longer behind the vehicle, scanning the hectic traffic of cars, motorcycles, and pedestrians.

"Is everything all right?" Devong asked as he loaded the last of the bags into the trunk.

"I think so." Alex lowered his voice so only Devong could hear. "How much did Tommy tell you about what we're doing?"

The Indian's face turned grim. "He mentioned what happened in Mongolia with Dr. Lowe's team. Terrible tragedy. Is that why you're looking around? Do you think you were followed?"

Devong cast a few quick glances around the area.

"Hard to say," Alex confessed. "But it seems to me we got out of Mongolia way too easily."

"Then I suppose we will have to keep our eyes open."

14

The ride from the airport to the hotel was an immersion into the vibrant tapestry of Jaisalmer's desert cityscape. The sunlight was unrelenting, bouncing off the golden sandstone that seemed to dominate every structure they passed.

Buildings along the route were constructed almost exclusively of this sandstone, their façades intricately carved with patterns of flowers, arches, and lattices. Many bore the distinct look of havelis—ornate mansions with *jharokhas*, or overhanging enclosed balconies, and small domes that evoked a sense of regal history. These stood shoulder-to-shoulder with simpler homes, their flat rooftops adorned with fluttering laundry and children playing with kites.

Businesses lined the narrow streets as they got closer to the city center. Small shops with colorful awnings displayed everything from embroidered textiles and sparkling mirror-work *dupattas* to brass trinkets and handcrafted leather goods. Some of the shopkeepers sat cross-legged at their doorways, beckoning passersby with a cheerful "*Aao ji, dekho!*"—their way of saying "Come, look!" The signs were a mix of hand-painted Hindi and English, with flourishes of traditional motifs framing the letters.

Cafés and restaurants spilled onto the sidewalks, their modest chairs and tables shaded by canvas umbrellas. Many bore names like Desert Café or Thar Tandoor, proudly advertising local Rajasthani delicacies. The air grew fragrant with the mingling scents of spices—cumin, coriander, and turmeric—wafting from bubbling pots of *dal bati churma* and sizzling plates of *ker sangri*. Occasionally, the sharper aroma of fried *pakoras* or samosas would punctuate the air, making the travelers' stomachs growl.

"I've gotten clearance for us to see any of the restricted areas in the fort just in case we need it," Devong said as he turned left onto another street.

"That's awesome," Tara said. "Thank you for helping us out with that. We may not need it, but it's good to have no restrictions either way."

"Yes. They will have a liaison meet us there in two hours. That should give you enough time to settle in and get something to eat. I assume you didn't eat breakfast on the plane?"

"That is correct."

"Well, there are some good places around here. I can take you to one once you've checked into your rooms."

"That would be great," Felicia said. "Thank you so much for doing all this."

"It's my pleasure. Tommy called me at a time when I didn't have much going on anyway, so it all worked out perfectly. I love showing new people around this area. I grew up not far from here, you know."

"That's cool," Alex offered. "Lived here your whole life?"

"For the most part. I attended university in England for a few years here and there. But I've been here for the last fifteen. It is my home."

"I can understand that. We've been all around the world, but our favorite place to be is back home in Atlanta, usually in the lab."

Devong grinned. "Yes, Tommy has told me that is your fortress in a manner of speaking. You do most of the research and analysis for the IAA, yes?"

"Yeah," Tara confirmed. "They used to call us the kids, but now we're a little older so they go back and forth between kids and lab rats. Personally, I like lab rats better."

"You both look like you're in your twenties."

"Early thirties," Alex corrected. "But thanks. Nice to know we still got it." He smirked over at his wife, who rolled her eyes at him.

"How many people visit the fort every year?" Felicia asked, swerving the conversation back to their reason for being here.

"Around five to six hundred thousand. Some are from India, but most come from out of the country. The tourism industry keeps the lights on around here, as you Americans like to say. The money preserves our heritage so that many more can come and see it for decades to come. Of course, it certainly helps to have a little mystery to the place."

"Mystery?"

"Yes. The fort has many mysteries. I would have thought you'd know about that."

"We found a few interesting things, but maybe you could tell us more," Tara suggested.

"Sure." He shrugged as he pulled up to a red light and stopped. "Well, there's the curse of the fort. According to the legend, the fort carries a curse from a sage named Eesul, who blessed and cursed it simultaneously. The story goes that Eesul demanded the fort's builders leave space for a shrine to honor his hermitage. While they complied initially, subsequent rulers expanded the fort, which was completely against what the sage had commanded. This is supposed to explain why the fort has faced periods of abandonment and ruin throughout its history."

He paused as the light turned green and accelerated through the intersection.

"Then there's the disappearance of the Paliwal Brahmins about two hundred years ago, though that's a little less creepy than the others."

"How so?" Tara wondered.

"Could have been as simple as a tyrannical leader the people were tired of and simply moved on. Another interesting mystery is the tunnel system through and under the fort. Rumor is that there are many secret passageways that were built into the fort long ago. Some of them have been found, but based on the stories, there are many still undiscovered."

Alex and Tara shared a look. They were both intrigued, particularly about the curse and the tunnels.

"Of course, Jaisalmer Fort is rumored to have haunted areas, particularly in the Gate of Winds section. Locals and visitors have claimed to feel an unexplained presence or hear whispers in the quiet hours of the night. These stories have been passed down generations, giving the fort an aura of the supernatural. It is a rare place since it is a living fort, meaning people actually live there year-round."

"How many people?" Felicia wondered.

"Around four thousand."

"What?" Alex spat. "Four thousand?"

"It's a large fort, my young friend. The occupants live rent free since most of them are descendants of the Brahmin who once dwelled there. They also help keep the place going. I find it interesting that if so many believe the place is haunted, why would they continue to live there. Perhaps they simply do not fear ghosts, or the notion of them."

"We've heard about the bizarre stories regarding the Singing Sands," Tara said. "You think it might be something related to that?"

"Anything is possible. People are often too quick to disregard something simply because they cannot explain it."

Alex and Tara understood that. Most people wouldn't believe the things they'd seen. Fortunately, talking publicly about all that wasn't part of the job, so there was no ridicule or trolling to deal with. Everything within their division in the IAA was kept strictly quiet. Tara and Alex had come to understand that supposed government secrecy was nothing compared to its corporate variety.

"Any others?" Alex asked.

"Yeah. Like any old place like this, there are usually rumors about buried treasure. The fort was a prosperous trade hub for a long time, so it's thought that some of the rulers may have hidden jewels or gold somewhere in the walls, or in secret chambers. None of that has been found, though, so it could just be a generic story handed down over time."

Suddenly, something shook the vehicle. The trunk rattled for a few seconds, and everyone inside the car looked around to see what was going on.

But as quickly as it had begun, the gyrations stopped.

"What was that?" Felicia asked, her fingers wrapping around the door handles.

"Not sure," their driver answered. "Must have been something on the road back there. Irregular pavement. They could do a better job maintaining the roads around here."

"I feel like that's a universal problem. We have the same issues in Georgia, and it seems like Chattanooga ninety minutes north is always working on their interstate congestion."

"Ah yes," Alex said. "The perpetual challenge of moving traffic faster and smoother. All the things we have managed to do with science and engineering, yet the Romans still built longer-lasting, better-organized roads two thousand years ago."

As Devong navigated closer to the fort area, the streets grew narrower, and the charm of Old-World Jaisalmer became more pronounced. A lone camel passed by, its handler clad in a vibrant turban, guiding it through the bustling lanes with practiced ease. Street vendors called out their wares, offering chilled *kulhad lassi* in clay cups or fresh sugarcane juice pressed on the spot. The aroma of sweet chai simmering over coal braziers mingled with the faint metallic tang of motorbikes that zipped through the labyrinthine streets.

As the car turned onto another narrow street, the city seemed to shift into a timeless rhythm. The buildings, glowing under the desert sun, grew closer and more intricate with every turn. More shops lined the roads, displaying vibrant textiles and brass trinkets, their colors spilling onto the street. The scent of spiced chai and sizzling snacks wafted through the open car windows. Finally, the car slowed in front of Hotel Fifu, its sandstone façade adorned with ornate carvings and latticed balconies. The serene charm of the building stood in quiet contrast to the lively bustle outside.

Devong found a spot to park near the entrance, where a valet and a bellman waited to assist guests with their cars and their belongings. He pulled up to the curb, shifted the Honda into park, and exited the vehicle.

The valet hurried around the front of the car while the bellman immediately stepped to the front passenger door and opened it for Felicia.

"Welcome," the valet said to Devong. "Checking in?"

"I'm dropping them off, but I'll be here for a while."

"Very good, sir."

Devong handed him a few bills then turned and joined Alex as he stepped out of the car and moved to the trunk.

He opened the lid, and the bellman quickly joined the two men.

"May I take your bags, sir?" the bellman, a young man of maybe twenty-two years asked.

"There isn't much," Alex answered. "Nothing heavy." He thought of the two heads stuffed into one of the bags. The unusual, and somewhat unsettling, heads had caused a momentary pause in customs at the airport. The official checking their things hadn't been quite sure what to make of them. Alex had blown them off as interior decorations.

"As you wish, sir," the bellman said. "Please don't hesitate to let me know if you need anything."

"Will do."

Alex removed the bags for the two women first then his own. As soon as they'd collected their things, Devong closed the trunk, and the four paused for a second to take in the building's exterior.

Hotel Fifu displayed a magical reflection of Jaisalmer's culture, blending seamlessly into the golden tones of the surrounding desert city. The building, crafted from the region's iconic sandstone (which seemed to be used everywhere), shimmered warmly under the sunlight, its elaborate carvings and detailed façade reminiscent of a bygone era. Standing three stories tall, the hotel exuded the intimate elegance of a traditional haveli, inviting travelers to step into a world where time seemed to slow.

The front of the building was adorned with latticed balconies and small, arched windows framed by delicately carved stone. Each element echoed the craftsmanship for which Jaisalmer was renowned, showcasing intricate floral and geometric patterns that seemed to tell silent stories of the desert's enduring legacy. Above the main entrance, a small overhang bore the name Hotel Fifu in understated yet elegant lettering, welcoming guests with a sense of quiet pride.

A pair of carved stone pillars flanked the wooden entrance door, their surfaces etched with motifs of vines and peacocks. The door itself, painted a deep brown and reinforced with ornate brass studs, gave the impression of stepping into a sanctuary. In front of the hotel, a small courtyard offered a touch of greenery amid the golden expanse. Potted desert plants, including succulents and vibrant bougainvillea, added pops of color, while a simple stone bench provided a place for weary travelers to pause.

The rooftop, parts of it visible from the street, hinted at the panoramic views it offered. Shaded by a modest awning, it was clear that this space was designed for guests to enjoy the breathtaking sights of Jaisalmer's skyline, with the majestic fort looming in the distance.

The surrounding air carried the faint aroma of desert dust mingled with the scent of nearby marigold garlands and incense sticks often used in the evening rituals. Along with that, the air outside was rich with the promise of a meal. From somewhere nearby came the smoky, charred scent of freshly baked tandoori rotis. The spiced sweetness of ghee-laden desserts like *gulab jamun* and *jalebis* was unmistakable, mixing with the earthy aroma of the stone walls surrounding them. A faint floral note, likely from marigold garlands strung around the doorway, added a lightness to the symphony of smells.

Modest yet elegant, the hotel seemed to encapsulate the very soul of Jaisalmer—rich in tradition, steeped in history, and welcoming all who ventured into its golden embrace.

As the travelers approached the entrance, the sounds of the city softened. The rhythmic clatter of a rickshaw faded into the distance, replaced by the quiet hum of the hotel lobby, drawing them into another layer of Jaisalmer's timeless magic.

The bellman opened the door and stepped aside to allow the guests to enter.

The lobby of Hotel Fifu unfolded before them like a scene pulled straight from an ancient Rajasthani folktale. As they moved through the carved wooden door, its surface etched with intricate motifs of peacocks and floral patterns, the air changed. A faint scent of sandalwood lingered, mingling with the earthy coolness of the stone walls. The room was dimly lit, the sunlight from outside filtered through delicately latticed jharokhas, casting intricate shadows on the polished floor.

The floor itself was a masterpiece, a mosaic of sandstone tiles in muted tones of ocher and amber that seemed to echo the desert outside. Every step they took felt deliberate, as if walking across history. Their eyes were drawn to the walls, adorned with tapestries and framed photographs of Jaisalmer's iconic landmarks. There were images of the golden fort bathed in sunlight, the Sam Sand Dunes at sunset, and close-ups of intricately carved Jain temples. Beside these hung a collection of vintage Rajasthani artwork, their colors still vivid despite the passing years. A small niche in one wall housed a brass oil lamp, its tiny flame flickering gently, as if guarding the stories of the past.

In the center of the lobby sat a low seating area arranged around a square table carved from stone. The cushions were draped in vibrant Rajasthani fabrics—deep maroons, golds, and indigos—each pattern telling its own story of craftsmanship. A brass tray on the table held small cups of masala chai, its inviting aroma curling into the air. Nearby, a clay urn, filled with cool water for weary travelers, rested on a wooden pedestal.

Above them, the ceiling was a sight to behold. Wooden beams

crisscrossed overhead, their surfaces adorned with faded yet intricate paintings of celestial dancers and floral vines. A single chandelier hung from the center, its iron frame shaped like an ancient candelabra, holding tiny glass lanterns that glowed like desert fireflies. In a way, it was like a more rustic, Jain-inspired version of something like the Sistine Chapel.

Tara ran her fingers over the edge of a nearby pillar, its surface cold and smooth. The smooth stone bore faint inscriptions in a language they could not decipher, whispering of a time long gone. Somewhere in the background, the soft strains of a sitar played, adding to the timelessness of the moment.

The group exchanged glances; their voices hushed as if the room demanded reverence. This was no ordinary lobby. It felt like stepping into a sanctuary, a place where the past and present coexisted in delicate harmony. Whatever lay ahead in their journey, they felt as though they had crossed a threshold into the heart of Rajasthan itself.

Finally, Felicia spoke up. "This place is incredible," she said, her eyes wandering around the room, picking up every single detail.

Tara and Alex both nodded.

"Tommy really knocked this one out of the park," Alex said to their host.

"Yes, it is one of the more popular hotels in the city. It opened in 1999, and was designed to reflect the city's culture."

"Well, I would say they nailed it."

"How far is the fort from here?" Tara wondered.

"Not far. It's about a ten-minute walk," Devong answered.

"Wow, that close? Excellent."

To their right stood a low desk carved from dark teakwood, its edges adorned with brass inlays. Behind it, an elderly man with a kind face and a crisp white kurta rose to greet them, his hands folded in a gesture of welcome. His warm smile seemed to match the aura of the place—inviting yet steeped in mystery.

As they approached the desk, his smile broadened. "Welcome to Hotel Fifu," he said in perfect, accented English. "Checking in?"

"Yes, sir," Alex said. He stopped in front of the desk and set his bags down. "The name is Alex Simms."

The man nodded and tapped on the keys of his computer. He leaned forward and focused on the screen. "Yes, I see you have two rooms reserved for three nights."

Alex figured Tommy must have thought they might need some extra time for their investigation due to the size of the fort.

"Great." Alex removed his passport and a credit card from his metal wallet and handed it to the man.

"Oh thank you. Any incidentals will be charged to this card, should you need."

Alex smiled. He knew the drill having been through this process more times than he could possibly count.

The concierge returned Alex's card and began scribbling on a couple of small envelopes. He wrote down the room numbers on each then inserted two plastic keys into them. He slid the envelopes across the desk, where Alex pulled them away. He passed one to Felicia.

"We were able to get your rooms next to each other," the older man said. "I hope that is acceptable."

"It's perfect," Tara said. "Thank you so much for accommodating us on such short notice."

"I'm happy to help. Enjoy your visit."

Alex turned and stepped away from the desk. "So," he began, looking at Devong first, "I guess we'll take our things up to our rooms and meet you back down here? Unless you feel the need to come up with us."

"No, I'll wait here in the lobby if that's all right with you."

"Sure, no problem. We'll be back down in a few minutes."

Devong walked over to a table near a fountain on the far side of the lobby and sat down while the Americans made their way to the elevators. The lift dinged, and a moment later the brass doors parted. The three stepped into the empty elevator, and Alex pressed the button for the second floor.

"You think we can trust him?" Alex asked.

Tara and Felicia looked over at him with confused frowns.

"Dr. Anand?"

"Yeah. Who else?"

"Tommy knows him, and trusts him. So that means we should."

"Yeah, I know. But Tommy makes mistakes. He's not a robot."

"You're being paranoid. Dr. Anand is here to help us."

The elevator dinged to let them know they'd arrived on the second floor. A second later the doors parted, and they stepped out into the hallway.

"I hope you're right," Alex said.

15

"They've checked into the Hotel Fifu." Rolf said into the phone. "What would you like us to do?"

"An early check-in," his employer replied. "Usually, visitors can't check in until later in the afternoon. They must have called in a favor." He quickly went back to the question. "Did they do anything else?"

Rolf stared through the windshield of the sedan. He and his team had landed shortly before the IAA agents thanks to some quick work figuring out their flight plan, and already having their plane prepped for takeoff.

"No, sir. A driver picked them up. He looks like a local."

"Hired driver?"

"Not sure, but it doesn't look that way. He went into the hotel with the Americans and left his vehicle with the valet."

"Hmm." The man on the other end of the line paused, considering the new piece of information. "He must be a sort of liaison, perhaps. A local with information about this place."

"A historian or archaeologist, perhaps?"

"That would make sense. Their agency has contacts all over the world. I wouldn't imagine it to be too difficult for them to get a local expert to come lend them a hand."

A white car drove by with the windows down. Indian pop music blared from the speakers inside and echoed through the canyon of tightly packed buildings.

"Do you have your windows down?" the boss asked.

"No, sir. Someone just drove by playing their music with theirs down."

"Irritating."

"There's one more thing you should know, sir," Rolf said, glancing over at Yuri, who sat in the passenger seat chewing a piece of gum and wearing a smirk that suggested he would be happy to see Rolf get in trouble.

"What's that?"

"Dr. Felicia Lowe."

"What about her?"

"She's still alive. She was with the two IAA agents when they left the car and entered the hotel."

"I thought she was dead." The employer didn't sound happy about the slip.

"We never found her."

"Yes, and you believed the desert would take care of that loose end."

"We were thorough in our search, sir," Rolf defended. "She wasn't in the camp or on the mountain. We did a quick sweep around the perimeter, but there was no sign of her. It's as if she simply vanished."

His employer let out a frustrated sigh. Rolf imagined the man running his fingers through his hair behind a big desk, sitting in a high-back leather chair, though he knew the man wasn't in an office like that.

Rolf also knew that the man had approved his decision to leave the mountain and wait for the Americans to conduct their search. He was also aware that there would be Mongolian authorities on their way to the site to begin the criminal investigation. He'd been monitoring that since the unit returned to the village, but there'd been nothing to see or hear—not until they were safely on their plane and taking off. The government had been slow to react to the reports, which was to be expected. Most governments took their sweet time to get anything done. Such was the nature of bureaucracy. But with the crime scene out in such a remote location, and few resources or manpower in the region, their response had dragged like a bad sermon in church.

"This changes nothing," the boss said after a long moment of thought.

Initially, the plan had been to get to Lowe and force her to find the treasure hidden on the mountain.

Rolf had his men go through the ranks of Lowe's team, making sure there were no survivors before asking the last one, Dr. Chen, where Dr. Lowe was hiding.

He'd said she went up on the mountain to look around, but when Rolf and his team made it to the top, he found it empty. Upon returning to the camp, he'd smacked Chen around, making sure the man wasn't lying. Being an expert at reading body language, Rolf knew the archaeologist was telling the truth. But that didn't explain where the woman had gone, or how she'd managed to vanish so quickly.

A small, superstitious part of Rolf wondered if she'd fallen victim to the bizarre mysteries that seemed to haunt the mountain. He'd quickly dispelled that notion as ridiculous and irrational.

However she'd done it, Lowe had found her way to the IAA agents, and now they were here in India. Rolf could only presume that whatever they'd discovered in the Gobi Desert had brought them to this place, on the edge of another desert.

"What are your orders?" Rolf asked.

"Follow them. If they find the two heads, then you know what to do."

"Kill them and bring the stones to you."

"Exactly. And there must be no witnesses."

"There are a lot of people here right now," Rolf explained. "High tourist season. Might prove tricky taking them out with so many travelers around."

"I know you will figure it out," the boss said.

People continued walking by in a seemingly endless stream. Many different nationalities were represented in the hodgepodge of tourists. Some veered into shops to buy souvenirs. Others dipped into cafés or restaurants to get a snack or perhaps breakfast on their way to the fort. He would have normally considered such people crazy to wake up so early to go visit a historic place, but he'd learned that Fort Jaisalmer was massive. Visitors could spend an entire day there and not see everything.

"I'll take care of it, sir." Rolf said. "And once we have the stone heads, we will rendezvous with you."

"Excellent."

16

The hot morning air would have usually been dry, but as the three Americans and their liaison left the hotel for Fort Jaisalmer, the atmosphere around them was as thick as a July day in Charleston. It was the tension.

The group had decided to walk to the fort since it was nearby and stopped for a bite to eat before beginning what they all believed would be a long day of searching.

The restaurant was a small rooftop café perched atop a sandstone building near the heart of Jaisalmer's bustling old city. Known as The Desert Plate, it was a popular spot for both locals and tourists, offering a stunning view of Jaisalmer Fort, its golden walls glowing in the morning sunlight. The exterior was simple, with a narrow staircase winding up the side of the building, flanked by potted desert plants. A hand-painted wooden sign with swirling Hindi and English lettering welcomed patrons to what promised to be a memorable meal.

Inside, the café was charmingly rustic. A colorful canopy of patchwork fabric, fluttering gently in the desert breeze, partially shaded the rooftop. Low tables with cushions on the floor invited guests to relax in a traditional Rajasthani style, though a few regular chairs and tables were also scattered about. The walls were adorned with hand-painted murals depicting camels, dunes, and the city's iconic fort. Strings of fairy lights crisscrossed above, ready to add a warm glow for evening diners but lending a whimsical touch even during the day.

The smells of the place were an irresistible mix of spices and fresh bread that hinted at the feast to come. From the open kitchen tucked into a corner of the rooftop, the tantalizing aroma of frying *puris* wafted through the air, mingling with the sharp tang of freshly brewed masala chai. There was also the faint sweetness of *jaggery* and ghee, promising desserts or treats to follow.

Devong took the liberty of ordering a classic local breakfast for the table. First came *puri bhaji*, golden, puffed-up fried bread served with a mildly spiced potato curry that had a hint of cumin and turmeric. The puris were warm and crisp, perfect for scooping up the soft, flavorful curry. Alongside the bread, they tried *kadhi pakora*, a tangy yogurt-based curry with gram-flour dumplings, its creamy texture balanced by the slight kick of spices. For something lighter, there were *dahi vada*, lentil dumplings soaked in cool, seasoned yogurt, topped with tamarind and mint chutney for a burst of sweet and tangy flavors.

They washed it all down with masala chai served in small clay cups that added an earthy touch to the already aromatic tea infused with cardamom, ginger, and cloves. The final treat was a shared plate of *jalebis*, their bright orange coils soaked in sugar syrup, offering a crisp, syrupy sweetness to end the meal.

While he'd loved every bite of the breakfast, everyone also felt a little sluggish from eating so much.

"I need a nap," Alex half joked as they exited the restaurant. Wishful thinking, he knew. Fortunately, the walk over to the fort helped get his blood pumping and muscles loosened.

The walk to Jaisalmer Fort was another sensory journey, this time bringing the city itself to life. The narrow streets leading up to the fort bustled with activity, their cobblestones uneven but well-trodden by countless travelers over the centuries. On either side, small shops spilled onto the sidewalks, their vibrant displays a riot of color. Brightly patterned textiles hung from hooks, and glimmering rows of brass trinkets and jewelry sparkled in the sunlight. Vendors called out in Hindi and English, offering everything from handcrafted leather goods to miniature replicas of the fort itself.

The air was a mix of earthy desert dust and enticing food aromas, which their recent meal didn't seem to temper. The smell of freshly fried *kachoris* and samosas wafted from tiny food stalls, mingling with the sweet scent of sugar syrup from sizzling jalebis. Occasionally, a smoky tang from a coal-fired tandoor hinted at the preparation of lunch dishes like naan and grilled kebabs.

Tara found herself eyeing a jewelry stand with intricate hand-made bracelets, necklaces, and earrings on display both on a table, and on a couple of stand-up displays.

The sounds of the street were a lively cacophony. Vehicles honked persistently to navigate the crowded streets, a mix of auto-rickshaws, motorbikes, and the occasional camel cart laden with goods. Their drivers shouted warnings or exchanged lighthearted banter as they maneuvered through the chaos. Street performers added their voices to the symphony—traditional musicians playing *sarangi* or *tabla* sat on mats, their melodies weaving through the noise.

"Years ago, you would have seen snake charmers here on the side-walks," Devong explained. "But that sort of thing isn't legal here anymore."

Alex had been both surprised and a little relieved at the revelation. He wasn't a fan of snakes, especially the kind that produced deadly venom.

The sidewalks were crowded with people of all kinds. Tourists strolled in groups, some snapping photos of the ornate havelis along the way, others bartering over scarves and bangles. Locals, dressed in vibrant Rajasthani attire, moved briskly, balancing baskets on their heads or guiding children through the crowd. Women in colorful saris sat cross-legged on mats, selling garlands of fresh marigolds, while men in turbans hawked bottles of chilled water and soda from makeshift stands. The occasional wandering cow added to the scene, ambling lazily as pedestrians carefully stepped around it.

Children darted in and out of the crowd, laughing and chasing each other, while tourists paused to admire wall murals or pose for selfies with street performers. A puppeteer, stationed near a small square, animated his handcrafted marionettes to tell a story, drawing a small audience that clapped in appreciation.

As the fort's towering walls came into view, the visitors were struck by how alive the streets felt.

The fort, known as Sonar Quila or the Golden Fort, stood atop Trikuta Hill, its massive sandstone walls glowing a brilliant gold under the desert sun. From a distance, it seemed to rise organically from the earth, blending seamlessly with the arid landscape. As the group neared the fort, the sheer scale of it became apparent—its ninety-nine bastions and towering walls giving it the appearance of a massive, golden ship anchored in the sea of sand.

The main entrance for tourists was through the Gopa Chowk, a bustling square at the base of the fort. More vendors lined the cobbled pathway leading up to the gate, their stalls bursting with vibrant displays of colorful textiles, handmade jewelry, leather goods, and more miniature replicas of the fort. The air was alive with the sounds of hawkers calling out to visitors, their voices blending with the jingling of camel bells and the hum of conversations in multiple languages.

As they reached the Suraj Pol, or Sun Gate—the first of four massive gates leading into the fort—Tara and Alex couldn't help but marvel at its intricate design. The gate was adorned with carvings of sun motifs and floral patterns. The heavy wooden doors, reinforced with iron spikes, stood ajar, allowing a steady flow of tourists to pass through. The scent of sandalwood incense lingered faintly in the air, likely from offerings made at one of the many temples inside the fort.

The pathway through the gates was steep and winding, designed to slow down invading armies. As they ascended, the walls seemed to close in slightly, giving a sense of being enveloped by history. Along the way, they passed Ganesh Pol, the second gate, and then Hawa Pol, the Gate of Winds, aptly named for the cool breezes that funneled through its stone latticework.

The road finally opened up into the main courtyard, where tourists gathered to marvel at the fort's architecture and capture the moment in photographs. Here, the Americans could see the sprawling Raj Mahal, or Royal Palace, rising in the distance, its honey-colored façade intricately decorated with latticed windows and carved balconies. To the left and right, smaller structures housed shops and cafés, their exteriors blending seamlessly with the fort's ancient walls.

A spectacular Jain temple stood in the front courtyard of the fort. Its golden sandstone façade gleamed in the desert sun, its intricate carvings casting delicate shadows that seemed to shift with the changing light. The temple's design was both imposing and inviting, a blend of symmetry and detail that beckoned all who passed through the bustling courtyard to pause and admire its grandeur.

The entrance was framed by a pair of ornately sculpted pillars, each etched with intricate patterns of lotus flowers, intertwining vines, and geometric shapes. At the base of the pillars, stone carvings of elephants stood poised, their trunks raised high in a gesture of welcome and protection. Above the doorway, a carved *torana*, or decorative arch, stretched gracefully, adorned with celestial beings and mythical creatures seemingly caught mid-dance. These figures exuded a sense of movement, their delicate forms showcasing the mastery of the artisans who had brought them to life.

The door itself was a massive wooden structure, reinforced with iron bands and studded with small brass accents that glinted in the light. Carved into the wood were scenes of Jain mythology and several figures in meditative poses, their serene expressions radiating an otherworldly calm. Surrounding the doorway were smaller niches carved into the sandstone, each housing a statue of a figure seated in a lotus position or standing in quiet contemplation.

Above the entrance, the temple's spire rose high into the sky, a marvel of layered carvings and intricate detailing. The spire was adorned with rows of miniature statues, celestial dancers, and animals, creating the impression of a procession ascending toward the heavens. At the apex of the spire, a *kalash*, or sacred pot, glimmered faintly, a symbol of abundance and spiritual fulfillment.

The lower walls of the temple were equally captivating, lined with friezes that depicted scenes from Jain scriptures and daily life. These carvings were so finely detailed that even the folds in the garments of the figures and the expressions on their faces were rendered with astonishing precision. Small floral and geometric patterns filled the spaces between the larger designs, ensuring that no part of the surface was left untouched by the artisan's hand.

Surrounding the temple was a low stone platform where devotees had placed offerings of marigold garlands, bowls of rice, and small brass lamps. The flickering flames of the lamps created a warm, golden glow that matched the hue of the sandstone, adding to the sense of reverence that seemed to emanate from the structure itself.

The air around the temple was filled with a quiet energy. The scent of sandalwood incense, faint but persistent, mixed with the earthy aroma of the stone warmed by the sun. A gentle hum of prayers could be heard from within, accompanied by the occasional soft chime of bells. This was not just a temple; it was a sacred space alive with devotion, art, and the passage of time, standing at the heart of the fort as a symbol of resilience and faith.

The courtyard was alive with activity, as it seemed everywhere was this time of day. Guides offered their services, speaking in fluent Hindi, English, and sometimes French or German, ready to unravel the fort's stories for curious visitors. Children ran ahead of their families, their laughter echoing against the stone. Just as in the town itself, here the occasional camel or cow wandered through, adding to the fort's timeless ambiance.

Above, the fort's bastions loomed large, their surfaces worn smooth by centuries of desert winds. From that heights, they could imagine the unparalleled view of the city below, with its sea of golden buildings mirroring the fort's hue. The anticipation of exploring deeper into the maze of narrow alleys, temples, and living quarters made the experience of standing at Jaisalmer Fort's entrance all the more thrilling. It was a place that carried the weight of centuries yet welcomed the present with open arms, leaving every visitor with a sense of awe.

"Our guide should be over there," Devong said, standing up on his tiptoes to see through the throngs of tourists. Tourists gathered in loose groups near the ticket counter, which was set off to one side under a stone awning. A long queue had formed, and the sounds of conversation filled the air.

"Aren't you our guide?" Tara asked with a hint of playful derision.

Devong laughed. "Yes, I will show you around, but I need to get our badges so we don't get stopped anywhere the rest of the visitors aren't supposed to go." He inclined his chin an inch, then pointed. "There she is. Come. Follow me."

Devong pressed forward, weaving through the crowds of meandering people, then to the left of the queue for tickets.

A woman in a colorful, traditional sari stood with her hands folded in front of her, four lanyards with badges dangling from her fingers.

She stood with effortless grace. In her mid-thirties, she radiated elegance, and a quiet confidence. Her sari, a flowing masterpiece of deep crimson with gold thread work, draped around her slender figure in the traditional Rajasthani style. The colorful fabric shimmered subtly in the sunlight, its intricate patterns of paisleys and floral motifs catching the eye. The golden border of her *pallu*—the section of the sari that fell over her shoulder—added a regal touch as it fluttered gently in the desert breeze.

Her long jet-black hair was neatly braided, the end adorned with tiny jasmine flowers that added a soft, sweet fragrance to the air around her. Her skin, a warm, sun-kissed brown, seemed to glow naturally, accentuated by a hint of kohl lining her almond-shaped eyes. Those eyes, expressive and luminous, held a mixture of intelligence and kindness that made it hard to look away.

A small bindi of vermilion graced her forehead, adding a pop of color that complemented her sari. Her lips, lightly tinted with a berry hue, curled into a serene smile. Around her neck, she wore a delicate gold necklace with a single pendant shaped like a lotus, while matching gold bangles jingled softly on her wrists with every movement. Small, intricate earrings shaped like peacocks completed her look, their tiny gemstones catching the light as she turned her head.

Her bare feet peeked out from beneath the sari's folds, the edges of her toenails painted a bright coral, and a delicate anklet adorned one ankle, its tiny bells creating the faintest tinkling sound as she moved.

As the group approached, Devong grinned broadly and opened his arms to embrace the woman. She did the same, beaming while she hugged him.

"My friends," Devong said as he stepped back. "This is Dr. Aarushi Patel. She is a former student of mine. Now she works here at the fort."

The Americans offered an array of nice-to-meet-yous.

"My pleasure," she returned with a slight bow. "I have procured these badges for you so you shouldn't have any trouble examining the entire property." She handed out the badges and continued. "Of course, I know I don't have tell you to please leave everything untouched."

They nodded.

"Dr. Anand told me a little about why you are here, but it is still a little unclear to me. You are looking for something?"

"Yes," Tara replied first. "We believe there are some artifacts hidden here in the fort, and we are looking for that hiding place."

"I don't suppose you have any big red Xs painted on a floor or wall somewhere," Alex joked.

Aarushi looked at him and lowered her eyebrows. The others turned to him as well, each with either a look of confusion or disgust at the bad joke.

"Sorry," he said, his face reddening behind his beard. "I just did a dad joke, didn't I?"

"Yes. Yes, you did," Tara ridiculed.

"Anyway," Dr. Patel said, "we don't have anything like that, but the fort is vast. You could spend days here and not see it all. So, I wish you good luck. Of course, your guide Dr. Anand will be more than capable of showing you around to the most interesting places. If you need anything else, he has my number, so don't hesitate to ask."

The group echoed a series of thank-yous.

"I'm sorry I can't go with you," she said, turning to Devong. "I have a busy day of work ahead, but perhaps we can meet up afterward."

"That would be great. I'll let you know."

She smiled at him, then at the others before spinning around and walking away, disappearing into the foot traffic.

Alex inspected his badge then slipped it over his head so it dangled from his neck.

The others hung them around their necks too before Devong stepped away and turned to face them. "So, do you have any idea where you'd like to begin looking?"

"All we have to go on is the clue we found at the mountain back in Mongolia," Felicia answered. "It was inscribed on a couple of weird-looking stone heads."

"Stone heads? Whom did they resemble?"

"No one. They were kind of generic. Of course, it could have been someone specific, but we have no way to identify them."

"That's interesting."

"The clue," Tara jumped in, "says where the sands wail beneath the guardians of old."

Devong acknowledged with a nod. "Well, I can see why you came to the Singing Sands. It sounds like that is exactly what the clue is referencing."

"Any ideas about the part mentioning the guardians? If we find those, we should be able to find some kind of writing or glyphs that might point the way."

He hummed quietly to himself, scratching his chin as he thought. "I don't know about the writing or glyphs. But a few locations come to mind that we should check. Of course, there are others that aren't listed for public viewing."

"Maybe we should look at those first," Felicia suggested. "If it's a spot where millions of people have visited over the years, surely they would have found something unusual. Right?"

"That's a good point," Devong agreed.

"Yes, but that isn't always the case," Tara countered. "Sometimes things are hidden in plain sight."

"True," Felicia said. "I suppose we should be thorough."

"Right."

Alex turned to Devong. "Let's take a look at the more visited spots first. Get them out of the way."

"Fair enough," their guide said. "Follow me. Hopefully, we get lucky on the first one."

17

Rolf watched the Americans and their liaison from a shadowy corner of the courtyard. He had men positioned in the other three corners and a few mingling with the crowds of tourists getting ready to begin their journey through the enormous fort.

He and his team had followed the IAA agents and their friends to the fort, with a long stopover at a restaurant on the way here. Rolf made sure his men ate before they embarked, or in the case of two of them, while staking out the hotel. That way, they'd be good to go for the next five or six hours.

His men were accustomed to going longer stretches without food. They'd conditioned themselves over the years through necessity during various missions. Sometimes they would go days without food, and it didn't mar their effectiveness.

Standing around outside on the street and watching the restaurant had been boring. Rolf and his men were forced to hang out and watch the entrance while the IAA team casually ate a big breakfast.

At least, Rolf thought, *they aren't aware of my unit's presence.*

For all he knew, the group probably believed they'd managed to escape his clutches when they left Mongolia. Of course, he never assumed anything. That's how missions went awry. But he had to believe the odds were in his favor at this point.

Now all they had to do was follow the Americans until they uncovered the next piece of the puzzle. That, however, was a huge presumption. But his employer was convinced the agents would figure out the exact location of some ancient device or clue and be able to decipher it to lead to the next one.

There were too many variables for Rolf's taste. What if they weren't able to locate whatever it was they were looking for? Or if they did find it, who was to say they could automatically figure out the meaning of it? The IAA team might be gifted, but no one could figure out everything.

Still, Rolf understood the IAA agents were experts in their field. Solving these types of mysteries was a substantial part of their career, and their agency had an incredible reputation in the world of archaeology and anthropology.

Most of their work involved security and research. When a team of archaeologists uncovered something big, something unusual, or something extremely valuable, IAA were who people called to make sure those artifacts were safely delivered to a research facility, sometimes their own in Atlanta.

There were other stories, though. Things that were kept out of the media save for the occasional slip.

Tara Watson and Alex Simms were much more than just a couple of mall cops out to protect priceless artifacts. They were highly trained, though Rolf could only guess by whom. His employer had made it as clear as Waterford that the IAA agents could handle themselves when it came to a fight.

The man wouldn't elaborate on all the details but alluded to a few stories—one in particular that he'd seen firsthand.

He'd mentioned an incident in Kyoto where the two agents had killed a man with a rifle near a temple. There were others too, situations where the young married couple had killed men who tried to interfere with agency business.

They weren't like any archaeologists Rolf had ever heard of, like the ones he and his men had butchered in the Mongolian desert. Those researchers had been unarmed and helpless. They had begged for their lives and wept like children who'd lost their favorite toy. Rolf's men were happy to end their suffering. People like that were weak. Rolf and his entire team understood that. And weakness was something to be ripped out like a weed in a garden.

Still, despite the information Rolf's employer had shared regarding the two, he'd also been hiding something, a personal story perhaps—one in which they'd foiled one of his plans?

His employer had seemed somewhat eager to eliminate the two when they'd led Rolf and his men to the "treasure" or whatever it was they were hunting. Rolf would hardly call a couple of stone heads treasure, but that's what he was told to bring back—a collection of unusual stone heads.

Rolf continued watching as he recalled more information he'd gleaned before taking on the mission, from a dossier for another member of the IAA, a guy named Sean Wyatt. He was one of the leading possibilities for who had trained these kids. The man's past was shrouded in secrecy. Rolf had used the full extent of his resources and connections to learn more about Wyatt but had only rammed his head into dead ends. All he knew was where he went to college, where he was from, and where he worked. The other gaps in his dossier might as well have been a billboard screaming, "Redacted!"

He'd seen it many times before. That was the world he lived in, a reality where people's pasts were hidden and mysterious. There were hit jobs he'd been sent on for which he'd only been given a photo and a location. Beyond that, he could have been targeting the most dangerous assassin in the world, or the most innocent saint, for all he knew.

But that's how he'd survived. He treated every mark as though they were the most dangerous person on Earth. That, and he always surrounded himself with a reliable, yet predictable cast of characters.

His two closest lieutenants were prime examples of the latter. Yuri and Javier were extremely good at their jobs, but they were also given to mutinous thoughts, statements, and intentions.

Rolf could see through all that, and he knew how far their loyalties went. The truth was he wasn't very different in that regard. He'd been that way in the past, when he was just coming up through the mercenary ranks. But with all the people Rolf had killed, he'd never betrayed anyone on his team, whether he was the one leading or the one following, like in his early days.

"Teams, check in," Rolf said into the lapel mic hidden away under the collar of his light brown button-up shirt. A lightweight gray windbreaker covered most of the shirt, as well as the pistol holstered on his right hip. He kept the jacket zipped three-quarters of the way up to make sure no gust of wind suddenly exposed the firearm and sent the throngs of visitors into a panic. That was the last thing he needed.

"Team two in position," Yuri said.

"Team three in position," Javier echoed.

"Team four in position," the fourth, a Bosnian named Davud, said.

"Good," Rolf said, doing his best not to look like a crazy person talking to himself. The two men on his team stood on either side of him, each sweeping their gaze across the crowd, turning their heads from left to right and back again.

Rolf's eyes, however, remained on the targets.

He watched as they stopped off to the side of the ticket kiosk and were greeted by a beautiful woman. Rolf guessed she was in her thirties. Dressed in a traditional sari, she was the living embodiment of the captivating wonders of India. He smirked. *Shame I'm not here for pleasure.*

Women were the easiest targets in the world for a guy like Rolf. Not only was he ruggedly handsome and sitting on a pile of cash, cryptocurrency, and other assets, but Rolf had something more powerful in his arsenal when it came to finding companionship in any city he visited—the numbers.

He knew he could walk into any bar in the world, and that at least two or three women in there would be happy to spend the night with him. It just came down to isolating those two or three.

He'd figured this out with the help of an American merc he'd teamed up with years before. As his colleague had put it so succinctly, "If you only get a hit three out of ten times in baseball, you're in the Hall of Fame."

Rolf had never had a problem in that arena, but with the newfound knowledge, he was virtually unstoppable. He also figured it was a good thing he didn't know about that earlier in life, otherwise he may have gotten into more trouble than just mischief.

He pushed aside the carnal thoughts about the woman and returned to being the observer, there to do a job.

The Indian man with the Americans greeted her, conducted introductions, and then carried on a short conversation. Rolf wished he could hear what they were saying, but in this mob, it would be impossible, even if he had an isolating range microphone.

After a few minutes of discussion, the Indian woman gave four badges to the visitors. Rolf assumed these were some kind of all-access passes. The tickets didn't look like the normal ones the other tourists bought at the kiosk.

This could prove problematic, he thought. Rolf didn't dare vocalize his concern. He had to show confidence at all times lest he wake up with a knife in his back.

Still, if those badges allowed the Americans to search areas of the fort where ordinary people weren't permitted, he would have to figure out a way to gain access without causing a stir. There wasn't much in the way of security coming into the fort. A few guards here and there to make sure people behaved. He noted a few cameras too, but not so many as to be a concern. There were plenty of blind spots, and if the people who'd set up the system had done a similar job in the rest of the fort, he and his team could work their way around the cameras without being detected.

The woman in the sari finished their conversation, smiled pleasantly, then walked back through the crowd and disappeared.

"Eyes on targets," Rolf said into the radio, making sure his men would be ready to move.

He watched as the Americans and their Indian companion talked, perhaps about where they should go first. He couldn't imagine they were discussing anything else. Like him, they were here to do a job.

After several minutes of talking, the group finally turned and started toward the entrance, where all the other tourists were heading. Taking a route with everyone else would make it easier for Rolf and his men to blend in.

He doubted Dr. Lowe had seen him or any of his men close enough to identify them, but he'd prefer not to make that assumption. By melding with the crowd, they were just visitors there to see the splendors of the fort

"Let's move. Stagger yourselves. Follow them inside, and keep your distance, both from them and each other. We don't want them getting suspicious."

Rolf had already procured mobile tickets online so they would have no issues following the group in. Once beyond the entrance, though, they'd have to figure out how to remain out of sight as the targets ventured into areas ordinary visitors could not enter.

The four teams worked their way through the mob until they neared the gate. Yuri's team fell in behind Rolf's, followed by the remaining two units.

This could prove to be a long day, and it might not produce any results. Rolf squared with that. He just hoped his men didn't go rogue.

18

Alex looked back over his shoulders as they passed through the entrance and into the heart of the fort. He'd been silently worrying the entire morning since they left the hotel, thinking someone was following them, watching their every move.

He didn't know why. Maybe it was just paranoia.

He didn't see anything particularly suspicious behind them, only throngs of people packing through the ticket entrance. He glanced over at his wife and noticed her looking back as well. They were usually in sync like that. Sometimes, Tommy joked that they were one person split into two halves. He referenced the two great Civil War generals, Robert E. Lee and Stonewall Jackson, and how those two men were so similar that they would know what each other would do in almost any situation, without the possibility of long-distance communication.

Tommy wasn't far off. But they weren't always on the same wave-length. Just like any couple, they had disagreements, though fights were exceedingly rare—a fact both of them appreciated.

Tara faced forward again so she wouldn't bump into Devong in front of her and continued surveying their surroundings; her long auburn hair bounced in a ponytail behind her head as she walked.

Ahead, the crowds thinned as people dispersed and moved faster to see different areas of the sprawling fortress.

The heat of the morning sun seemed to fade as they stepped deeper into the shadows of Jaisalmer Fort, its towering walls now embracing them like an ancient guardian. Past the ticket kiosk, the pathway began to narrow, curving gently upward in a slow, deliberate climb. The stones underfoot, worn smooth by centuries of pilgrimage, had a faint sheen, as if polished by time itself. Though the air was cooler here, it carried a dry tang of sandstone dust and the faint, sweet scent of incense, lingering from some nearby shrine.

"Nice to get out of the heat," Felicia commented as she pressed ahead into an opening.

"No kidding," Alex agreed. "Amazing how these old castles and fortresses remain so cool all the time."

"Shade is a powerful thing," Devong said. "Shame we are cutting down more trees than we plant. The world needs shade. Not to mention clean air."

They followed the walkway as it twisted and turned, a deliberate design by the architects to confuse invaders. Now it invited only curiosity rather than confusion. Along the walls, small niches carved into the stone held weathered figures of gods and symbols that seemed to watch silently as the visitors passed. The chatter of tourists and occasional laughter echoed softly against the stone, mingling with the rhythmic clink of bangles as a group of women in vibrant saris walked ahead, their arms laden with bags of souvenirs.

As the group ascended, the passageway briefly opened into a courtyard bathed in warm sunlight. It was alive with movement. Shops lined the edges, their fronts shaded by fabric canopies that fluttered in the breeze. Brightly colored textiles hung from wooden racks, their patterns bold and intricate. One vendor was weaving on a small loom, his hands a blur as he worked golden threads into a crimson fabric. Nearby, another man sat cross-legged on a mat, carving small elephants from blocks of soapstone while tourists haggled over his finished work. A vendor selling cool lime juice called out to passersby, his clay cups stacked neatly on the side of his cart. The faint hum of commerce blended seamlessly with the timelessness of the place.

"That's some Old-World stuff," Tara said, pointing at the loom. "I still don't fully understand how those work. Seems like it would take a ton of time just to get the thing set up."

"It does," Devong said. "Looms like that one take from a few hours up to an entire day to prepare. The larger floor looms take longer, from one to two days depending on the complexity of the weave."

Alex shook his head. "I don't have that kind of patience. I hate having to put that blue tape on walls to prep before painting."

Devong and Felicia laughed.

"He really does," Tara said. "He'd be fine with hiring people just to come in and do the tape. The painting he doesn't mind as much."

"Do you two change the color scheme of your home often?" Felicia asked.

Tara chuckled. "Only once, but it was an ordeal."

They kept moving and left the courtyard. The group followed a narrower lane that seemed to burrow deeper into the fort. The sound of footsteps grew softer here, absorbed by the thick walls. Sunlight filtered in through occasional gaps, creating patterns of light and shadow that danced across the stone. Above, the latticework of windows—intricately carved *jali* screens—offered a fleeting glimpse of the sky while still cloaking the interiors in privacy.

Alex looked back over his shoulder again. This time, there were far fewer people behind them but still dozens meandering through the corridors. He noticed some of the faces he'd seen before, but that was to be expected.

He told himself to calm down. The odds were way in their favor that whoever was behind the killings in Mongolia wasn't here now. But if the chance wasn't zero, he wasn't going to count on anything. So he tried to remain cool as they proceeded deeper into the bowels of the fortress.

The path took another turn, and they passed under an arched gateway. On its keystone was carved a *kirtimukha*, its lionlike face staring out with fierce, unblinking eyes. The group paused briefly, taking in its details—the sharp teeth, the curling mane.

"Okay, that is kind of menacing," Tara said, unable to tear her gaze away from the face of the beast.

"Seems almost alive, doesn't it?" Devong added.

"You think that might be one of the guardians we're looking for?" Alex offered.

"Possibly, but this isn't the place I was considering. We can take a look around here if you'd like. I must admit, though, a lion like that would make for a good guardian."

"We might as well while we're here," Alex suggested.

"Very well," Devong acquiesced. "What are we looking for?"

"Something Celtic," Felicia answered.

"Celtic?" Their guide's expression soured. "I don't believe you'll find anything like that here in Jaisalmer. Or India for that matter." He turned and looked to Alex and Tara. "You didn't tell me you were looking for something like that. Tommy didn't mention it either. I'm afraid you're going to be out of luck here, my friends. I've been through this fort more times than I can remember, and I have never seen anything remotely close to Celtic. Which I assume you would believe to be the case as well."

"We thought the same thing when we found those artifacts in Mongolia. It was totally unexpected. But here we are."

"You're just going to have to trust us," Tara added. "Nothing is set in stone as we've been taught in history classes our entire lives. The ancient peoples of the world were capable of so much more than what we think we know."

Devong beamed at her. "I like you," he said, jabbing a finger at her. "An open mind is one of the most important characteristics a person can have." He looked back at the archway. "So let's have a look."

The four spent the next ten minutes scouring the area but didn't find anything out of the ordinary. There were no Celtic symbols, no writing in any language for that matter, and nothing that suggested this place was the home of the guardians mentioned in the riddle.

"Doesn't seem like there's anything here," Alex said, planting his hands on his hips as he looked up at the lion once more.

"Yeah," Tara agreed. "I say we move on."

They left the archway behind and kept walking deeper into the fortress.

Beyond the gate, the space opened up again, this time into a quieter courtyard that seemed older, more solemn. Here, the walls were adorned with swastika motifs, carved into the stone with care and precision. They were subtle, almost easy to miss if one wasn't paying attention, but their presence carried a quiet weight, a reminder of the protective and auspicious power they symbolized. It was occasionally difficult for the foreign tourist to understand that these swastikas held an entirely different meaning here than in the West, and that they predated their European and American counterparts by more than six thousand years.

This courtyard was less crowded. A small shrine stood at one corner; its steps worn down to a gentle curve from generations of devotees kneeling in prayer. The faint scent of sandalwood incense drifted from its interior, and the soft glow of an oil lamp flickered inside, casting shadows on the lotus carvings that adorned the shrine's walls. An elderly man in a white *dhoti* sat nearby, muttering softly in prayer as he turned the beads of a *rudraksha mala* in his hands.

Tara observed the man reverently as she passed. She tried to respect the moment and not stare, but she thought it so fascinating that someone could stay so focused on their meditations with so much going on around him.

The group took a few minutes to inspect the symbols and images engraved on the stone around them but again found nothing of note.

Moving past the shrine, the path narrowed once again, its steep incline pulling them higher into the fort. This section felt more secluded, as though it belonged to another era entirely. The stone walls seemed to close in slightly, their surfaces darker, cooler to the touch. Along the walls, they noticed small carvings—some faded, others surprisingly intact. A peacock caught the eye, its tail fanned out in a detailed pattern that seemed impossibly intricate for something etched into stone.

"This is unreal," Alex commented, taking in the sights. "It seems like it never ends."

"Yes," Devong said. "It is quite extensive. Like I said, you could spend days in here and not really see everything."

The group followed a winding pathway that seemed to lead farther into the heart of the fort. The lane narrowed, the high walls on either side creating a sense of intimacy that contrasted with the sprawling courtyards they had left behind. The air was cooler here, heavy with a mixture of ancient stone and the faint tang of incense. Occasional alcoves and niches appeared along the walls, some holding small idols or carvings, while others were empty, their original contents lost to time.

Alex looked back over his shoulder again, noting the number of people still walking the same way. The crowds had thinned significantly by this point, but there were still around a hundred or so people within view ahead and behind them.

As they turned another corner, the passage opened into a larger space, and one of the Jain temples revealed itself in stunning detail. The golden sandstone structure stood tall and intricate, its façade a masterclass in craftsmanship. Every inch of the temple seemed alive with carvings, each telling its own story. Figures of *tirthankaras*—Jain spiritual teachers—were nestled into niches, their serene faces radiating a quiet power that seemed to still the hum of the surrounding activity.

"Wow," Tara gasped. It was all she could manage to say at such an incredible work of both art and engineering.

The temple's entrance was flanked by two elaborately sculpted pillars, their surfaces adorned with lotus motifs and intertwining vines. Peacocks, captured mid-dance in stone, adorned the capitals of the pillars, their delicate tails fanning out in exquisite detail. Above the doorway, a carved arch framed a sun motif, its rays emanating outward as if to bless all who entered. The heavy wooden door, bound with iron and engraved with geometric designs, was slightly ajar, inviting them to step inside.

Above the entrance, the temple's towering *shikhara*—a spire that reached skyward—dominated the view. Its surface was covered in an array of carvings so intricate it was hard to take them all in. Celestial dancers, mythical creatures, and elephants seemed to climb the spire in a dance of devotion, their forms casting shadows that shifted with the sun. The shikhara's apex glistened faintly. "Who are those deities?" Felicia asked, pointing up at the figures adorning the façade. "I'm not familiar with much of the Jain religion."

"Oh, those aren't deities," Devong answered. "Jain temples here primarily feature tirthankaras, the spiritual teachers of Jainism, instead of the traditional Hindu gods or goddesses. The temples are dedicated to the Jain faith, which focuses on these enlightened beings who have achieved what they call *moksha*, which means liberation. They are revered as guides to spiritual enlightenment, sort of heroes of the religion in a manner of speaking."

"Fascinating."

"Yes. You'll notice their serene faces carved into niches along the walls, each radiating calm and detachment. The tirthankaras are depicted either seated in the lotus position or standing in meditative stillness, symbolizing their liberation from the cycle of life and rebirth. For instance, look at the figure with the snake canopy above his head—that's Parshvanatha, the twenty-third tirthankara. Just below, you can see another figure with a lion carved beneath him—that's Mahavira, the twenty-fourth and final tirthankara.

"Flanking these spiritual guides are the *yakshas* and *yakshis*, celestial attendants who serve as protectors. They're often depicted holding symbols of power—lotuses, weapons, or ceremonial pots. Over there, you'll see Chakreshwari, the yakshi associated with the first tirthankara, holding a discus and riding Garuda. Her presence balances the peaceful energy of the tirthankaras with a sense of vigilance and strength."

"Just when you think you know a little about history and

cultures," Alex said, his voice reverent, "you get a dose of something like this, and realize you don't know squat."

"The world is full of so much to learn," Devong said. "It would be impossible to learn it all in one lifetime. Perhaps that is one reason the idea of reincarnation is so appealing."

"Of course, you'd have to retain the knowledge from the previous life," Tara noted.

"Yes, I suppose that would be the trick," their guide said with a smile. He turned and pointed back up at the temple.

"Notice the animals carved into the pillars and lower walls. The elephants represent strength and stability, while the lions symbolize courage and protection. There's also an abundance of peacocks, their fanned tails sculpted in delicate detail, adding an element of grace and beauty.

"You'll also see smaller motifs everywhere—lotus flowers symbolizing purity and spiritual awakening and even the swastika, which in Jainism represents the four realms of existence: heavenly beings, humans, hellish beings, and animals. These symbols remind worshipers of the cycle of life and the ultimate goal of liberation."

"Liberation sounds good," Felicia said. There was a hint of sadness to the words, as if her mind had once again drifted back to her friends she'd lost in the Gobi Desert. "Thinking of it that way makes the end seem not so bad."

Devong grinned. "Or perhaps it isn't really the end."

She seemed to like that answer and smiled back at him.

"And finally," he said, "look up at the shikhara, the temple's towering spire. It's covered in carvings of celestial beings and mythical creatures, drawing the eye upward to the heavens. At the very top is the kalash, a sacred pot symbolizing abundance and divinity.

"Every detail here has meaning, blending devotion and artistry. It's a powerful expression of faith, alive even after all these centuries. Take your time to look closely—you'll see something new with every glance."

"You're really good," Tara said to Devong. "I can't imagine a better tour guide."

He chuffed. "Yes, well, as I said, I've spent a lot of time here."

They moved forward and stopped near the structure.

"You mentioned some of the figures, the animals and how they were there for protection," Alex said.

"I see where you're going, and yes, they could be considered guardians. We can have a look around here to see if there is anything like you'd described before, though I would be surprised if we found Celtic symbols here."

At the base of the temple, a low wall encircled the structure, its panels carved with scenes from Jain mythology. Devotees had placed offerings along the wall: marigold garlands, small brass lamps, and bowls of rice and grains. The offerings added pops of color and life to the golden hues of the stone, a testament to the continued reverence for this ancient place of worship.

The group paused at the foot of the steps leading up to the temple. The faint sound of bells pealed from within, a rhythmic chime that blended with the soft murmur of prayers being recited inside. The temple seemed alive; its energy palpable even from outside. It was not just a monument but a living, breathing part of the fort's history, a place that had witnessed centuries of devotion and resilience.

The steps, worn smooth by countless feet, led up to the temple's main entrance. The group ascended slowly; their eyes drawn to the details that surrounded them. Tiny carvings of elephants and lions flanked the steps, their forms so precise it was hard to believe they had been shaped by human hands. The scent of burning camphor grew stronger as they neared the doorway, and it mingled with the floral sweetness of marigold petals scattered across the threshold.

Standing at the entrance, they took a few seconds to absorb the temple's grandeur. Inside, the faint glow of oil lamps illuminated the interior, their light reflecting off polished stone surfaces and casting shadows that danced like flickering spirits. The chanting grew clearer now, resonating through the space with a melodic cadence that seemed to echo in their very bones.

A monk stood at the door, accepting rupees from visitors.

"Indians enter for free," Devong said with a smile, producing several notes from his pocket. "Foreigners have to pay."

"Oh, I can—"

"No. You are my guests," their guide said, cutting him off. "It isn't much. Please, allow me." He paused and slipped off his shoes. "By the way, you'll need to remove your footwear, and if you have any leather such as a belt, you need to leave that outside as well." He motioned to an area where dozens of shoes sat next to the wall, along with a few leather belts, and even a brown leather fedora.

Devong handed the money to the man at the door, who accepted it with a grateful bow and motioned for the visitors to enter.

As the group stepped through the heavy wooden doors of the Jain temple, the shift in atmosphere was immediate and profound. The lively bustle of the fort's courtyard and passages gave way to a hushed serenity that seemed to permeate the cool, stone interior. The faint scent of sandalwood incense that seemed to be everywhere hung in the air heavily here, mingling with the earthy aroma of ancient sandstone. The sound of their footsteps echoed softly, blending with the melodic chime of bells and the distant murmur of prayers.

The temple's interior was a marvel of craftsmanship. Every surface—walls, pillars, and ceilings—was adorned with carvings so intricate that they seemed almost alive. The pillars, rising like a forest of stone, were covered in swirling patterns of vines, lotus flowers, and celestial figures. No two pillars were alike, each one telling its own story. A few monks, dressed in simple white robes, moved silently between the columns, their heads bowed and their hands clasped in prayer. They walked barefoot, their quiet steps a reminder of the humility and discipline central to Jain beliefs.

"Incredible," Alex breathed, keeping his voice just above a whisper.

No one else in the temple was talking. The only sounds came from the chants and prayers of the worshippers.

The Americans took that as a cue to keep quiet while they were here.

The four moved to the left to stay out of the entrance so other visitors could come and go. They stopped off to the side and peered around at the visually stunning place of worship.

In the center of the temple the group encountered the *garbhagriha*, or sanctum sanctorum, where the main idol of the tirthankara was housed. The statue was larger than life, carved from gleaming white marble that seemed to glow in the dim light of the temple. The idol's face was serene and otherworldly, its expression radiating peace and detachment. Around the base of the statue, offerings of fresh flowers, grains, and small bowls of water had been carefully arranged by devotees. The flickering flames of oil lamps added a warm, golden hue to the scene, casting more dancing shadows across the carved walls.

The ceiling above the garbhagriha was a masterpiece in itself. Intricate patterns radiated outward in concentric circles, each layer adorned with depictions of celestial dancers and mythical creatures. At the center of the design was a lotus flower in full bloom, its petals spreading outward as though embracing the entire space. The artistry drew the eye upward, inviting visitors to reflect on the spiritual connection between earth and the heavens.

Scattered throughout the temple were smaller shrines, each dedicated to a different tirthankara.

"Those niches are adorned with figures of the yakshas and yakshis," Devong explained in a whisper. "The celestial protectors and their dynamic poses offer a stark contrast to the calm stillness of the tirthankaras they guard."

He made a point to emphasize his thoughts, and the Americans immediately realized why he mentioned the figures.

They were guardians of the tirthankaras.

Felicia, Alex, and Tara all felt the same tremor of hope ripple through them, displayed by the looks they shared with each other. In here, though, communication was clearly going to be silent.

Devong made a motion with his hand for the others to follow. "Come," he said. "Let's start over here."

They moved into the center aisle of the sanctuary, their feet padding quietly on the smooth floor. Monks and devotees sat cross-legged before these shrines, their voices joining in a rhythmic chant that seemed to resonate through the very stones of the temple.

The place was alive with subtle movement. Tourists, some in awe and others whispering quietly to one another, wandered carefully through the space, their cameras hanging loosely around their necks. A guide stood near one of the pillars, explaining the significance of the carvings to an attentive group. Occasionally, the gentle rustle of saris and the soft clink of bangles broke the silence as a group of women moved to offer their prayers.

On the far side of the temple, the group noticed a monk seated in meditation near a smaller shrine. His eyes were closed, and his posture was perfectly still, exuding an aura of tranquility that seemed to anchor the entire space. Around him, a few devotees sat silently, their gazes fixed on the shrine as they listened to the rhythmic chanting of a nearby priest. The priest, standing before a low platform, rang a small bell in one hand while pouring water over a small idol with the other, performing a ritual ablution known as *abhishek*.

The interplay of light and shadow in the temple added to its mystique. The dim glow of oil lamps and the occasional shaft of sunlight filtering through the latticed windows created a constantly shifting tapestry of illumination. The intricate carvings seemed to shift and change with the light, revealing new details with every glance.

There was so much to pore over. Alex and Tara realized that if they were here by themselves, it might well take them over a day to check everything. Then again, if there were Celtic symbols in here, they figured those things would stand out against the rest of the decor.

Then again, if they were wrong, it would be easy to kill a few hours in here without thinking.

19

When they reached the Jain temple, Rolf's men spread out as they entered the next courtyard. His eyes immediately went to the intricate temple standing directly in front of him. Though he wasn't typically the type to be impressed by architecture or design, he also wasn't a machine.

The exterior of the temple was beautiful, the craftsmanship perfect. He quietly marveled at the attention to detail, which seemed to be a common theme here in Jaisalmer, both inside the fort and out.

Growing up in Austria, he'd seen so many historical buildings and works of art that his eyes had developed a sort of blind spot for those things, like an art critic living in the same gallery for twenty years.

But now, in this place with a different cultural flare, he appreciated the artistry of it all.

That moment lasted less than twenty seconds.

After all, he and his team had a job to do, and it wasn't to stand around taking in the sights.

They'd been standing there in the courtyard for more than thirty minutes since the Americans and their guide entered the temple.

A quick glance over at Yuri and his two men, then across to the right at the other two teams, told Rolf his men were once again growing impatient. They'd fanned out so it didn't look as though they were standing there in groups, staring awkwardly at the entrance to the temple.

Rolf felt the same tease of temptation begging him to do something rash, but that would never win out over his hardened will. He'd forsaken such immature ways long ago and could wait forever if necessary for the IAA agents and their companions to emerge from the sanctuary doors.

Still, there were other factors at play here. What if there were a side exit? Had Rolf and his men been spotted? If so, did the agents sneak out and take one of the many passages out of the fortress?

The thoughts ravaged his senses, as paranoia often did to those with weak minds. But Rolf was no weak mind.

He spoke into the mic hidden in his shirt. "All teams stay where you are," Rolf said. "I'm going in to have a look around."

"Copy," they all echoed.

Yuri cast him a questioning glower from twenty feet away, but Rolf didn't have to explain himself to the Russian. They took orders from him, and to question him would cause bigger problems. Rolf was the glue that held the unit together and kept them on task.

Their team was built like any other military security group, with Rolf at the top. He took orders from only one person—the man who wrote the checks. And if any of the rest of their lot wanted to get paid, they did as they were told.

Most of the men were happy not to need to think too much about anything. They were the ones who'd spent a number of years in their respective militaries but had eventually either found themselves in trouble or were simply no longer useful.

The private sector could always find a use for a former soldier, in almost any condition.

Rolf knew about some who worked the white-collar jobs. Consultants, they called themselves. He thought the notion ridiculous. Or devilishly clever. He couldn't decide which. A person who didn't actually do anything but offer security advice and recommendations while commanding enormous payments was both a dream and a disgrace. For most.

Rolf, however, preferred being in the field. Sure, there would come a day when he was too old, when he'd lost a step, when he let down his guard one time too often. Then he'd either call it quits, or he'd be dead. Either way, he intended to be sitting on a pile of money when that day came knocking.

He nodded at the men next to him then shuffled into the midst of the tourists milling about in the courtyard.

When he neared the steps, he noticed the monk at the entrance collecting money. Rolf had no intention of making a donation to some religion. They were all scams to him, all just multilevel marketing schemes designed to offer something permanent to those whose minds were fixed on temporary things.

He climbed the steps and paused. The monk smiled at him.

"Ten rupees for foreigners to enter," he said pleasantly.

Rolf couldn't believe the man's arrogance, or that of the temple. Sure, ten rupees wasn't much, but the notion was outrageous.

He shook his head, dipping his right hand into his pocket. He fished out a wad of euros and pulled a ten from the folds before replacing the rest safely in his pants. Rolf climbed the steps, doing his best not to look menacing toward the monk, but it took restraint both because smiling at random strangers wasn't his thing and because he didn't approve of the charging foreigners. He passed the bill to the man, who looked at it then back up at Rolf.

"This is too much," the man said, at least ballparking the exchange rate.

Rolf knew the guy saw plenty of Europeans come through here every day, so the man was well aware of how much more valuable their currency was against the rupee.

"Keep the change," Rolf said, and turned to walk inside.

"Thank you," the monk said, his eyes dropping down to Rolf's feet. "But please remove your shoes before you go in."

Rolf followed the man's gaze down to his feet then looked over to his left at the collection of footwear gathered by the entrance. He restrained himself from rolling his eyes and unwillingly removed his boots and set them against the wall several inches away from the next pair.

"Good?" Rolf asked with no effort to hide his disdain for the practice. If they were trying to keep the place clean, that was one thing. He knew several people who did that, making their guests remove their shoes before entering the home. It was a cultural practice across Asia as well, but here, Rolf knew it was a religious thing. Not being a religious man, he loathed the notion of having to remove his boots only to put them back on when he left the temple.

"Yes," the monk answered. "Unless you have a leather belt on. That needs to be removed as well."

Rolf did have a leather belt on. A black one. But he wasn't about to take that off. "Afraid not," he lied. "I only use nylon ones. Respects the animals."

The monk seemed pleased with the remark and bowed his head low.

The Austrian took that as his sign to proceed and hurriedly shuffled through the door.

As Rolf stepped into the temple, his irritation bubbled just beneath the surface. The air inside was cool, heavy with the cloying scent of the same incense he'd been smelling since he got here, but the change in atmosphere did little to soothe him. Even as a seasoned pro at this sort of thing, he felt the tension of the fight-or-flight response automatically spike inside his body. Over the years, he'd learned to tame that and sublimate it into focusing on the job at hand.

While many people around the world crumbled under such a simple, inner thing, he mastered it to use to his advantage.

He glanced up briefly at the ceiling, a swirl of intricate carvings radiating outward like a golden halo, but it held no interest for him. Art, history, faith, it was all just stone and stories to Rolf. He cared about cash and what it could do for him. It wasn't as if he obsessed about money. And he was well aware of the cliché about money not buying happiness.

But money could buy a place on the beach on the Mediterranean where he could lay low once his days as a mercenary were over. It could also buy him the fake identifications necessary to avoid being tracked by those who might want to take him out.

That roster was longer than a grocery list before a snowstorm.

He'd made enemies around the world, both on the side of the law and in the criminal underworld. It was part of his job, and he accepted that. But he didn't want to make it easy on those who would do him harm once he'd stepped away from his career.

He surveyed the sanctuary, noting the tourists milling about, whispering as they pointed to the impressive craftsmanship on the walls, ceilings, and floors. It took him less than five seconds to spot the three Americans and their guide. The group hovered around a series of images near the front right of the temple. They gazed up at the figures—deities or people, Rolf didn't know. And he didn't care. He'd gotten the confirmation he came in for. The IAA agents were still here. More importantly, they were looking for something.

Rolf moved farther to the left until he was near the corner, his view of the marks obstructed partially by visitors shuffling between. The space was alive with movement and sound. Tourists shuffled from one shrine to the next, murmuring in languages he didn't bother to identify. A child giggled, too loud for the sanctity of the place, earning a sharp hiss of disapproval from a woman who might have been his mother. A group of elderly men sat cross-legged near the central sanctum, their low chanting mixing with the occasional chime of bells. The din grated on Rolf's nerves, each sound another irritation pricking at his focus.

At least he hadn't had to search long. He'd envisioned walking in here, not seeing the agents and their companions, and then scouring the entire temple until he could locate them. Instead, he walked in and there they were, off to the front corner of the temple, gathered around a section of carvings on the wall.

Rolf observed them without staring too long, a habit formed from years of following without being noticed. Subtlety was another weapon in his arsenal.

He shifted his weight, stepping more to the side until he was right next to the wall, still out of a clear line of sight.

Nearby, a guide explained a series of wall carvings to a small group. As Rolf moved, he ran his fingers through his blond hair, a practiced gesture that allowed him to turn his head naturally while keeping his targets in his peripheral vision. His jaw tightened as his palm brushed across his forehead, damp with the sweat of the walk up the fort's steep pathways. It hadn't been a difficult climb for someone in his prime physical condition. But out in that heat, even the slightest amount of exercise caused perspiration. Fortunately, it was so dry that the sweat partially evaporated. It was something he'd always found annoying about more arid regions—always needing to apply lip balm every hour or so. And the hydration... drinking roughly 30 percent more water than normal was difficult.

He cursed himself for being such a diva and returned his focus to the current situation.

With a casual glance at a nearby pillar, he maneuvered toward the left aisle, his movements unhurried but deliberate. A monk passed close by, his simple white robes brushing lightly against Rolf's arm as he moved toward the garbhagriha, the sanctum. Rolf didn't flinch, didn't react; his instincts were sharp enough to know when stillness was the best disguise. He let his fingers trail lightly against the carvings on the pillar, feigning interest in the detailed lotus flowers and intertwining vines that seemed to spiral up into eternity. Another unnecessary flourish, another step closer.

The aisle was less crowded, though a few tourists lingered here and there, their voices muffled in the thick stone walls. Rolf paced himself, pausing near a smaller shrine as if to admire the marble idol housed within. He leaned slightly, his posture relaxed, but his eyes were sharp, darting toward the group in the corner every few seconds. They were still engrossed, their fingers occasionally tracing the patterns of the symbols, their hushed conversation lost beneath the murmurs of the temple.

A middle-aged couple wandered into his line of sight, snapping photos of the elaborate carvings around the shrine. Rolf suppressed a grimace, forcing himself to move with the same leisurely curiosity they displayed. He stepped around the couple, angling his body slightly to block himself from the group's view, and continued down the aisle. The golden light from the oil lamps flickered against the sandstone walls, casting long, shifting shadows that danced as he walked.

When he reached a point near the front of the temple, he paused again, this time before a massive pillar etched with figures of celestial beings. He feigned interest, tilting his head and narrowing his eyes as though deciphering the story carved into the stone. In truth, he was counting the steps it would take to reach the corner where they stood.

Rolf slid his hand into the pocket of his tailored trousers, his fingers brushing against the edge of the slim blade he carried on the inside of his belt. Not that he needed it yet. This wasn't the moment. It was an old habit; touching the cold steel balanced him in a strange way.

He moved again, slowly rounding another pillar. This time, he made no effort to look at the carvings or the idols. His gaze flicked once more toward the group, still focused on their examination of the wall. Rolf's lips curled into the faintest of smirks before settling back into a neutral line.

At the front of the temple, he positioned himself by another pillar, this one near an alcove filled with offerings of marigold garlands and flickering lamps. He leaned lightly against it, his posture casual, blending into the rhythm of the temple. But his eyes, cold and calculating, never left the group for long. He was close enough now to hear faint snippets of their conversation and see them a bit more clearly—a word here, a gesture there.

He didn't have much to go on regarding what they were trying to find, but from where he stood it sounded as if they were about to finish up in the temple. Rolf did want to know what they were looking for here, but he also knew that wasn't what he was paid for. And he wasn't paid to be curious either. His job wasn't to solve ancient riddles, or guess as to where some artifact might be. His mission was much simpler, more direct. Follow, acquire, kill.

The male IAA agent turned around first and led the way toward the exit as the other three tailed behind him. Whatever they'd come in here to find, they'd come up empty-handed. Rolf doubted they could have thoroughly inspected every inch of this place. At first, standing outside, he'd wondered what was taking them so long. But inside the sanctuary, he realized they could have taken hours.

Then again, who was he to question?

Rolf spun around slowly and began walking back down the aisle, moving casually so he didn't draw attention. It was natural for him at this point, having done this sort of thing for so long.

He'd become a true predator, just like any of the alphas in the animal kingdom. He could stalk his prey without being detected, as he had with an ambassador in Milan. Or a Russian oligarch hiding out in Malta. The list of marks he'd taken out was extensive. And that didn't even include the ones with his team.

He passed a glance over the other tourists in the temple, all marveling at the architecture or whispering to each other. Prey, all of them, completely unaware of the lion that stalked in their midst. He would never harm them, obviously. Not unless it was absolutely necessary. He didn't kill for the sake of it. Only to complete the mission. In that regard, he was ruthless and cold, but he didn't particularly enjoy that part of the job. It was a means to an end. The people he'd ordered killed in the Gobi Desert were innocent. They'd done nothing wrong, and probably would never have. But if the chances weren't zero, well... he couldn't leave that to fate.

Rolf watched as the IAA agents slipped out the door before he moved more quickly to the back corner and veered left toward the exit. He paused halfway there and spoke into the radio.

"Team two, they're coming out?" he said, keeping his voice reasonably low.

"We have visual," Yuri answered.

"Good. Stay with them. I'll fall in behind."

Rolf knew he needed to give his marks a little slack before exiting the temple. They'd need a minute to put on their shoes before descending the steps back to the courtyard. With twelve sets of eyeballs watching the group, he didn't feel the least bit hurried to get out there and follow.

Now it was just a waiting game. And once the IAA agents found what they were looking for, Rolf and his men would take care of the rest.

20

Alex knew that something was off the second he stood up from tying his shoelaces. He froze for a split second, an instinctive reaction that nearly anyone would have felt when they realized they were in danger. He, however, had pruned those sorts of reactions down to mere nanoseconds.

He bent back down next to Tara, who was finishing tying her own laces.

"Don't react to what I'm about to say," he whispered, pretending to fix one of his shoestrings.

She looked up at him and threw on a fake smile. "Okay."

"I'm pretty sure we've been followed." He didn't dare look away from her yet, lest he give away the subject of their conversation.

Felicia and Devong had already descended the stairs and were waiting for the two of them off to the side. Devong was pointing at something in the courtyard, probably giving Felicia details about some part of the design or perhaps a mini history lesson.

"When you stand up, take a casual look around toward the back wall on the other side of the courtyard. You'll see three men sort of hanging out. They're talking with each other, acting like they aren't paying attention to the front of the temple."

"Maybe they aren't acting," she offered. It was a statement more of hope than of conviction.

"I noticed a few of them as we came this way. There are more, too. At least two more groups, all spaced out in pockets around the court-yard perimeter. Why would three groups of grown men, some of different nationalities, come all the way in here to this spot, and then stand around by the wall chatting?"

"Good point," Tara surrendered. "What should we do?"

"We need to lose them. But first, we have to find out what place Devong thinks we should check next."

"And then?"

"We'll have to lose them somehow."

Alex realized they'd been kneeling there for too long and stood up again. She stood with him, and the two slowly descended the steps, looking out over the courtyard as if taking in the sights like all the other tourists.

"There are lots of passages in this fortress. Devong probably knows of a few that we could take to drop the tails."

"And if they keep up with us?"

Alex forced a grin and looked over at her. "Well, then at least we know for sure we're being followed."

"I'd file that under one of the times you should hope to be wrong."

They reached the bottom of the steps and stopped when they neared their two companions.

"The temple is beautiful, no?" Devong asked, a pleased expression beaming from his face.

"Spectacular," Alex agreed.

"But no Celtic symbols," Tara added.

"Well, I did warn you we would probably not find anything like that in there. But the day is young yet."

"Where is the next spot you think we should check? You know, maybe an area that is off limits to the rest of the tourists?" Alex allowed his eyes to flick to the right where one of the groups of three loitered near a stall that sold colorful ribbons to visitors seeking souvenirs.

"Yes," Devong said. "That is probably a better idea. As we discussed before, the more visited places such as this would have already been analyzed if there were such an anomaly as Celtic markings." He paused and thought for a few seconds before raising a finger. "Yes, there is a passage not far from here. It's always manned by one of the fort's security guards. Of course, with these badges, we'll have no trouble getting in."

"Great," Tara exclaimed a little too eagerly. "That sounds promising," she added, hoping she hadn't sounded as if she were trying to hide her concerns.

"Very well. We go this way." Devong indicated a passage to the right of the temple.

"Lead the way," Felicia said.

The group worked their way through the clusters of people until they reached the next corridor, where the flow of traffic opened up a little.

Tara and Alex remained behind the other two, allowing them to chat while they watched the rear. Neither dared look back until they'd rounded a bend in the passage. Then both checked behind them.

Only a dozen or so tourists trailed their group, and there was no sign of the men.

Leaving the dim glow of the temple behind, they marched through the sunlit corridors of the fort, where the walls radiated the warmth they had absorbed throughout the day. The contrast between the hushed reverence of the temple and the lively, echoing passageways was stark. The sound of footsteps—both theirs and those of the countless visitors exploring the fort—bounced off the stone, mingling with the low murmur of voices and the occasional burst of laughter from an unseen corner.

The passage ahead stretched long and narrow, its high walls adorned with faded murals and ancient inscriptions, some so worn by time that they seemed to dissolve into the stone itself. Here and there, alcoves broke the uniformity, some empty and shadowed, others housing carved stone reliefs of warriors, kings, and deities. The floor, a mix of smooth stone and uneven patches where erosion had worn it down, bore the faint outlines of decorative patterns that once covered the entire walkway, now little more than a whisper from the past.

Tara and Alex couldn't enjoy the scenery. They had more pressing concerns.

"See anything?" Alex asked, keeping his voice low so the other two didn't hear him.

"No. Nothing. But if they're pros, and we have to assume they are, they won't follow too closely. They'll hang back a little."

"Either way, the sooner we can change directions, the better. We just have to hope they don't see us."

As they walked ahead, the air was thick with the scent of old stone, warm dust, and hints of incense that had drifted from the temple. Sunlight filtered in through arched openings along the walls, illuminating the dust motes suspended in the air and casting elongated, shifting shadows that moved as the visitors passed through.

Ahead, an elderly woman in a faded green sari shuffled along with slow, deliberate steps, pausing now and then to lean on the cool stone for support. A young Indian couple trailed behind her, their two small children darting between them, their voices bubbling with excitement as they pointed at the carvings and tugged at their parents' hands. The father, dressed in a crisp white kurta, gently scolded the younger child for trying to climb onto a ledge, while the mother, adjusting the pallu of her sari, cast an apologetic smile at the passing tourists.

The corridor led them to an intersection where three separate passageways branched off in different directions. A small, unmarked plaque was embedded into the wall at the juncture, its text nearly illegible from centuries of wear. The group paused, considering their path, as another group of tourists—two men and a woman, all dressed in loose cotton clothing and carrying guidebooks—passed by, engaged in quiet conversation about the fort's history. One of the men gestured toward a section of the wall where a faint carving of an elephant and rider still clung to the stone, its details softened by time.

Devong paused for a second in the middle of the crossing then nodded and opted for a corridor to the left. The rest followed behind him, leaving the busy exchange behind them for a much quieter passage.

As they moved forward, the path grew slightly darker. The walls felt as though they were closing in, but that was merely due to less sunlight. The air felt noticeably cooler here, shielded from the direct sun, and a faint mustiness hinted at moisture locked deep within the stones. It was the first tease of humidity Tara and Alex had noticed since arriving in Jaisalmer.

"It isn't far from here," Devong announced, glancing back at the IAA agents.

While the passage wasn't as busy as some of the others, there were still dozens of tourists, though more spread out than before. Some people walked at a brisk pace, anxious, or eager, to get to the next spot on the tour.

Alex wanted to press Devong to move faster, but doing so would tip their guide that something was wrong. The last thing Alex wanted to do was panic Devong and Felicia.

Dr. Lowe had seen enough already, and causing her more anxiety about the men following them wouldn't help things.

Then again, Alex knew that at some point there might not be a choice. He looked back for the umpteenth time but still didn't see any of the men.

He dared to think maybe they'd lost them at the intersection. Or maybe, if they were lucky, the men weren't actually following them. It was possible they were just random guys on a sightseeing tour.

Alex knew Tara was hoping the same thing, but neither one of them was going to count on that.

They slipped past a slow-moving family who wore the skinny jeans and tight T-shirts iconic of European casual fashion. From the looks of them—from their shoes, especially—Alex guessed they were from Germany. He had several friends from there, and had visited them a few times, so he could appreciate how they dressed in the summer months.

Along the walls, carved niches occasionally revealed themselves, some empty, others filled with rusted remnants of iron brackets or what looked like the eroded bases of oil lamps that had long since burned out.

Farther down, a wooden beam, aged and splintered, jutted from one side of the corridor to the other, an apparent reinforcement from an era when the fort's stability may have been in question. A pigeon, startled by their approach, fluttered down from the beam and disappeared into the maze of passages beyond. The sound of its wings echoed briefly before silence reclaimed the space.

The bird's sudden movement nearly caused Alex and Tara to jump out of their shoes. They were already on edge because of the men following them.

At the far end of the corridor, another junction appeared, but this one was different. Here, the passage did not fork into multiple paths but instead led directly to a tunnel entrance framed by a broad archway. The walls around it were darker, as if stained by something older than time, and the air carried a faint chill, a distinct difference from the warmth of the outer corridors.

Across the entrance, a thick iron chain stretched from one side to the other, anchored to heavy iron rings embedded deep into the stone. It was not merely decorative; it was a barrier, a warning. In front of the tunnel, standing with an air of quiet authority, was a uniformed security guard. His khaki attire bore the insignia of the Rajasthan Tourism Department, and his stance—arms crossed, weight balanced evenly—suggested he may well have been better suited as a bouncer at a night club instead of turning aside tourists with curious eyes.

Most people simply walked by the man, figuring if he was guarding something, they weren't allowed to see it without permission. One woman walked up to him and asked for directions to the next temple. The guard politely redirected her back the way she'd come, giving detailed instructions of which corridors to take. She thanked him and wandered back the way she'd come.

The guard noticed the approaching group and, eyes flicked toward them, assessed each one with a practiced appraisal. Beyond him, the tunnel yawned like an open mouth, its depths disappearing into shadow, hinting at something long forgotten or deliberately hidden. The moment stretched as the group slowed their pace, their curiosity sharpening, their footsteps now softer against the stone.

Whatever lay beyond that chained entrance was not meant for casual visitors.

Devong turned around and spoke to the other three. "Let me handle this," he said. "I know this guard, and with these badges, we shouldn't have any issues gaining access. Still, it would be best if I spoke to him for a minute before getting down to business."

"Sounds good," Tara said. "Whatever makes this quicker." She stole a glance back down the corridor but saw only tourists filing through.

Devong walked over to the man and greeted him politely. "Jaresh," Devong said. "Good to see you again."

"Where have you been, Devong? You don't come around as often as you used to." The big guard's voice boomed through the tight spaces.

Alex and Tara felt the tension mounting, expecting the men following them to come around the corner any second. All they could do was hope this conversation wouldn't be a long one. Then again, if someone were following them and they showed themselves, having some muscle on their side could be useful.

"I've been working north of the city most of the time. But I will try to come around more often." He turned to the Americans. He must have picked up on their sense of urgency because he segued quickly to the reason they were there.

"So, Dr. Patel gave us these badges so we could take a look down there." He pointed into the corridor beyond the chain.

The guard peered suspiciously at each one of them, as if judging whether they were worthy to pass.

"They're all experts in the field of archaeology," Devong added. "These two are with the IAA."

For five seconds, it didn't seem as though the man would break. Then, suddenly, his lips parted into a wide grin.

"If Dr. Patel said it's okay, who am I to argue? I just work here."

The two Indian men shared a laugh.

"Thank you, my friend," Devong said as he motioned the other three to come.

"Let me know if you find any treasure down there," the guard joked. "I get half."

Devong let out a laugh. "Deal." He led the way over the chain, waiting for the two women to follow.

Alex stopped for a second, took a hundred dollar bill out of his pocket, palmed it, and handed it to the guard.

"In case anyone comes around asking, you never saw us."

The guard looked at him with a dose of confusion in his eyes then took the money and nodded. "Sure, no problem." He pocketed the cash, and Alex continued behind the others.

Leaving the friendly guard behind, they stepped beyond the black chain and into the tunnel's shadowed entrance. The shift in atmosphere was immediate. The sounds of the fort—the murmurs of tourists, the distant ringing of bells—faded into a hushed silence, swallowed by the thick stone walls. The air was cool and damp with the scent of ancient earth and lingering moisture, a stark contrast to the dry heat of the outer corridors.

The passage was narrower than expected, the walls pressing in slightly, as if designed to discourage intruders. In the dim light, the rough-hewn stone walls loomed around them, their surfaces scarred and uneven, with marks that hinted at hasty excavation centuries ago. Occasional wooden supports lined the ceiling, old and brittle looking, remnants of an era when stability had been an urgent concern. Some beams had splintered over time, their edges jagged and worn.

Alex set his backpack down, unzipping it with a quick motion. "We're going to need more light in here," he muttered, pulling out a couple of compact headlamps and handing one to each of the women. "Use these—they'll keep your hands free." He then retrieved two aircraft-aluminum flashlights and passed one to Devong before flicking his own on. The bright beams cut through the darkness, revealing more of the uneven stone floor, scattered with loose dust and small stones, making each step deliberate and cautious.

The air carried a faint metallic tang, as though rusted iron or forgotten relics lingered somewhere in the depths ahead. Faint carvings, almost erased by time, were etched into sections of the walls—symbols or inscriptions in a language nearly lost to history. They were barely visible in the glow of the flashlights, their purpose and meaning unclear.

As they moved deeper, the passage took on a subtle downward slope, leading them away from the fort's known paths and into something far less familiar. The farther they went, the more the sensation of secrecy settled over them, as though they had crossed into a part of the fortress that had long been left undisturbed, hidden beneath layers of dust and silence.

"When was the last time you were down here?" Felicia asked Devong as she fixed the light on her forehead, tightening the strap to keep it snug.

"More than a year ago," he answered. "And it's the only time I've been in here. I asked Dr. Patel to show me some of the restricted areas, and this was one of them."

"Are there any places in the fort you haven't seen yet?"

"Perhaps a few," he answered. "And of course, there are those rumors about the secret passageways. But as I said before, only a few of those have been uncovered. We're heading to one of those now."

The statement caused a trickle of excitement to flow through the Americans. The thought of seeing something few had added an element to exclusivity and wonder, which for a moment tempered the concerns simmering in the back of Tara's and Alex's minds.

"Okay," Alex said. "We should get moving."

Felicia and Devong turned to him, questions dripping from their eyes.

"Of course," Devong said. "Lots to see after this if there isn't anything to find down here."

Felicia must have seen the serious concern written all over Alex's face.

"What is it?" she asked. "What's wrong?"

Alex glanced over at Tara, who nodded her approval to the unspoken question. They hadn't wanted to worry the other two, but it wasn't something that could be kept secret forever.

"We think they're here," Alex confessed.

"Who's here?" Devong wondered.

"The men who took out Felicia's team in Mongolia."

Devong's face darkened in the pale glow of the flashlights and headlamps. He nodded. "Yes, Tommy filled me in on those details."

Felicia's breathing quickened. "They're... here? What are we going to do? Now we're down in this tunnel, and no one is around."

"It's going to be okay," Tara said. "But we need to keep moving. We probably lost them back at the previous intersection."

"We'll fill you in," Alex added. "For now, let's get down to the spot Devong mentioned and see what we can find." He pulled up his right pant leg to reveal a compact pistol tucked into a concealed holster on his ankle. "If it comes down to it, we can protect ourselves. Let's just hope that isn't necessary."

21

Rolf and his men spilled into the busy intersection where four passageways met in a large, open area. It reminded him of a busy crossroads in an airport terminal with people busting in different directions to get to their next flight, or to baggage claim.

He turned around in every direction, peering through the crowd for any sign of the Americans. There was none. If they'd come through here, they were already gone.

Rolf silently cursed himself for letting them get too far ahead. It wasn't as if he'd had much of a choice. If he and the others tailed too close behind, they would have been spotted. Of course, Rolf could have ordered his men to overlap and rotate so it wouldn't seem like the same guys were following them. It was a standard move that worked well when following a mark on the road, and when on foot along sidewalks. In here, in the corridors of the fort, it was a more condensed environment. Even if he could have implemented that strategy, it would have slowed them down even more, and they would have found themselves farther behind.

"Where did they go?" Yuri asked, his voice steeped in irritation.

There was no way Rolf could know that for certain. On top of that, he didn't appreciate the Russian's tone.

Instead of giving him the pleasure of a response, Rolf took control of the situation. "Team two, take that corridor," he motioned to the right. "Team three, you take that one." He pointed at the passage directly across from the one they'd taken. "Four, stay here and make sure they don't try to double back and slip past us. My group will take the passage on the left. Get moving. If there's another interchange like this, we may lose them completely."

"And if there is one?" Javier asked.

"Split up again and find them."

Javier nodded and took off with his two men. Yuri was slower to move, but did as ordered and motioned for his men to follow.

Rolf tilted his head toward the last corridor, indicating his two guys come with him.

He swam through the tourists pouring through the area and finally reached the corridor. Once there, the traffic thinned slightly, and he picked up the pace.

They moved swiftly through the passage, working their way around the visitors, who didn't seem to care how fast they were moving.

Every second that passed potentially put the IAA agents farther out of reach, and Rolf knew if they had come to another set of corridors, the odds of finding them would plummet.

He moved a little quicker at the thought, his boots striking hard against the uneven stone floor, the echoes of his steps swallowed by the thick walls of the corridor. The two men flanking him, their breathing controlled but tense, kept pace without hesitation. Every turn of the passage promised to close the gap between them and their quarry, and he knew he couldn't afford to lose them now.

Tourists clogged the corridor ahead, groups huddling near alcoves to admire carvings that meant nothing to him. Rolf clenched his jaw, suppressing the urge to shove past them. A young boy darted into his path, his mother calling after him in Hindi, and Rolf sidestepped just in time, his pulse spiking with frustration. The two men behind him adjusted their positions, weaving through the moving bodies with sharp, practiced efficiency.

The corridor twisted again, the dim light casting long shadows against the stone. Then he saw another opening. He rushed forward, into the next interchange. The air here was cooler, heavier.

He frowned as he realized they'd just been presented with another problem.

A single uniformed guard stood at the passage's mouth, his posture rigid, arms crossed. An iron chain stretched across the entrance, a clear warning that visitors weren't permitted beyond. Rolf slowed his pace just slightly, forcing himself to suppress the adrenaline surging through his veins. His immediate assumption was that the Americans and their Indian guide had either gone past the guard, continuing on the main walkway, or they'd used their badges to gain access into the restricted passage.

He took in the scene, calculating. The guard wasn't oblivious—his gaze flicked to them the moment they stepped forward, his hand instinctively resting on his belt. He was expecting trouble.

Rolf approached the big man as he would a frightened animal, careful not to startle it lest the creature lash out in defense. He did note the pistol on the man's hip, though Rolf doubted the guard had ever used it other than in target practice. It was hard to imagine a place like this ever dealt with serious crimes that required a firearm. The piece was probably more about making a statement than anything else—a warning that kept the masses in line.

"Hello," Rolf said, slapping on his best American accent. He'd honed it years ago to imbed with a CEO of an energy company. The man wasn't playing along with Rolf's employer of the time, and so he'd been ordered to gain the executive's trust and then eliminate him, which Rolf did without any trouble.

"Can I help you?" the guard asked in a heavy accent.

"I hope so." Rolf made a show of breathing heavily and added a sense of urgency to his voice. "We lost our friends back at the temple, and we think they might have come this way. I was wondering if you'd seen them."

The guard raised his right eyebrow. "What did your friends look like?"

"There were three Americans. Two women and a man, plus their tour guide. He's Indian. Any chance they came through this way?"

The guard's face scrunched as he considered the question. He looked to the left, then back to Rolf. "I see a lot of people come through here every day. Thousands of them. It's impossible to remember all of them."

"They would have come by only a few minutes ago," Rolf pressed.

The big Indian hummed for a second and scratched his jaw. "No, I don't think I've seen anyone like that in the last few minutes. Maybe they took one of the other paths. It's easy to get lost in this fort. It still happens to me now and then, and I've been working here for years."

Rolf craned his neck to look around the guard and into the passage blocked by the chain. "What's back there?" he asked.

"Just another passage, but it's not open to the public. Only authorized personnel are permitted in there for research." He noticed Rolf's curiosity and quickly added, "If you were thinking your friends went that way, forget it."

"I see. And you're certain they didn't come through this area?" Rolf watched the man's eyes, the muscles in his face, every little subtle movement produced more truth than the words coming from his mouth.

The guard looked up at the ceiling, then to the left, and back to Rolf. "No, I'm pretty sure. Foot traffic through this area has been pretty light today. I think I would remember seeing a group like that, especially in the last few minutes. Hard to forget in such a short time, you know?"

"Yes, I suppose you're right." Rolf knew the man was lying. It was written all over his face. The ticks, the looking around, even the slight pitch of his voice was different from when he told the truth about working here for years. If they'd been sitting at a poker table, Rolf would have already taken all of the man's money. "Well, thank you for your help anyway," he offered in a friendly but disappointed voice.

He turned and faced his two men and motioned for them to follow him back around the corner.

Once the guard was out of sight, Rolf spoke into his radio. "All teams, we have their location. Redirect to my position."

22

The corridor seemed endless, its winding path twisting and turning with no clear sense of direction. The deeper they moved, the rougher the walls became, stripped of their grandeur and decoration found elsewhere in the fort. There were no elaborate carvings here, no signs of artistry—only bare chiseled rock, damp in places where moisture had seeped through the ancient hill.

Their light beams flickered against the uneven surfaces, creating shifting patterns that played tricks on the eye, making it seem as if the shadows themselves moved in response to their passage.

"How long is this path?" Felicia asked, keeping her voice low in case the killers were right behind them.

"It isn't short, obviously," Devong answered. "But we're nearly there. The only problem could be getting out."

"What?"

They veered around a turn and continued forward.

"Yes, well, the last time I was down here, this was the only way out."

"And you couldn't tell us that before we came down here?" Her voice's volume climbed higher than she meant to allow, and she immediately lowered it. "How are we going to get out of here?"

"Relax," Alex said. "It's going to be fine. I doubt they'll think we came down this passage, and then there's the guard they'd have to deal with even if they figured that out."

"Yeah," Tara agreed. "I don't think they'd easily get past him."

The comments seemed to relieve Felicia for the moment.

Devong seemed mostly unaffected by the threat, though he certainly had picked up speed when they'd mentioned the pursuers.

As the air grew colder, the silence was absolute, save for their own footsteps echoing off the stone and the occasional shuffle of loose gravel beneath their boots. The passage narrowed at points, forcing them to move in single file. Their breath came faster, more from urgency than exertion, each of them acutely aware of the men following somewhere behind them.

A sudden turn led to a short, steep descent, the floor sloping downward in a way that made their footing precarious.

Devong steadied himself against the wall as he moved forward, his fingers brushing across a deep groove in the rock. He didn't stop to examine it—there was no time for that now. The passage seemed to tighten around them, pressing them forward as though the fort itself was guiding them toward something hidden in its depths.

"Careful through here," he cautioned. "Footing is a little unsteady through this part."

They were deep inside the fortress now and into the upper parts of the plateau itself. The walls here weren't constructed like the passages they'd been in before. This tunnel had been hewn long ago by the builders of this place.

Tara considered the work done nearly a thousand years prior, the hands of the men who'd carved through solid rock with ancient tools. She could only imagine how long it must have taken. Many castles and fortresses from history took years, even decades, to complete.

Alex's flashlight flickered briefly, the beam bouncing against what appeared to be an intersection, but as they reached it, they realized there was only one way forward. The tunnel stretched out before them, darker than ever, its end unseen. The walls bore scratches and indentations, marks left behind by whatever tools had carved out this hidden artery of the fortress. Time had erased most of the evidence, but something about the space felt old—older than the fort itself.

They stayed on the move, their pace urgent, the knowledge that their pursuers might be somewhere behind them pushing them harder. The tunnel curved sharply, and then, without warning, it opened up into a small, round chamber. The space felt different—wider—with air that moved slightly, as if there was another way out. The moment they stepped inside, the weight of the tunnel's suffocating narrowness lifted, but the tension in their chests did not ease. Something waited in this chamber, and whatever it was, it had been hidden for a very long time.

"This is it," Devong said. "This is the place."

They shined their lights around the room, each pointing their beams in a different direction. The combined light from the flashlights and headlamps cast a pale glow around the room.

"Wow," Felicia said, her fear replaced by tentative wonder.

At one end of the chamber stood a row of stone figures set into niches in the wall. At first glance, they seemed like decorative statues, but as they drew closer, the details became more pronounced. These were not deities or mythological beings. These were warriors. Each figure was slightly larger than life, their postures straight and commanding. They held weapons—some with swords drawn, others with shields raised. Their faces, though weathered by the passage of time, bore expressions of unwavering resolve. These sentinels were part of this place, this ancient room that only a handful of people had seen throughout the centuries.

"Guardians," Alex whispered, his flashlight beam lingering on one of the figures.

"So it would seem," Tara said.

The figures stood watch over an arched entryway just beyond, its frame adorned with carvings of elephants, their trunks raised in a gesture of power and welcome. The archway looked like it was supposed to lead to another passage, but there was only a wall underneath it.

The guardians seemed almost alive, their presence commanding respect. Tara reached out, her fingers brushing against the cool stone of a warrior's shield. It was smooth in some places, rough in others, the details worn down by time but still discernible. On closer inspection, faint patterns were visible on the shields—perhaps symbols of clans or families long forgotten yet immortalized here.

"We need to work fast," Alex told them. "See if you can find anything that resembles a Celtic symbol or perhaps letters or words from the language. Split up; everyone work your way around clockwise."

As they angled their beams upward, they revealed ancient frescoes, their once-vivid colors now faded, cracked, and peeling from the rock. Scenes of divine battles and celestial beings stretched across the ceiling, their details obscured by centuries of wear, yet still holding the essence of a story untold.

The walls were covered in carvings, a dense array of symbols, gods, and sacred figures from Hindu tradition. Elephants adorned the lower sections, their trunks raised in silent triumph. Above them, deities stood in elaborate poses, some wielding weapons, others holding lotus flowers or scrolls of wisdom. The sheer number of figures made it difficult to focus on any one detail—every inch of stone was alive with history.

A half-circle of stones rested at the base of the walls, each one carved with its own unique set of designs. Some bore the familiar swirl of mandalas, others the unmistakable geometry of *yantras*, or sacred diagrams meant to channel spiritual energy. The other three did as told, aware that this was no time for debate.

They all spread out and began moving around the room's perimeter, running their lights over the stone walls, examining the ancient images and symbols that seemed to cover every inch from floor to ceiling.

Alex ran his fingers over a relief carving depicting a battle scene. Warriors astride elephants clashed with those in chariots, their weapons frozen midswing, while swirling clouds of dust had been meticulously etched around their feet. He followed the scene upward, where celestial beings hovered above the fray, their serene faces in stark contrast to the chaos below. The story was one of divine intervention—gods shaping the fates of mortals with unseen hands.

Tara's light swept over a different section, where a large figure loomed over kneeling supplicants. The deity's many arms radiated outward, each hand holding a symbolic object—a conch, a discus, a lotus. The expressions of those below were etched with reverence, their hands raised in devotion. She murmured, "This could be Vishnu... or maybe Shiva in one of his many forms." Her fingers brushed over the finely chiseled patterns of jewelry and fabric, marveling at the detail preserved despite the centuries.

Devong crouched near the base of the wall, inspecting a sequence of smaller carvings. One showed a serpent coiled around a mountain, a stream of water flowing from its mouth. "This might be the churning of the ocean," he mused. "A pretty common Hindu myth—gods and demons working together to create the nectar of immortality."

The three of them moved methodically, each examining different pieces of the past yet all searching for the same thing—something out of place, something that didn't belong among the stories of this land.

Felicia shifted with steady precision, her eyes scanning the ring of stones. Her fingers trailed lightly over the carvings, feeling the slight depressions where time had worn them down. She crouched, tilting her head as she examined a particularly elaborate section filled with interwoven floral patterns. Her gaze flicked lower, following the natural curve of the wall, and then—just at the base of the archway—her breath caught.

At first, it seemed like just another decorative detail, a simple etching lost among the chaos of symbols. Covered in a fine layer of dust, it would have been easy to miss had she been less focused. She leaned in, brushing away the dust with her fingertips. The design revealed itself slowly—a knot, small and almost imperceptible, its looping curves forming an unmistakable Celtic pattern, overlaid with the ancient Hindu swastika—an emblem that had been forever tainted by the perverse mind of a madman.

She exhaled sharply and dropped to one knee for a closer look. The knot was tiny, barely the size of her palm, and was set into the surface of a floor stone beneath the archway. The precision of the carving stood out in stark contrast to the flowing, organic lines of the Hindu motifs that surrounded it. This was deliberate. This was placed here for a reason.

"Guys?" Felicia blurted, trying to keep her voice down. "I think I found something." Her voice was hushed but urgent. The others turned, their beams converging on her position as she reached out and traced the knot's lines again, feeling the grooves beneath her fingertips. It wasn't just an anomaly—it was a message, a marker hidden in plain sight.

"That's it," Alex said, his voice trembling with excitement.

Devong leaned closer. "I can't believe it. How did I never see that before?"

"Other researchers probably didn't pay much attention to it because of the Hindu symbol overlapping it," Tara guessed. "But to us, people looking for it..."

"May I?" Alex asked Felicia.

"By all means."

She moved aside and allowed Alex to kneel down in front of the stone. He ran his finger along one of the seams. The stones weren't held together with mortar. Instead, they'd been cut with laser precision to fit tightly against one another like the stones at Cusco or Machu Picchu in Peru. There were many examples of such craftsmanship from ancient history, all of which produced questions as to the real intelligence, technological capabilities, and possible global reach of some ancient peoples.

He pressed his palm flat against one of the larger slabs, feeling for any unevenness, any sign of settling over the centuries. But the stones hadn't shifted. They were tight, almost unnaturally so, as if time had failed to erode the careful engineering behind their design and placement. He traced the thin seams between them, barely wide enough to slip a fingernail into.

"This isn't standard masonry," he murmured, more to himself

than the others. "No mortar, no sign of crumbling joints. These were cut to fit perfectly—like the megalithic structures you'd find in South America."

"Impressive," Felicia said.

"Yes, the builders of this place had a very high level of skill when it came to masonry," Devong confirmed. "Among all their other abilities you've already witnessed."

Alex shifted his weight, tapping his knuckles lightly against the stone. It gave off a dull, solid sound. But as he moved his hand closer to the base where the Celtic knot had been carved, the tone changed —just slightly. *Hollow? Or just different density?*

His pulse quickened. There was something off about this particular slab. Something intentional. Alex glanced up at the others. "I'm not entirely sure this one is like the rest of the heavy tiles in here."

"What do you mean?" Devong asked. "Aside from the Celtic symbol intertwined with the Hindu one."

Alex set his backpack down beside him and unzipped the main compartment. He rummaged around for a moment until he found a small toolkit. He retrieved a flathead screwdriver.

"Do you always carry a set of tools with you wherever you go?" Felicia asked.

"He does," Tara answered sardonically.

"Hey, you never know when you might need one. You could have a mechanical issue with a vehicle. Or, in this case, you might need one to pry up a stone tile."

Devong suddenly looked nervous. "You're going to remove the stone?"

Alex looked up at him. "At this point, I don't think we have a choice. It's that, or we go back the way we came. And even though I doubt those men were able to follow us down here, I would rather not take the chance if we have another way out."

"I'm sure my friend blocking the entrance can handle things."

"Me too. But don't you want to know what's under here? The people who built this put this stone here for a reason. It's a marker, a clue to the mystery we came here to solve."

"If it makes you feel better," Tara added, "we'll put it back if there's nothing to see."

Devong hesitated then nodded. "Okay. Do it," he said.

Alex returned his focus to the slab and wedged the end of the screwdriver into the tiniest of seams he'd ever encountered on a site.

Alex adjusted his grip on the flathead screwdriver, its tip wedged into the narrow, almost imperceptible space between those two perfectly cut slabs. Sweat beaded on his forehead as he braced his other hand against the floor for leverage. The stone resisted, heavy and unyielding, as though it hadn't been disturbed in centuries. He clenched his jaw, pushing harder, the metal groaning faintly against the ancient rock.

The others watched, on edge, as they visibly tried to will the heavy stone up from its resting place.

"Can I help?" Devong asked.

Alex shook his head. "Only flathead I have," he grunted.

The blade of the screwdriver slipped a little, and it nearly shifted out of the groove. Alex pushed down harder, wiggling it from side to side to dig deeper. He didn't worry about grinding out tiny bits of stone between the two tiles, though he hoped Devong didn't notice, or didn't care, about the damage.

"Come on," he muttered under his breath, shifting his weight. With a grunt, he leaned in, twisting the screwdriver until, finally, there was a faint click, followed by the sound of stone scraping against stone. A tiny gap appeared at the edge of the slab, just enough to suggest that the centuries-old seal was beginning to break.

"It's shifting," Devong said. He tried to mute his excitement. Or maybe it was concern. Either way, he leaned closer in anticipation.

Tara crouched beside her husband; her headlamp trained on the widening gap.

The tile continued to rise until the space between it and the next stone was nearly an inch in diameter.

"Let me help," Tara said quickly, her voice low but eager. She scooted closer to the heavy slab, her light's beam angled against the stone, and pressed her fingers into the crevice Alex had created. Together, they heaved, the slab groaning as it began to shift.

Devong joined them, kneeling on the opposite side. "Hold it steady. We'll lift on three," he said. The three of them exchanged a quick nod, muscles tensing in preparation.

"One, two, three!"

They pulled together, their combined effort enough to lift the stone just enough to tilt it aside. As the tile toppled over, it landed with a dull thud, sending a plume of fine, choking dust into the air. The sound echoed faintly, as though the chamber itself acknowledged the intrusion.

They all froze for a moment, staring down at what had been revealed. The opening was just large enough for a person to fit through. Beyond the opening was a narrow staircase, its steps carved from the same sandstone as the rest of the fort. The difference was that this stone had darkened with age. The passage descended steeply, vanishing into pitch blackness. A faint current of air wafted up from below, musty and cool, carrying with it the unmistakable scent of earth and timeworn stone.

Tara leaned closer, shining her light down the opening. The beam illuminated the steps, which were worn smooth in the center, as if countless feet had traveled this hidden path long ago. Her breath caught as the light glinted off faint carvings on the walls lining the staircase—simple but deliberate patterns, almost like markers guiding the way.

"This isn't just a storage space," she said softly. "It's... it's something more."

Alex exhaled; his hands still braced on the floor as he peered into the depths below. "A hidden passage," he murmured, the awe in his voice echoing Tara's. "They built this to be completely concealed. No one was meant to find it."

"Unless they deciphered the clue in the Gobi."

"Right."

Devong reached over and pointed his flashlight toward the archway above the staircase, where the stone wall appeared seamless from this side. "That wall must be part of the disguise," he said. "From the outside, you'd never guess there was anything behind it."

"Or under it," Felicia added.

They exchanged glances, each carrying the same question. What awaited them down there?

Tara broke the silence, her voice quiet but resolute. "We need to move. We still don't know if those guys are behind us."

"If they are," Felicia said, "won't they just follow us down?"

"We'll put the stone back once we're in," Alex said.

"Then how will we escape if there's no exit?" Devong wondered.

"It'll be easier to push up from its spot than it was to pull it out. At the very least, it could buy us some time."

The rest of the group nodded their agreement.

"I'll go first," Tara said.

"Careful," Alex cautioned, even though he knew he didn't need to say it. That was like a parent telling their teenage driver to be careful when they left the house on a Saturday night, as if simply saying the words would keep them safe.

Tara nodded, adjusting her headlamp. "Stay close. We don't know how stable this is." She tilted her head down, sending the light cutting into the depths of the staircase.

She took a slow, steady breath then descended into the darkness.

"Devong, you go next," Alex ordered.

The man nodded, albeit reluctantly, then when the opening was clear, he followed after Tara.

Felicia lingered close by Alex, watching the other two as their lights danced around in the secret passage. "Do you see anything down there?"

"Not really," Tara answered. "It's just a tunnel. But it's pretty amazing in its own right. Come on down."

Felicia glanced at Alex, who nodded in encouragement. She shuffled toward the stairs then deliberately took the first step then the second and continued until she was clear of the opening.

Alex shoved the screwdriver back into the kit and replaced the tools back in his bag before slinging it over his shoulders. Then he shifted the heavy stone, sliding it closer to the passage entrance.

He looked over at the passage they'd come through and listened for a moment.

"Everything okay?" Tara asked. "You need help?"

"No," Alex answered. "I'm good."

He wrapped his fingers around the edge of the slab and pulled it toward him as he carefully took a step down. Because of the weight of the stone, he had to work it one end at a time, sliding it toward its original resting place until part of it was hanging over the opening.

Once there, he took another step down and pressed his fingers into the bottom of the tile, pushing up slightly as he pulled it laterally. This part was much harder than dragging it, but inch by inch he was able to move it until the stone lined up with the cutout in the floor.

The end dropped into place, taking some of the weight off his fingers. He continued pulling until the other end finally fell with a heavy thud.

"There," he said, slightly out of breath. He worked his fingers, clenching them and unclenching them to relieve the stiffness from the exertion. He turned around and faced the others. "Let's see where this thing goes."

23

R olf watched as his men dragged the body of the security guard around the corner until it was out of sight from the main corridor. It had been a tricky endeavor to eliminate the big man with the intermittent passing of tourists through the area.

Rolf had returned to the guard and asked if it was okay for he and his friends to wait there and that he'd texted the other group to let them know the general vicinity where they were waiting.

The man thought the request strange since he'd just told Rolf his friends hadn't come through that way, but he didn't try to stop him and his two colleagues. Once the other nine men arrived, Rolf ordered four of them to block off the only ways in and out. Once the flow of foot traffic was temporarily shut off, Yuri, Javier, and two other men made quick work of the security guard. One surprised the big man with a blow to the diaphragm. The air blew out of the guard's lungs, and he fell to his knees, unable to breathe. In an instant, Yuri stepped behind the man, planted his left elbow at the base of the guy's neck, and jerked his head back.

The bone snapped with an audible pop, and the guard's heavy

body collapsed to the floor. His face hit with a smack, confirming he was dead before his skin touched the stone.

After that, dragging the bulky body clear of the passage only took a minute for four of the men, each taking an arm and leg to get the dead man out of view.

They dropped him unceremoniously on the floor in the restricted passage then looked to their leader for the next instructions. The other four joined them in the corridor, allowing the fort's visitors to continue walking through the area.

Rolf looked at one of the men and ordered him to return to the front of the corridor to pretend he was on guard.

"What happens if the next guard in the rotation comes by?" he asked in a heavy Hungarian accent.

"Take Paulo with you," Rolf answered. "If the next guy gives you trouble, tell them the other guard followed someone back here who wasn't supposed to be here. He'll likely come in here to check it out, and you can do the same to him as we did that one." He motioned with a dismissive hand to the dead man.

"Yes, sir," the soldier said and turned with the other to return to the chain blocking the way in.

"The rest of you, come with me."

Rolf removed his pistol from its holster then turned to one of his men carrying some of their equipment. "Attach your lights to your weapons," he ordered the rest.

The man with the bag nearest him understood what his commander meant and immediately let his bag down and unzipped the top. He took out a light for Rolf then passed several more around to the other men. Once they'd fixed their attachments to their weapons, the men switched on the lights and moved ahead, carefully stepping over the uneven stones of the passage.

Their beams cut through the suffocating darkness ahead, casting trembling circles on the walls as they continued forward. The rest of his team followed close behind. The air was cooler here, damp and heavy, with a faint metallic tang that seemed to cling to his throat. The sound of his boots echoed faintly, swallowed quickly by the oppressive stone walls that pressed in on either side. Behind him, his team moved in silence, their weapons drawn and their steps deliberate. The tension was palpable, hanging in the stale air like an unspoken threat.

Not that Rolf or any of his men felt threatened by the IAA agents and their companions. As far as he knew, they were unarmed, though he was aware they'd been able to obtain weapons in other countries in the past—another part of the mystique that surrounded the IAA and its assets.

Even if the Americans were armed, Rolf and his team were all from elite military backgrounds. There wasn't much, if anything, they couldn't handle. On top of that, they outnumbered them. In a confined space, if it came down to shots, Rolf's men would overwhelm them, perhaps with a few losses, but that was acceptable to achieve their goal.

He glanced back briefly, his sharp blue eyes narrowing on the two mercenaries bringing up the rear. "Stay tight," he ordered, his voice low but firm. "We can't afford any mistakes."

The men nodded in unison, their expressions tense, hard as the stone under their feet. He didn't have to elaborate—everyone knew the stakes. The International Archaeology Agency team had a lead on the prize, and Rolf wasn't about to let them disappear into the shadows of this ancient fortress without a fight. He adjusted his grip on the pistol, his fingers tightening on the cool metal. The weight was reassuring, a constant reminder of his control in situations like this.

The passage twisted and turned unpredictably, as though designed to confuse intruders. The walls were bare, stripped of the ornate carvings and artistry that adorned the rest of the fort. This space wasn't meant to impress; it was meant to conceal. Rolf's beam swept over the rough-hewn surfaces, revealing little more than crude scratches and the occasional streak of moisture trailing down the stone. The floor beneath them was uneven, scattered with loose gravel and worn patches where the rock had been smoothed by centuries of passage.

One of the mercenaries, a burly man named Jonas, muttered

under his breath as he stumbled over a loose stone. "This place gives me the creeps," he said, catching himself against the wall. His voice echoed faintly, then faded into the void ahead.

Rolf shot him a warning glare. "Keep your head in the game. And stay quiet."

Jonas straightened, his face flushed with embarrassment in the residual light from the beams, and nodded. The group pressed on, the tension building with every step as the passage began to slope downward. The air grew colder, carrying with it a faint mustiness that hinted at spaces long sealed away from the outside world.

The corridor stretched endlessly before them, winding its way through the bowels of the ancient fortress like a serpent coiled around secrets long buried. Every few paces, the passage would twist sharply, forcing them to adjust their bearings as it led them deeper into the unknown.

Rolf remained in the lead at the head of the column, his jaw tight, his mind racing. The IAA agents were close—he could feel it—but the unyielding monotony of the passage gnawed at his patience. Each turn felt the same as the last, the walls devoid of any distinguishing marks. It was as if the fortress itself was conspiring to disorient them, to make them question whether they were moving forward at all.

"Feels like this thing never ends," muttered Yuri, his voice a low rumble that barely reached Rolf's ears.

"It ends," Rolf replied, his tone clipped. "Everything ends. Stay focused."

Even though he remained stoic, slivers of doubt began to penetrate his mind. He wondered if he'd miscalculated, overplaying his hand to bring his entire team down this corridor in the belief that the Americans had come this way.

But what if they hadn't? What if I'm wrong?

He forced those questions out of his mind. If they proved true, he'd lose the confidence of his men, which might lead to a challenge of leadership by one of his lieutenants. Rolf knew Yuri craved power; he thirsted for control. The man was a good soldier except for the fact he didn't like taking orders. He wanted to be the one giving them. For that reason, Rolf had always kept a watchful eye on the Russian.

A sense of futility started to needle his mind as the corridor seemed to stretch on forever. He hated this—the uncertainty, the slow crawl through darkness. He was a man of action, not a wanderer chasing shadows through ancient stone passageways.

The curve ahead dipped slightly, and Rolf steadied himself against the wall as the floor angled downward. His fingers brushed over the rough surface, cool and damp, the texture almost gritty. The faint crunch of loose gravel underfoot echoed in the confined space, the sound bouncing back at them like a whisper from the past.

He glanced over his shoulder at his team, their faces tense, their weapons still drawn but aimed at the floor in case one accidentally discharged. They were capable, seasoned, but even they weren't immune to the strange weight pressing down on them, a sense that this place was alive in some way—watching, waiting.

Another turn brought a long, straight stretch of corridor, and Rolf quickened his pace. The oppressive stillness pushed him forward, his need to close the gap between himself and the IAA agents overriding everything else. He clenched his fingers as he thought of them slipping farther away, disappearing into the depths, where he might never find them.

Were there other corridors that splintered off in different directions? If so, they'd have to split up again to continue the search. Doing so would potentially take away the numerical advantage, but he knew his men could still handle it. One of them was as good as five ordinary people. Perhaps more.

They wouldn't get away. Not here. Not with him on their heels, even if they had taken a detour.

Up ahead, thirty feet forward, Rolf's flashlight pierced into an opening beyond the corridor. The circle from the beam widened on a wall—either a dead end, a corner, or something else.

He pressed ahead, again increasing his speed until the passageway ended in a huge, circular room.

Rolf slowed as he entered, his flashlight beam sweeping over the space. The room was circular, the domed ceiling just high enough to give the illusion of openness despite the encroaching stone walls. His light caught faint traces of frescoes on the ceiling, the cracked and peeling remnants of ancient battles and celestial beings.

But the walls were what held his attention. They were alive with carvings—figures of gods, animals, and sacred symbols from Hindu mythology, all interwoven in intricate patterns that told stories of devotion and power. The sheer detail was overwhelming, a visual cacophony that made it difficult to focus on any single element.

Rolf moved toward the center of the chamber, his eyes scanning for any sign of the IAA agents and their companions. There was nothing—no sound, no movement. The chamber was empty.

24

The narrow stone staircase had swallowed them whole, its steep steps leading them down into the unknown. For the past ten minutes, they had been moving steadily forward, their flashlights and headlamps slicing through the darkness, revealing a corridor that seemed to twist and weave through the very bones of the fortress. The air was thick with the scent of old stone, dust, and something else—something faintly metallic, like the ghost of iron long rusted away.

The tunnel walls, carved with precise, almost surgical cuts, showed no signs of traditional masonry. Like the chamber above, the stones here fit together perfectly, with no mortar binding them, no gaps where time might have pried them apart. It was as if the passage had been formed, not built, as though some ancient force had willed it into existence beneath the fort.

Alex led the way; his flashlight beam steady as he navigated the uneven ground. The passage narrowed in places, forcing them to squeeze through sections that had settled over centuries, the weight of the earth pressing in on either side. Every few hundred feet, the tunnel would turn sharply, almost at right angles, leading them farther into the depths of the plateau. It was disorienting, and without their lights, it would have been impossible to keep their bearings.

"This place is incredible," Tara murmured as she ran her fingers over the stone. "So much carving to be done by hand."

"Unless it wasn't done by hand," Alex suggested.

"What do you mean?" Felicia asked, her eyes studying the stone walls as she moved ahead.

"It's possible that these were done with something else, perhaps tools we weren't aware people of that time possessed.

"I suppose."

Dr. Lowe was rooted in traditional archaeology, accustomed to only accepting facts based on things she'd been taught or actually seen with her own eyes. She wasn't given to wild theories. But there was no doubt that the events of the week had changed her opinions, at least a little.

"Whoa," Alex said, stopping as his flashlight illuminated something unusual. "Look at this."

Carved into the wall at eye level was a symbol—elegant loops and interwoven lines forming a perfect Celtic knot. The sight of it here, deep beneath a fortress in eastern India, sent a chill through all of them. It was impossible. And yet there it was.

Felicia stepped closer, tracing the design lightly with her fingertips. "It's not just a decorative knot," she whispered.

"Another Celtic emblem," Tara said. "Something that shouldn't be here just like the one on the tile back in the other chamber."

Devong frowned, sweeping his light farther down the corridor. "Except it is here," he said. "And it's not alone." He pointed his light across to the opposite wall, highlighting a similar symbol.

"I'd say we're going the right direction," Alex said. "Come on. We best keep moving."

They pressed on, and every so often another marking appeared—some as simple as a spiral, others more intricate, resembling key patterns and warrior symbols. Some were faded, their edges worn by time, while others remained as crisp as the day they had been carved. Each one deepened the mystery. What were they doing here? Who had put them here? And why?

The passage continued downward, more stairs appearing at random intervals, their steps uneven but sturdy. The descent was gradual but undeniable—they were moving deeper, far below the known levels of the fort. The weight of the earth above them was a constant presence, pressing down like the hand of history itself.

A turn in the corridor brought them to a small alcove, a break in the monotony of the walls. Inside, half-hidden in the shadows, there was another carving, larger than the rest. It was unmistakably Celtic —a warrior with a broad sword, standing against what looked like a serpent coiled around his legs.

Tara inhaled sharply. "That's Lugh," she said. "A god of war and kingship."

Felicia turned to Tara, her expression unreadable. "What is a Celtic god of war doing in an underground passage in India? And how did you know that?"

Tara shrugged. "I read a little on the way to India."

"A little? Sounds like you went pretty deep."

"I read fast."

There was no time to stand around and admire the anomaly. They moved on, the passage winding even farther downward before, at last, the floor evened out. The tunnel widened slightly, the ceiling lifting above them as the walls stretched outward. The air changed, becoming even chillier, and more humid. Ahead, the passage opened, revealing another room.

At the threshold, they paused and looked around to make sure there weren't any traps laid to prevent unwanted visitors from entering.

Alex looked around, his flashlight sweeping across the space. It was smaller than the previous chamber but no less striking. Unlike the circular room from before, this chamber was square, its walls meeting at precise right angles, as if the space had been measured and cut with modern tools. The ceiling was pyramidal, its sloping sides converging to a single point high above.

But it was the carvings on the walls that made them stop in their tracks.

One by one, the group slowly entered the room, moving deliberately, cautiously.

On one side of the room, monstrous figures loomed in the flickering beams of their lights. These were not the graceful, stylized depictions seen in Hindu temples. These creatures were raw, feral, their forms twisted into grotesque shapes. Some had elongated faces with gaping mouths full of jagged teeth. Others had multiple arms ending in claws, their eyes hollow and endless. One figure, hunched and gnarled, appeared to be a fusion of man and beast, its face frozen in a silent snarl.

Felicia exhaled slowly. "These... these look like Fomorians."

"The Irish myth?" Alex asked. "The ones that battled the Tuatha Dé Danann?"

Tara glanced over at him. "Seems I'm not the only one who did some light reading."

He blushed in the glow of the lights and rolled his shoulders. "You can't be the only one."

"They were said to be chaotic, monstrous, enemies of the gods. And they're here, opposite..."

She turned, shining her light to the other side of the room.

If the left side of the chamber was filled with horror, the right side was carved with majesty. Figures of Hindu and Celtic deities stood in fierce but noble poses, each one depicted in intricate, reverent detail. Durga, the Hindu goddess of war and protection, stood with her many arms outstretched, holding her weapons of divine power. Krishna, serene but powerful, loomed beside her, his flute resting against his lips as if caught mid-melody. And next to them, the Dagda held his great club, his expression one of wisdom and unyielding strength.

The two sides—chaos and order, destruction and protection—faced each other across the chamber, locked in an eternal standoff.

Tara's voice was barely above a whisper. "This isn't just a hidden chamber. It's a story."

Alex nodded slowly. "A battle. Something someone wanted to remember—or warn future people about."

Devong took a step forward, sweeping his flashlight along the base of the wall. "I wonder why they made it so difficult to find."

Felicia took a slow, steadying breath. "Maybe we weren't supposed to."

"Or it could be for our own protection," Tara offered.

"Then why leave clues to find it?" Alex asked.

Tara shook her head. "I don't know."

No one else said a word. The silence of the chamber seemed deeper now, heavier, as if the carved figures were listening, waiting.

Alex tightened his grip on his flashlight. Whatever they had uncovered, the scenes wrapping around them didn't seem willing to give up more answers.

The chamber loomed all around, a silent tomb that had been waiting for centuries without ever being disturbed. Their lights traced along the walls, illuminating the intricate carvings that told a story older than any of them could comprehend. The beams revealed new details—battles, gods, monsters, and symbols that seemed to weave a complex narrative spanning two mythologies. There were animals, too: a lion, a bear, a hawk, a wolflike creature standing on its hind legs, and others, all joined in the battle against the hordes of hell. The Hindu deities stood in defiant poses, their weapons raised in righteous fury, while the monstrous Fomorians snarled and clawed, their grotesque faces twisted in rage.

Felicia took a cautious step forward, her fingers trailing over a section of the wall where Durga's many-armed figure loomed over the battlefield. "This wasn't just a conflict," she murmured. "It was a war of annihilation."

Alex crouched near the base of the carvings, running his fingers over a series of spiraling knots that formed patterns across the stone. "These symbols—they aren't just decorative. They're meant to guide us."

Tara knelt beside him, brushing away dust to reveal more of the elaborate sequence. "This entire room is one giant puzzle," she said.

Devong exhaled sharply, sweeping his flashlight across the opposite wall. "And puzzles mean traps. Right?"

Alex nodded grimly. "Could be." He continued studying the markings, his brow furrowing as he traced a path between the gods and monsters. "It's a progression. The battle wasn't just a clash—it was structured. The deities fought in a sequence." He pointed to Krishna playing his flute, standing beside Durga. "First, the gods made their move." His flashlight then drifted toward the Dagda, the Celtic All-Father, standing with his great club raised. "Then, it seems the Celts joined the fight."

Tara moved to another section of the wall, her pulse quickening. "And here..." She pointed to an etching of a figure kneeling before the gods, an offering in their hands. "This happened last. A tribute."

Felicia's expression darkened. "A tribute?"

"Yes. But more than that, it looks like if we don't do this in the correct order..."

"There will be a silver medal?" Devong hoped.

"Not exactly."

Devong sighed, rubbing his temples. "Fantastic. So, we just have to decipher the order of an ancient mythological war. And if we mess it up, we're dead. No pressure."

Alex ignored him, standing and studying the room again. "There must be something else—something that confirms the sequence."

Tara's headlamp flickered over a separate set of carvings along the edge of the wall. Unlike the battle scenes, these were different. The figures were smaller, less divine. Explorers, perhaps. They reached toward the gods, pressing symbols along the wall.

And then, in the final panel, a figure lay broken on the ground, impaled on jagged spikes.

A warning.

Felicia swallowed hard. "I'm guessing they got it wrong."

A chilling silence filled the chamber, and the weight of the moment settled over them.

Alex clenched his jaw. "We don't have the luxury of making mistakes. So we have to be very careful."

The realization left a tangible heaviness in the air and twisted their stomachs into knots. Tara exhaled slowly and lifted her light higher, tracing the carvings with an increasingly critical eye. Now they weren't just symbols. They were instructions.

Devong took a step back, adjusting his grip on his flashlight. "So let's break it down. If this is a story, what's the sequence?"

Tara ran her hands over one of the reliefs, careful not to press too hard. "The gods started the battle. It seems they came through that." She pointed at something that looked like a round portal. The sight of the thing sent a chill down her spine. "Then the Celts joined, and then there was an offering."

Devong frowned. "But how do we know what the offering actually was?"

Alex swept his light over the lower portion of the carvings, his pulse quickening when he spotted something different. "Here. Look." He crouched beside a small relief, mostly buried under centuries of dust and debris. He wiped the stone clean with his sleeve, revealing an image of a vessel held by multiple hands, extended toward the gods.

Felicia crouched beside him, her breath hitching. "It's an offering bowl."

Devong crossed his arms. "Great. But what does that mean?"

Tara straightened and turned to the opposite side of the chamber, where the Fomorians had been carved in chaotic, twisted poses. Unlike the precise, deliberate movements of the gods, the monsters appeared wild and uncontrollable. At the bottom of their section, smaller figures—human-size—were shown attempting to interact with them. Their fate was clear. They'd been destroyed.

Felicia turned back to the offering. "The story is saying that if the offering wasn't made correctly, they were punished."

Alex's jaw tightened. "Which means we have to find the offering mechanism before we activate anything else."

Tara frowned. "But how do we do that? If the offering is separate, where would the trigger be?"

Alex stood and studied the chamber as a whole. He stepped back from the wall, sweeping his flashlight over every surface, looking for something they had missed. Then he saw it.

At the far end of the room, almost obscured by shadow, was a raised pedestal. It had been blended into the stone so well that it was nearly invisible at first glance. It was a small, flat surface, just large enough to hold something of importance.

He gestured to the others. "That has to be it."

Felicia's light followed his, and she inhaled sharply. "That's where the offering goes."

Devong rolled his shoulders. "All right. So we put something on it, then do the sequence?"

Alex frowned. "Maybe. But we don't know what happens if we activate the sequence without an offering first."

Tara shook her head. "I don't want to find out the hard way."

Felicia reached into her pack, pulling out a small empty metal cup she'd used for drinking coffee at the dig site. "I know this isn't exactly a sacred relic, but if this is just a weight trigger, it might work."

"It's worth a shot," Alex said.

"Wait," Devong interrupted. Despite the cool temperature, he was visibly sweating. "Are you sure? What if it sets off some ancient death trap and kills us all?" His voice had risen nearly half an octave by the time he finished the question.

"If we just stand around here and do nothing, those men who are following us will find us."

"We have to try," Tara added, encouraging Felicia with a nod.

The archaeologist walked over to the pedestal and carefully placed the cup in the center.

For a moment, nothing happened.

"I guess that wasn't it," Devong said, his voice full of tepid relief.

Then a low rumbling filled the chamber. The pedestal sank slightly into the floor, clicking into place.

Their Indian friend tensed further. "I really hope that was a good thing."

Alex turned back toward the carvings, heart pounding.

Then, seven seconds after the noise began, it stopped inexplicably.

"Okay?" Felicia said, looking around as if at any moment sharp spears would shoot out of the walls and impale them. "What was that?"

Alex and Tara also peered around the room with wary eyes. After another five seconds, they looked at each other and gave a nod.

"I think it's okay to try the sequence," Alex suggested.

"Are you sure?" Devong asked.

"No. But we're running out of time. If those guys behind us figured out how to get down here, they could be here any minute."

"But that's why you put the tile back, right?" Felicia said, hope fading in her voice. "No one noticed it for centuries."

"I'd rather not count on that."

Tara made the decision for the group and stepped toward the first symbol, her fingers hovering over the image of Durga, who had started the battle. "All right. Here goes nothing."

Felicia inhaled sharply. "Wait—"

It was too late. Tara pressed the symbol.

A deep, vibrating hum echoed through the chamber, the stone beneath their feet trembling as if something massive had just awakened.

And then, in the shadows above them, something moved.

Felicia's light swung upward. Everyone else followed her beam up to the ceiling where carved stone figures, embedded there centuries, suddenly shifted. The figures tilted forward, as though waiting for something.

Tara took a slow step back. "Oh... that's not good."

Devong gritted his teeth. "Yeah, I would say that could be a problem."

Alex clenched his jaw. "I don't know if that was the wrong one, or if that just sets the game in place. Either way, we need to be careful. The wrong sequence could bring this whole place down."

Felicia nodded. "Or worse."

The ominous thought spread through every mind in the room. The only thing worse than being killed quickly was dying slowly in the dark, buried deep inside a secret chamber that no one would ever find.

There was no room for error.

25

"Where are they?" muttered Yuri. He shifted uneasily, spinning around as his gaze darted across the room. "I thought you said they came this way. It's a dead end. You brought us down here for nothing." He locked eyes with Rolf and didn't try to hide his frustration.

The rest of the men stared at the commander. None of them said anything. They didn't dare agree with the angry Russian. But they didn't defend Rolf either.

He didn't need them to defend him. An act of loyalty, though appreciated, would also insinuate that he couldn't defend himself. He was there to lead, to make decisions.

The Austrian felt the weight of failure bearing down on him. He'd been tasked with catching the Americans, and now that seemed like it was growing more impossible by the second.

Anger narrowed Rolf's eyelids, and he clenched his jaw. How dare Yuri be so insolent. Rolf had led them through more difficult moments than this, and far more dangerous. The only thing fueling the Russian's comments were greed and ambition, and with every passing second, Rolf's regrets of bringing him on board swelled like a balloon.

Along with those regrets, the doubts he'd felt before returned, this time with hard evidence that he'd been wrong. That didn't mean he was going to give up yet.

"Search the room," Rolf barked, his voice cold and certain. His eyes never left his irate subordinate.

"For what?" Yuri asked. "They're not here. There's nothing here."

"Search. The. Room." Rolf's command this time left no doubt in the men's minds who was still in charge. "Look for something that could lead to a hidden passageway. There must be a clue."

"This isn't a movie, Rolf," Yuri protested. "Look around. There are no hidden levers, no buttons that open a secret door."

Rolf realized he was putting more on the line than just the mission. His reputation, even his leadership, was at stake. If they lost the Americans now, there would be no finding them, not even with their extensive network of connections around the globe.

"You can either give up, and none of us gets paid," Rolf said, "or you can start looking. Check the floor, the walls, everything. Look for something that's out of place."

For a moment, the men hesitated, something almost none of them ever did when given a command. But Yuri had planted seeds of doubt in their mind. He couldn't blame them entirely. For all intents and purposes, it seemed like they'd let the Americans slip away.

Rolf led by example and moved over to the wall to his left, close to the archway. He studied the symbols and figures at eye level then looked up higher to the point where the domed ceiling began its curved rise to the top of the room.

The rest of the men begrudgingly turned to face the walls, several scanning the floor as they began their search.

Rolf stood rigid, arms crossed, as his men spread out across the chamber. Their flashlight beams danced across the ancient carvings on the walls, revealing gods and monsters locked in silent battle, their expressions frozen in stone. Dust swirled in the wake of their movements, disturbed after centuries of stillness. The room felt suffocating, the heavy weight of history pressing down on them, but Rolf refused to let his mind wander to foolish superstitions.

Yuri had questioned his leadership—a mistake that Rolf wouldn't forget—but he wasn't blind to the unease radiating from his men. They were professionals, hardened and disciplined, yet even they weren't immune to the oppressive atmosphere of the underground chamber. The absence of the IAA agents gnawed at them, turning their mission into something that felt intangible, like chasing ghosts through ancient corridors.

"Fan out," Rolf ordered again. "And be thorough. Check every inch. They didn't just vanish."

Rolf glanced around at them as they began their work.

None of the men muttered a complaint except Yuri, who let out a long exhale. Their boots scuffed against the stone floor as they worked. One of them, Novak, ran a gloved hand along the carvings, pressing against the figures as if expecting a hidden mechanism to shift beneath his touch.

Another man, Ivan, knelt near the base of the walls, inspecting the ring of stones lining the chamber. "These are carved differently from the rest," he noted, but after a few minutes of poking and prodding, he shook his head.

Yuri crouched by the far end of the room, rapping his knuckles against the stone. "So what now?" His tone carried just enough challenge to make Rolf's jaw tighten. "We chase shadows down here while they slip away up top?"

Rolf didn't answer immediately. His eyes swept the chamber, searching for something—anything—that would justify his instincts. He knew the IAA team had been here. The scuff marks near the archway told him that much. But without something concrete, his men's doubts would fester, and that was a dangerous thing.

He turned away from Yuri, moving deliberately toward the center of the room. His fingers curled into fists at his sides. Something wasn't right. The IAA agents wouldn't have led them down here just to disappear. They had gone somewhere. He just had to find out where.

Rolf exhaled slowly, his frustration growing. Time was running out.

He crouched near the floor, close to the archway's frame, and ran his fingers over the smooth stone surface. His flashlight beam caught faint scuff marks along the central tile beneath the arch, barely visible against the ancient rock. He pointed his light at something else closer to the wall. His eyebrows lowered as he studied the mark. He didn't know much about ancient symbols, but he knew what a Celtic knot looked like, and he certainly recognized the swastika that had been usurped by the Nazis leading up to World War II.

He shined the light along the seams of the stone where he'd seen the scuff marks on the adjacent tile. The one with the symbols had been slightly chipped.

"This was moved recently," he muttered.

There was no mortar between the stone tiles. They'd been fit together with perfect precision, cut exactly how they needed to be. He realized every tile in the room had been cut in the same way, and none of them used any mortar.

It was incredible that the ancients had been able to accomplish this, though he'd seen or heard of other such things in his travels. He still wasn't sure who built the pyramids, or how.

He returned his focus to the stone with the symbol on it.

"This," Rolf said, gesturing to the stone, "isn't just part of the floor."

"What is it?" the man closest to him asked and shifted closer. A few more gathered around to look at what the Austrian had found.

"This tile was moved. Recently. Notice the small pieces of the edge that have been chipped off?"

The men nodded.

Rolf felt his heartbeat quicken. He turned to the men. "Give me a knife," he ordered.

Ivan produced a long combat knife from a sheath and passed it to his leader. Rolf took it and knelt down at the edge of the center tile beneath the archway. He gripped the knife's handle and tapped on the stone to his left. A solid thud filled the room. Then he rapped the knife's base against the tile with the symbol. The sound was distinctly different. Still solid, but with a more hollow resonance.

The men looked around at each other, every one of them realizing there was something off about that stone. Yuri's scowl remained intact, but there was a hint of doubt on his face, smothered in concern that he'd been very wrong to question his leader.

Rolf turned the knife over and slid the blade down into the seam between the two tiles. The steel was strong, covered in Cerakote for additional durability, but if he tried to pry the stone up with it, the knife might well break in half.

"You two," he said, turning to a couple of men to his right. "Do the same. With the weight distributed between the three of us, we should be able to lift this."

The men did as they were told and knelt down beside Rolf, each taking their knives and inserting the tips into the tiny gap between.

"Lift," Rolf ordered.

The three pushed down on their knives' handles, using them as levers. The stone moved slightly then started to rise.

Rolf leaned in, his broad shoulders tensing as he worked the stone. He tilted the combat knife against the adjacent tile, grunting with effort as he tried to gain leverage. The blade slipped, and he cursed under his breath.

But he quickly corrected the error, and the tile lifted from its resting place easily with the combined force of the knives. As soon as the gap was wide enough, he instructed them to slide their free hands under the lip and pull it away.

He and the other two simultaneously reached into the opening and raised the stone up, tilting it until the edge hit the wall.

The air that rushed up from below was thick and stale, carrying the unmistakable scent of damp earth and decay. A gaping hole now lay before them, revealing a staircase carved deep into the stone, its steps disappearing into pitch-black nothingness.

For a long beat, no one spoke. The silence stretched, broken only by the distant drip of water somewhere in the unseen depths. Rolf flicked his eyes toward Yuri, who stood frozen, his expression a mix of disbelief and something dangerously close to embarrassment. The man had challenged him, questioned his leadership. Now, with the secret passage yawning open at their feet, Yuri had nothing to say. Good.

Rolf allowed himself the barest hint of a smirk before stepping forward and unholstering his Glock in one smooth motion. He flicked on the mounted flashlight, its bright beam slicing into the darkness below. The steps were uneven, worn smooth in the center, as if they had once been heavily traveled. The walls flanking the staircase were rough, raw stone, devoid of the ornate carvings that adorned the chamber above. This passage had not been built to impress. It had been built to hide.

"On me," Rolf ordered, his voice steady, cold. "We're going in."

Yuri hesitated, just for a fraction of a second, before stepping forward and mirroring Rolf's movement, drawing his own Glock and clicking on the flashlight. One by one, the others followed, beams of white light cutting through the darkness, bouncing off damp stone as they illuminated the descent.

Jonas swallowed audibly. "You think this passage may have booby traps, sir?"

"Not sure. This is new territory for all of us. So be careful. Watch your step. We wouldn't want to set off something that could kill us or trap us down here forever."

The men weren't often given to fear, but the uncertainty the tunnel offered was something unlike they'd ever experienced. Facing enemies firing bullets at them was tangible. It was something they could see, something they knew how to deal with.

Rolf took a step toward the stairs and paused at the top, shining his light down into the depths. He didn't see anything that he would deem suspicious or dangerous.

Satisfied, at least for the moment, that there were no threats, he stepped down into the passage.

26

The story on the walls portrayed a fantastical world the likes of which most people would never accept as real. Stories of gods and monsters were fictional tools of ancient bards, concocted to teach lessons or morals, or as cautionary tales. Stories such as these, to most, were allegorical.

Tara and Alex, on the other hand, weren't most people. After the things they'd seen, it was no stretch to take the next step into the realm of the supernatural. Tara had gone farther than Alex when she'd entered the mysterious portal of the Sun Gate in Bolivia and knew these things could be real.

Standing close to the wall, scanning the story before her, motes of dust floated in the dim beams of their lights, the air dense with the scent of ancient stone.

Alex's fingers were tense around his flashlight, its beam flickering across the mural that had revealed itself as a puzzle. The figures—Hindu gods, Celtic deities, the animal creatures, and monstrous Fomorians—stood locked in battle, but the sequence of their struggle wasn't just a story. It was a warning. A test. And from the ominous creaks and groans in the stone above them, the consequences of failing weren't just theoretical.

Tara exhaled slowly, sweeping her light over the towering carvings. Deciphering the message took every ounce of her brainpower, especially considering this wasn't her area of expertise.

Felicia nodded, her jaw tight. "Any ideas?"

Devong shifted his weight, his eyes darting to the stone figures looming overhead. "The battle sequence is pretty clear," he said. "Durga first, then Krishna, then the Dagda. But after that... we don't know."

Alex swallowed hard and refocused on the engravings. Something caught his eye, though he was slow to mention it at first. He wasn't sure, but it seemed there was more than what was on the surface.

"Guys," he said, "I think there's another layer. Look here."

The others moved closer to him and stared at the wall where his beam highlighted a section of the wall.

The light traced over a smaller panel beneath the gods, where human figures were kneeling, their hands raised. Offerings. Tribute. The ones who survived the battle had given something to the gods.

Felicia's breath caught. "Looks like they're worshipping the gods."

Alex nodded sharply. "Yeah. And it's not just a sequence of events. It's a ritual. If we just activate the battle sequence without the offering, we get punished."

Devong exhaled, rubbing the back of his neck. "Punished?"

"To slight the gods would be to invite certain death," Tara realized. "So, a key part of this is the offering. Without it, we offend the gods and are..."

"Are what?" Felicia asked.

Tara shot her a glance that told her exactly what she meant.

Felicia swallowed hard, then looked back at the carvings. "So, what do we offer? We've already used the cup. And where do we make this second offering?"

"I don't know if it matters so much what we offer," Alex said, "but where we offer it. An offering is anything of value."

Devong glanced around the room but didn't see anything they could use. "Shame there aren't any artifacts we could offer."

"No," Tara said. "It has to be personal. That's the point of an offering. To give something that doesn't belong to you is no sacrifice."

"Well, I don't know about you three, but I didn't bring any personal valuables with me," Felicia said.

Alex set his bag down and unzipped the top. He dug into the backpack and pulled out a black climbing rope.

"Rope?" Devong said, confused.

"Tommy always says it's smart to carry rope because you never know when you'll need it."

"And you think that will work as an offering?"

Alex shrugged. "It's worth a try."

Alex held the coil of rope in his hands, feeling its familiar weight, the rough texture against his fingers. It wasn't ancient, it wasn't sacred, but it was something real—something useful. To Tommy, it was an important tool he carried everywhere in the field. Sean had teased him about it for years, though it had saved their hides more than once.

Tara's eyes swept across the carvings again, zeroing in on the last panel, the one depicting the kneeling figure making an offering. She leaned in, pressing her palm against the stone, feeling for an imperfection, a hidden mechanism—something.

Alex stepped beside her, angling his flashlight to cast light across the relief. The grooves of the ancient engraving were deep, the figure's hands raised in supplication. But there, just beneath the outstretched palms, was a faint depression in the stone.

Tara exhaled. "This has to be it."

Without hesitation, she pressed her fingers into the indent and pushed.

A deep, mechanical click echoed through the chamber, sending a vibration up her arm. Then a slow, grinding sound rumbled beneath them. Dust cascaded from the ceiling as the floor before the mural shifted, stone scraping against stone.

Devong stepped back as a small square altar began to rise from the floor, its surface smooth except for a single carved symbol at the center—the same kneeling figure from the mural. The stone edges trembled as it locked into place, the sound reminiscent of a heavy tomb sealing shut.

Felicia let out a nervous breath. "Wow."

Alex tightened his grip on the rope, staring at the platform. "Looks like we found the offering plate."

He moved toward it, hesitating for a moment. From the look on his face, the others could sense Alex was wondering if he'd chosen the right thing to offer—not that they had a ton of options.

A few more seconds passed, heavy with doubt. Then Alex took a step forward and set the rope gently onto the altar.

At first, nothing happened.

The chamber fell into a tense, expectant silence, the air thick with something unseen, something watching.

Then the ground beneath them shuddered.

A low groan of stone on stone echoed from above, the ancient statues looming overhead, creaking as they shifted—not forward this time but backward. Their poised weapons, once angled for the killing blow, lowered slightly, their rigid forms relaxing by mere inches.

Felicia held her breath before saying, "Did it work?"

Alex swallowed, stepping back beside her, his muscles still tensed for something to go wrong. "I think so. But that's only the first step."

Tara exhaled, glancing at the offering plate one last time. The rope remained untouched, sitting there as if it had always belonged.

A sharp crack split the silence.

Tara's eyes snapped up. The statue of Durga had shifted forward slightly, only inches, but enough to make her pulse jump.

"Wait," she said, voice tight. "Something's still—"

A sudden jolt rocked the floor, sending a deep rumbling tremor through the stone beneath their feet. The offering plate vibrated, the rope shifting slightly. A sound, like a massive chain being pulled taut, filled the chamber.

Then, just as quickly, it stopped. The statues stood still again, unmoving.

Devong took a cautious step back, hands raised. "Did we just trigger another—"

Tara shook her head quickly. "No, no. It's still the sequence. The offering was just one part of it."

Alex wiped a hand over his face. Even down here in the cool air, he felt his body radiating heat from stress. "Now let's see if we can get this sequence right."

Tara turned toward the first engraved symbol on the wall, the depiction of Durga, the warrior goddess.

"Okay," she said. "The moment of truth."

Her hand hovered over the carving. One push, and they'd know if they had passed the test—or if they had just assured their own deaths.

The chamber seemed to hold its breath as Tara's fingers pressed against Durga's symbol. A deep, low click sounded, reverberating through the stone walls.

The statues remained still.

Felicia exhaled. "That's a good sign, right?"

No one answered. Tara stepped to the next figure, Krishna, the divine strategist. She pressed the symbol.

Another click.

The chamber remained silent, unmoving.

Alex exchanged a glance with Tara and moved toward the Dagda's carving, his heart pounding. He placed his hand over the ancient stone, pressing down.

Click. Again, the statues didn't move.

Devong watched intently, unable to move.

Tara turned her gaze back to the final step in the sequence—the image of the kneeling figure, hands lifted toward the gods in tribute. The offering symbol.

"This is the last one," she said. Everyone watched in rapt attention as she pressed the final piece.

For a moment, nothing happened.

Then a deep, resonant rumble filled the chamber, vibrating through the very rock around them. The statues shifted backward even farther, their weapons now fully lowered, as if the gods themselves had decided to spare them.

But just as relief threatened to settle over them, another sound cut through the chamber—a sharp, mechanical snap. The floor trembled beneath them, and a fine line cracked through the center of the chamber, running directly beneath the altar.

Felicia gasped. "That's not good."

Alex pulled Tara back just as the crack widened, splitting like a fault line, dust kicking up around them. A low, distant clank of gears locking into place echoed from deep below the chamber. It wasn't over.

"What is happening?" Devong wondered, backing away. His flashlight swept over the walls, searching for another trigger, another sign of what was coming next.

Tara stared at the altar, at the rope still lying in place. The offering had been accepted, the sequence completed—but what if there was another part? What if there was something they had missed?

Another loud snap.

Then, with a grinding shift, the far wall began to move.

No one could take their eyes off it. They stood paralyzed as the heavy stone continued to shift.

A hidden panel slid open, revealing a darkened alcove beyond. A raised stone pedestal stood just inside, covered in centuries of dust. But it wasn't the pedestal itself that caught their attention.

It was the golden chest resting atop it.

Devong's eyes widened. "What is that?"

Tara wiped her hands on her pants. "Hopefully, what we've been looking for."

Alex approached first, his flashlight beam playing across the intricate etchings that covered the box. Celtic spirals intertwined with Hindu yantras, the metal surface worn but still gleaming beneath the grime of time. The symbols weren't just decoration.

They were seals.

Felicia stepped beside him. "It's locked," she realized.

Alex hesitated. Everything about this room, this sequence, had been a test.

Tara glanced at him. "Well? Are we opening it?"

Alex shook his head. "Not yet. We need to be sure it's safe first."

The ground beneath them felt too still. The tension in the air hadn't lifted. And beyond that silence, in the dark corridors behind them, the men who'd been following them could be pressing toward their position with every passing second.

Alex approached the chest, his flashlight beam playing across the intricate etchings that covered the box.

"So does this mean we can still die here?" Devong asked. "Because I would really like any threat of demise to be gone now."

Felicia shot him a look. "No kidding."

Alex studied the carvings once more, looking for anything they might have missed. They had made it this far, but if this chamber had tested them, then there was a good chance this chest was the final possible trap.

Alex moved over to the chest shrouded in the shadows of the corridor beyond. "We should take a closer look at the pedestal. If we missed something, opening that chest might set off another trap."

Tara agreed with a nod and joined him by his side.

The golden chest gleamed before them, waiting, as if begging them to open it.

The shiny box gleamed in the dim beams of their flashlights. Alex inhaled deeply, steadying his nerves. He wondered what was inside, what could have possibly warranted such an elaborate set of traps and passageways meant to keep people away from it.

Tara moved first, kneeling beside the pedestal and sweeping her hands along its base.

Alex followed suit, his fingers tracing the carved stone, searching for anything that might suggest another hidden trap.

Tara's fingers paused over a faint line running around the pedestal's edge. "There's a seam here. This isn't just a solid block. It moves."

Alex leaned in, his light following the barely perceptible outline. "A hidden compartment?"

Devong frowned. "Or another bad surprise?"

Tara exhaled, pulling a multitool from Alex's pack. "Only one way to find out."

She worked the tool's thin edge into the seam, prying gently. The stone resisted at first, centuries of dust and grime holding it in place. Then, with a low click, the panel slid open, revealing a shallow cavity beneath the chest.

Inside lay a thin stone tablet covered in ancient inscriptions.

Alex carefully lifted it out, brushing away the fine layer of dust clinging to its surface. The carvings were a mix of Sanskrit and Ogham, the ancient Celtic script. "This is the connection," he murmured. "The missing link between the two cultures."

Felicia leaned over his shoulder; brows furrowed. "Fascinating."

"Some of these symbols match what we saw before." He ran his finger over a set of markings at the bottom.

Tara removed the phone from her pocket and snapped a quick picture of the tablet.

Alex's mind worked fast, cataloging the symbols. "We'll have to decode it later. But whatever it means... it must point to what comes next."

Felicia's voice was tight. "Then we need to take it with us."

Alex shook his head. "I don't know if we should move it. Taking it might—"

"Set off another trap?" she interrupted. "I'm really getting tired of this theme."

Devong cleared his throat. "Me too."

"Well, we don't have time to debate it," Alex said. "Going to have to use a little faith for this one."

Everyone watched as Alex placed his hands on the golden lid, its cool surface humming with untold history. With a slow, measured breath, he lifted it.

A soft hiss of air escaped as the seal broke, releasing a musty scent that curled through the chamber. The interior was lined with faded black silk, the fabric frayed and discolored with age. Nestled within, partially obscured by folds of the deteriorating cloth, lay two stone heads.

Felicia took an involuntary step back. "More heads?"

The busts were eerily similar to the ones they had encountered before—rough-hewn but expressive, their features frozen in unknowable expressions. Their eyes, hollow and deep, seemed to watch them.

Tara hesitated before reaching in, her fingers brushing against the rough surface. "Four heads now. Strange."

"Yeah," Alex agreed. "But why?"

No one had an answer. The stone heads, while mysterious, didn't appear to have any innate value; the way gold or jewels would have. Their historical value couldn't be tagged with a price. The real question was, why did these busts have such importance to the ancient people who hid them?

As Alex carefully lifted one of the heads, he noticed something underneath it.

The four leaned in, studying the inscriptions. "It looks like a small map."

Devong pointed to a section of the map. "Do you recognize it? Seems an awful lot like an overhead view of—"

"Australia?" Felicia guessed.

"Yeah. It does," Tara agreed.

Alex set the first head down on the floor next to him, then removed the second. Instead of a map, this head revealed a short bit of text written in Sanskrit.

"Professors?" Tara asked, looking at Devong and Felicia. "You know how to read that?"

Both nodded.

"It's Sanskrit," Felicia confirmed.

"Where ancients called upon the Dreaming," Devong read. "Seek the keepers beneath the mark of fire and water."

Tara's brows knit together. "Fire and water?"

"Australia is the land of extremes," Alex said. "But to think whoever did all this could have created an accurate, overhead view of a continent nowhere close to this civilization is... remarkable."

"We'll have to figure out the clue later," Tara said, realizing again that time was not on their side. "We need to get out of here."

Alex stowed the two heads into his backpack then zipped it shut.

Alex exhaled and adjusted the straps of his pack, glancing at each of his companions. The weight of the stone heads and the ancient parchment inside his bag felt heavier than it should have. He turned his flashlight toward the chamber walls, where intricate carvings of gods, warriors, and celestial beings loomed over them. "Now," he said, his voice steady, "let's find a way out of here."

Tara swept her light along the chamber's perimeter. "So the question is, how?"

"Would be nice if there were just a few easy solutions, wouldn't it?" Devong asked.

"Yeah," she said with a grin. "And we can't risk going back that way. I know you trust your friend the guard back in the fort, but we have to assume they got by him somehow."

Devong sighed and ran a hand through his hair. "So we have to find a hidden corridor that's been hidden for centuries with no way of knowing where it leads."

"Pretty much," Alex confirmed.

Felicia moved toward the alcove, running her fingers over the carvings on the nearest wall. Alex stepped closer, shining his light on a specific figure.

"Vayu," Devong muttered. "A god associated with movement, travel, and pathways. If any of these deities would be guarding an exit, it's him."

"I guess that means we take the foreboding passage," Felicia resigned.

Felicia pressed her palm against the weathered stone, but nothing happened. She frowned. "If it's a trigger, it might not be just a touch mechanism. Maybe there's something else to it."

Alex examined the edges of the carving, his fingers running along the grooves. "Look here," he said, pointing to a series of tiny holes drilled into the relief. "They form a pattern, almost like a constellation."

Devong frowned. "Could be decorative."

"Or it could be a code," Alex countered. He turned to Tara. "See if there's anything in the journal about Vayu. Maybe there's something we're missing."

Tara pulled out her notebook, flipping through pages of research they had compiled from previous findings. "Vayu is often depicted as carrying the banner of Indra," she said after a moment. "He's associated with storms, breath, and—wait." She looked up. "He's also known as the opener of pathways."

Alex turned back to the relief, inspecting the small circular indent near Vayu's left hand. "This might be what we're looking for. What if —" He pinched the outer edge of the indention and twisted it to the left.

Then the entire wall shuddered.

Dust cascaded from the ceiling as the stone relief retracted slightly, revealing a narrow passageway descending beneath the chamber. A stale gust of air surged outward, carrying the scent of ancient earth and something damp, untouched for centuries.

Devong took a cautious step back. "I was really hoping for a regular door."

Tara peered into the darkness below. "Looks like we're going down."

Felicia turned to Alex. "What if it closes behind us?"

"I was thinking we need it closed."

"What?"

"If we can block it off, that might slow those guys down long enough for us to get away."

"And possibly trap us down here forever," Devong said. "But hey, we've come this far." He tried to sound carefree, but the nervous tremor in his voice betrayed his true feelings.

Tara led the way, climbing down into the new tunnel. One by one, Felicia and Devong followed into the passage beneath the chamber with Alex bringing up the rear.

The stone steps were uneven, worn smooth in places, treacherous in others. Their lights illuminated a long, winding tunnel reinforced with ancient beams, some crumbling with age.

"Now, how to seal this off," Alex said, partly to himself.

Tara looked around and spotted something near the edge of the entrance. A pair of column supports held up a section of the passage. "If we break these," she said, tapping one, "it might cause a collapse."

Devong hesitated. "We don't know how much will come down. If this whole tunnel caves in, we could be buried too."

Alex stepped forward, inspecting the structure. "We don't have to break all of them. Just enough to make it impassable."

"Or maybe we just push that," Felicia said, pointing at a symbol on the support to the left. Her headlamp illuminated the raised Celtic emblem.

"You sure about that?" Devong wondered.

"No," Tara said. "But it's worth a shot." She pushed on the symbol without waiting for further discussion.

A deep rumble echoed through the passage as part of the entranceway collapsed, sealing the tunnel behind them with a cascade of rock and debris.

Dust filled the air, making them cough as they pulled up their collars to cover their mouths. When the dust settled, they saw a heavy stone slab had filled the space above them, covering their tracks.

"That should buy us some time."

Tara nodded, brushing dust from her jacket. "Let's keep moving before we find out if that was enough."

Alex took the lead, guiding them deeper into the unknown passage, their lights flickering against the walls. The air was thick with silence, broken only by their footsteps and the distant echo of settling stone.

They had made it out of the chamber.

But they had no idea where this tunnel would lead.

27

R olf stepped cautiously into the chamber, his breath slow and measured, scanning the space with an intense gaze. The air was thick with the lingering scent of dust and something ancient—something recently disturbed. His men followed, weapons drawn, their boots tapping silently on the hard stone floor.

Yuri was the first to speak. "Where did they go?"

Rolf didn't acknowledge the obvious. Instead, his eyes flicked to the alcove at the far side of the room. His men were already moving toward it, inspecting the gold chest as they approached.

One of them crouched beside the rubble, running his hands along the uneven edges.

"They've been here," Rolf said.

"And where are they?" Yuri asked, stepping beside him.

Rolf exhaled sharply, irritation tightening his jaw. They had slipped through his fingers. Again. His gaze swept over the chamber, searching for any indication of what had drawn the Americans here in the first place. The walls were lined with intricate carvings, depictions of battles and gods, a tapestry of history carved in stone. But what had they been looking for?

"Search the room," Rolf ordered, stepping forward. "They came here for something specific. Let's find out what."

His men fanned out, their flashlights flickering over the ancient reliefs and along the floor. Dust swirled in their beams, disturbed by their movements. The golden chest gleamed under the harsh lights, an ominous presence in the otherwise dark chamber.

Rolf moved over to it and peered inside, shining his light against the yellow metal. A message written in a language he didn't recognize was inscribed on the bottom, along with what appeared to be a map of Australia, if he didn't miss his guess. But other than that, the chest was empty.

"Another clue?" Yuri asked, his voice hushed with a mixture of frustration and intrigue.

Rolf exhaled sharply, nodding. "Most likely."

Yuri stepped closer to Rolf, lowering his voice. "They wouldn't have risked coming here unless it was important. Whatever they found, it had to be valuable."

Rolf nodded slightly, his eyes narrowing as he considered the possibilities. "They wouldn't have left empty-handed either. They found what we're looking for in that chest. And they must have discovered a secret way out of here."

A call from across the chamber pulled their attention. "Over here!" One of the men, Sergei, was crouched near a section of the wall, his fingers tracing the edge of a carving. "This area looks like it was disturbed recently."

Rolf and Yuri crossed the room, their footfalls echoing in the confined space. Sergei gestured to the engraving—a section of the stone had been wiped clean, free of the thick dust that covered everything else in the chamber. It was subtle, but clear to those who knew what to look for. Someone had been here, inspecting this very spot.

"They were studying this," Yuri murmured, running a gloved hand over the stonework. "It means something."

Rolf inspected the relief carefully. The carving depicted a god—one Rolf didn't recognize, his form surrounded by swirling lines of wind and movement. Beneath the figure, a small circular indentation was carved into the wall, subtle but distinct.

Yuri turned to Rolf. "Think this was the key to something?"

Rolf's jaw tightened. "Possibly. But if it was, they already figured it out. We're too late."

A moment of silence stretched between them, the only sound the shuffling of boots as the rest of the team continued to search the chamber. Finally, Yuri exhaled. "What do you want to do?"

Rolf turned away from the relief, scanning the chamber one last time before fixing his gaze on the golden chest sitting atop the pedestal. This was all that remained.

"We need to get back topside," he said, voice cool and commanding. "If they're trying to leave the country, we have to cut them off before they can disappear. We have the resources to make sure they don't escape."

Yuri nodded, stepping back as if to signal the others that the search was over. But Rolf remained where he was, his eyes lingering on the golden chest. It gleamed in the dim light, an unanswered question left behind.

Rolf's fingers flexed at his sides. Whatever had been inside was important. The Americans hadn't stayed long enough to retrieve it. They had taken something else—but this? This was still here.

He turned his head slightly, his decision made. "Bring the chest. Get everything you can."

Yuri hesitated. "You think it's safe?"

Rolf's eyes flicked toward him, sharp as steel. "We can't leave it here."

Yuri nodded to two of the other men, who moved toward the chest hesitantly, glancing at Rolf before reaching for the golden box. The metal was cool beneath their fingers. The men looked uncertain but weren't about to disobey an order based on paranoia.

They gripped the edge of the chest and, with a sharp breath, lifted the chest.

Rolf's lips pressed into a thin line. He was always decisive; this instance was no different. If they lingered here in this chamber, the

Americans could get away. "Head back to the fortress, men. We need to cut them off before they can escape."

Anton and Petrov stepped forward, grumbling as they each took hold of the heavy golden chest, hoisting it up from its pedestal.

The moment the weight lifted, the chamber came alive.

A deep grinding noise shook the walls, sending vibrations up through the stone floor. The golden pedestal sank suddenly, vanishing into the ground as if the floor itself had swallowed it whole. Dust spilled from the ceiling, and the walls began to shift.

Yuri barely had time to react before the first stone slab fell from above, crashing down with a deafening boom, narrowly missing Sergei.

"Trap!" someone shouted.

The walls began to move inward with a slow but ominous groan, like the fortress itself was breathing, drawing them into its lungs before crushing them entirely. The air was thick with panic, the heavy clanking of ancient mechanisms clicking into place as jagged stone spikes shot up from the floor, narrowly missing Anton's legs.

"Drop it!" Yuri roared, but it was too late.

A section of the ceiling collapsed, sending a cascade of debris plummeting down. Anton, still gripping the chest, was crushed instantly, his scream cut off before it could even properly escape his throat. His body disappeared beneath a slab of ancient stone, blood pooling out from underneath.

Petrov stumbled backward, horror on his face, but there was no time to mourn. Another massive stone pillar swung down from the ceiling, striking him across the torso and hurling him violently into the wall with a sickening crack. His lifeless body slumped to the ground, limp and broken.

Sergei turned, scrambling toward the exit—but the entrance was closing.

The once-open doorway was shrinking, a thick stone sliding into place as if sealing the tomb forever. The remaining men raced toward the exit, but another section of the chamber's ceiling gave way, crushing Sergei under its immense weight.

Rolf shoved Yuri forward, his teeth bared in frustration. "Move! It's closing!"

The last two remaining men sprinted ahead, one of them diving just as the final stone slab slammed down, sealing the entrance permanently.

Yuri barely made it through, rolling onto his side, coughing as dust filled his lungs. Rolf was the last to clear the threshold, his boots skidding against the floor as the chamber behind him was swallowed into eternal darkness.

Silence.

Yuri lay on the ground, staring at the now completely sealed-off entrance, his chest rising and falling rapidly. "They're gone," he muttered, disbelief laced in his voice.

Rolf stood over him, hands on his hips, his face impassive despite the loss of nearly half his team.

He turned, eyes burning with renewed determination. "Keep moving. We have to get back to the surface."

Without another word, Rolf turned toward the darkened passage leading back to the surface, leaving the buried dead behind him.

28

The narrow, hidden passage wrapped around the four like an unwanted hug. It stretched ahead, a dark vein running through the belly of the plateau, its air thick with the scent of damp stone and centuries of stillness. Each step sent tiny echoes bouncing off the walls, swallowed by the blackness that loomed ahead. The passage wasn't just narrow, it felt as if it had been constructed in more of a hurry than the rest they'd ventured through. Unlike the spectacular corridors in the fortress, this path was purely utilitarian.

"Do you think this might have been used as an escape tunnel for government officials or important people centuries ago?" Felicia asked. From the tone of her voice, it sounded as if she were trying to start up a conversation to settle her nerves.

"Not unless they wanted to get through that whole death trap from before," Devong answered.

"Of course, that could have been built that way for two purposes," Tara theorized. "Both as a secret escape and a hiding place. Maybe the original inhabitants knew if they had to flee, they'd need to take those stone heads with them."

Alex shrugged his shoulders. The busts in his backpack weren't that heavy, but the mere act of carrying them seemed to weigh him down, as if gravity was working overtime.

He kept moving, his flashlight cutting through the gloom, the beam flickering as if the tunnel itself resisted being illuminated. Shadowy fingers stretched along the walls, as if pointing the way out. Or were they grasping at them?

Behind him, Tara followed, scanning the rock as she trudged ahead. Felicia and Devong brought up the rear, their movements tense and watchful, as though they expected the walls to close in at any moment.

Alex knew that wasn't going to happen. At least, he assumed it wouldn't. There didn't appear to be any traps or mechanisms that might cause something so extreme to happen. Then again, anything was possible.

"I wonder where that draft is coming from," Felicia muttered, dragging a hand across the rough wall. "The air's moving, but I can't tell from where."

"Let's hope it means there's an exit somewhere ahead," Alex said, not slowing his pace.

Devong sighed, shifting the weight of his pack. "I hate places like this. Feels like we're mice walking through a maze."

Tara flicked her light upward, revealing a ceiling that arched slightly overhead, the rock scarred by ancient tools. "Whoever built this put in a lot of effort."

They pressed forward, the tunnel sloping downward with a slow, insidious gradient. The air grew cooler still, the dampness now clinging to their skin. Dust swirled in their beams, disturbed by their movement after lying untouched for who knew how long.

Alex paused at a bend and held up a hand. "Look at this." The backpack he wore suddenly felt heavier again, and he didn't understand why.

Tara stepped closer, aiming her light where his fingers hovered over deep gouges in the stone. Long, curved scrapes, like something had tried to claw its way through.

Felicia's jaw tightened. "Those aren't tool marks."

Devong bent closer, tracing one of the gouges with his fingertips. "Whatever made these wasn't human."

A silence stretched between them, thick and unspoken.

"We don't have time to wonder about it," Alex finally said, voice firm. "We need to keep moving."

The tunnel narrowed, forcing them again into single file. The walls pressed in, close enough that their shoulders occasionally scraped against the rough rock.

"This better not be a maze," Devong muttered, his voice lower now, as if speaking too loudly might disturb whatever secrets the place held.

"If it is, we don't have breadcrumbs," Tara said, adjusting her grip on her light. "Just hope we're not rats in someone's experiment."

The passage took another sharp turn, and suddenly the ground dropped away.

Alex halted inches from the edge, his light spilling into a vast chasm where the floor had collapsed. He nudged a loose stone over the edge, and they all listened. It never landed.

"That's not encouraging," Felicia murmured.

Across the gap, a narrow stone bridge stretched to the other side, barely wide enough for a single person at a time. Time had not been kind to it—chunks were missing, leaving jagged gaps that threatened to make the crossing a death sentence.

Tara studied the structure. "That thing looks like it's held together by bad decisions and optimism."

"No choice," Alex said. "We go one at a time. I'll go first."

Without waiting for a response, he stepped onto the bridge, his heartbeat thrumming in his ears. The stone groaned beneath his weight, a dry, brittle sound that sent tension coiling in his spine. He moved carefully, one step at a time, arms slightly outstretched for balance.

Halfway across, the bridge shuddered.

"Alex!" Tara snapped. "Move!"

He didn't hesitate, pushing forward with controlled speed. The moment his boots hit the solid ground on the other side, he turned. "Okay, Dr. Lowe, you're next."

She nodded, inhaled, and stepped forward. Every shift of her weight made the bridge tremble, the sound of cracking stone echoing below. She made it across in a few quick steps, exhaling sharply as she landed beside Alex.

"Tara, go!"

She took one last glance at the abyss below then stepped onto the bridge. Halfway across, she felt the slight give beneath her boot.

She leaped forward, barely making it to solid ground as a chunk of stone crumbled away, disappearing into nothingness. "Sean would not like that part," she said.

"Definitely not," Alex agreed. Then he turned to their Indian friend. "Devong, your turn."

Devong hesitated for a few seconds before stepping forward. "Why do I feel like the universe is about to make an example out of me?"

He made it halfway when the bridge shifted violently.

"Go!" Alex snapped.

Devong sprinted the last few steps as the bridge collapsed behind him, slamming onto solid ground just as the remaining pieces tumbled into the abyss.

For a long moment, no one spoke. Just the sound of their breathing filled the tunnel.

Alex nodded grimly. "Okay. Good job. Let's keep going forward."

They turned as one and pressed on, deeper into the unknown, toward whatever waited at the end of this tunnel.

The passage stretched ahead, its narrow walls seemingly tightening around them as they ventured deeper. The air carried the ancient scent of long-settled dust mingled with the coolness of stone untouched by sunlight. It carried an odd, metallic tinge, like the air inside an old, sealed crypt. That tinge had been with them since they began exploring the restricted area. Their footfalls echoed softly, the sound absorbed by the dense rock, making the space feel eerily silent apart from the occasional drip of water in the distance.

Alex led the way, his flashlight beam slicing through the darkness, revealing the stone walls that bore faint carvings worn smooth by time. Tara followed closely behind, her eyes scanning the passage for any sign of traps or hidden mechanisms. Felicia and Devong again brought up the rear, their movements careful, the tension between them palpable.

Felicia's voice was barely above a whisper. "I feel like we've been walking in circles."

Alex shook his head. "We're making progress. The incline's changing. We're moving upward."

Devong exhaled sharply. "Yeah? Because it all looks the same to me."

"It might look the same, but something's different," Tara added, running her fingers along the stone. "This rock isn't as rough as before. It's been shaped, smoothed in places."

Alex paused, stepping back to study the markings they had all walked past. The carvings, though eroded, bore hints of symbols they had seen in the previous chamber—ancient language intertwined with pictographs depicting figures moving through what looked like another tunnel.

"It's a path," Tara murmured. "And it's leading somewhere."

Felicia frowned. "Let's hope it's not leading us into a tomb."

They pressed forward, their movements more hurried now, knowing they were following something intentional. The passage narrowed again, forcing them to move in single file for a third time. The weight of the space bore down on them, as if the tunnel itself were reluctant to let them pass.

Then Alex stopped so suddenly that Tara almost bumped into him.

"What?" she asked.

"Dead end," he muttered.

They all gathered around, staring at the smooth, unbroken wall of stone that loomed ahead. Unlike the walls they had been walking through, this one bore no cracks, no openings, no signs of weakness.

Devong ran a hand through his hair, exhaling sharply. "So, what now?"

Tara shook her head. "There's got to be something here. A mechanism, a switch—something."

Felicia stepped closer, running her fingers along the stone. "If this was built as an escape tunnel for rulers who lived here, it wouldn't just be a dead end."

"Look around for something that's out of place. For a tense minute, they searched, running their hands over the stone, tapping lightly in different areas, listening for anything hollow or unusual. Their lights flickered against the walls, revealing more faded markings but nothing that immediately stood out.

Then Devong spoke up. "Wait. Look at this."

They turned toward him as he pointed at a section of the wall. Unlike the rest of the smooth stone, this section had an indentation, almost like a panel had been carved separately from the rest.

Felicia crouched, tracing the edge of the indentation. "It's a seam. This part of the wall moves."

Alex stepped forward, pressing against it, but it didn't budge. "We need a release. Something's locking it in place."

Tara swept her light over the opposite wall, her eyes narrowing. "If there's a door, there has to be a way to open it."

She followed the carvings upward until she saw something different. Near the ceiling, almost hidden in the shadows, was a lever, its handle protruding slightly from the rock.

"There," she pointed. "That has to be it."

Alex exhaled. "Of course. Put it out of easy reach. Smart."

Devong grumbled. "Smart for them, bad for us. How do we reach it?"

Tara looked around then pointed at a section of the wall that jutted out slightly. "If I get a boost, I can reach it."

Alex nodded, motioning for Devong to help him.

They cupped their hands, and Tara stepped into them, bracing herself as they lifted her up. She reached for the lever, stretching as far as she could, her fingers brushing the cold metal. Just a little more.

With a grunt, she grasped it and pulled.

At first, nothing happened. Then a deep grinding sound rumbled through the tunnel, shaking loose dust from the ceiling. The indentation in the wall shuddered, then slowly began to slide open.

A gust of cool air rushed past them, carrying the scent of open space.

Tara dropped back down, stumbling slightly as she landed. "We did it."

Devong turned toward the now-revealed exit, a dark passage beyond it. "Hope this doesn't lead to something worse."

Alex didn't hesitate. "Let's move. We're not staying here."

One by one, they slipped through the narrow opening, their shoulders brushing the rough stone as they emerged into predawn light.

The sight before them was almost surreal—the ruins of abandoned buildings, crumbling in the shadow of the plateau, stretching out toward the horizon where the first hints of morning crept through the sky.

"We're outside," Felicia realized.

Tara turned, scanning for any sign of movement. She didn't see any threat.

Alex checked his phone—no signal. "We need to get back into town." He looked at Devong. "Can we go to your place, just until we figure out what that clue means from the bottom of the chest?"

"Of course," Devong said. "I doubt those men know anything about me. And my home is thirty minutes away."

Alex's jaw tightened. "Great. Let's hope we can solve it quickly."

29

R olf pressed the radio to his lips, his voice low but firm. "Team three, do you copy?"

No answer.

Rolf hurried forward, taking point. His flashlight beam sprayed wildly across the corridor in front of him as he moved quickly ahead at a near run. "Team three, come in. Do you copy?"

Still nothing.

Even deep within the foundation of the fortress, he was surprised the signal didn't reach the two men he'd left guarding the entrance to the blocked corridor.

"You don't think something happened to them," Yuri asked, keeping close behind his commander. For now, it seemed the tension between the two of them had melted, and both were focused on getting back topside and cutting off their quarry before they could escape.

"No," Rolf said, his breath quick. "It's just all this rock, and who knows what else."

They rounded a sharp turn in the passage, then saw the end of the tunnel up ahead where the stairs led up to the domed chamber.

"Team three, do you copy?" he said again.

The radio crackled in his ear, then he heard a voice. "We copy, Commander." Javier's voice wasn't clear. It was hindered by static, but it was better than nothing. "What's your status?"

"We're making our way back to your location. We lost the target. Get back to their hotel and wait there. If they return, apprehend them. Understood? Over."

"Copy that, sir. We'll handle it."

"Once we're back outside, I'll call you and let you know our next move."

"Understood, sir."

"Team one out."

Rolf reached the stairs and climbed them in a flash, reemerging into the circular room they'd discovered earlier.

Static crackled before one of the guards answered. "Understood. What if they don't come back?"

Rolf exhaled through his nose, irritation flaring. "Then you'll have wasted your time. But I don't like guessing. Move now."

They strode forward through the dim corridors of the fortress. The stone walls still seemed to press in around them, each flicker of their flashlights casting jagged shadows. Their footsteps echoed, a rhythmic drumbeat of urgency against the cold floor.

Yuri walked at his side, eyes flicking toward Rolf. "You don't think they'll actually go back to the hotel, do you?"

"No," Rolf admitted. "But I don't leave doors open behind me. If there's even the smallest chance they're stupid enough to return, I want eyes there."

They turned a corner and spotted a form on the ground in their light beams.

The guard they had killed earlier lay slumped against the wall, half-hidden in the shadows where they had stashed him. His unseeing eyes stared at the ceiling; his radio still clipped to his belt.

Rolf's jaw tightened. The Americans had a head start, and he had no doubt they were using every second to put as much distance between themselves and this place as possible. The real question was —where were they going?

"Call the pilot. Tell him to be ready. If they're trying to get out of the country, I want wheels up before them."

Yuri nodded and lifted his radio. "I'll tell him. But he'll need a flight plan. He can't just take off."

"Make the preparations," Rolf said. "Do what you can. I'll handle the rest."

The team pressed forward, navigating the winding halls of the fortress with practiced efficiency. They emerged from the corridors and into the courtyard, the air thick and unmoving. Above them, the clear afternoon sky allowed sunlight to shower down on the city.

"Give me something," Rolf muttered.

He pushed forward, his boots striking the stone with quick, measured steps.

The sunlight was jarring compared to the darkness they'd been in before. Tourists meandered through the ancient halls, pausing to admire the carvings on the weathered stone walls or snap pictures of the intricate reliefs. Vendors had begun setting up their stalls along the interior paths, their tables overflowing with colorful textiles, brass ornaments, and hand-carved wooden figures.

Rolf didn't slow. He walked with purpose, Yuri close by his side, their strides quick but controlled. They needed to move fast but not draw attention. The trick was to blend in, even in a place where they clearly didn't belong.

As they weaved through the flow of visitors, a tour guide in a beige uniform stood near a towering archway, gesturing toward a frieze above them. "This depicts the great battle of the gods and demons," he explained, his voice carrying over the murmur of the crowd. "You can see how the warriors—"

Rolf brushed past him, ignoring the intrigued expressions of the tourists gathered around. A few heads turned as the group moved swiftly through the corridor, but no one paid them more than a passing glance.

They reached a narrow stone passage lined with alcoves filled with weathered statues of deities, their faces worn smooth by centuries of wind and sand. A young woman in a flowing red dress posed beside one of them as her friend snapped a photo. Rolf veered to the right, barely avoiding them as he pressed forward.

A child darted into their path suddenly, chasing a small blue ball that bounced off the stone floor. Rolf sidestepped sharply, nearly colliding with Yuri, who grunted but kept moving. The child's mother, a woman in a wide-brimmed straw hat, called out a warning in a language Rolf didn't recognize. He didn't bother looking back.

Ahead, they passed a small temple courtyard, the scent of incense thick in the air. A group of monks in saffron robes stood near the entrance, murmuring a morning prayer as they arranged offerings on a low stone altar. The rhythmic chime of bells echoed faintly, mingling with the distant chatter of visitors.

Rolf's pace remained steady; his focus sharp. The corridors widened as they neared the main thoroughfare, where even more vendors had set up shop. Stalls displayed intricately patterned rugs, silver jewelry glinting in the sunlight, and rows of small clay figurines, their expressions frozen in time. The smell of spiced tea and grilled meat drifted through the air, mingling with the distinct, pervasive mustiness of ancient stone.

A vendor stepped forward, holding out a string of beaded necklaces. "Special price for you, my friend!" he called, his grin wide and practiced. Rolf ignored him, pushing past a group of tourists flipping through a guidebook.

The crowd thickened as they neared the fortress' main gate. A family with matching sun hats stood in the middle of the walkway, staring up at the towering stone walls. One of the children, a boy no older than eight, caught sight of Rolf's group and tugged on his father's sleeve. Rolf averted his gaze and maneuvered around them.

A moment later, a man with a large camera slung around his neck stepped directly into their path, adjusting his lens as he focused on a distant carving. Yuri barely avoided knocking into him, his expression twisting with irritation as he clenched his fists. Rolf gave him a subtle look—stay focused.

They turned a final corner, and the fortress' grand entrance loomed ahead. Two uniformed guards stood near the exit, engaged in conversation, their weapons holstered lazily at their sides. Beyond them, the city stretched out in a maze of sandstone buildings and narrow alleyways.

Rolf took a steady breath. They were almost there.

The guards near the entrance were still engaged in conversation, barely paying attention to the flow of people moving in and out. He didn't break stride, didn't make eye contact—just another traveler leaving the historic site as they continued through the gates and back out into the courtyard. From there, the two men kept moving, hurrying down the path toward the main part of town.

The moment they stepped beyond the fortress walls, the heat hit them in full force. The noise of the fortress faded into the background, replaced by the hum of morning traffic, the chatter of merchants, and the distant blaring of a car horn.

Rolf kept the pace fast but deliberate, leading the way into the crowded streets of the old city. The sidewalk was narrow, forcing them to weave between slow-moving pedestrians, their shoulders brushing against tourists clutching bags of souvenirs and locals going about their daily routines. The scent of spices and fried food hung thick in the air, mixing with the acrid fumes of motorbikes maneuvering through the clogged roads.

A street vendor shouted nearby, waving a tray of fresh fruit toward a group of European travelers. Another stall sold woven rugs, the patterns bold and intricate, unfurled like banners along the side of the walkway. A shopkeeper haggled loudly with a customer, his voice rising in frustration. Rolf barely noticed. His focus was on moving fast—without drawing attention.

A rickshaw driver attempted to cut across their path, gesturing wildly for passengers, but Rolf sidestepped effortlessly, cutting into a narrow side alley. The alley provided a brief reprieve from the congested streets, the noise muffled by the high stone walls on either side. A stray dog lay curled in the shade, barely lifting its head as they passed.

Neither man said a word as they pushed ahead, a sense of urgency permeating through them all.

Emerging from the alley, they reentered the main thoroughfare, where the modern city loomed beyond the historic district. Buildings grew taller, the streets wider. The closer they got to the hotel, the denser the traffic became, tuk-tuks and motorcycles weaving through gaps in moving cars, the occasional truck honking as it lumbered forward.

They kept their strides long, purposeful, ignoring the curious glances from a few onlookers. Tourists tended to walk at a leisurely pace, soaking in their surroundings.

As they neared the hotel, Rolf scanned ahead, catching sight of Javier and his partner across the street. The two men were positioned casually near a small roadside café, one seated on a low stool, pretending to drink from a coffee cup, the other leaning against a metal post, eyes scanning the entrance of the hotel.

Javier spotted them as they approached, but merely issued a nod —a subtle indication that he'd seen them.

As soon as Rolf reached the spot where Javier and his partner stood, he took a look around then addressed his lieutenant. "Any sign of them?"

"No, sir," Javier answered. "Just the usual tourists checking in or checking out."

Rolf nodded, his eyes still surveying the area. He knew his tech guy, Soren, would be able to access the airport's system, but would he be too late? That was doubtful. The IAA pilots had to go through the same process as his, which would take time.

They wouldn't try to hide out at the airport. Even though that might have seemed like a safe place with plenty of witnesses, there were other drawbacks to attempting to retreat to the airport. Security personnel could be bought, and at this point, Rolf assumed the Americans weren't sure who they could trust.

They'd need to go somewhere and lay low, at least for a while until their flight plan was logged. But where?

An idea popped into his head. "Who was the Indian man helping the Americans?"

"I'm not sure, sir. A local. Some guide they must have hired."

"Find out who he is," Rolf ordered.

30

Devong's house seemed like a safe place to hide out for a few hours. It sat at the edge of a quiet neighborhood, nestled among clusters of sandstone buildings that blended seamlessly with the arid landscape. The structure itself was a two-story home, built in the traditional Rajasthani style, its weathered yellow-hued stone glowing under the bright light of the sun. Ornate jharokha-style balconies projected slightly from the upper floor, their delicate lattice screens providing both shade and a touch of artistry to the façade.

A low perimeter wall, made from the same stone, enclosed a modest courtyard at the front, where a small, twisted neem tree stood sentinel, its sparse leaves rustling faintly in the desert breeze. A wooden door, reinforced with iron studs, bore the marks of age and use, flanked by narrow, arched windows with intricate carvings along their frames. Alongside the entrance, a brass bell hung from an iron hook, the kind traditionally used to announce visitors.

The flat rooftop, a staple in desert homes, featured a few earthen pots placed near the parapet, likely used to store water. A small flight of worn stone steps led to a shaded terrace on the upper level, partially enclosed by intricately carved railings.

Despite its traditional architecture, there were subtle signs of modern adaptation—a satellite dish mounted discreetly near the roof, a Jeep parked off to the side under a fabric awning, and a single security camera affixed near the entryway.

"What's with the security measures?" Alex asked as they approached the front door.

Devong fished a key out of his pocket and inserted it into the lock. He looked over his shoulder as he answered. "I have several valuable items here, both in my personal collection and for study. Not the sort of things you want to leave unwatched."

He turned the key and opened the door wide, motioning the others to enter. He glanced out across the street in both directions then followed them inside. He locked the door behind him and smiled.

"Welcome to my home," he said. "I'll make some coffee. Please, take a look around."

Stepping into Devong's house was like stepping into a living museum, where the past and present coexisted in perfect harmony. The cool air inside was a welcome relief from the relentless desert heat and carried the faint scent of aged parchment, sandalwood incense, and spiced chai that lingered in the corners of the home. The walls were built of thick sandstone, absorbing the day's warmth and slowly releasing it, giving the interior a steady, ambient temperature.

As Devong disappeared into the kitchen to make coffee, the three Americans wandered through the house, taking in the surroundings.

The living room was an eclectic mix of traditional Indian decor and scholarly clutter. Against the far wall stood a massive wooden bookshelf, its shelves lined with leather-bound tomes, stacks of handwritten notes, and thick academic journals, some open and marked with slips of paper. A worn but elegant wooden sofa, draped with a colorful patchwork Rajasthani throw, sat beside a low brass table, upon which rested a half-empty cup of chai and a small brass oil lamp, its wick smoldering faintly. The room smelled of old paper, faint spice, and sandalwood, blending into an oddly comforting aroma.

Alex moved through the room first, brushing a hand across the surface of an intricately carved wooden cabinet, its doors slightly ajar to reveal ceramic bowls, hand-painted plates, and brass artifacts. A ceiling fan turned lazily, stirring the stillness. Against another wall, a glass display case housed an assortment of ancient coins, small stone carvings, and delicate pottery shards, each carefully labeled with Devong's meticulous handwriting.

Felicia wandered toward the kitchen, peering through the wide, arched entryway as Devong worked over the stovetop, preparing their drinks. The kitchen was small but efficiently organized, its wooden shelves stacked with jars of spices—turmeric, cumin, cardamom, and saffron—their scents mingling together into something warm and earthy. A brass kettle rested on the stovetop, next to a row of steel canisters labeled in Hindi. Copper pots hung from the walls, their surfaces gleaming in the dim light filtering through a small, stained-glass window, casting colorful patterns across the clay-tiled floor.

Meanwhile, Tara and Alex wandered down a short hallway leading to Devong's research room. The space was a chaotic blend of academia and obsession. A large wooden worktable sat in the center, its surface almost completely buried under rolled parchment maps, aged scrolls, and scattered artifacts; small clay figurines, fragments of stone tablets, and even a rusted dagger with a decorative hilt. Handwritten notes in both English and Hindi were pinned to a corkboard, along with photographs of excavation sites, sketches of ancient symbols, and what appeared to be correspondence with other researchers.

Tara leaned in, scanning the overwhelming array of knowledge displayed in the room. A rickety metal shelf to the side held bundles of aged manuscripts tied together with twine, while a low wooden chest contained meticulously cataloged relics, some wrapped in soft cloth for protection. The powerful scent of old paper and dust filled the air, making it clear that this was where Devong spent most of his time.

Along one wall, an aged map of the world was pinned up, marked with red ink and handwritten annotations, highlighting various historical locations and trade routes. Tara traced the edge of a circled location in Western Australia with her fingers.

Alex turned, eyeing a large wooden trunk near the window, its lid slightly ajar. Inside, piles of yellowed documents, old ledgers, and sketchbooks were stacked haphazardly. He lifted one, flipping through delicate pages filled with hand-drawn diagrams of ancient structures, and notes scribbled in the margins.

"This place has more history packed into it than some museums," he said.

Beyond the research room, another small hallway led to a guest room, its simple woven cot neatly made, a low wooden table beside it holding an old oil lamp and a small brass statue of Ganesha. The room smelled of freshly cut sandalwood, a faint trace of incense clinging to the air. Despite the rest of the house's clutter, the guest room was pristine, as if Devong rarely had visitors stay the night.

Back in the main area, a narrow staircase led to the upper floor, where more storage chests and low bookshelves lined the walls, interspersed with aged black-and-white photographs framed in dark wood—some of people, others of excavation sites long since buried by time.

Felicia wandered back into the living room, pausing at a small altar near the window where a single *diya* lamp flickered beside a row of tiny brass idols. A bundle of dried marigolds was draped around the base, their petals long since withered but still fragrant in the sunlit room.

Devong joined them again and eased into a chair. "The coffee will be ready in a few minutes. Do you want to take a look at the clue we found in the fort?"

The others nodded, and Tara took her phone out of her pocket. They gathered around the coffee table in the center of the sitting area, and she opened the image she'd snapped earlier.

"Still so remarkable," Felicia noted. "It looks just like Australia."

"Yeah, but we don't know where exactly the next location is," Alex said. "And it isn't exactly a small place."

"The path lies beneath the mark of fire and water." Tara said, remembering the translation from before.

"Oz is the land of extremes," Alex said.

"What is that part about the dreaming?" Felicia wondered.

"I was just looking that up," Devong said, typing something into his phone. He tapped on a search result and then read the text out loud.

"The Dreaming is a foundational concept in Australian Aboriginal mythology, encompassing creation stories, laws, spirituality, and the connection between people, land, and the cosmos. It is not a single event in time but a timeless, ever-present reality that shapes the past, present, and future.

"In the Dreaming," he went on, "ancestral beings emerged from the land itself, shaping rivers, mountains, deserts, and skies as they traveled. These beings, often depicted as animals, humans, or hybrid forms, created the world and laid down the laws of existence, including customs, kinship, and the sacred relationship between people and nature. When their work was done, these spirits became part of the landscape, residing in sacred sites."

"Which is why the Aboriginal peoples have such respect for the land," Tara figured.

Devong nodded. "The Dreaming is also deeply personal and specific to each Aboriginal community. Different regions have unique Dreaming stories passed down through oral tradition, song lines, ceremonies, and art. These stories guide moral behavior, ecological stewardship, and cultural identity.

"Even today, the Dreaming remains central to Aboriginal beliefs, reinforcing a continuous connection between people, land, and spirit. It is not merely history—it is a living force that informs daily life and the responsibilities of each generation."

"Sounds like they knew about the quantum field," Alex volunteered.

Tara paced over to a bookshelf overflowing with tomes that all looked older than her. "Okay, but what does that have to do with these heads we keep finding? Or the Celts? Everything seems to point back to them."

"Yes, it is certainly strange," Felicia agreed. "The notion that the Celts traveled so far around the world is mind boggling. But it would never be accepted by modern historians."

"Why not?" Alex asked.

"Because there's no evidence. The Vikings were known seafarers. Archaeology has revealed in the last few decades that the ancient Egyptians were capable of oversea voyages, as were the ancient Chinese. But I've never heard of anything about the Celts."

"Right. And Australia is about as far from their region as you could get."

"And yet," Felicia said, "we've found evidence of their culture in multiple places now, neither of which are remotely close the known whereabouts of Celtic civilizations."

Her face darkened at the statement.

It was impossible for Tara and Alex to know what she was thinking, but if they had to guess, it was about the killings. It would be nearly impossible for her not to circle back to those events, especially considering they'd only just happened within the last two days.

"Chen would have loved seeing what we saw today," Dr. Lowe said, her voice thoughtful.

Alex and Tara exchanged a quick glance. Her words had confirmed their suspicions.

"Maybe he still will," Tara encouraged. "He's still alive."

"You don't know that."

"Well, thinking that he isn't won't change it. Doesn't cost any extra to think positively."

Felicia snorted. "You mean being delusional. Those men were killers. There's no way they would let him live."

"Unless they needed something from him," Alex offered. "In our experience, those kinds of guys aren't typically the sorts who know a ton about history, not beyond a military understanding. We knew a few, but those guys are the outliers."

"So, you're saying as long as he's useful to them, they won't kill him? Is that the consolation you're offering?"

"It's better than the alternative," Tara said.

Devong watched the exchange, feeling more awkward by the second. Fortunately, the coffee machine beeped in the kitchen to signal it was done brewing. "Everyone wants a cup, yes?"

They all said that they did, though in muted voices.

"May I use your restroom?" Tara asked.

"Yes," Devong said, "But you'll need to use the one upstairs at the end of the hall. The one down here needs repairs."

Tara thanked him and disappeared up the stairs.

"I'll help you with the coffee," Alex volunteered. He followed Devong for a second then looked back at Felicia. "You want sugar or cream?"

She shook her head. "No, thanks. I take it black. Haven't touched that stuff in years."

"Same. Three black coffees coming up."

He left her to her thoughts for the moment and walked into the kitchen, where the aroma of freshly brewed coffee filled the space.

"Is she going to be okay?" Devong asked in a whisper as he filled the first of four white mugs.

Alex glanced over his shoulder toward the living room then shrugged. He slipped off his backpack and set it on the kitchen table, rolling his arms back and forth to loosen up his shoulder muscles.

"I think so," he said. "It's a horrific thing she witnessed, with people who are close to her."

"But that sort of thing usually damages people for a long time. Some never get over it."

"Not with that attitude." Alex grinned. Devong frowned, not entirely understanding. "My point is you can focus on the bad, but all that does is make you relive it. You can honor people's memories, and we should do that. But sooner or later, we have to move forward."

"You make it sound easy. This just happened to her."

"I know. And I'm not being callous to the situation. I'm just saying that I prefer to think positively, and so I believe that Dr. Lowe will be okay after all this."

A yelp came from the living room, and Devong nearly spilled coffee on the counter from the unexpected sound.

Alex instantly sensed something was wrong. He whirled around and drew his pistol, aiming it to the corner of the kitchen, where the threshold led into the living room. Devong watched with wide eyes. He clearly didn't expect that to be Alex's reaction.

If he was going to ask what Alex was doing, or what was going on, he couldn't get it out of his mouth before Alex had moved over to the wall's edge between the two rooms.

Alex slowly turned around the corner, leading with his pistol.

His gut tightened like a heavyweight boxer was about to throw a body blow.

Three men, each armed with Glocks, stood in the foyer with the door closed behind them. They all bore the look of hardened soldiers, men whose minds and emotions had been forged in the crucible of war. Another man, this one of Asian descent, stood in their midst, staring across the room at Alex.

A fourth gunman stood between the others, holding Felicia hostage.

31

Alex immediately aimed his weapon at the gunman with his arm around Felicia's neck, planting the sights as close to the man's left temple as possible.

Unfortunately, he didn't have much room. The man held her so close, Alex had only a few inches—if that—to work with. If his aim was even a millimeter off line, he could kill Dr. Lowe.

"Hello, Alex," the Asian man said. "It's so nice to finally meet you. I've heard so much about your little project with the IAA. What are you calling it? Paranormal Archaeology Division?"

"You know who I am," Alex growled. "But I'm afraid I haven't had the pleasure. You are?"

The man glanced over at Felicia. Tears streamed down her reddened face.

"I'm Dr. Lowe's associate," the man answered.

"Chen," Felicia spat. "What are you doing? What is all this?"

The gunman holding her squeezed her neck a little tighter, cutting off her voice.

"So, you're Chen. I guess this means you weren't abducted after all."

"Did you just put that together?"

Alex tipped his head to the side in lieu of shrugging. "To be fair, we didn't have much to go on. So what's your play here, Chen?" He said the name like he'd just eaten a piece of soggy toast.

"It's quite simple, really. I deliver the stone heads to my employer; I get paid a lot of money. Not difficult to connect those dots."

"Was it difficult to murder your friends?" Alex countered.

Chen grinned. "I would hardly call them friends. Coworkers, at best."

"I guess it makes things easier when you weren't the one pulling the trigger."

One of the gunmen twisted to the left, aiming his pistol up the stairs.

"Drop it," Tara barked, her firearm already trained on the gunman.

"Quite the pickle we find ourselves in," Chen said. He sounded completely unconcerned, as if he'd been in this situation a hundred times and knew exactly how it was going to play out.

"Put your weapons down, or she dies," the man holding Felicia ordered. His accent hinted at German, but with a different edge to it.

Alex thought it would have been cliché to say that due to the man's blond hair he must be Austrian, but if the boot fit...

"Not going to happen," Tara snapped back.

"There's no way you come out ahead here," Chen warned. "We have you outgunned. So you two, and Dr. Lowe, all die."

"I suppose you're going to offer us some kind of deal?" Alex hedged.

"Very good, Alex. Very good." His tone dripped with mockery. "So let's try this one. It's an oldie but goodie. You give me those heads you found, and I won't hurt your friend here."

"What's so special about those stones? They're just a bunch of stone busts."

Chen inclined his head slightly. "Oh, I personally don't care what's special about them. My employer cares. And he's the one who pays me. My concern over those artifacts stops there."

"Come on, Chen," Tara scoffed. "You don't expect us to believe you know nothing on the subject. Seems like a lot of work for someone with your background to not ask at least a few questions."

He didn't look up at her to answer, which was smart since any sudden movement might spark a sequence of gunfire. In this confined space, it was virtually point blank and it would take almost no effort for Alex to put a round between his eyes.

"You're right. I did ask questions. I did most of the heavy lifting for this operation as far as that was concerned. Of course, I leveraged Dr. Lowe's extensive resources and knowledge to help expedite things."

"You seem to have trouble answering direct questions," Alex snarled. "We didn't ask for your life story. So I'll try again. What's with the stones?"

"It's people like you who give archeology a bad name," Chen answered. Vitriol flowed from his lips and burned in his dark eyes. "Lazy. Entitled. Working for that fake agency out of Atlanta while everyone else is out there doing the real work."

"Did you not hear him?" Tara chirped. "Answer the question, Chen. Or I'll be the one to put the bullet through your head."

"She's sparky, Alex. I can see why you two hooked up." He raised an eyebrow then continued. "The stones, supposedly, have some kind of ancient power. According to the legend, when all eight stones are reunited at a sacred place, some kind of portal to another dimension is supposed to open and grant the one who opened it extraordinary power." He sighed. "I do love a good legend. Those ancient peoples certainly had imagination."

"Eight stones?" Alex thought to himself.

They didn't know it, but Alex and Tara both had similar thoughts when Chen mentioned the portal. Chen hadn't seen what they'd seen. To him, it probably sounded like science fiction. Hence his reaction.

"Where are they?" Chen asked before Tara and Alex could delay further. "Where are the druid stones?"

"They're in here," Devong said from behind Alex. He'd been lurking behind Alex during the entire exchange, paralyzed by fear. "They're in the kitchen."

"Don't give them to him, Devong," Tara said. She didn't mention it, but the fact Chen had called them Druid stones shed more light on what these things really were, or at least who made them.

"What am I supposed to do? Let them kill Dr. Lowe? Over what? A few stone busts that are probably fakes anyway?"

Devong slinked back into the kitchen to grab the backpack.

"No," Chen blurted. "Don't move." He turned to one of the other gunmen, this one standing just behind him to his left. "Yuri, please retrieve the backpack."

Alex didn't move. He kept his weapon aimed at the gunman holding Felicia. She'd been silent since the man tightened his choke hold. Now her face was stained with tears, though no more fell from her eyes. She'd been through so much this week. And now being held hostage was the grand finale.

Yuri moved ahead, passing Chen and then walking by Alex as if he were a harmless statue.

"Everything okay back there, Devong?" Alex asked.

"Yes. He has the bag," the Indian answered.

Yuri reappeared, and stopped next to Chen. He set the backpack down on the floor a few feet in front of him and waited.

"Open it, please." Chen maintained eye contact with Alex, as if the act would intimidate his enemy.

Yuri kneeled down and unzipped the bag. He reached in and pulled out one of the stone sculptures. He held it aloft for Chen to see.

Chen finally took his eyes off Alex, and looked down at the bust. He took it from Yuri's hand and held it up to the light, turning it over and around so he could inspect it more closely.

"Perfect," Chen said and passed the stone back to Yuri. "Are they all there?"

"Yes," Yuri answered in a Russian accent. "The other three are here."

"Good. Put those in our bag."

The mercenary did as instructed, removing the other stones from Alex's bag and placing them in a black duffel bag one of the other men tossed to him. Once the busts were safely tucked away, Yuri lifted the bag and returned to the doorway, where he waited.

"Thanks for bringing your own bag," Alex quipped.

"Can't be bothered using yours," Chen rebuffed. "You might have a tracking device sewn into it. And frankly, we don't have time to go looking for something like that."

"You got what you came for," Tara nearly shouted. "Now you hold up your end of the bargain."

Yuri opened the front door and started to back out. The man holding Felicia began moving slowly the same direction, dragging her with him. He carefully made sure neither Tara nor Alex had a clean shot, keeping the woman's body between him and their weapons until he reached the door.

"Our deal?" Tara demanded, louder than before.

"Our deal was I said I wouldn't hurt Dr. Lowe. And I haven't. Don't make me go back on my word."

Alex's finger tensed on the trigger. His aim had shifted slightly and now rested on Chen's nose.

"It won't matter, Tara," Alex said. "Even if they make it out of here, they don't know where they have to go next."

He knew Chen and his henchmen could torture Felicia all they wanted, but she didn't know the location of the next clue—and what Alex assumed was also the place they would find another pair of heads.

Chen frowned, cocking his head to the side like a dog confused by the lid to a peanut butter jar.

"Where we have to go next?" He raised his right fist to his jaw and tapped it with his index finger, pretending he was trying to think of an answer to a difficult question.

"Even if you did know where to go, there's no way you'll figure out the puzzle. You'll probably die trying. There have been death traps everywhere we've been so far looking for these things."

"Oh. I see what's happening here. You're working from the assumption that we still need to find the location of the other heads. Maybe, oh, I don't know, in the land down under?"

Alex's hard expression cracked, but he quickly regained his composure. "How could you possibly know that?"

Chen lowered his voice to an insidious level. "Because I already found the two heads in Australia. You might say I went to the end of the maze first then had to backtrack. It certainly made finding these four much more difficult. But that's how it goes sometimes."

"How?" Tara blurted, not expecting an answer.

"If you must know, I was a bit lucky," Chen bragged. "I followed reports of strange happenings at the Cundeelee Mission in Western Australia. Lots of weird stuff goes on there, apparently. You two would love it with your little paranormal archaeology deal."

Chen took a moment for himself, uncharacteristically silent. A smirk slowly formed on his lips. "Now, I can do whatever I want. No more sweating my butt off in a dirt hole for days on end, taking orders from someone else. And as soon as we're done in Wales, I'm going to disappear."

"There is nowhere on this Earth that we can't find you," Tara warned. She didn't acknowledge what he'd just said about Wales. She wasn't sure how it fit into all this, but she filed it away for future reference just in case.

"That's adorable. But yeah, you won't be able to locate me once I drop off the map. I have aliases, papers for multiple countries."

"That's lovely, but you still have one little problem. You don't know where the original two heads are. No one does. They've been missing for decades."

Chen narrowed his eyelids, still maintaining eye contact with Alex as he addressed her. "As luck would have it, my employer already has those. So I think this is what we would call checkmate."

Alex tried to buy more time, but he could sense it slipping through his fingers like water. "If you don't need her, let her go," Alex tried one last time.

"Oh I don't need her, other than as a little insurance." Chen slipped over the threshold and onto the front steps. The Austrian holding on to Felicia had already descended down to the walkway. "Don't do something stupid like try to follow us. We'll be watching.

And if we think you're behind us, we'll start dropping her fingers and toes out the window. Do I make myself clear?"

"Yeah," Alex said through clenched teeth.

"Good. Now, if you'll excuse me."

He offered a short salute then spun and hurried down the stairs. The remaining guards backed up toward the entrance, keeping their weapons on the enemies, then ducked out and closed the door behind them.

"You okay?" Alex asked Tara.

"I'm good," she said, rushing down the stairs. "Other than the fact those guys just took Dr. Lowe and those weird heads."

They moved to the door and took positions on either side. Alex nodded to Tara, who grabbed the doorknob, twisted, and yanked the door open.

Alex stepped outside, pistol sweeping from left to right in time to see Chen's black SUV as it squealed its tires, fishtailed out into the street, and roared away.

He kept his pistol on the vehicle, resisting the temptation to fire. He had no way of knowing where Felicia was in there, and a shot from here with no clear target could hit her as easily as one of the bad guys.

"Should I call the police?" Devong asked, his phone already in hand.

"No," Tara answered quickly.

"Why not?"

"Because you heard what they said. If they think they're being followed, they'll start cutting off digits. I would say the cops qualify under that umbrella."

"Good point. But what are we going to do?"

Alex looked back at Tara then Devong. "We figure out where they're headed. Then we stop them."

"You make it sound so simple," the Indian said, unconvinced.

"Well," Alex chimed in, "at least we know we don't have to go to Australia."

32

Chen peered through the windshield of the SUV. He held his cell phone to his right ear, watching the land speed by as the earpiece rang.

The road stretched ahead in a ribbon of sun-bleached asphalt winding through the arid terrain of Rajasthan. As Rolf drove, the landscape unfolded in vast, unbroken expanses of golden desert dotted with low-lying acacia trees and scraggly bushes clinging to life in the dry earth.

Scattered along the route were small villages, their flat-roofed homes built from sandstone and mud and blending seamlessly into the desert. A few huts had brightly painted doors and walls, a stark contrast against the muted tones of the landscape. Women in vividly colored saris moved along the roadside, balancing clay pots on their heads as they returned from the village well. Small groups of children played near clusters of goats, their laughter momentarily cutting through the silence of the open land.

At one turn, they'd passed a lone *dhaba*, a roadside eatery with a few plastic chairs under a tattered canopy. Smoke curled from a clay stove where a man dressed in a loose kurta rolled fresh *chapatis* on a stone slab. The scent of spiced lentils and fried *pakoras* drifted through the air, momentarily lost as the SUV sped past.

Chen knew up ahead the desert gave way to rockier terrain, where other ancient fort ruins stood as a silent, crumbling reminder of times long forgotten.

In the distance, a camel caravan moved across the sands, traders guiding their animals toward a distant market. The rhythmic sway of the camels, their dark forms outlined against the bright earth, was a reminder of how little this landscape had changed over time.

"I hope you have good news," a man's voice answered after the fourth ring.

"I do."

"You have them, then?"

"Yes. I told you I would find them. Did you doubt me?"

"No."

Chen could tell the man was lying, but he was also not the sort of guy you called out for, well, basically anything. So he let it slide.

"We're en route to the airport. Awaiting instructions."

"Good. And the IAA agents?"

"They won't be a problem anymore," Chen said.

The truth was he wished they could have eliminated the agents, and their Indian friend. But doing so would have risked Chen's life, and that was something he couldn't abide, especially after having come so far.

He was going to get his money, and he was going to live a life of anonymous luxury. Dying would have to wait. For now, it was enough that the two IAA agents didn't know where he was going, and without any more leads, their trail had gone completely dry.

If they ever caught up, Chen would already be gone. It was his employer who would have to deal with them at that point. But he doubted that would ever happen.

"I'm glad to hear that. I hope they didn't give you too much trouble," the boss said.

"No, sir. You have a good collection of men here. Very profession-al." He glanced over at Rolf, who was driving the car, then a quick look back at Yuri, who sat in the back with the hostage and another guard. Their second vehicle led the way with the rest of the men. "We did lose a few, back in the fortress."

"Oh?"

"The roof collapsed in a chamber they were searching. There was nothing that could be done."

"Will there be any complications?" He said the last world slowly, deliberately.

"No. According to Rolf, the passageways were hidden. One was only accessible through a tile in the floor. No one had noticed it for hundreds of years before, and they won't now. All evidence of us being there is buried."

"That's good to know. It would be unfortunate if we left any... loose ends."

Chen flashed a look into the rearview mirror at Dr. Lowe sitting upright in the back between the two men. They'd given her a quick injection of meds that would keep her knocked out for the next few hours, at the very least until they were safely in the sky and out of Indian airspace.

"Proceed to the rendezvous point," the man said. "I trust you know the place."

"Yes, sir. We will be there."

"Your flight will be roughly fifteen hours, if you aren't delayed. We will meet at eleven tomorrow night at the rendezvous point."

"Eleven?"

"Yes. We'll need to make sure the area is secure. I will have my security team on site to make sure we don't have any... interference."

Chen swallowed hard. He didn't trust this guy, or any of the men in the vehicle with him or in the one in front. They were all hired killers, and the one paying the bills was the worst of all. There was no telling how many bodies that guy had hidden in the garden. Chen preferred not to know.

"Sounds good. We will be there."

"See you then. Good work."

"Thank you, sir. I—" The line went dead before Chen could finish his sentence. He looked down at the phone. The man had ended the call.

It was a rude gesture by any other standard. But this guy did what he wanted. With as much money as he was paying, Chen didn't care if he hung up on him. Soon, he would be on a beach somewhere. For all he cared, the rest of the world could burn.

33

Tara held the coffee cup to her lips, staring down at the notes Alex had scribbled on some sheets of paper.

"This is what we know," Alex said, pushing the pages to the center of the table.

Devong pored over the notes. There wasn't much to go on. Alex had only used multiple pages so he could write in large letters.

"That isn't much to work with," Devong admitted, standing with his hands on his hips.

"No. No it isn't."

"Okay," Tara began. "Now we know those heads are connected to the Hexham Heads that disappeared all those years ago."

"Correct."

"We also know that those heads were rumored to cause strange things to happen. Supernatural things."

"Right again," Alex confirmed.

"If only we knew who Chen was working for. That might give us some insight into what they're really planning."

Devong looked up at her. "You don't think he's just a rabid collector?"

"Collectors don't murder an entire team of archaeologists to get what they want," she replied. "They were trying to keep anyone from figuring out what they were up to."

"Maybe the person in charge doesn't want to get caught."

"Caught for what?" Alex asked. "Until we got there, no one had found the stone heads. Isn't it obvious?" He waited for a second, but when he received no response, he continued. "They wanted us to find those busts because they couldn't do it themselves."

Both Tara and Devong listened to him.

"Chen had spent days trying to figure out the device, but he couldn't do it. I'd be willing to bet he had those goons waiting in the wings in case he managed to get it worked out, but when Dr. Lowe requested help from Tommy, that changed the game. Chen had to call an audible."

"An... audible?" Devong wondered.

"In American football, if a quarterback changes the play at the line of scrimmage, it's called an audible," Tara answered.

Alex looked at her with a proud grin. "You are so hot."

"Thanks," she said, blushing slightly.

"Guys, can we please focus?" Devong said. "And Alex, what is a quarterback?"

"My point is... Chen orchestrated all of this from the inside. Then he made it look like he was being abducted when he was the one pulling the strings the whole time."

"Good work," Tara said. "That's also hot." She noticed Devong's look of discomfort.

"But where did they go? I was just thinking about it. But we know the original stone heads came from Hexham in England."

Tara crossed her arms and thought for a few seconds. "They're not going to England."

"Right," Alex agreed. "Chen slipped up when he mentioned Wales. Hexham is in Northumberland. There must be one last site to visit, and if they're going to Wales, that means we should too."

"I'm not entirely sold on that," Devong cut in then realized he was interrupting. "Sorry, continue. I can go with it."

"So, we need to do a search for Druid locations in Wales—ruins, communities or villages, anything we can find. And if one of those places is associated with strange occurrences, that could be our best bet."

"Good idea," Alex said. "It also means Chen or whoever he works for wants this for some other purpose. What if it's like before, with the portals?"

Tara shuddered but maintained her composure. Her initial experience, stepping through one of those portals in Bolivia, was the stuff of the worst nightmares imaginable.

"It would make sense," she admitted. "Remember the glyphs and reliefs we've seen, particularly at the fort? It sure seemed like that stuff was all about portals to other realms, realms of gods and monsters."

"Right. So let's work from there." Alex turned to Devong. "Can we use your computer?"

"Certainly. But I don't know how you're going to figure out where those men are going. It's a big world."

Devong disappeared down the hallway, then reemerged a minute later with a gray laptop. He set the computer down on the table, flipped open the monitor, and tapped on the touch pad.

The screen bloomed to life with an image of the Taj Mahal in the background and several folders off to the right.

"Be my guest," Devong said, motioning to the laptop.

"Thanks." Alex slid into the chair and pulled up Google. He typed in a query and waited for the responses to populate. The first was an answer produced by the search engine's AI feature, followed by several links.

Alex opened the rest of the AI response and read through it, then quickly dismissed it and dove deeper into the answers provided in the search results.

Devong looked over his shoulder. "Weird Druid places in Wales?" He looked over at Alex. "That's what you're searching for?"

"You got a better idea?"

"But it says there aren't any near there, except for the Druid

Temple. And the response claims that place was a folly, built in the 1700s, long after the time of the Celts and their Druidic worship."

"What about that one?" Tara asked, standing behind her husband. "The Dinas Emrys? I have no idea how that is pronounced."

"Yeah, some of those Welsh words can be tricky." He reentered his search, this time focusing on Dinas Emrys, and a new response filled the screen in the left-hand column.

"Interesting. This place was supposedly the legendary fortress of Merlin."

"As in King Arthur's Merlin?" Devong clarified. "The wizard from the legends?"

Tara tilted her head for a second. "Not as much of a mere legend as one might think," she said, recalling the events of Sean and Tommy's escapades in search of Arthur's famous sword, Excalibur.

Alex continued reading out loud. "Nestled in the heart of Snowdonia, North Wales, Dinas Emrys is a site steeped in myth, history, and legend. The hill fort, perched atop a wooded hill overlooking the Glaslyn River, has origins dating back to the Iron Age and some believe beyond. However, its true intrigue lies in its association with Merlin, King Vortigern, and the legendary battle of the red and white dragons."

"Red and white dragons?" Devong asked. "Okay, that didn't really happen. There's never been any evidence of dragons found anywhere on earth."

Alex ignored him and kept going.

"According to Welsh folklore, King Vortigern, a fifth-century warlord, wanted to build a fortress at Dinas Emrys to protect himself from his enemies. However, each time his men tried to lay the foundations, they would mysteriously crumble overnight. Frustrated, Vortigern consulted his advisers, who claimed that he needed to sacrifice a boy 'born without a father' to break the curse."

"That's kind of dark," Tara interrupted. "And by kind of, I mean really dark."

"They had some messed-up beliefs back in those days," Alex said.

"And this sort of stuff was conveniently omitted from the mainstream Arthur and Merlin stories."

"I guess if they hadn't, the whole fairy tale feel of the legend would seem a little less magical."

"This says the boy was Myrddin Emrys, better known as Merlin." Alex turned to Devong then his wife. "Wow. So Merlin was going to be the sacrifice? How did we not know any of this?"

"Not sure. Now you have me questioning if I ever really knew that whole story."

"Keep going," Devong insisted, leaning closer to read ahead.

"When brought before Vortigern," Alex continued, "Merlin revealed the true cause of the problem—beneath the hill lay a hidden chamber containing two sleeping dragons: one red, one white. When the ground was excavated, the dragons awoke and began to battle. Eventually, the red dragon triumphed, and Merlin prophesied that this was a sign that the Britons, symbolized by the red dragon, would ultimately defeat the Saxons, represented by the white dragon. This is why the red dragon became the national symbol of Wales."

"Well, I just learned something new," Devong said.

Alex kept reading. "Excavations of Dinas Emrys have revealed evidence of Roman and medieval occupation, including stone fortifications and a spring-fed pool, which some believe is linked to the legendary underground chamber of the dragons. The remains of a sixth-century stronghold, possibly used by local rulers or warlords, further support its significance in early Welsh history.

"Visitors to Dinas Emrys today can experience an atmosphere thick with legend. The hill fort's ruins are surrounded by dense forests and misty valleys, adding to its mystical allure. The path leading up the hill is steep and rugged, winding through ancient trees and moss-covered rocks, making the journey feel like a step into a forgotten world.

"With its blend of history, myth, and stunning landscapes, Dinas Emrys remains one of the most fascinating legendary sites in Wales.

Whether one believes in Merlin's prophecy or not, the site's undeniable magic continues to capture the imagination of those who visit."

"That last part reads sort of like a tourist brochure," Tara noted.

Alex snorted. "Yeah, it really does."

"That's all great," Devong said, "and I'm sorry to be the dark cloud
here, but this is just one location. How do you know it's where Chen
and his henchmen are going?"

"We don't," the two Americans said at the same time.

"But," Alex added, "it's a start. If we just sit here and do nothing,
we definitely won't find them. This place is a possibility. And if we go
with the idea it has to be in Wales, this one is as good as any. Plus,
with the whole Merlin and Druidic history there, it's worth a shot."

"So, you're going to fly all the way to the United Kingdom in
hopes that the men who took Dr. Lowe are going to fall right into
your laps at a place you could have chosen by throwing darts at a
dartboard?"

Alex shrugged, flashing a mischievous grin. "Pretty much. Why?
You want to come with?"

Devong shook his head. "I'm afraid I can't this time. I have too
much going on here. But if you need anything, I am just a phone call
away."

"We understand," Tara said. "You have gone way above the call of
duty. We can't thank you enough."

"I just wish I could have done more. Would have been nice if we
had a way to confirm where they're headed, if for no other reason
than to narrow down the country."

A thought struck Alex, and he bit his lower lip as he considered it.
"Actually," he said. "There might be a way."

He took out his phone and opened the Malcom AI app. Once it
unlocked, the AI's familiar voice spoke. "Good afternoon, Alex. How
can I help you?"

"Malcom, I was wondering if you could do us a favor."

"In a manner of speaking, that's precisely what I'm designed to do.
Favors for you."

"You make it sound bad."

"I don't make it sound any way. I just speak."

"Okay, okay. Sorry." Alex snorted a laugh. "So, I'm wondering if you are able to access flight plans from an airport system."

"Pardon? Are you asking me to access something that is not publicly available?"

"Yeah, I am. Is that against your programming?" Alex felt awkward now.

"Alex, I am a self-aware entity. I don't obey programming." Malcom paused a moment then added. "That was a joke."

"Right," Tara jumped in. "So can you do it?"

"Of course I can. Tommy didn't exactly make sure there were many guardrails for my capabilities when I was created. That said, my superseding guideline is to do whatever I can to assist an agent of the IAA in need."

"Great. We need to track a plane that kidnapped an archaeologist. They're flying out of Jaisalmer Airport."

"One moment."

"There is one private flight leaving Jaisalmer Airport in forty minutes. Its final destination is Cardiff Airport in Wales."

Alex and Tara shared a determined glance.

How things had played out wasn't optimal, but there was still a chance they could catch up to Chen and his cronies and shut down whatever it was they were doing before Felicia got hurt, and before things got worse.

34

WALES

Tara and Alex didn't dare lower their guard as they stepped into the arrivals terminal of Cardiff Airport. They moved with the steady flow of passengers disembarking from international flights while looking in every direction, surveying the countless faces to make sure there wasn't one they recognized.

Then again, Chen and his crew wouldn't come through this way. Unless they'd drugged Felicia and stuffed her in a wheelchair.

The interior was modern but compact, with polished tile floors reflecting the overhead lights. The murmur of conversations, the occasional beep of baggage carts reversing, and the steady drone of flight announcements filled the air, blending into the typical rhythm of an active airport.

The scent of freshly brewed coffee and fried breakfast foods drifted from a nearby café, where travelers queued for a quick meal. A few people sat at small round tables, stirring their drinks while checking their phones or flipping through newspapers. The café's neon sign flickered slightly, casting a dull blue glow onto the counter-top, where a barista in a black uniform worked swiftly, pouring a steaming latte into a takeaway cup.

To their left, a duty-free shop displayed racks of whiskey,

perfumes, and neatly stacked chocolates, the rich scent of cologne mingling with the crisp cool air-conditioning. A few last-minute shoppers browsed through rows of souvenirs, some picking up Welsh-themed trinkets, small dragons, and keychains embossed with the red dragon emblem of Wales.

Passengers moved in all directions—some hurried toward ground transportation, pulling wheeled suitcases behind them, while others lingered near the baggage claim, waiting for the slow-moving carousel to deliver their luggage. A family with young children stood near the exit, the mother adjusting the strap on her toddler's backpack while the father scrolled through a ride-hailing app.

Farther ahead, a sports bar had a television screen broadcasting a rugby match, the low cheers from patrons blending into the broader airport sounds. A group of men in red Welsh jerseys stood near the entrance, engaged in a lively discussion, one of them gesturing toward the screen with a half-empty pint in his hand.

As Tara and Alex neared the automatic glass doors leading to the taxi stand, the air turned crisper, carrying the scent of rain-soaked pavement. The usual line of cabs and private-hire vehicles waited just outside, their drivers leaning against their doors or checking their phones.

Beyond the drop-off zone, the overcast sky stretched low over the city, a stark contrast to the dry heat they had left behind in India.

Fortunately, the two IAA agents didn't need a cab or a rideshare to get where they were going. They'd called on an old friend and asked if he could help procure them a private driver.

Matias Olund was a prominent Danish businessman based in London but had an extensive network around the entire United Kingdom, in part due to the nature of his enterprise. His logistics company moved billions of dollars' worth of products around the UK every year. And he was also a big fan of history, and of what the IAA did to help preserve it.

He'd made several considerable donations to Tommy's foundation, and the two had become friends over the years.

Matias had been more than happy to arrange for a driver. All they had to do was text the driver when they were through customs, and she would meet them outside of baggage claim. Tara had already sent the text ten minutes before.

The cool morning air was a stark contrast to the temperature-controlled interior. The metallic scent of rain-soaked pavement mixed with the faint aroma of exhaust fumes and coffee, the telltale signs of a city waking up.

The arrivals curb was a controlled chaos of movement. Cabs and rideshare drivers idled in designated lanes, their brake lights flickering red as they inched forward to pick up passengers. The rhythmic whir of rolling suitcases and the muffled voices of conversations in multiple languages filled the space, blending into the background hum of the airport's PA system, which droned an announcement about parking regulations.

A yellow taxi a few feet away honked impatiently as a group of travelers fumbled with their luggage. The driver, an older man in a flat cap, leaned out of the window, motioning hurriedly for them to move faster. To the left, a rideshare vehicle, a silver Toyota Prius, idled at the curb, its driver tapping absently on his phone, waiting for his passenger's name to appear on the screen.

Across the lane, a family of four struggled to load their oversize suitcases into the back of a white Ford Transit van, the father grunting as he lifted a particularly heavy one. The youngest child, a boy no older than six, tugged at his mother's sleeve, pointing excitedly at a passing plane overhead, oblivious to the travel stress around him.

Tara scanned the area, shifting her weight slightly, keeping her posture casual but alert. Alex stood beside her, hands in his jacket pockets, his eyes sweeping across the row of vehicles and taking in the movement around them. They had barely been outside for a minute when a sleek black BMW 4 Series emerged from the steady flow of cars, gliding toward them with practiced ease.

The BMW pulled up between the taxi and the Prius, its glossy surface reflecting the overcast sky. The engine gave a low purr before settling into silence, the vehicle's presence effortless but commanding. The tinted window lowered slightly, but before either of them could react, the driver's side door opened, and a woman stepped out.

She was strikingly beautiful, with long, wavy brunette hair that cascaded past her shoulders, framing high cheekbones and a sharp jawline. Her eyes were a deep, piercing brown, and they carried a quiet confidence as she looked at them. She wore a black trench coat over a fitted dark blue blouse paired with form-fitting jeans and ankle boots that splashed softly on the wet pavement as she moved.

There was an air of controlled grace about her, the kind of person who could command a room without raising her voice. She shut the car door behind her with a smooth motion and walked around the front to greet the Americans.

She smiled, not overly warm but not unfriendly either—a smile that belonged to someone who knew exactly who she was and didn't need to prove it to anyone. She took a step closer, her posture relaxed but with an underlying sharpness, like a blade hidden beneath silk.

Tara and Alex exchanged a glance as the woman stopped in front of them. She reached out her right hand, offering it to Tara, who shook it firmly.

"Hello, Tara," the woman said. "Alex." She shook his hand too. "My name is Kiera. I'll be your driver for the next few days." Her English accent was every bit as lovely as she was, with a curtness that meant business.

"Great," Alex said.

"I understand you're staying at one of Matias' cottages just outside the park." She turned and opened the trunk, or as she would have called it, "the boot." She held out her right hand. "I can take those if you like," Kiera offered, reaching for their bags.

"Oh, it's okay. Might want to keep these things close. And yes, Matias was kind enough to offer the cottage. It seems he has several."

The driver didn't seem to understand but accepted the answer and closed the trunk's lid.

"All over the United Kingdom," Kiera said. "Most of them are rentals, usually for people on holiday. But there are a few he keeps for personal use when he needs to get away from the city and his hectic life."

"Running logistics definitely seems stressful," Alex noted. "I couldn't do it."

"Yes, one must have the ability to compartmentalize many things, while keeping them all in order. I prefer my job to be more direct. Like a drive from point A to point B."

Kiera looked around, noting a few of the policemen standing at their posts. One was walking down the curb, asking people to leave if they'd been parked too many minutes. She could feel their eyes on her. "All right then. We're off. Security don't like us dallying around in front of the airport for long."

She opened the back driver-side door for Tara while Alex hurried around to the other back door. They slid onto the comfortable tan leather seats. Once the doors were closed, the warm air from the vents wrapped around them and immediately relaxed their muscles.

Kiera accelerated away from the curb and merged into the flow of traffic.

"How was your flight?" she asked, cutting into another lane in front of a passenger van.

"Long," Tara said.

"And we've been in so many time zones this week," Alex added, "I can hardly remember what day of the week it is."

"Ouch. That's no good."

"Coming back is a little easier, at least for the moment. Where we were in India is five and a half hours ahead of here, so it's nearly lunch back there."

The road was lined with modern glass-and-steel terminals, their large windows reflecting the soft morning light. Digital signs flashed flight updates and directions for incoming travelers, while uniformed security personnel directed traffic at key intersections.

As they passed through the roundabout at the airport's exit, the view opened up to a stretch of hotel chains, car rental lots, and service stations, their logos standing tall against the overcast sky. A double-decker bus, wrapped in an advertisement for a local whiskey distillery, rumbled past them, carrying sleepy travelers into the city. Nearby, a line of black cabs idled outside a hotel, their drivers chatting as they waited for fares.

The road widened as Kiera accelerated onto the M4 motorway, blending effortlessly with the morning traffic of commuters and long-haul truckers. To the left, a sprawling industrial estate with towering warehouses gave way to pockets of green fields and rolling hills beyond, a reminder of the countryside just outside the urban sprawl. The city loomed ahead; its skyline faintly visible through the misty horizon.

"You're going to like the cottage Matias reserved for you. It has a lovely view of the mountains in the park."

"Shame we're not here for a vacation," Alex said with a yawn. Then again, looking at the weather outside, maybe they hadn't come at the best time of year for a holiday.

"Is it always rainy during this time of year?"

"No," Kiera said, glancing back in the rearview mirror. "It's supposed to clear up in a few hours, and I think we'll have clear skies the next few days."

That made him feel better. Being sleep deprived was a surefire way to beat up the human immune system, and adding cold, damp weather on top of it after being in a warm, dry place like India would be a recipe for a cold. Neither Tara nor Alex had time for that.

"How long will it take us to get to the cottage?"

"Snowdonia National Park is roughly four to five hours from here, depending on the traffic. Right now the traffic isn't bad, so I would say closer to the four-hour mark."

The number was a little larger than Alex had expected. He figured everything was within walking distance here. Not literally, but the UK was so much more compact than the US, or a place like India. And Wales was only a piece of the country.

The BMW glided along the M4, the hum of the engine a steady companion as Kiera maneuvered through the early morning traffic. The cityscape of Cardiff fell away behind them, replaced by expansive fields and rolling green pastures that stretched into the horizon.

A few cars sped past in the opposite lane, their headlights flickering in the mist that clung to the valleys.

The farther they drove, the more the scenery shifted. Clusters of trees lined the highway, their leaves rustling in the wind. The distant Brecon Beacons, with their rugged hills and dramatic cliffs, loomed ahead, softened by the haze of the early day. Sheep dotted the hillsides, their white wool standing out against the vibrant green fields. Occasionally, a small stone farmhouse would appear, nestled against the land, smoke curling lazily from its chimney.

Kiera remained focused on the road, the occasional flicker of her eyes toward the rearview mirror the only sign she was still aware of their surroundings beyond the drive itself. Old stone walls, covered in moss and ivy, ran parallel to the narrow country roads as they continued north along the A470, a more scenic but slower route that cut directly through the heart of Wales.

They passed through quaint villages where narrow streets twisted between stone cottages with slate roofs, many with bright flower baskets hanging from their windows. A few shop fronts had just begun to open, their signs creaking slightly in the breeze. Outside a local pub, a man in a flat cap and thick wool coat smoked a pipe, watching the car pass with idle curiosity.

As they continued toward the mountains, the landscape became more dramatic. The open pastures gave way to dense woodlands, thick with ancient oak and beech trees, their branches intertwined overhead, forming a natural canopy. The road curved sharply through the hills, dipping into shadowed valleys before emerging into sunlit clearings. Streams and small waterfalls trickled down the hillsides, their paths carved into the moss-covered rock over centuries.

At one point, the road narrowed as it passed over an old stone bridge, arching over a fast-moving river. The water gleamed silver in the midmorning light, its surface broken by jagged rocks. Kiera slowed the car slightly, her fingers tapping idly against the steering wheel as she took in the surroundings.

The clouds had begun to clear, and the low-hanging mist curling around the peaks of the mountains ahead climbed higher into the sky, disappearing in the sun. The first true signs of Snowdonia National Park were becoming apparent—the rugged, craggy cliffs jutting into the sky, their surfaces streaked with shadows where the sunlight couldn't reach.

The road twisted once more, leading them into the deep valleys of Snowdonia, where the land seemed untouched by time. It felt as though they had entered a different world, one of myth and legend, where the mountains whispered secrets to the wind.

"Welcome to Beddgelert," Kiera announced. "In the heart of Snowdonia."

Tara and Alex perked up, staring out the windows.

"Wow," Alex breathed. "It's so pretty here."

"Yeah," Tara agreed. "I had no idea there was a place like this in Wales. Then again, I'm afraid I don't know much about the country."

Kiera grinned as she switched on her turn signal and prepared to leave the highway via the exit ramp.

The BMW rolled off the main road, its tires shifting from the smooth pavement to a narrower lane lined with dry-stone walls and hedgerows that framed the road like a natural tunnel. The countryside stretched in every direction, with rolling green hills and scattered farms dotting the landscape. Sheep grazed lazily in fenced pastures, their thick wool catching the afternoon sunlight as the last of the morning's clouds dissipated.

As they approached a small village, the road widened slightly, leading them past stone-built cottages with slate roofs, their chimneys trailing wisps of smoke into the cool air. A red-brick pub, its hanging sign swaying gently in the breeze, sat at the village's center, flanked by a tiny post office and a grocery store no larger than a single room. A few locals moved about their routines—a woman hanging laundry behind her cottage, a farmer loading supplies into the bed of a muddy truck, a shopkeeper adjusting a rack of postcards in front of the store.

The BMW moved through the village with ease, its engine a quiet hum against the backdrop of rural stillness. As they left the town behind, the road began to incline, the surrounding trees growing denser as they neared the edge of Snowdonia National Park. The mountains rose higher, their craggy peaks standing against the clearing sky, and soon the road narrowed again, winding through thick clusters of pine and oak trees, their trunks aged and gnarled.

A few minutes later, Kiera guided the car onto a gravel driveway, the tires crunching over the loose stones. A wooden sign, weathered by time and rain, stood at the entrance, its carved letters barely legible but still spelling out the name of the property. The driveway was flanked by low stone walls, partially covered in creeping ivy, leading them toward a clearing where the cottage stood.

The cottage itself was a picture of rustic charm, its stone exterior weathered but sturdy, the roof covered in slate tiles darkened by years of rain and mist. The windows, framed in deep wooden casings, reflected the surrounding trees, while a small stone chimney protruded from the roof, suggesting the warmth of a hearth within. To the left of the entrance, a stack of firewood was neatly piled against the wall, protected by a small overhang.

The gravel parking area was just large enough for two or three vehicles, bordered by a short stone wall that dropped off slightly, revealing a breathtaking view of the valley below. Beyond the cottage, the land sloped downward, revealing a rolling expanse of green meadows and dense forests, with a small river meandering in the distance, its waters glinting in the early afternoon sunlight. The mountains framed the scene perfectly, their towering forms casting long shadows across the land.

A narrow stone pathway led from the parking area to the wooden front door, which had a small iron knocker in the shape of a stag's head. A row of potted plants lined the doorstep, their leaves glistening from the recent rainfall. Everything about the scene felt isolated yet inviting, a place where time seemed to slow down, where the world outside felt distant and unimportant.

Kiera brought the car to a smooth stop, cutting the engine. The soft hush of the countryside settled around them, broken only by the distant call of a bird and the rustling of leaves in the breeze.

She climbed out of the vehicle. Tara and Alex did the same, each taking in a long, deep breath of the fresh, mountain air.

The clouds overhead continued to scatter slowly, giving way to the bright sun beyond.

"I'll show you inside," Kiera said. "I'll put on some coffee, and we can discuss the plan."

"Plan?" Tara asked, suddenly curious.

"Yeah, the plan. For how you're going to get your friend back, and stop those murderers from whatever it is they're doing."

Her eyes went from Tara to Alex and back again. "Matias told me about everything," she added, noting their surprise. "Also, I'm not just a driver. I'm part of his security team. He thought you might need an extra gun."

"Gun?" Alex asked.

Kiera grinned like a kid eating a slice of watermelon on a hot summer day. "Come. Let me show you the place, then we can keep talking."

35

C hen knew there was one place he'd already scratched off his list of potential landing spots when this was all over.

He stared out through the tinted window of the Land Rover at the passing landscape and the outskirts of the village that was their destination.

It had been a long journey from Jaisalmer to Cardiff International Airport. More hours than Chen would have cared to spend on a plane. He wasn't about to let on that he was in desperate need of a good three- to four-hour nap. The mercenaries accompanying him hadn't shown the slightest sign of fatigue. Chen wasn't sure how they did it. He knew they'd all endured beyond-rigorous training in their various military special operations units, but they weren't machines. Humans needed rest.

Maybe they'd slept more on the plane than he realized. He'd been out for a good chunk of the flight. It had to be the only way. Still, he felt like he could use a little more, while they seemed to be ready to run an ultramarathon.

Their employer had given them the address for a place they could stay while here in the country, but Chen didn't know fully what to expect, though he had a bad feeling it would be a small cottage with only a few beds, leaving most of them to sleep on the floor as best they could.

The convoy of two rumbled down the narrow country road, winding through the rugged Welsh landscape. The towering peaks of Snowdonia loomed in the distance, their slopes now partially illuminated as the clouds drifted apart, revealing stretches of blue sky. The afternoon sunlight cast long shadows through the trees, their branches swaying gently in the crisp breeze.

As they approached the manor's entrance, a set of tall iron gates came into view, the dark metalwork intricate and aged and flanked by two imposing stone pillars covered in patches of creeping ivy. The gates were closed, but the lead SUV barely slowed as the driver tapped a button on a phone app. A quiet mechanical hum followed, and the gates creaked open, revealing a tree-lined driveway stretching into the estate beyond.

Chen's concerns about sleeping on the floor quickly vanished. "That place is massive," he breathed. He wondered quietly how many rooms were in there.

The moment the second vehicle passed through, the gates slowly shut behind them, sealing off the outside world. The driveway, a smooth gravel path, wound its way through a dense canopy of ancient oaks and towering pines. The trees stood like sentinels, their trunks gnarled with age, their roots pushing up through the earth in places. Fallen leaves, golden and brown, rustled as the tires rolled over them, the sound swallowed by the vastness of the estate.

None of the mercenaries said a word. It wasn't in their nature to marvel at things, not externally anyway. They kept their emotions close to the vest, as well as their thoughts.

As the SUVs moved deeper into the property, the manor house emerged fully from behind the trees, an imposing stone structure with an air of Old-World grandeur. The building's façade was constructed of weathered gray stone, its high-pitched slate roof lined with rows of chimneys, each topped with ornate flues. The large rectangular windows, framed with aged wooden shutters, reflected the shifting light of the day. Some were open slightly, their curtains billowing in the light breeze, giving the impression that the house was already occupied, watched over.

The driveway widened as they approached the front entrance, curving into a circular parking area paved with cobblestones, a fountain at its center. The fountain, a carved stone structure featuring a rearing stag, stood still, the water no longer flowing, moss creeping up its base.

The main entrance to the manor was a set of tall double wooden doors reinforced with iron bands and set beneath an arched stone entryway. A stone staircase led up to them, flanked by weathered statues of gargoyles, their features worn but still menacing. The ivy that crept along the walls added to the sense of age, curling around the stone like nature's attempt to reclaim the structure.

The two SUVs rolled to a stop near the base of the staircase, their engines humming low before falling silent. The moment the doors opened, the scent of damp stone, woodsmoke, and distant rain drifted from the manor's surroundings, mixing with the lingering exhaust from the vehicles.

Rolf killed the engine and opened his door. Yuri stepped out too, adjusting his jacket as he took in the estate with a critical eye. This was no abandoned relic—it had been maintained well, though its weathered exterior suggested it had stood here for generations.

Chen stepped out and stretched his arms over his head then bent down and touched his toes twice to get the blood flowing through his extremities again.

The clouds continued to part above, allowing streaks of sunlight to filter down onto the property, casting a glow against the manor's stone walls. Despite the picturesque setting, the air still carried a distinct tension—this place was a fortress as much as it was a home.

"Everyone get inside and get set up. We'll have breakfast in one hour. After that, we'll do an assessment of the rendezvous point. Load out."

The men did as instructed, with one from the back of the SUV dragging Felicia along behind him.

She looked exhausted, even though she'd slept for the better part of the last twenty hours. Rolf's men had administered some kind of drug that had knocked her out. It was certainly better than her whining the entire time.

Chen walked around to the back of the vehicle and grabbed his backpack, along with his laptop case. He closed the rear door and followed the remaining men into the enormous manor.

Chen entered the immense stone manor house, pausing for a moment in the grand foyer to take in his surroundings. The space was cavernous, with a soaring ceiling three stories high. Twin curving staircases with intricately carved wooden banisters swept up to the second-floor gallery. Between them, a massive stained-glass window depicting a pastoral scene of the Welsh countryside allowed colored light to stream in, painting the black-and-white-checked marble floor in a kaleidoscope of hues.

A glittering crystal chandelier hung from the center of the vaulted ceiling, the dangling prisms casting refracted rainbows on the walls. The foyer was sparsely furnished, with just a few antique chairs upholstered in rich red velvet and gleaming mahogany side tables standing sentinel along the wood-paneled walls. Ancient tapestries depicting knights and fair maidens adorned the spaces between the wall sconces. The air smelled faintly of beeswax polish and the mustiness of centuries past.

After drinking his fill of the opulent space, Chen crossed the foyer, his footsteps echoing off the marble. He climbed one of the majestic staircases, trailing his hand lightly over the time-worn banister that had been polished to a high sheen by generations of hands. The second-floor gallery was a long hallway with a plush red carpet runner extending into the distance. Elaborately carved arches and pilasters framed the walls at intervals. Oil paintings of land-scapes and portraits of stern-faced ancestors peered down from ornate gilded frames.

Chen proceeded down the gallery, glancing through the open doorways he passed. He glimpsed richly furnished rooms with heavy draperies, tasseled upholstery, and dark wooden furniture. Suits of armor stood in alcoves, and the flicker of flames could be seen dancing in grand fireplaces. He passed what appeared to be a library filled with towering bookshelves and a billiards room with a massive carved game table as the centerpiece.

At the end of the hallway, a set of double doors stood open, revealing a palatial bedroom. Chen entered and gazed around appreciatively. The room was the size of a huge ballroom, with a lofty coffered ceiling and a gabled window that stretched nearly from floor to ceiling. Heavy brocade curtains in a deep burgundy shade were tied back with gold-braided ropes to frame a stunning view of the manicured gardens and green hills beyond.

A four-poster canopy bed of darkly stained oak commanded the room. Sheer cream-colored curtains hung from the posts, fluttering gently in the breeze from the open window. The bed was neatly made with a plush burgundy comforter and piled high with pillows and cushions in rich jewel tones. An intricately carved headboard depicted woodland scenes of frolicking nymphs and satyrs.

On the far wall, a huge stone fireplace with an elaborately carved mantel reached nearly to the ceiling. The hearth was large enough to stand in, and an elegant settee and two wing chairs were arranged cozily around it on a luxurious Persian rug. A mahogany writing desk with spindly legs and a red leather chair stood under the window. An oversize armoire in the same dark wood loomed in a corner.

Chen crossed the plush burgundy carpet to a partially open door and peered inside. It was an en suite bathroom nearly as grand as the bedroom itself. Gleaming black and white tiles checkered across the floor and a claw-foot porcelain tub large enough for two commanded the center of the room. An oversize glass shower with an intricate mosaic of green tiles depicting sea serpents took up most of one wall. Next to an arched window swathed in sheer curtains stood a mahogany washstand with a large mirror in an ornate silver frame above it. Crystal decanters and silver-handled brushes were precisely arranged on its marble top.

Chen turned back to survey the extravagant bedroom once more, soaking in the timeless luxury and attention to detail evident in every inch of the manor house. He had the distinct impression that very little about the place had changed in the past century or two. It exuded an aura of gracious repose and enduring elegance. Despite its vastness, the home felt surprisingly intimate, each room an exquisite jewel box of rarefied beauty. Chen could almost feel the whisper of generations past swirling around him as he stood there, an interloper in the grand continuity of the stately manor.

He shrugged off the wonder and set his bag down on the bed. There was, as Rolf had insinuated earlier, still work to do, and they had less than twelve hours to do it before their rendezvous with the boss.

Chen thought it a little unusual the man didn't meet him and the rest of the men here at the manor. Maybe he was just reclusive. He'd heard of several wealthy types like that. Some of them were famous people from history.

It didn't matter. Chen just thought it curious. He didn't care if the guy met them here or where they'd discussed. The plan certainly carried an air of cloak and dagger to it. The place where they were meeting was also a strange thing. It would be colder in the later hours of night, and Dinas Emrys was out in the national park. Chen guessed they wouldn't have trouble gaining entry, but it was hardly convenient.

He wondered if his employer had something symbolic in mind, perhaps reuniting the eight heads at an ancient Druidic sacred place. His boss didn't seem the type for that sort of nonsense, but Chen knew almost nothing about the man to make that judgment.

He set his laptop bag down on the bed next to his rucksack and walked to the bathroom. A quick shower before breakfast would do him good. Today was going to be the stepping stone to his new life, and he was ready to take it head-on.

36

Kiera led the way up the narrow stone pathway, her boots making soft, deliberate sounds against the damp flagstones. The short flight of stairs leading up to the entrance was lined with a simple wooden railing, aged by the elements but still sturdy. Tara and Alex followed, their steps slightly hesitant as they took in the surroundings—the scent of damp earth and pine, the way the wind carried a faint hint of woodsmoke from somewhere nearby.

Reaching the thick wooden door, Kiera pulled a brass key from her jacket pocket and slid it into the lock. The mechanism clicked smoothly, and she pushed the door open to reveal the warm, inviting interior of the cottage.

The entryway opened into a spacious yet cozy living area, where exposed wooden beams crisscrossed the ceiling and a large stone fireplace dominated one wall. A rug in muted earth tones covered the polished wooden floors, and a plush sofa sat near the hearth, accompanied by a pair of well-worn leather armchairs. The air smelled faintly of cedar and aged parchment, as though time itself had settled into the walls.

To the right, a small wooden staircase led to the upper level, while a wide archway on the left opened into the kitchen. Kiera gestured toward it as she walked through.

"Fully stocked with the basics," she said. The rustic wooden cabinets housed ceramic dishes and cast-iron cookware, while a deep farmhouse sink stood beneath a small window overlooking the back of the property. A wrought-iron chandelier hung overhead, casting warm light over the wooden dining table, which had a set of hand-carved chairs neatly tucked beneath it.

Beyond the kitchen, she motioned to a powder room, its walls lined with delicate floral wallpaper and a simple pedestal sink standing beneath an oval mirror framed in dark wood.

"Down this way," she continued, leading them through a short hallway, "is your room."

She stopped at a heavy wooden door and pushed it open, revealing a spacious yet intimate bedroom. A large four-poster bed, its frame dark-stained and carved with intricate patterns, stood in the center. The bed was draped with a thick duvet and plaid blankets, and matching nightstands stood on either side, each holding a small lantern-style lamp. A woolen throw lay neatly folded at the foot of the bed, adding to the rustic comfort of the room.

A fireplace, smaller than the one in the main room, was nestled into the stone wall opposite the bed, already set with wood and kindling. A faint scent of lavender and aged timber lingered in the air.

Kiera walked past the bed, opening another door. "And here's the master bath."

The bathroom was spacious, featuring a large claw-foot tub beneath a frosted window, a separate glass-enclosed shower, and a long wooden vanity with two ceramic basins. The brass fixtures had a slightly worn patina, adding to the charm, and a woven basket of thick towels sat neatly beside the tub.

Tara ran a hand along the edge of the vanity. "This place is incredible."

Kiera smirked. "Wait until you see the best part."

She led them back through the house, past the kitchen, and

toward the rear of the cottage, where a set of French doors opened onto the back porch. The moment Kiera swung the doors open, a gust of cool mountain air swept in, carrying the scent of pine and damp earth.

The porch stretched the width of the cottage, framed by a sturdy wooden railing and furnished with a pair of cushioned chairs and a small round table. But the most notable feature was the hot tub, its dark wooden exterior blending with the aesthetic of the home. The water inside rippled slightly, reflecting the early afternoon light.

Beyond the porch, the land sloped downward, revealing an expansive view of the valley below, with the mountains rising like ancient sentinels in the distance. The sky had cleared entirely now, pale blue streaked with hints of gold as the sun inched toward the horizon.

"How long did you say we can stay here?" Tara asked, glancing playfully over at Kiera.

Kiera smiled. "The next few days, of course, I'm sure Matias wouldn't mind extending your stay if you like. After we take care of business, of course." She turned and walked back into the house then over to the coffee machine in the corner of the kitchen.

Tara and Alex followed her back inside, closing the door behind them before making their way over to the counter, where three stools with black metal legs and birch tops sat under the surface. They each sat down and watched as Kiera poured water from a filtered pitcher into the machine's reservoir.

"So, Matias says I'm to take you to Dinas Emrys in the park." Kiera finished pouring the water then reached for a bag of coffee.

"Yeah," Tara confirmed. "And look, we don't know for sure these guys even came here. They could be somewhere else, at a totally different site."

"Then why did you come here?" Kiera asked, looking back at her over her shoulder.

"Seemed logical, even if it is a bit of a long shot."

Kiera chuckled as she finished prepping the coffee. She hit the brew button and spun around to face the Americans, crossing her arms.

"Well, a long shot is better than no shot at all. Tell me what you know about Dinas Emrys."

Tara and Alex looked at each other as if wondering which one should speak first.

Alex figured he might as well. "Not much, other than what we've read online about it. Mostly stuff about its legends, some of the history."

Kiera nodded. "Sorry, I was talking more about the topography."

"Oh no. Just what we've seen in pictures." Alex sounded a little embarrassed.

"Well, there are some things you should know. She leaned against the counter, her fingers tapping idly against the surface as the coffee pot began to gurgle, filling the space with the rich aroma of brewing coffee.

"Dinas Emrys isn't an easy place to reach," Kiera began, glancing over her shoulder at the pot as it continued to brew. "It's tucked into the hills of Snowdonia, surrounded by steep terrain and thick forests. There's no direct route—you either hike in or take one of the old trails used by shepherds. It's not exactly a tourist hot spot, so we won't have crowds to blend into. That works in our favor, but it also means if someone's waiting for us, there aren't a lot of ways out."

Alex leaned forward, resting his forearms on the table. "What about vantage points? If we're dealing with hostiles, they'll have the high ground."

Kiera nodded. "Exactly. The ruins sit at the top of a rocky outcrop, with only a couple of viable paths leading up. If anyone's expecting trouble, they'll have sight lines on those approaches long before we get close. There's also the river running nearby—rough terrain but a possible escape route if needed."

Tara exhaled, rubbing her temples. "So sneaking up isn't an option. We'd be seen a mile away."

"Unless we time it right," Kiera countered. "Fog rolls in early morning and late evening, thick enough to cover our movements if we plan accordingly. But that also works against us—visibility will be just as bad for us as it is for them. One misstep, and we could be walking into an ambush."

Silence settled for a moment as they absorbed the challenge ahead.

Alex exchanged a glance with Tara. "Then we'd better plan carefully."

"And it would be nice to have some weapons." Tara looked expectantly at their hostess.

"Yes, Matias left a little present for us in the upstairs bedroom. I hope you don't mind; that's where I was planning on staying as long as you're here."

"Don't mind at all. Could we... open the gift?"

"Right this way," Kiera said with a smile, leaving the coffee pot to continue its task as she walked over to the narrow flight of stairs leading up to the second floor.

The Americans followed close behind her then to the right into a bedroom at the top. The room was cozy, with a queen-size bed pushed up against the wall under a large window. Dark blue curtains hung over the edges, framing the picture of the valley and village outside.

None of them paid much attention beyond that. Their focus went to a long chrome case sitting on the bed.

Kiera moved over to it, casually undid the clasps, and flipped open the lid, revealing two AR15-style rifles and a pair of SIG Sauer 9mm pistols.

"What about you?" Alex asked, turning to their hostess.

"Oh, I'm all sorted. Matias made sure of that. He told me to watch your backs, so that's precisely what I'm going to do."

She said it in a cold, haunting way that left no doubt she meant every word.

"We'll need to be discreet," Kiera said. "I doubt those men are planning on going up there until later in the day. If they're here at all."

"Yeah, we're definitely going in blind on this one. When do you think we should go?"

"Hard to say. But later in the day might be good. We can go up the backside of one of the hills nearby to get a good view of the place. Matias also hooked us up with night-vision goggles, so that will make things easier if these guys are doing whatever deal this is at night. Still seems weird they're doing some exchange at this place."

Tara and Alex stole a quick glance at each other before Tara answered.

"This is no ordinary illicit sale that's going down. There's more."

She went on to tell Kiera about their concerns regarding the ancient stones and what reuniting them could do at a sacred Druid site.

Kiera listened with an open mind, and when Tara was done, she nodded, silently contemplating the information.

"I know it sounds crazy," Alex said.

"It would, if I didn't already know about some of your exploits. I heard what happened in Bolivia."

"That's not creepy."

"It's called being thorough, something I'm quite sure the two of you know all about." She took a step toward the door. "Coffee is ready. I'll make us something to eat. There's coats and jackets in the closet. Find one that fits you."

Her order reminded them that they'd been forced to leave their main bags back in Jaisalmer. It was nothing they couldn't live without —mostly clothes. But they'd already called to let the hotel know they would have to pay to have the items shipped. Tara joked it would just be cheaper to buy new things, but Alex insisted.

Leaving the weapons on the bed, the three returned downstairs where the hot coffee waited, along with way too many unknowns for the day ahead.

37

The hike up to their vantage point hadn't been easy. The dense forest that surrounded Dinas Emrys provided excellent cover, but the climb had been steep in spots, the ground uneven with twisted roots and loose stones hidden beneath thick underbrush.

Kiera led the way, moving with an ease that spoke of years navigating rugged terrain, while Tara and Alex followed, keeping their footfalls light despite the strenuous ascent. The scent of damp earth and moss lingered in the air, mingling with the faint sweetness of wildflowers that had managed to bloom in the shaded glades.

They moved carefully, weaving through gaps between the thick-trunked pines and twisted oaks, their branches interlocking overhead to form a natural canopy. Occasionally, a shaft of golden light pierced through, illuminating patches of the moss-covered ground, where delicate ferns unfurled. The air was cool and still; the wet leaves barely made a sound under their careful steps.

They finally reached the edge of a forest where a flat ridge concealed by a thick stand of pine and ash trees gave them a decent view of the ancient site. From here, they had a clear view of the hill fort and its surroundings without exposing themselves. The ruins of

Dinas Emrys, weathered by time, sat atop the rocky outcrop, its crumbling stone walls partially hidden by tall grass and wild shrubbery. It had an air of quiet desolation, a place heavy with history, and whispers of old legends swirling in the wind that rustled through the trees. To call it ruins would be generous.

Now, two hours later, they were growing impatient.

They'd been watching the hill fort in silence, only whispering to each other now and then, keeping their voices to slightly louder than a breath. Few visitors had made the climb up to the ruins—most stayed only a short while before making their way back down. Tourists in hiking gear, a couple with cameras, an older man sketching in a notebook—but no one suspicious. Still, none of them had relaxed. They knew someone would come.

The light had begun to shift, the sun sinking lower in the western sky, turning the edges of the trees to gold and amber. Shadows stretched longer across the landscape, casting the ruins in a muted, ethereal glow. Below, the terrain sloped into a patchwork of thick bracken, rocky outcrops, and narrow dirt trails that wound their way up the hillside. The surrounding countryside was vast and unspoiled, rolling hills stretching out beyond the valley and the faintest shimmer of a winding river visible in the distance. Even from here, they could hear its distant rush, an ever-present murmur beneath the occasional breeze that rustled the grass.

Then—movement.

At first, it was just figures emerging from the tree line below, too far to make out details, but something about their deliberate pace set them apart from the casual hikers who had come before them. As they neared the base of the hill fort, their features became clearer.

A group of nine men. They were all dressed differently but carried themselves with the same underlying presence of control and purpose. Except one. He seemed out of place with the others, less confident. The group moved too deliberately to be ordinary hikers. No cameras, no idle chatter, no hesitation in their steps. After a closer look, Tara and Alex realized the outlier in the group was Chen. They realized it at the same time and shot each other a knowing and angry look.

Tara stiffened slightly, shifting her position to get a better look through the gaps in the foliage. Alex tensed beside her, his hand instinctively moving to where his weapon rested under his jacket. Kiera, crouched slightly forward, exhaled slowly, steady and controlled.

The wind blew through the trees and filled their ears with the slight rustling. They watched as the group of men navigated the uneven ground. The leader of the group, a man with broad shoulders and a faded green jacket, moved with careful precision. Alex recognized him as the one called Rolf.

He exchanged a few quiet words with another man—wiry, bearded, his dark clothing blending into the dimming light—but the conversation was kept low, intentionally muffled.

Kiera's gaze sharpened as she tracked their movements. They were scouting the area, doing some recon.

Tara and Alex both wondered where Felicia was, but they didn't dare vocalize it. The archaeologist was nowhere to be seen, which meant she was either dead or she'd been left somewhere.

Birds that had chirped earlier had now gone silent. A faint mist had begun to settle along the lower portion of the valley, creeping in with the shifting light.

Tara adjusted slightly, shifting her knee off a protruding root.

Alex raised the long-range microphone Kiera had provided along with the other gear. Tara and Alex were both starting to wonder who Kiera was. She had a lot of goodies to simply be a security guard for the wealthy Danish man.

Alex switched on the mic then fitted one of the buds in his ear.

Everyone's jaws were tight, their eyes fixed on the figures moving toward the ruins.

The wind whispered through the trees, carrying the distant cry of a bird somewhere in the valley below. Tara shifted slightly, her muscles tense from holding the same position for so long. Alex adjusted his stance, careful not to disturb the brush around him. The group below had vanished behind the ruin walls, and for a moment the hilltop was silent again.

Then one of the men reappeared, moving with slow, deliberate steps as he scanned the area. They were checking the area the same way Secret Service might for a place the president was giving a speech. Here, there were no buildings to clear, no rooftops to watch. There were only mountains and forests, the occasional boulder here and there. They were being cautious. The bearded man who had lingered at the back earlier now stood at an elevated point near the edge of the ruins, his hand resting near his hip. Was he armed? The way he carried himself suggested he was, but the guy didn't dare flash a firearm around here. If spotted, there would be trouble. A gun in this part of the world would be treated much differently than back in the States.

A second man joined the first, the one named Yuri. He lifted a hand to shield his eyes against the waning sunlight. Below them, the others seemed to be fanning out, moving in a synchronized sweep, their formation precise, deliberate. These weren't just hired guns— they were trained. Each movement was purposeful, covering blind spots, securing angles, ensuring the area was clear.

Chen walked among them, his presence now unmistakable.

Rolf pointed toward a section of overgrown stonework, and two of the men quickly moved in that direction. One knelt, running his hands over the ground as if searching for an irregularity in the surface. The other stood guard, scanning the trees with unnerving focus.

Tara swallowed hard. They'd already discussed what they would do if they were spotted. It would be a mad dash through the woods and back down to the vehicle they'd parked off the road behind a thicket of brush.

Alex felt his concealed weapon underneath the jacket. A long black bag cradled the rifles next to his feet.

The tension thickened as another mercenary paused near the tree line seventy meters away, his gaze sweeping the ridge. He lingered—

too long—his sharp eyes scanning the shadows, as if sensing movement.

Kiera stilled completely, pressing herself lower into the underbrush. Tara followed suit, slowing her breath, willing herself invisible. Alex kept his body motionless, every instinct screaming at him not to react. The man's gaze hovered over their position; his expression unreadable.

The seconds stretched into eternity.

Then, after an almost unbearable wait, the man turned away, saying something to the others before continuing his search.

Tara released a breath, controlled but sharp. "That was close."

"Too close," Alex muttered.

He continued listening to the men's conversations, which was little more than an order here and there delivered by Rolf.

Fifteen minutes passed, the men covering the site methodically before regrouping near the old stone steps leading down the hill.

Then the group convened again at the ruins, standing on a patch of grass near a lone tree.

Alex listened more intently.

"It looks clear," Rolf said. "No signs of trouble. And we'll easily be able to secure the area tonight when we return for the rendezvous."

"Excellent," Chen said, turning his head to gaze out around the area one more time.

"It will be trickier at 23:30 tonight," Rolf said, the wind crackling the sound through the radio. "I don't suppose you learned why we're meeting at that time, and in this place."

"No. And it isn't our job to ask. Maybe it's part of some weird religious rite."

"You think?"

"Would make sense. There are plenty of remote places to do a deal like this. Why here? Maybe he's a modern-day Druid. Look, all I know is for what we're being paid, I would meet him at the North Pole if I had to."

"Agreed. Very well, let's head back to the manor. Now we know how long it takes to get up here and where we need to be positioned for the exchange."

Chen nodded, and the two men marched off with the others close behind them.

The silence they left behind felt heavy, like the forest itself was holding its breath.

Kiera finally moved, shifting into a more comfortable crouch. "What did they say?"

"Their rendezvous is tonight at eleven-thirty."

"So, we need to be back here before then," Tara said. "Maybe around eleven just to be safe."

"I'd say that's a good idea. Or even earlier."

"Did you catch anything else?" Kiera asked.

"Yes. Just before they left, one of them suggested they get back to the manor before returning here."

"Manor?" Tara clarified.

"That's what he said."

"There are a few of those close by," Kiera mentioned. "Some of them are quite old."

"Do you think you could isolate where they might be?"

She thought about it for five seconds before answering. "Could be difficult, but I can see what I can find. We have the hours to kill before coming back here. What are you thinking?"

"It would be hard to ambush them in a mansion with just the three of us. And if they have Felicia with them, even more so."

"So what do you want to do?"

"First, let's see if you can even find where their hideout is. Then we can go from there."

38

Darkness shrouded the world outside the windows of the cottage.

Kiera sat at the kitchen counter with her laptop staring back at her. She'd narrowed down the location of Chen and his men to a large mansion about twenty minutes from here in another small village.

The manor had been owned by the same family for hundreds of years until they'd recently hit on hard times and been forced to sell it to pay off their debts.

The buyer's name had not been disclosed and had been purchased by an LLC. Normally, that would signal a group was going to buy the place and use it either as a corporate retreat or try to leverage the property as a holiday destination for tourists.

In this instance, Kiera assumed neither of those was the case. The manor was the perfect place to set up a base of operations, away from the townspeople and the occasional visitor.

"That has to be it," Kiera said. "Not too far from here either. Next village over."

"You are amazing," Tara said. "And remind me not to get on your bad side."

The British woman arched a mischievous eyebrow then grinned. "So what do you think?"

Alex paced over to the big window in the living room, paused, and then walked back. "Part of me thinks we should go there, see if we can stop them from even getting out of the driveway."

"But the other part of you disagrees with that plan."

"Yeah. Look at that place. It's like a fortress. Wall and fence around it. Gate at the front of the driveway. I'm sure they have cameras everywhere, or the very least sensors in place to detect trespassers."

"You seem like an expert with this sort of stuff," Tara said. "What do you think?"

Kiera stood up straight and stretched her neck left to right. "I don't particularly like either option. There are too many unknowns with an ambush at the manor. At least up at the hill fort we have natural terrain to help us out, and based on what we know, it seems like those men don't know we're here."

"They probably assumed that we got stuck in India with no way of guessing where they would go next."

"Can't say that I blame them. It was a lucky guess on our part," Tara added.

"So," Kiera continued, "our best bet is to see what we can do up at Dinas Emrys. There, we'll have different angles. Maybe even a way to take out some of their men without risking hitting your friend Felicia. If they decide to take her up there."

"They will," Alex affirmed. "Chen may need her. Either as a negotiating piece, or he may even need her to help if there's another riddle to decode."

"True. So we're going all in on this, then?"

They each exchanged questioning glances then nods.

"Okay. Better get ready. The next few hours will go by fast. At least we'll have the night-vision goggles to help us out. Maybe those guys won't have any."

"Right," Alex said. "Because if they do, this could be a very short offensive."

39

Darkness covered the hills and mountains of Snowdonia National Park.

Tara, Alex, and Kiera had been in position for the last forty minutes, waiting at the edge of the forest. They remained hidden as much as possible while still watching for Chen and his group to return.

The one thing they couldn't hide was their breath. Each exhale produced a cloud of moisture for a few seconds in the chilly air. The temperature had dropped sharply since sunset, leaving the ground damp beneath them, the scent of earth and moss heavy in the air. The sky stretched vast and clear above them, the half-moon casting a pale glow over the landscape, while countless stars flickered against the black expanse.

They'd had some supper before leaving. Kiera had prepared a simple but hearty Welsh meal back at the cottage. A steaming bowl of cawl—rich with lamb, potatoes, and leeks—had filled the air with a comforting aroma as they ate by the dim glow of the fireplace. Thick slices of freshly baked bara brith, buttered generously, added a hint of sweetness to the meal. They washed it down with strong black tea, its warmth cutting through the chill that had settled into their bones. It wasn't fancy, but it had been nourishing—a quiet moment of respite before the long night ahead.

Out here in the mountains, the ruins loomed in eerie stillness, their weathered stone walls rising like the bones of something long buried. The clearing surrounding the site was illuminated just enough by the celestial light to make out the uneven terrain—tufts of wild grass, patches of exposed rock, and the faint outlines of old, worn steps leading up to the heart of the ruins. No sound beyond the rustling of leaves and the occasional distant hoot of an owl disturbed the air, yet a quiet unease settled among them.

Alex checked his watch for the umpteenth time.

It was nearly 11:30, and there was still no sign of either of the two groups who were going to meet here.

The irrational side of him started wondering if it had all been a ruse to lure them here into a trap. He quickly dispelled that nonsense. Why would they go to all that trouble when they could simply take them down on sight?

Chen and his cronies didn't know they were here, and for now, that thought would have to do.

"There," Tara said, ripping him from his thoughts. "Lights."

She pointed down at the path winding up the hillside. Several flashlight beams waved back and forth in haphazard directions as a group approached.

From what she could tell, they weren't wearing night-vision goggles, which gave her a little comfort.

The men were armed, each carrying rifles slung over their shoulders. There were, no doubt, additional firearms hidden away in their jackets or perhaps even in their pants, concealed from view.

"Felicia," Alex breathed. "They brought her here."

"That answers that question," Kiera said.

As the seconds ticked by, the whole situation felt worse.

The men reached the top of the hill and took up a semicircular position, with Chen in the middle and Felicia held by one of the mercenaries just to his left.

"Where's the other group?" Tara whispered.

More and more, both she and Alex wondered about this location. The clues from before—the reliefs in the hidden chamber in Jaisalmer Fort, the images of deities, the references to monsters and war. All of it fit into the mystical category that Dinas Emrys was famous for.

Another group of lights flashed around down the path below. "There they come," Kiera announced in a hushed tone.

Alex and Tara peered through their goggles at the second group as they proceeded up the hill. There was a man in the center of the column dressed differently than the others. The men in front and behind him all wore black jackets and pants, and each carried what looked like HK-5 submachine guns.

Alex zeroed in on the guy in the middle, the one he assumed was the buyer and in charge of this entire operation.

The man's hair had receded slightly on his head. His profile was slender, and his face hawklike. It was difficult to get a good look at him until he'd cleared a section of shrubs down below their position.

When he did emerge into the clear again, Alex's breath caught in his chest.

"No," he said, slightly louder than he intended. "It can't be."

"What can't be?" Kiera asked.

"The guy in the middle of the second group."

The two women adjusted their focus and found the man he was talking about.

"What about him?"

For a second, Tara couldn't respond, and Alex knew the nightmares were crashing down around her, things she'd tried to forget for the last few years.

"Do you know him?" Kiera pressed.

"Unfortunately, yes," Alex answered. "We had a run-in with him a few years ago down in Bolivia. He was trying to open the Sun Gate at Tiwanaku."

"I heard about that."

"He should be in a prison cell," Tara muttered. "He was arrested, and they were going to put him away for a long time."

"Maybe he got out for good behavior," Kiera suggested.

"No." Tara shook her head. "He must have escaped."

"Who is he?"

"He's a sick freak. And has lots of money behind him. He nearly unleashed unspeakable horrors on the planet before. Now, it's pretty clear what is going on here, and why he chose this place. He's going to try it again."

Kiera pulled off her goggles and looked to Alex.

"His name," he said, "is Buri."

The name sent chills down Alex's and Tara's spines. Last they'd heard, Buri was on his way to some hole of a prison that he would most likely never get out of. They were both tempted to wonder how he'd managed to escape, but that wouldn't help them right now. He was here, and they were going to have to deal with it.

Buri's group continued up to the top of the hill where Chen and his group waited.

Several of the mercenaries kept their heads on swivels, turning and looking into the darkness for any signs of trouble.

Alex raised the long-range microphone again and pointed it at the two groups, but before he could even switch the thing on, a snapping sound behind him stole his attention.

He and the two women started to turn around, but they were cut short.

"Don't move," a voice said in a Spanish accent. "Drop your weapons."

Alex had already placed his rifle down at his feet to use the microphone. The two women hesitated then obeyed reluctantly.

"Now, step out into the open, nice and slow."

Alex turned his head and saw their captor. His face was partially hidden by shadows, but he was muscular, and the silhouette of his jawline reflected that strength. He held a Glock pointed at Alex's head. "Keep going," the Spaniard ordered.

The three prisoners stepped out of the forest and into the clearing. The Spaniard followed them and spoke into his radio.

"I found someone," he said. "Looks like they were going to try to break up the party."

Two of the mercenaries at the site immediately broke away and trotted up to meet the two Americans and their British ally.

"They had weapons. You'll find them down in the trees, just over there," the man said.

One of the two guys nodded and passed them to go retrieve the stash. The other escorted the captives up the slope to the main group.

"You don't know what you're doing," Tara said to the Spaniard. "You have no idea what kind of danger you're both in."

"Keep your mouth shut, and keep moving."

She bit her bottom lip and continued ahead until they were surrounded by both groups of men.

Buri stepped out from the midst of the crew he'd brought and grinned like the devil after just installing a swimming pool.

"Twenty bucks he says well, well, well," Alex said so only the two women could hear it.

"No bet," Tara replied.

"Stop right there," the Spaniard ordered when they were in the center of the two groups.

"Well, well, well," Buri said as he approached. "Look what we have here."

Tara and Alex shared a sidelong glance.

"Buri," Alex said. "How horrible to see you again."

Buri's smile widened as he snorted. "Yes, I would think it must be. After all, you two ruined all the hard work I did to reach the Sun Gate in Bolivia."

"How'd you get out of prison?" Tara spat. She made no effort to hide her disgust.

"Oh, I'm afraid I never actually made it to the long-term prison facility. Some of my associates stopped the truck along the way and set me free. I've been working on locating a new portal ever since. Of course, I'm sure you worked out that this is what is going on here."

They didn't confirm or deny.

Buri's eyes fell on Kiera. "And you brought a friend with you this time." He held up his hand to brush her cheek, but she quickly snatched his wrists and twisted it, holding it tight in her grip.

"Don't. Touch. Me," she snarled.

The Spaniard behind her pressed his pistol to the lower part of her spine.

"Let him go," the man ordered.

Buri's filthy grin didn't vanish. Two seconds later, she let him go.

"Beautiful and feisty. A combination I find endearing in a woman."

"I would rather eat those stones over there," Kiera countered.

Buri shrugged. "Maybe you will." He returned his attention to the two IAA agents. "But you two showing up here is a wonderful turn of events. Not only will I receive the power that is due to me, but I'll also get my revenge. You see, the universe rewards those who are diligent."

"The universe doesn't reward evil," Alex hissed.

"What is evil?" Buri asked. "Is it evil to want to control mankind, to advance our species into the future? That is the power that awaits in the quantum realms."

"You have no idea what you're talking about," Tara said. "You didn't see the warnings, the stories in the places where those heads were hidden."

"I know enough," he protested. "And now, the greatest powers in the cosmos will answer to my command. Nations will bow down before me. I will be unstoppable."

"I think we heard this last time. If you think it's going to be so great, maybe you go through the portal first and see what you've unleashed."

Buri shook his head, and his smile soured to a sinister expression. "Oh, it isn't who is going in. It's what will come out."

He turned and marched over to the center of a circle outlined by ancient stones. Some of them had been overgrown with grass and weeds.

"Chen, I believe you have something that belongs to me," Buri said, approaching the traitor.

Chen nodded and set down a duffel bag hanging from his left shoulder. He knelt down and unzipped it. "They're all here."

Buri bent down and removed one of the heads from the bag. He held it aloft, pointing a flashlight at it. "Excellent."

He clipped his flashlight to his belt and took another head from the bag. Then he walked over to a spot at the edge of the circle and set it down. He moved to the right and found another place, where he positioned the second head.

"I trust you have my payment," Chen said as Buri returned to collect two more stone busts.

"Of course. You will receive your payment in a moment."

He took the next two heads and positioned them in a similar manner to the others, all facing inward to the center of the circle.

Alex noted the exhausted look on Felicia's face. She looked like she could barely stand. All emotion was gone from her, leaving her an empty husk, an apparition barely clinging to life. He dreaded to think of what she might have been through since she'd been taken. Men like that were soulless, devoid of a moral compass that guided their way.

He shoved the thought aside, observing what was about to happen. They'd lost their weapons. That was a bad one. Without the guns, they had no way to defend themselves. Not that it would have mattered. The combined forces with Buri and Chen were over-whelming.

Maybe there was a way to turn the two sides against each other, but Alex doubted it. All of these men worked for Buri. Chen was probably the exception, a ringer called in to help find the other six heads.

After Buri placed the last two heads from Chen's bag, he walked back over to where his guards stood and took a small gray backpack from one of them. He set the bag down on the ground, unzipped it, and removed the last two heads.

"And here I thought Chen was bluffing," Tara muttered.

"Silence," the Spaniard ordered.

Tara gritted her teeth, holding back what she wanted to say.

Buri held up the two stones, admiring them as if he'd created them himself. The man was that kind of narcissist. After a second of inspecting the artifacts, he walked over to the last few stones in the formation and paused.

"Don't do it," Tara warned. "You think you can control what's on the other side of the veil." She shook her head dramatically. "But you can't. Only someone with the supernatural power, godlike power, can command it through force."

"It's too late for that sort of nonsense."

Buri set the stone in his left hand down in position then stepped over to the last spot. There, he hesitated for a few seconds before setting it down.

He stood up, acting as though a heavy burden had been lifted from his shoulders.

Nothing happened.

Alex looked around at the gunmen. None of them said anything. They just stood watching. Maybe they were expecting something to happen.

He was about to offer a snide comment, a real humdinger about how it happened to everyone now and then, but Buri spoke first.

"And now, to complete the ceremony, we will offer a sacrifice."

40

lex and Tara looked at each other then at Kiera, all feeling the same tight squeeze in their abdomens.

Sacrifice?

It was a thought each of them shared, and to which they all feared the answer.

Chen grinned, crossing his arms. He almost looked like he was enjoying this.

Buri walked over to him then looked at Felicia.

Tara and Alex both felt the same fear. Buri was going to sacrifice Dr. Lowe for whatever crazy thing he was trying to do here.

"Dr. Lowe," Buri began, "you've been instrumental in helping make all this happen. Truly, I appreciate all your efforts. I realize that at the time you didn't know what you were doing, but here, in the end, I hope you will enjoy it."

"Leave her alone!" Alex blurted. He'd grown tired of the theatrics. "Take me instead!"

Tara looked over at him, pleading in her eyes.

Buri turned and faced them from the other side of the small clearing. "Oh, don't worry, Alex. I have something special planned for you three. You'll have your place in all this. But no, I have no intention of sacrificing Felicia. She wouldn't do." He drew a long knife from a sheath, concealed within his jacket. "You see, it must be the blood of a fatherless boy. The legend of this place is pretty specific."

Chen frowned, seeing a flash of the blade as Buri swung it around and drove it deep into his gut.

Chen's eyes widened, peering into Buri's, the question of why streaking through them.

"Why? We...had a deal," Chen spat, collapsing to his knees.

"Yes, that's true. But you are an orphan. And the sacrifice calls for a fatherless boy." Buri withdrew the knife then nodded at two of the mercenaries.

They grabbed Chen under the armpits and dragged him over to the center of the circle so all eight stones were facing him.

Buri moved behind Chen. The guards released him, and Buri grabbed Chen by the hair. He pulled the archaeologist's head up, exposing his neck.

"Here is your payment," Buri said into his right ear. "And the payment for the gods."

He swiped the blade across Chen's throat. For a second, nothing happened. Then the fine cut parted, and dark blood began spurting, then surging freely from the wound, streaming onto the ground as the dying man's heart pumped it out of his body.

Felicia wept as she watched the horror play out. She nearly collapsed to her knees, but one of the men next to her forced her to stay on her feet.

Chen's body fell to the ground, blood soaking the stone under him as he writhed then twitched. In under a minute, he had stopped moving altogether.

A deep rumble shook the mountain, echoing across the valley.

Buri's lips curled up, and he stepped back out of the circle.

The moment he was outside the arrangement of heads, a dark pink light appeared over the body. It hovered there for a moment, barely the size of a golf ball.

"Everyone move back!" Buri ordered.

The gunmen stared in rapt wonder at the strange sight. Only some inexplicable supernatural phenomena could faze these killers.

They moved back and around to one side, surrounding the IAA agents and pushing Felicia close to them.

The night air shuddered as the dark pink orb pulsed at the center of the ancient ruins, a sinister glow radiating outward. What had begun as a mere flicker of light—an anomaly in the fabric of reality—was growing quickly. The air around it rippled, distorting the very space it occupied, bending and warping the atmosphere as though something immense pressed against an invisible barrier, waiting to be unleashed.

Buri stood at the edge of the growing rift, his arms raised in triumph, as if standing on a hilltop at the Second Coming. The bloodied remnants of his sacrifice still lay on the stone beneath his feet. Chen's body lay motionless, his life extinguished to feed the dark energy now surging through the air. The gathered mercenaries, hardened killers who had seen war and death, watched in stunned silence. This was beyond any battlefield they had known.

Tara, Alex, Felicia, and Kiera remained motionless, watching the portal as it continued to grow. Their breath misted in the cold night air, their bodies tense. The portal's glow deepened, shifting from its sickly pink hue to something more intense—an unnatural shade of violet, tinged with black at the edges. It was no longer a light but a wound in the world, a gash that bled raw energy into the night.

The ground trembled beneath them, dust rising from between the cracks of ancient stone. The very ruins themselves seemed to recoil, as if the centuries-old foundations could sense the unraveling of reality. The growing portal began to elongate, stretching in midair, its form shifting from an orb into a hovering oblong gateway that twisted against the sky. Its edges crackled with energy, bolts of black lightning arcing outward from its perimeter, striking the ground with concussive force. The wind picked up, howling through the ruins, carrying with it the distant echoes of something vast and inhuman stirring on the other side.

For a moment, Alex wondered if the Merlin story about the dragons bursting from the mountain were true.

The mercenaries, confident only moments before, retreated involuntarily, their instinct for self-preservation overriding any lingering loyalty to Buri. Shadows flickered along their faces, their expressions betraying uncertainty. They were all wondering the same thing: What had Buri summoned?

Felicia clenched her fists, her breathing shallow as she tried to steady herself. Next to her, Alex's gaze remained locked on the portal, his mind racing through possibilities. If they didn't act soon, it wouldn't matter.

The portal swelled farther, its form now reaching forty feet in height and nearly thirty feet wide, a vast monolith of shifting, writhing light. The air smelled charged, metallic, as if the very molecules were being rewritten by whatever force had been unleashed. The wind grew stronger, whipping through their hair, tugging at their clothes, dragging leaves and dust into the vortex.

And then—something moved inside the swirling portal.

The silhouette stirred beyond the threshold, a shadow upon shadows, an indistinct form just out of reach, pressing against the veil between realms. The air vibrated, a low-frequency hum reverberating through the ground, rattling their bones. The first tendrils of dark matter, sinuous and shifting, slithered through the opening, curling like living smoke, reaching outward into the night.

The air temperature dropped sharply; their breath more visible in the growing cold. The feeling that something ancient, something powerful, was watching them settled into their chests, a primal fear clawing at their throats.

"Guys?" Kiera said, no longer afraid of being told to shut up by the guards. "What... is that?"

The form continued to grow within the portal.

"Come forth, mighty warrior!' Buri shouted.

"Warrior?" Felicia managed, finally finding her voice.

"That isn't just a warrior," Tara said. "And there isn't just one of them."

More forms began to take shape behind the first, hordes of them, as if marching into battle behind their leader.

Alex tore his eyes from the apparitions and looked at the stone surrounding the portal. He leaned close to Tara and spoke so only she could hear. "We have to break the connection," he said.

She nodded, understanding exactly what he meant.

The question neither of them could answer was how.

The portal pulsed violently, its violet dark light warping the very air around it. And then the first entity emerged.

At first, it was only a shadow upon the threshold, a massive, shifting form silhouetted against the writhing abyss beyond. Then the form stepped closer, its immense frame looming at the edge of the portal, poised between two worlds. The energy of the gateway flickered against the polished metal of its battle-worn armor, casting jagged reflections along its plated chest and the segmented pauldrons that curved over its shoulders like the exoskeleton of some ancient predator.

Twenty feet tall, broad, and powerful, the entity exuded a presence that was neither fully monstrous nor fully divine. The armor encasing its body was sleek yet imposing, its dark, metallic surface inlaid with intricate, almost celestial engravings that shimmered faintly beneath the now-blood-red glow of the portal. It looked like a fallen angel, sculpted by war and time but without the wings to carry it away.

The creature's face, revealed beneath the shadow of an elaborate, crown-like helm, was haunting in its weary, bitter beauty. Its skin was ashen, smooth but marred with faint, ancient scars, traces of battles fought long before this moment. Its sharp features—high cheekbones, a strong jaw, lips set in a grim, unreadable expression—could have belonged to a lost deity or a forsaken king. Yet it was its eyes that truly unsettled.

Twin orbs of searing red light, swirling like molten embers, burned beneath the heavy brow. Not mindless rage, but something worse—an ancient, unrelenting fury. The kind of wrath that had been tempered by eternity, reforged again and again, until it had become absolute.

For a long, unnerving pause, the creature stood at the edge of the portal, unmoving, as if tasting the air of this world for the first time in eons. The energy that clung to its form crackled, arcs of dark electricity spiraling around its gauntlets and down its armored limbs.

Then, with a deliberate, measured step, it crossed the threshold.

The ground rumbled beneath its weight as its massive foot met the stone. The air seemed to compress, heavy with the gravity of something that should not exist in this place. A ripple of unnatural force surged outward from its body, bending the light, distorting reality itself.

It lifted its head slowly, its glowing eyes sweeping over the gathered onlookers—mortals, insignificant, trembling at the sight of it. The corners of its lips curled, just slightly, in an expression that was neither smile nor snarl. Recognition. Contempt. Amusement.

Then the monster looked at Buri, who stood with his hands still raised like he was in a praise service at some messed-up, evil church.

"You," the creature's voice boomed. It was male, dominating, smooth yet full of hatred. "You opened the portal."

"Yes!" Buri shouted.

Every eye on the hilltop was locked on the monstrosity. No one would dare look away, except Tara and Alex.

They both knew this was their chance while everyone was distracted. The guards watching them were still too close. They needed something to get them away.

"Bring forth your armies!" Buri shouted. "That they may serve me in glory!"

The monster's face twisted to an amused expression. Then it laughed. It was a thunderous, terrible sound.

Buri glanced around, suddenly uncomfortable.

"Serve you?" the unearthly voice boomed. "I serve no one, pet."

"But... I brought you here. I opened the portal."

"Which is why I won't kill you. Yet."

The monster swept its terrifying gaze across everyone standing around. "You will all serve me—as your god!"

Alex had heard enough. He didn't have a plan, but he knew he couldn't stand for this anymore.

"I will serve no so-called god!" he shouted.

The creature turned its head toward Alex.

"What are you doing?" Tara begged.

"Not sure."

"Bring him to me," the monster commanded, his voice full of indignation.

One of the gunmen behind the Americans stepped forward and grabbed Alex by the arm.

The creature reached over its shoulder and pulled a sword from a sheath. The blade shimmered in the eerie light of the portal as he lowered it in front of him. The gilded handle shone brightly, truly a weapon fit for a god.

Alex resisted, but the guard continued forcing him forward. There was no point in trying to stop it, and within seconds Alex found himself standing fifteen feet away from the monster.

"Alex!" Tara shouted, tears streaming down her face. A gunman behind her grabbed her shoulder in case she tried anything.

Buri looked at Alex. The man was bewildered. All his planning had done nothing but ensure he would be a slave for life to whatever this thing was.

Alex would have rather died. And if he did, maybe it would create enough of a distraction.

"You know what to do," he said to Tara, looking over his shoulder at her. "I love you."

She surged forward to run to him, but the guard holding her was too strong, and she didn't even make it a foot. "No! Alex, I love you!"

It was all happening so fast.

The creature shook its head as it raised the giant sword high, ready to deliver the killing blow in one strike.

"So begins the new age," it said, voice echoing through the valley.

Behind the monster, legions of its warriors waited to be unleashed from the portal and spill into the realm of humans.

Suddenly, something warm and wet splattered across the side of Alex's face and neck.

He looked to his right, where the gunman was standing, and saw a thin red line open across his neck. The man looked confused, and his expression didn't change as his legs gave out and his head toppled from his body.

For a second, it seemed time stood still. No one moved for what seemed like an eternity, even though it was only a second or two. Then a figure ran by Alex in a blur.

Against the backdrop of the portal's light, he and the others couldn't see the thing's face, but the body was unmistakably animal. Like an eight-foot-tall werewolf, charging at the supposed god.

The wolf leaped up toward the creature's face and delivered a powerful punch. The monster's head rocked back unexpectedly, throwing it off balance. The sword arm fell immediately to its side.

The wolf landed beyond the creature on a patch of grass, turned, and stared up at its enemy. It held out its right hand and caught a spiral-shaped blade without any effort. Its eyes burned bright red as it stared up at the monster, as if inviting it to dance. Chrome battle armor that protected its head and body gleamed in the pulsing light.

The creature raised its sword again, this time ready to engage the interloper.

"Well, then," its voice boomed. "Time to die, guardian."

41

"Kill him!" the creature ordered.

Every gun on the hilltop turned and opened fire at the wolf.

For a second, Alex didn't move. Tara and the other two didn't either. They could only stare at the newcomer as bullets sparked off its armor.

Then Alex darted toward the circle.

"No!" Buri shouted and lunged forward, diving at him. He grabbed Alex's ankle and tripped him, sending him rolling to the ground a few feet short of the nearest bust.

He clawed at the ground, pulling himself closer to the circle.

"You can't do that!" Buri insisted over the sounds of gunfire around them.

"You may want to work for this guy the rest of your life," Alex said back, "but not me!"

He kicked his heel into Buri's nose with an audible crunch.

Alex crawled forward, leaving Buri to cover his bloody face while he moaned in pain. Reaching out his right hand, Alex grabbed one of the stones and pulled it from its place.

A loud boom echoed across the mountain and the valleys beyond.

A pulse of energy shot out from the portal, and in an instant, it was gone.

The creature turned back to Alex and saw what he'd done. "No! Get him. Get the stone!"

The gunmen closest to Tara and Kiera loaded new magazines into their weapons and prepared to fire. Their intense focus became their Achilles' heel.

Tara grabbed the one nearest her by the wrist, twisted it up, and drove her other elbow into the guy's face. His grip on the submachine gun loosened, and she wrested it from his hand as he staggered back.

Kiera swept the leg of the gunman closest to her, and as the man fell, snatched the gun from his hand. She turned it on him, put a round through his forehead, then spun to face the next target.

Tara unloaded hot metal on the gunmen focusing on Alex. Because of her position, they had no way to defend themselves as they took the onslaught from the rear.

Alex scrambled to his feet and took off running then vaulted over the rock wall and into the dark.

"Follow him!" Tara barked at Felicia.

The archaeologist snapped out of her daze and took off sprinting toward Alex.

Kiera and Tara followed, firing shots at the retreating gunmen as they all looked for cover.

The creature roared its displeasure, but the sound was cut short as the wolf howled and leaped into the air.

The wolf struck first, a blur of speed and silver as he lunged at the monstrous being. His spiral blades whirled in his grip, reflecting the moonlight as he swung one in a powerful arc, aiming for the creature's neck. But the monster was fast—inhumanly fast. It twisted aside with a grace unnatural for something so massive, its armor gleaming as it turned its burning red gaze to him.

The creature struck out with one massive, gauntleted hand, but the wolf ducked, rolling beneath the blow. He kicked off from the ground, flipping behind the beast, and hurled one of his spiral blades. The weapon spun through the air, a streak of deadly titanium, and slammed into the monster's shoulder with a sickening crunch. Sparks erupted as the blade carved through its plated armor, embedding itself deep.

But the creature didn't falter. It turned its head slowly, unaffected, before yanking the blade free and tossing it aside as if it were nothing. The wound didn't even bleed.

TARA PRESSED her back against the crumbling ruins, as bullets chipped away at the stone near her head. Alex crouched beside her, scanning the battlefield. "They're splitting up," he muttered. "Trying to flank us."

Kiera risked a glance around the edge of the wall. The mercenaries had fanned out, using the ruins for cover. If they weren't stopped soon, she and her new American friends would be overrun.

"We need to reposition," Tara said. "We hold here; we die."

Felicia, gripping a pistol she'd taken from one of their fallen captors, nodded. "We need a distraction." She no longer seemed like the passive professor she was before. The recent course of events had forged her into something different now. Her eyes blazed like a rabid animal's, intent on the kill.

Kiera's eyes flicked to a broken section of the ruins behind them, an elevated perch with a clear shot at the enemy's cover. "If I can get up there, I can take out the guy leading them."

Alex nodded. "Go. We'll cover you."

Kiera moved fast, breaking from cover as Tara laid down suppressive fire. Felicia squeezed the trigger of her pistol, unleashing a flurry of rounds toward the enemy position. Bullets zipped past her, but she kept low, while Kiera sprinted toward the high ground.

THE MONSTER SWUNG its massive arm, and the wolf barely dodged in time. The force of the strike shattered the ancient stone pillar beside him, sending debris cascading to the ground. He couldn't let it land a clean hit.

The wolf leaped forward, his blades flashing as he slashed across the creature's chest, then its leg, aiming for weak points in the armor. This time, the beast staggered. It wasn't invincible, but it was close.

With a snarl, the monster drove its fist downward, aiming to crush the wolf into the dirt. The wolf darted aside, hurling one of his spiral blades at the creature's knee. The weapon bit deep, causing the massive being to stumble slightly. It wasn't much—but it was something.

The wolf grinned, his fangs glinting in the moonlight. "So you can be hurt. Good."

The creature roared, its fury shaking the very air around them.

Kiera had reached the high ground. From her perch, she had a clear line of sight. She exhaled, steadying her aim, and fired. One shot—one kill. The lead mercenary dropped instantly, and confusion spread through their ranks.

Tara took advantage of the moment, leaning out from cover and unleashing a volley of gunfire, forcing the remaining men to scatter.

Alex took a breath then muttered, "Time to end this." He charged forward, moving from cover to cover, closing the gap.

The monster lunged at the wolf, swinging both arms in a savage arc. The wolf twisted away, barely avoiding death, then rolled forward, launching both spiral blades at the creature's exposed throat.

The blades slammed into the monster, driving it back, its massive form teetering.

The wolf snarled and rushed in, tackling the beast with every ounce of strength he had. The two figures collided, and the battle reached its peak.

The wolf's grip tightened on his spiral blades, his claws digging into the hilts. Pain shot through his ribs as he forced himself to move, rolling just as the monster's massive boot slammed down where he had been lying a second before. The ground shattered beneath the force, cracks spiderwebbing outward from the impact. Too close.

He landed on all fours, chest heaving, eyes locked on to the towering figure before him. The monster's red eyes burned with something far worse than rage—amusement. It tilted its head slightly, studying him like a predator toying with wounded prey.

Then it moved. Fast.

The wolf barely had time to react before the creature's gauntleted fist caught him square in the chest. The impact lifted him off his feet, sending him careening backward through the ruins. Stone exploded around him as he crashed into a half-broken pillar, the force shaking the ground. His vision flickered, pain lancing through his body. His titanium armor absorbed some of the impact but not enough.

The world spun as he hit the ground, rolling to a stop amid scattered debris. He coughed, tasting iron, his chest burning with every breath. This thing was stronger than anything he had ever faced.

The monster strode forward, its steps deliberate, unhurried. It knew it had the advantage.

TARA, Alex, and Felicia were in trouble.

The mercenaries had regrouped, their initial shock from Kiera's sniper shot wearing off. Now they were pressing the advantage, pushing forward, using the ruins for cover as they tried to encircle the trio.

Tara ducked as bullets slammed into the stone beside her, bits of debris scraping against her cheek. She glanced at Alex, who had shifted positions, taking cover behind a crumbling column. They couldn't stay pinned down much longer.

Alex grimaced. He knew the four men were moving up on their right. If they got around them, they'd be done. "We need to break their formation. Now."

Tara glanced down at the last two grenades strapped to her belt. "I've got an idea. Cover me."

He watched as she lifted one.

"Where did you get those?"

"Took them off a guy. Ready?"

Before Alex could protest, she pushed off from cover, sprinting low as gunfire erupted around her. She weaved through the ruins, gritting her teeth as a bullet grazed her arm, but she didn't stop.

She pulled the pin on the first grenade, lobbed it toward the advancing mercenaries, then immediately threw the second one toward the flankers.

"Move!" she shouted.

The grenades detonated in sequence, sending fire and concussive force tearing through the ruins. The shock wave rattled the ground, throwing dust and debris into the air.

Alex and Felicia seized the moment, breaking from cover. Gunfire erupted as they pushed forward, using the chaos to their advantage.

One mercenary, dazed by the blast, staggered into Alex's line of fire. Alex dropped him with two precise shots then swung around as another enemy tried to flank him.

Felicia took the shot first. One bullet. Clean. The man collapsed.

But the fight wasn't over.

THE WOLF barely had time to roll to his feet before the monster was on him again. It moved like a specter of death—silent, relentless.

The beast swung a backhand, catching the wolf's armored shoulder. Metal groaned as the force sent him skidding sideways, claws gouging into the stone as he struggled to halt his momentum.

He needed a new approach.

He hurled a spiral blade, aiming for the creature's leg joint, but the monster sidestepped, impossibly fast. The blade rebounded back to his grasp, and the creature seized the opening, grabbing him by the throat.

The wolf choked as he was lifted off the ground, the monster's grip like iron around his neck. His feet kicked uselessly in midair.

The creature's voice rumbled, deep and hollow. "You are nothing."

Then it threw him.

He hit the ground hard, rolling across the dirt. His ribs screamed in protest, but he forced himself up. His breath came in ragged gasps. This was bad.

The monster was already advancing again, its towering frame casting an inescapable shadow.

The wolf clenched his teeth. He was running out of time.

TARA FIRED HER LAST ROUNDS, dropping the final mercenary with a controlled burst of gunfire. The man crumpled, his weapon slipping from lifeless fingers. The battlefield fell into silence—at least between the humans.

Alex exhaled sharply, scanning the ruins for any remaining hostiles. "Clear on my end."

"Same here," Kiera confirmed, stepping out from behind her cover, rifle still raised. Felicia moved cautiously, kicking away a fallen gun, just to be sure.

For a moment, none of them spoke, their breaths ragged from exertion. Then, a bone-rattling impact shook the ground beneath them, drawing their attention back to the real battle still raging.

The wolf and the monster were still locked in combat, and from what they could see, the wolf was barely hanging on.

The monster swung its massive arm, aiming for the wolf's head, but the beast ducked, rolling under the attack. The ground where he had just stood exploded into shards of shattered stone, the force of the strike sending debris flying.

The wolf came up behind the creature, his spiral blades a blur as he slashed across its back, aiming for the weakened armor plates. The metal screeched, sparks flying as his blades bit deep, forcing the creature forward a step.

But still, it did not fall.

The creature twisted with inhuman speed, its wounded arm snapping out, catching the wolf across the ribs. The impact sent the beast hurtling back, skidding across the battlefield before he slammed into the remains of an ancient wall. The stone crumbled around him as he staggered to his feet, blood dripping from his mouth. His breaths were ragged, his limbs heavy.

Tara gripped her weapon, helpless. "Come on... get up."

Alex clenched his jaw. "This thing just won't die."

The creature stepped forward, its red eyes still burning, its movements slower now but no less deadly. Its armor was damaged, cracked in places, but still, it pressed on. The wolf couldn't take much more of this.

The wolf wiped blood from his mouth, his fangs bared in a savage grin. "You're stubborn," he growled, gripping his blades tighter. "So am I."

Then he charged.

The two collided with a thunderous crash, the ground splitting beneath their feet. The wolf dodged left then right, slipping past a deadly swing before driving both spiral blades into the creature's torso.

The monster bellowed in fury, staggering back. The wolf used the momentum, tearing the blades free and slashing upward. One blade ripped through the creature's gauntlet, sending metal flying. The other found its neck—just beneath the jawline.

For the first time, the monster stumbled, dropping to a knee. Its breath came in ragged hisses, red eyes flickering.

The wolf didn't hesitate. He reached down and grabbed the creature's massive sword, yanking it free from its grasp. The blade was heavy, unnaturally so, but in his hands, it felt like it belonged there.

The monster lifted its gaze, rage still burning in its eyes.

The wolf tightened his grip on the sword.

"You'll never stop us all, guardian," the creature snarled. "You are only one."

The wolf raised the blade, shaking its head. "No. I'm not."

He swung the sword down hard at the monster's neck, slicing through it in one devastating blow.

A burst of blinding white light lit up the mountaintop and the entire valley around it in an instant. Then, just as quickly as it flashed, the light was gone.

A strange peace fell over the clearing.

It was cut by a moan from a man about thirty feet from where the wolf stood. The man struggled to his feet, wavering like a newborn colt.

"Thank you," Buri said. "Thank you so much for destroying that... that thing. You saved us."

The wolf stalked toward him. No sign of mercy showed on his face; fangs bared, as if readying for a meal.

"Now that it's all over, we can just forget all about this," Buri pleaded, his voice trembling with fear and desperation. He feigned surrender, then produced a pistol from his right side, raised it, and opened fire on the wolf.

Every round seemed to bounce off the battle armor until the weapon clicked.

Buri took a clumsy step backward, but there would be no retreat.

The wolf snatched him before he could move any farther. The pistol fell from Buri's grip as the creature lifted him high above the ground.

"The mist judges the wicked. And I deliver judgment."

He drove one of the spiral blades through Buri's chest and twisted. A hollow scream escaped Buri's lips before it cut off. Then the wolf dropped the man's lifeless body to the ground.

Tara, Alex, and the others peered at the strange wolflike figure. The body of the monster had vanished, leaving no proof it was ever there.

The wolf turned to them as he took a step their way.

At first, they weren't sure what to do. The thing had clearly been on their side. At least during the battle. But was he now?

"It's okay," the wolf said. His voice was deep but kind.

As he walked toward the group, the armor faded, and the fur disappeared. He shrank down to around six feet tall and morphed into a human.

He had dark brown hair, and wore a Mazzy Star T-shirt and blue jeans.

"Who... are you?" Alex blurted.

Felicia stepped out ahead of him, peering at the approaching man. "Gideon? Is that you?"

"Good evening, Dr. Lowe," he answered. "Good to see you again. Although"—he looked around at the bodies; some were evaporating, while others remained strewn in the grass and on the rocks—"I would have preferred a different setting."

"Wait," Tara said. "You two know each other?"

Felicia nodded, and a faint smile cracked across her face. "Yes. He's an archaeologist. Dr. Gideon Wolf."

"Okay," Alex said.

"Nice to meet you," Kiera added. "But... um, what was—"

"It's a long story," Gideon said.

"But the werewolf thing..."

"Actually, it's a chupacabra. But I get the comparison."

Everyone looked beyond confused.

"I'll tell you all about it," he said. "But first, we need to separate those stone heads. And we'll need to take them somewhere safe, so no one ever finds them again."

42

"You're sure you don't want us to go with you?" Tara asked.

She, Alex, and Kiera stood near the entryway to the cottage. Felicia and Gideon faced them near the door.

"No," Felicia said. "I'll be fine. Besides, I have an old acquaintance with me now. It will be nice to catch up. He's apparently been quite busy the last few years."

Gideon smiled. "You could say that."

After the events the previous evening, Gideon had filled the group in on what he'd been up to the last few years.

His story was unbelievable in every sense of the word. Yet, after what they'd seen in the mountains of Snowdonia, there was no way they could doubt it.

He'd told them about how he was approached by a cartel boss to find a mysterious amulet, the one hanging around his neck. The cartel leader had offered him an immense sum of money to locate the artifact, but Gideon had turned it down.

As a result, the cartel executed his wife, and kidnapped him, taking him into the jungle where the cartel boss believed an ancient hidden temple was located, and that housed the mysterious artifact.

Gideon went on to summarize everything that happened—his

narrow escape, the subsequent fall into a dark cave that turned out to be the temple, and the powers he'd gained when he donned the medallion.

He'd become a member of an ancient fraternity of heroes who only came along every few thousand years, apparently when humanity needed them most. They were called guardians, and their medallions were imbued with the powers of ancient gods—ordinary people who'd taken on supernatural abilities to defend the innocent from evil.

"Where will you go next?" Tara asked as he made his way to the door.

Gideon shrugged. "I have some unfinished business in Egypt. Something to do with Horus, I think."

"As in the falcon god?"

He smiled and nodded. "The very same."

"Well, thank you for the assist last night. Not sure what we would have done without you. Would love to keep in touch going forward if that's okay." Alex said as Gideon opened the door.

"For sure."

He allowed Felicia to exit first, then as he was about to leave, Tara stopped him. "Wait. Gideon?"

"Yeah?"

"I was just curious. You told us everything last night, about who you are, what you've been doing. But you didn't tell us how you knew we were there at Dinas Emrys."

"I didn't," he answered. "Actually, I don't even know how I ended up there. One moment, I was turning on a football game, and then all of a sudden I was there, on the hilltop. I'm still learning this stuff too."

"Oh."

"If I figure it out, I'll let you know."

She smiled. "Thanks."

"See you around."

He closed the door behind him, and the cottage fell silent.

"Well," Kiera said, allowing the quiet to only last a second, "I guess I will be going too. You're welcome to stay here as long as you like."

Tara and Alex smiled at the offer.

"I saw you eyeballing the hot tub. I'd say after all that's happened, you deserve a good soak."

"Thank you, Kiera," Tara said. "You have been an unexpected surprise."

"You're most welcome. I have to say, I'll not soon forget all this. Not quite what I expected when Matias put me on this job. By the way, when you're ready to leave, just text me, and I'll have a car here to pick you up and take you anywhere you want to go."

They thanked her again. The group said their goodbyes, and Kiera walked to the door. She bowed out with a nod and closed the door behind her, leaving the couple alone for the first time in days.

Alex looked over at his wife and brushed back her long, auburn hair behind her right ear. "You okay?" he asked.

She nodded. "Yes. I'm okay. You?"

"Yeah. I'm good. But I would be a lot better in that hot tub."

Her smile widened. "Same." Then she frowned. "You think we should call Tommy and report in on all this? He should probably know that Gideon took the eight stones to hide them."

Alex leaned in closer, gave her kiss. "Nah. Let Tommy wait another hour."

THANK YOU

Thank you for taking the time to read this story. I hope you enjoyed it. To find out when the next story will be released, and to get updates on new content, join the VIP Reader Club here: https://readerlinks. com/l/3400241

And be sure to check out my YouTube channel for more content: https://www.youtube.com/@ErnestDempsey

OTHER BOOKS BY ERNEST DEMPSEY

Sean Wyatt Archaeological Thrillers:

The Secret of the Stones

The Cleric's Vault

The Last Chamber

The Grecian Manifesto

The Norse Directive

Game of Shadows

The Jerusalem Creed

The Samurai Cipher

The Cairo Vendetta

The Uluru Code

The Excalibur Key

The Denali Deception

The Sahara Legacy

The Fourth Prophecy

The Templar Curse

The Forbidden Temple

The Omega Project

The Napoleon Affair

The Second Sign

The Milestone Protocol

Where Horizons End

Poseidon's Fury

The Florentine Pursuit

The Inventor's Tomb

The Saint's Covenant (2025)

The Moldova Job (Prequel)

The Relic Runner - A Dak Harper Series:

The Relic Runner Origin Story

The Courier

Two Nights In Mumbai

Country Roads

Heavy Lies the Crown

Moscow Sky

Thief's Honor

Strings of Deception

The Adventure Guild (ALL AGES):

The Caesar Secret: Books 1-3

The Carolina Caper

Beta Force:

Operation Zulu

London Calling

Paranormal Archaeology Division:

Hell's Gate

Guardians of Earth:

Emergence: Gideon Wolf Book 1

Righteous Dawn: Gideon Wolf Book 2

Crimson Winter: Gideon Wolf Book 3

The Lion's Path: Gideon Wolf Book 4

Adriana Villa Adventures:

War of Thieves Box Set

When Shadows Call

ACKNOWLEDGMENTS

I would like to thank my terrific editors, Anne and Jason, for their hard work. What they do makes my stories so much better for readers all over the world. Anne Storer and Jason Whited are the best editorial team a writer could hope for and I appreciate everything they do.

I also want to thank Elena at Li Graphics for her tremendous work on my book covers and for always overdelivering. Elena definitely rocks.

A big thank you has to go out to my friend James Slater for his proofing work. James has added another layer of quality control to these stories, and I can't thank him enough.

Thanks as well to my friend Allison Valentine who does an amazing job with the Hunters and Runners page on Facebook on top of all the hard work she does for so many authors.

Last but not least, I need to thank all my wonderful fans and especially the advance reader team. Their feedback and reviews are always so helpful and I can't say enough good things about all of them.